LITTLE MAN,
WHAT NOW?

LITTLE MAN, WHAT NOW?

HANS FALLADA

TRANSLATED BY **SUSAN BENNETT**
AFTERWORD BY **PHILIP BRADY**

 **MELVILLE HOUSE**
BROOKLYN · LONDON

Little Man—What Now?
First published as *Kleiner Mann—was nun?*
by Rowohlt, Berlin, 1932
© Aufbau-Verlagsgruppe GmbH, Berlin 1994
(Published with Aufbau; "Aufbau" is a trademark
of Aufbau Verlagsgruppe GmbH)

Negotiated by Aufbau Media GmbH, Berlin

This edition © 2009 Melville House Publishing

Translation © Susan Bennett, 1996
This unabridged translation first published by Libris, 1996

Afterword © Philip Brady, 1996

Melville House Publishing
145 Plymouth Street
Brooklyn, NY 11201
www.mhpbooks.com

ISBN: 978-1-933633-64-0
8 9 10

Library of Congress Cataloging-in-Publication Data is available

CONTENTS

LITTLE MAN — WHAT NOW?

TRANSLATOR'S NOTE

In the German original Johannes Pinneberg generally calls Emma Morschel (later his wife) 'Lämmchen' (lambkin) as a term of affection. This has been lightly anglicized here by omission of the umlaut. Lammchen in turn often calls Johannes 'Junge' (laddie). This somewhat old-fashioned term of endearment is translated as Sonny. German place-names have been preserved except where relevant English equivalents exist – like Market Place for 'Marktplatz'.

I would like to thank Dr Jenny Williams, of Dublin City University, whose specialized knowledge of Hans Fallada and his times and close familiarity with the original *Kleiner Mann* have contributed greatly to this translation. Thanks also – posthumously – to Eric Sutton whose racy, albeit abbreviated, thirties translation was often a helpful and sometimes a conclusive point of reference if I was stuck for a word.

LITTLE MAN – WHAT NOW?

PROLOGUE

BLITHE SPIRITS

It was five past four. Pinneberg had just checked his watch. He stood, a fair-haired, neatly-dressed young man, outside number 24 Rothenbaumstrasse, and waited.

Five past four; and he and Lammchen had agreed to meet at quarter to. Pinneberg had put away his watch and was staring earnestly at a nameplate on the entrance to number 24. He read:

DR SESAME
Gynaecologist,
Consulting hours 9–12 and 4–6

'Exactly! And it's five past four. Now if I light another cigarette, Lammchen's going to come round the corner for certain. So I won't. It's going to cost enough today as it is.'

His eyes wandered away from the nameplate. Rothenbaumstrasse had only one row of houses. Across the road, and the strip of green, was the embankment, and beyond that was the Strela, flowing fine and broad here as it neared the Baltic. A fresh wind was blowing towards him which gently bowed the bushes and set the trees lightly rustling.

'That's the way to live,' thought Pinneberg. 'I'm sure that Dr Sesame there has seven rooms. He must earn a packet. What sort of rent would he pay? Two hundred marks, three hundred? Uh. How would I know? – Ten past four!'

Pinneberg fished in his pocket, took a cigarette out of his case and lit it.

Round the corner wafted Lammchen, in pleated white skirt and art-silk blouse, hatless, with her blonde hair all blown about. 'Hello, Sonny. I really couldn't make it any earlier. Are you cross?'

'Not really. But we'll have ages to wait. At least thirty people have gone in since I've been here.'

'They won't all have been going to the doctor's. Anyway we've got an appointment.'

'You see. It was right to make an appointment.'

'Of course it was right. You're always right, Sonny.' And there on the doorstep, she took his face in her hands and covered it with a storm of kisses. 'Oh God, Sonny, I'm so glad to see you again. It's been nearly a fortnight. Can you believe it?'

'I know, Lammchen,' he replied. 'I'm not cross any more now.'

The door opened, and a white shape stood before them in the dim hallway and barked: 'Medical cards!'

'Let us in first if you don't mind,' said Pinneberg and pushed Lammchen in front of him. 'And we're private. I have an appointment. My name is Pinneberg.'

At the word 'private' the apparition raised a hand and switched on the light in the hall. 'The doctor's just coming. Please wait a moment. In there please.'

As they went towards the door they passed another which was half open. That must be the ordinary waiting-room, and all the thirty people who Pinneberg had seen coming in past him seemed to be sitting in it. They all looked at the two of them, and a buzz of voices arose:

'That's not fair.'

'We've been waiting longer!'

'What do we pay into the public health scheme for?'

'I'd like to know what makes that stuck-up pair any better than us.'

The nurse appeared in the doorway: 'Can we have a bit of quiet, please? You're disturbing the doctor! It's not what you think. This is the doctor's son-in-law and his wife. Isn't that so?'

Pinneberg smiled, flattered. Lammchen hurried towards the other door. There was a moment's quiet.

'Oh, do hurry up,' whispered the nurse, pushing Pinneberg from behind. 'Those medical-card patients are so common. What on earth do they think they're entitled to for the pittance we get from the public scheme?'

The door swung shut, and Sonny and Lammchen found themselves surrounded by red plush.

'This must be his lounge,' said Pinneberg. 'How d'you like it? I think it's dreadfully old-fashioned.'

'I call that disgusting,' said Lammchen. 'We're usually medical-card patients. Now we know how those women at the doctor's really talk about us.'

'What are you getting so worked up for?' he asked. 'That's how it is. If you're a nobody, they can treat you as they like.'

'But it does get me worked up. . .'

The door opened and another nurse came in. 'Mr and Mrs Pinneberg, please? The doctor says he won't keep you a minute. May I take the particulars while we're waiting?'

'By all means,' said Pinneberg. 'Age?' asked the nurse briskly.

'Twenty-three.'

'First name: Johannes.'

After a moment's hesitation: 'Book-keeper.'

Then, more smoothly: 'I've never had any health problems – apart from the usual childhood illnesses. So far as I know, both in good health.'

Another hesitation. 'Yes, my mother's still alive. My father's not. Can't say what he died of.'

Now it was Lammchen's turn. . .

'Twenty-two, Emma.'

This time she was the one to hesitate: 'Maiden name Morschel. No serious illnesses. Both parents alive. Both in good health.'

'All right. It won't be long now. The doctor will be with you in a minute.'

'I don't know what all that's for,' he growled, as the door swung shut. 'When all we want. . .'

'You weren't too keen to say "book-keeper".'

'And what about your "maiden name"?' He laughed. 'Emma Pinneberg. Known as Lammchen. Maiden name Morschel. Emma Pinne. . .'

'Shut up, you. Oh God, Sonny, I've simply got to go again. Have you any idea where it is?'

'Not again: Why ever didn't you. . .'

'I did, Sonny. Really. Just now in the Rathaus Square. It cost a whole groschen. But it always happens when I'm nervous.'

'Lammchen, do please make an effort. If you've really only just been. . .'

'But I have to. . .'

'This way please,' said a voice. In the door stood Dr Sesame, the famous Dr Sesame, whose reputation as a sympathetic and, according to some, also a kind-hearted man had spread throughout the town and beyond. He had also written a popular pamphlet on sexual problems, which had given Pinneberg the courage to write making an appointment for Lammchen and himself.

This, then, was the Dr Sesame at present standing in the doorway, and saying 'This way, please.'

Dr Sesame searched on his desk for the letter. 'You wrote to me, Mr Pinneberg. . . saying you couldn't have any children just yet because you couldn't afford it?'

'Yes,' said Pinneberg, dreadfully embarrassed.

'You can start undressing,' said the doctor to Lammchen, and carried on: 'And you want to know an entirely reliable means of prevention. Hm, an entirely reliable means. . .' He smiled sceptically behind his gold-rimmed spectacles.

'I read about it in your book. . . These pessoirs. . .'

'Pessaries,' said the doctor. 'Yes, but they don't suit every woman. And it's always a bit of a business. It depends on whether your wife would be nimble-fingered enough. . .'

He looked up at her. She had already taken off her blouse and skirt. Her slim legs made her look very tall.

'Well, let's go next door,' said the doctor. 'You needn't have taken your *blouse* off for this, young lady.'

Lammchen went a deep red.

'Oh well, leave it off now. Come this way. One moment, Mr Pinneberg.'

The two of them went into the next room. Pinneberg watched them go. The top of the doctor's head reached no farther than the 'young lady's' shoulders. How beautiful she was! thought Pinneberg yet again; she was the greatest girl in the world, the only one for him. He worked in Ducherow, and she worked here in Platz, and he never saw her more than once a fortnight, so his joy in her was always fresh, and his desire for her absolutely inexpressible.

Next door he heard the doctor asking questions on and off in a low voice, and an instrument clinking on the side of a bowl. He knew that sound from the dentist's; it wasn't a pleasant one.

Then he winced violently. Never before had he heard that tone from Lammchen. She was saying in a high, clear voice that was almost a shriek – 'No, no, no!' And once again, 'No!' And then, very softly, but he still heard it: 'Oh God.'

Pinneberg took three steps towards the door – What was that? What could it be? What about the rumours that those kind of doctors were terrible lechers? But then Dr Sesame spoke again – impossible to hear what he said – and the instrument clinked again.

Then there was a long silence.

It was a glorious summer day, around the middle of July, with brilliant sunshine. The sky outside was deep blue, a few twigs poked in at the window, waving in the sea breeze. An old rhyme from Pinneberg's childhood came into his head:

> Wind, don't blow
> Wind, don't puff
> Wind, don't knock my child's hat off.
> Wind, be kind
> Wind, be mild
> Wind, be gentle to my child.

The people in the waiting-room were talking. Time must be dragging for them too. They didn't know how lucky they were. How lucky. . .

The doctor and Lammchen were returning. Pinneberg glanced at her anxiously; her eyes were opened wide, as if she had just had a fright. She was pale, but she smiled at him, wanly at first, but then the smile spread, becoming wider and wider until it lit up her whole face. . . The doctor stood in the corner and washed his hands, glancing sideways at Pinneberg. Then he said rapidly: 'It's a bit too late for prevention, Mr Pinneberg. Nothing to be done now. Beginning of the second month, I'd say.'

Pinneberg couldn't breathe, he felt as though he'd been struck. Then he gabbled, 'But Doctor, it's impossible. We were so careful. It's absolutely impossible. You tell him, Lammchen!. . .'

'Sonny!' she said. 'Sonny. . .'

'It's true,' said the doctor. 'No doubt about it. And believe me, Mr Pinneberg, a child is good for a marriage.'

'Doctor,' said Pinneberg and his lip trembled. 'I earn one hundred and eighty marks a month! Please, Doctor!'

A weary look came over Dr Sesame's face. He knew what was coming next. He heard it thirty times a day.

'No,' he said. 'No. Please don't even ask me. It's out of the question. You are both in good health. And your income is not at all bad. Not – at all – bad.'

'Doctor!' cried Pinneberg feverishly.

Lammchen stood behind him and stroked his hair. 'Leave it, Sonny, leave it! It'll be all right.'

'But it's absolutely impossible!' exclaimed Pinneberg – and then stopped. The nurse had come in.

'You're wanted on the phone, Doctor.'

'You wait and see,' said the doctor. 'You'll be glad in the end. And as soon as the baby arrives, you come straight to me and we'll see about prevention then. Don't think it's safe just because she's feeding the baby. So, there we are. . . Courage, young lady.'

He shook Lammchen by the hand.

'I'd like to. . .' said Pinneberg, taking out his wallet.

'Ah yes,' said the doctor, half-way through the door, and looked once more at the two of them, appraisingly. 'Well, fifteen marks, sister.' 'Fifteen. . .' said Pinneberg slowly, and looked towards the door. But Doctor Sesame had already gone. Pinneberg took out a twenty-mark note with a great deal of fuss and watched frowning as the sister wrote out the receipt and handed it to him.

His forehead cleared a little. 'I'll get that back from the health insurance, won't I?'

The nurse looked at him, then at Lammchen. 'Confirmation of pregnancy?' She didn't even wait for the answer. 'No, you won't. None of the insurance schemes pay out for that.'

'Come on, Lammchen,' he said.

They went slowly down the stairs. Lammchen stopped at a landing, and taking one of his hands between her own, said: 'Don't be so sad. Please don't. It'll be all right.'

'Yes, yes,' said he, deep in thought.

They went a little way along Rothenbaumstrasse, then turned off into Mainzerstrasse. There were tall buildings there and a great many people. Lines of cars drove past. The evening papers were out. Nobody paid any attention to the two of them.

'"Not a bad income", he said, and then took fifteen marks out of my hundred and eighty. Daylight robbery!' 'I'll manage,' said Lammchen, 'I'll manage somehow.' 'Dear Lammchen!' said he.

They turned out of Mainzerstrasse into the Krumperweg, and there it was suddenly quiet.

Lammchen said: 'That explains a lot of things.'

'What do you mean?' he asked.

'Oh, nothing really, just that I've felt sick every morning. And things were funny, generally. . .'

'But you must have noticed something.'

'I just kept on thinking, oh, it will come on soon. It's not the first thing you suspect, is it?'

'Perhaps he's made a mistake!'

'No. I don't think so. It all fits.'

'But it could be a mistake.'

'No, I believe. . .'

'Listen to me, will you! It is possible.'

'Everything's possible.'

'Perhaps your period will start tomorrow. If it does, I'm going to write that man such a letter!' He relapsed into thought. He was composing the letter.

After the Krumperweg came Hebbelstrasse with its beautiful elm trees. The two of them walked deep in thought through the summer afternoon.

'I shall ask for my fifteen marks back as well,' said Pinneberg suddenly.

Lammchen did not reply. She was concentrating on placing one foot in front of the other and taking great care where she walked. Everything was so different now.

'Where are we going?' he suddenly inquired.

'I've got to get home,' said Lammchen. 'I told mother I'd be back.'

'That's all I need!' he said.

'Oh don't start scolding me, Sonny,' she pleaded. 'I'll make sure I can get down again at half-past eight. What train are you catching?'

'The half-past nine.'

'Then I'll go with you to the station.'

'And that's it, is it?' he said. 'That's all for another two weeks. What a life!'

Lütjenstrasse was a real working-class street, always teeming with children, impossible to say goodbye properly there.

'Don't take it so hard, Sonny,' she said, taking his hand. 'I'll manage.'

'All right,' he said, and forced a smile. 'You're the ace of trumps, Lammchen. You win every trick.'

'And at half-past eight I'll be down again. Promise.'

'Can't you kiss me now?'

'No, I can't, honestly. It would be all over the street in a minute. Cheer up! Do cheer up!'

'Well, all right then, Lammchen,' he said. 'Don't you take it too hard either. It will all work out somehow.'

'Of course it will,' she said. 'I'm not going to go all soft just like that, am I? Well, bye-bye for now.'

She whisked up the dark stairway, her vanity-case knocking against the banisters, tap, tap, tap.

Pinneberg stared after the gleaming legs. How many thousand times had Lammchen vanished out of his reach up those damned stairs.

'Lammchen!' he bellowed. 'Lammchen!'

'Yes?' she inquired from above, leaning over the banisters. 'Wait a moment!' he called. He stormed up the stairs, stood breathless before her and gripped her by the shoulders. 'Lammchen!' he said, panting from excitement and lack of air. 'Emma Morschel! Why don't we get married?'

MOTHER MORSCHEL – MR MORSCHEL – KARL MORSCHEL:
PINNEBERG GETS DRAGGED INTO MORSCHELLAND

Lammchen Morschel said nothing. She disengaged herself and sank gently onto a stair. All the strength had suddenly gone out of her legs. She sat and looked up at her young man. 'Oh God!' she said, 'Sonny, would you really do that?'

Her eyes lit up. She had dark blue eyes with a green tinge. And now they were fairly overflowing with light.

As if all the Christmas trees of her life were glowing inside her, thought Pinneberg, so moved that he felt embarrassed.

'Right you are then, Lammchen,' he said. 'Let's get married. As soon as possible, eh?'

'You don't have to, Sonny. I can manage. But you're right – it'd be better for our Shrimp to have a father.'

'"Our Shrimp",' said Johannes Pinneberg, 'of course, our Shrimp.'

He was quiet for a moment. He was struggling with himself. Should he tell her that his proposal had had nothing whatever to do with the Shrimp and everything to do with the fact that it was very unfair to have to wait three hours out on the street for his girl on a summer evening? But he didn't tell her. Instead, he pleaded: 'Do get up, please, Lammchen. The stairs are bound to be all dirty. Your best white skirt. . .'

'Who cares? What do we care about any old skirts! I'm so happy. Johannes! Sonny!' Now she was well and truly on her feet, and threw her arms around his neck again. And the house was good to them: out of the twenty sets of tenants who went in and out by these stairs not one person came by. Despite the fact that it was the early evening rush hour when the breadwinners were coming home and the housewives were running out for some forgotten ingredient for their evening meal. No one came by.

Then Pinneberg broke free and said: 'Surely we can be doing this upstairs now we're engaged. Let's go up.'

Lammchen asked dubiously: 'D'you want to come with me

straight away? Wouldn't it be better for me to prepare Father and
Mother first? They don't know anything about you.'

'Best to get it over and done with,' declared Pinneberg, still quite
determined not to go onto the street. 'Anyhow, they're bound to be
pleased, aren't they?'

'Maybe,' said she, thoughtfully. 'Mother will be. Very. But father,
well, you know, he really likes getting a rise out of people, but he
doesn't mean it. You mustn't take offence.'

'I won't,' said Pinneberg.

Lammchen opened the door onto a little hall. A voice rang out
from behind another door which was slightly ajar: 'Emma! Come
here! This minute!'

'Just a moment, Mother,' called Emma Morschel. 'I'm just taking
off my shoes.'

She took Pinneberg by the hand and led him on tiptoe into a little
room with two beds in it which looked out into the yard.

'Put your things down there. Yes, that's my bed. That's where I
sleep. Mother sleeps in the other bed. Father and Karl sleep across
there, in the big bedroom. Now come with me. Wait a minute, your
hair!' She quickly ran a comb through the tangles.

Both their hearts were beating hard. She took him by the hand,
they crossed the hall and pushed open the kitchen door. A round-
shouldered woman stood bent over the stove, frying something in a
pan. Pinneberg saw a brown dress and a big blue apron.

The woman did not look up. 'Emma, run down into the cellar
now and fetch me some briquettes. I can ask Karl till the cows come
home. . .'

'Mother,' said Emma, 'This is my friend Johannes Pinneberg from
Ducherow. We want to get married.'

The woman at the stove looked up. She had a brown face with a
strong mouth, a sharp, dangerous mouth, a face with bright sharp
eyes and thousands of wrinkles. An old working woman.

The woman shot a sharp, angry glance at Pinneberg. Then she
turned back to her potato-cakes.

'Silly young fool,' she said. 'So now you're bringing your
blokes home, are you! Go and fetch me some coal. The fire's nearly
out.'

'Mother,' said Lammchen, trying to laugh, 'he really does want to marry me.'

'Get the coal, will you, girl!' shouted the woman, working away with her fork.

'Mother!. . .'

The woman looked up. She said slowly, 'Haven't you gone yet? Do you want a slap on the face?'

Lammchen gave Pinneberg's hand a fleeting squeeze. Then she took up a basket and shouted, as cheerfully as she could 'Back in a moment.' Then the hall door slammed.

Pinneberg stood, abandoned, in the kitchen. He looked cautiously towards Mrs Morschel as if the very act of looking at her might irritate her, then across towards the window. There was nothing to be seen but a blue summer sky and a few chimneys.

Mrs Morschel pushed the pan aside and fiddled with the stove rings. There was a lot of clanging and clanking. She prodded the fire with the poker, muttering to herself.

'Excuse me. . .?' asked Pinneberg politely.

These were the first words he spoke at the Morschels. He shouldn't have said anything, for the woman descended on him like a vulture. In one hand she held the poker, in the other the fork she had been turning the potato-cakes with, but that wasn't the worst, despite the way she was brandishing them. Her face was worse, with all the wrinkles twitching and leaping; worse still were her cruel and angry eyes.

'If you bring shame on my girl!' she cried, beside herself with rage.

Pinneberg took a step back. 'But I do want to marry Emma, Mrs Morschel,' he said nervously.

'You think I don't know what's up,' pursued the woman undeterred. 'I've stood here for two weeks and waited. I've thought: she's going to tell me something. I've thought: soon she's going to bring me the fellow. I've been sitting here waiting.' She drew breath. 'She's a good girl. You man, you, my Emma's not some piece of dirt for you to play with. She's always been cheerful. She's never said a cross word to me – Do you mean to bring shame on her?'

'No, no,' whispered Pinneberg nervously.

'Oh yes, you do,' shrieked Mrs Pinneberg. 'You do. For two weeks

I've been standing here and waiting for her sanitary towels to put in the wash, and nothing. How did you do it?' Pinneberg had no reply.

'We're young people,' he said softly.

She was still angry: 'You. . . what sort of a person are you to get my girl to do that!' Then she began muttering to herself again: 'Pigs, all you men are pigs. Ugh.'

'We'll be married in as short a time as it takes to get the papers,' explained Pinneberg.

Frau Morschel had gone back to the stove. The fat was spitting. 'What are you anyway? Can you afford to marry?'

'I'm a book-keeper. In a grain merchants.'

'So you work in an office?'

'Yes'

'I'd have preferred a man from the shop floor. What do you earn then?'

'A hundred and eighty marks.'

'After deductions?'

'Before.'

'That's all right,' said the woman. 'It's not too much. My daughter should stay the down-to-earth girl she is.' And then, flaring up: 'And don't think we've anything to give her. We're working-class people and we don't do that kind of thing. She's only got the bits of linen she's bought herself.'

'It's not necessary,' said Pinneberg.

Suddenly the woman flared up again: 'You haven't anything either, have you? You don't look the thrifty kind. No one who goes around in a suit like that has money left over.'

Lammchen's arrival with the coal spared Pinneberg the necessity of confessing that Mrs Morschel had about hit the mark with her comment. Lammchen was in the best of moods. 'Has she eaten you alive, you poor boy?' she asked. 'Mother's a real tea-kettle, always boiling over.'

'Don't cheek me, you young scallywag,' scolded the old lady. 'Or you'll get that slap after all. Go into the bedroom and have a kiss and cuddle. I want to talk to father alone first.'

'Well, have you asked my fiancé whether he likes potato-cakes? Today's our engagement day.'

'Get along with you!' said Frau Morschel. 'And don't lock the door. I want to be able to keep an eye on the pair of you and see you're not getting up to anything.'

They sat facing each other across the table on the little white chairs.

'Mother's just an ordinary working woman,' said Lammchen. 'She has a sharp tongue but she doesn't mean it.'

'Oh, she meant it all right,' said Pinneberg, grinning. 'D'you realize your mother knows what the doctor told us today?'

'Of course she knows. Mother always knows everything. I believe she liked you.'

'Oh, come on! It didn't sound like it.'

'Mother's like that. She's always telling people off. I don't notice it any more.'

They were silent for a moment, sitting opposite each other like good children, their hands outstretched on the little table.

'We'll have to buy rings,' reflected Pinneberg.

'Heavens, yes,' exclaimed Lammchen. 'Tell me, what kind do you like best: shiny or matt?'

'Matt!' he said.

'Me too, me too!' she cried. 'I believe we've got the same tastes in everything. That's great. What will they cost?'

'I don't know. Thirty marks?'

'As much as that?'

'Will we have gold ones?'

'Of course we'll have gold ones. Let's take measurements.'

He moved over to her. They took a length of cotton, but it wasn't easy. Either it cut into them or it was too loose.

'Looking at hands brings strife,' said Lammchen.

'But I'm not looking at them,' he said. 'I'm kissing them. I'm kissing your hands, Lammchen.'

A sharp knuckle rapped on the door. 'Come out. Father is here.'

'Right away,' said Lammchen, and slid out of his arms.

'Quick, let's tidy ourselves. Father's always quick to make remarks.'

'What's he like, then?'

'Oh God, you'll see soon enough. It's neither here nor there anyhow. It's me you're marrying. Father and Mother don't come into it.'

'The Shrimp comes into it.'

'Oh yes, the Shrimp. Nice sensible parents he's going to have. Can't even sit properly for a quarter of an hour. . .' At the kitchen table sat a tall man in grey trousers, grey waistcoat and white singlet, without a jacket or a collar and wearing slippers. A sallow wrinkled face, small sharp eyes behind drooping spectacles, grey moustache and almost white beard.

He was reading the Social Democratic *Volksstimme*, but when Pinneberg and Emma came in he let it drop and surveyed the young man.

'So you're the young fellow that wants to marry my daughter? Pleased to meet you. Sit down. You'll soon change your tune.'

'What?' asked Pinneberg.

Lammchen had put on an apron to help her mother. Mrs Morschel said crossly: 'Where's that boy got to again? The potato-cakes are getting hard.'

'Overtime,' said Mr Morschel laconically. And then, winking at Pinneberg: 'You do overtime too, sometimes, I suppose?'

'Yes,' said Pinneberg. 'Quite often.'

'But without pay. . .'

'I'm afraid so. The boss says. . .'

Mr Morschel wasn't interested in what the boss said. 'There, you see, that's why I'd prefer a working man for my daughter. When my Karl does overtime he gets paid for it.'

'Mr Kleinholz says. . .' began Pinneberg again.

'What the employers say, young man – we've heard it all before,' declared Mr Morschel. 'And we're not interested. All we're interested in is what they do. There must be a wage agreement in your place, eh?'

'I believe so,' said Pinneberg.

'Believe! Belief's a question of religion, and a working man has no truck with that. I'm sure you have a wage agreement. And it says that overtime has to be paid. How come I end up with a son-in-law who isn't paid overtime?'

Pinneberg shrugged his shoulders.

'Because you're not organized, you white-collar workers,'

explained Mr Morschel. 'Because you don't stick together; you've got no solidarity. So they can push you around just as they like.'

'I'm organized,' said Pinneberg resentfully. 'I'm in a union.'

'Emma! Mother! Our young man is in a union? Who would have thought it! So natty and in a union.' Morschel senior turned his head to one side, and surveyed his future son-in-law with half-closed eyes. 'And what's your union called, my lad? Out with it!'

'Clerical, Office and Professional Employees Association of Germany,' said Pinneberg, getting crosser and crosser.

At this Mr Morschel almost doubled up with laughter.

'The COPEA! Mother, Emma, hold me up! Our young man's a boss's lap-dog. Call that a union? Doesn't know which side it's on. The bosses have got it in their pocket. God, what a joke.'

'Hold on, just a minute' cried Pinneberg furiously. 'We're not lap-dogs. We're not financed by the bosses. We pay our own dues.'

'Oh yes, and to whom? A bunch of stooges. Oh Emma, you picked a right one there. The COPEA! What a lap-dog!'

Pinneberg looked over at Lammchen for support, but Lammchen wasn't looking his way. Perhaps she was used it, but that didn't make it any less of an ordeal for him.

'I hear you white-collar workers think you're a cut above us working men.'

'That's not what I think.'

'Oh yes, you do. And why? Because you give your boss not just a week but a whole month's grace before he has to pay you. Because you do unpaid overtime, because you take less than the agreed wage, because you never strike, because you're always the blacklegs.'

'It's not just to do with money,' said Pinneberg. 'We think differently from most working men. We have different needs. . .'

'You think differently! You don't. You think just like a proletarian.'

'I don't believe it's so,' said Pinneberg. 'Take me, for example. . ..'

'Yes, take you for example,' said Morschel, with a mean smirk on his face. 'You helped yourself to an advance, didn't you?'

'What d'you mean?' asked Pinneberg, confused. 'An advance?'

'Yes, on Emma.' The man's smirk widened. 'Not very nice, sir. And a very proletarian habit.'

'I. . .' began Pinneberg, growing very red. He wished he could slam the doors and roar: 'Oh, go to hell all of you. . .!'

But Mrs Morschel said sharply: 'Now you be quiet, Father, and stop baiting people. That's all settled. It's none of your business.'

'Here comes Karl,' called Lammchen, as the door banged outside.

'Well let's have the food, woman,' said Morschel. 'And I am right, son-in-law, you ask your pastor. It's not nice.'

A young man came in, but young only in years; in appearance he was totally un-young; even more sallow and distempered than the old man. He growled 'Evening', and taking no notice at all of the guest proceeded to take off jacket and waistcoat, then his shirt. Pinneberg watched with growing amazement.

'Been doing overtime?' asked the old man.

Karl Morschel growled something inaudible.

'Leave off cleaning up for now, Karl,' said Mrs Morschel. 'Come and eat.'

But Karl had the tap already running, and had begun washing himself very thoroughly. He was naked from the hips up. Pinneberg felt a little embarrassed on account of Lammchen. But she didn't seem to mind; that was the way things were, to her.

It wasn't the way things were to Pinneberg: the ugly earthenware plates, all chipped and stained, the half-cold potato cakes which tasted of onions, the pickled gherkins, the lukewarm bottled beer, which was only put out for the men; and on top of all that this miserable kitchen, and Karl, washing. . .

Karl sat down at the table and said disagreeably, 'I need a beer.'

'This is Emma's fiancé,' explained Mrs Morschel. 'They're getting married soon.'

'Oh, so she's landed one after all,' said Karl. 'A bourgeois, I see. A proletarian isn't good enough for her.'

'See what I mean,' said father Morschel, highly satisfied.

'You'd better pay your keep before you open your mouth here,' declared Mrs Morschel.

'I don't see what you mean,' said Karl sourly to his father. 'I'd rather have a real bourgeois than you social fascists.'

'Social fascists!' retorted the old man angrily. 'I'd like to know who's the fascist here, you Soviet slave.'

'Oh, so we're the slaves? What happened to the Social Democrats' promise to build bonny babies, not battle-cruisers, then?'

Pinneberg listened with a certain satisfaction. What the old man had been handing out to him he was now getting back from his son with interest. But it didn't improve the taste of the potato-cakes; it wasn't a nice dinner; he had imagined his engagement party quite differently.

A NIGHT-TIME CHAT ABOUT LOVE AND MONEY

Pinneberg had let his train go without him; he could get one at four in the morning and still be at work in time.

The couple were sitting in the dark kitchen. Mr Morschel was asleep in one room, Mrs Morschel in the other. Karl had gone to a Communist Party meeting.

They had drawn two kitchen chairs up to each other and were sitting with their backs to the cold stove. The door to the little kitchen balcony was open and the wind was gently moving the thin curtain over the door. Outside, above the hot courtyard full of the din of radios, was the night sky, dark, with very pale stars.

'What I would like,' said Pinneberg softly, squeezing Lammchen's hand, 'would be to have somewhere nice. I mean,' he tried to describe it, 'somewhere bright, with white curtains, and as clean as clean.'

'I know,' said Lammchen. 'It must be awful for you in our house, not being used to it.'

'I didn't mean it like that, Lammchen.'

'Yes you did. And why shouldn't you say so? It *is* awful. Karl and Father always rowing, Father and Mother always quarrelling, Karl and Father always trying to diddle her over the housekeeping money, Mother short-changing them over the meals. It's awful, awful.'

'But why are they like that? There are three people earning in your home; things ought to be quite easy.'

Lammchen didn't answer him. 'I simply don't belong here,' she carried on. 'I've always been the Cinderella. When Father and Karl

come home, their day's work is done. I have to start in on the
washing up and ironing and sewing and darning socks. Oh, but it's
not really that!' she cried aloud. 'I wouldn't mind that. It's being
taken for granted, being pushed around and never getting a kind
word, and Karl behaving as though he was keeping me because he
pays more for his board and lodging than me. . . But I don't earn as
much as him. . . What sort of money can you get as a shopgirl these
days?'

'It will be over soon,' said Pinneberg. 'Very soon.'

'It's not really that either,' she cried desperately. 'Not really. You
see, Sonny, they've always despised me, "Dummy" they call me. Of
course I'm not that clever. There's lots of things I don't understand.
And then, not being pretty. . .'

'But you are pretty!'

'You're the first one who ever said so. If we ever went to a dance, I
was always a wallflower. And if Mother told Karl to send his friends
over, he would say, "Who'd want to dance with a nanny-goat like
her?" You really are the first. . .'

A feeling he didn't quite like came over Pinneberg. 'She really
oughtn't to be telling me this,' he thought. 'I'd always thought she
was pretty. Perhaps she isn't pretty after all.'

But Lammchen talked on: 'Dear Sonny, I don't want to moan to
you. I just wanted to tell you this one time, so that you know I don't
belong here, I belong to you. Only to you. And I'm so so grateful to
you, not just because of the Shrimp, but because you've come and
rescued Cinderella. . .'

'Oh, you're so. . .'

'Let me finish. And when you say we want our place to be bright
and clean, you'll have to be a bit patient: I've never learned to cook
properly. And if I do anything wrong, you'll have to tell me, and I'll
never lie to you. . .'

'Now, now, Lammchen, that's enough.'

'And we'll never, never, quarrel. Ah God, Sonny, how happy we're
going to be, just the two of us. And then there'll be three, with our
little Shrimp.'

'What if it's a girl?'

'This Shrimp's going to be a boy, I tell you. A lovely little boy.'

After a while they stood up and stepped out onto the balcony. Yes, the sky was there over the roofs and the stars. They stood a while in silence, their hands on each other's shoulders.

Then they came down to earth, and the cramped yard with its many lighted window-squares, and the squawking jazz.

'Shall we get a radio?' he asked suddenly.

'Yes, of course. That way I'll not be so lonely when you're at work. But not to start off with. There's such a dreadful lot we have to get first!'

'Yes,' he said.

Silence.

'Sonny,' began Lammchen quietly. 'I've got to ask you something.'

'Yes?' he said, uneasily.

'But don't be cross!'

'No,' he said.

'Have you any savings?'

There was a pause.

'A bit,' he said, hesitantly. 'What about you?'

'I've got a bit too,' and then, very quickly, 'But only a very, very little bit.'

'Tell me,' he said.

'No, you tell me first,' she said.

'I. . .' he began, then broke off.

'Oh, please tell me!' she begged.

'It's really very little. Perhaps even less than you.'

'It can't be.'

'Oh, yes, it can.'

There was a pause. A very long pause.

'Ask me,' he begged.

'Right,' she said, and took a deep breath. 'Is it more than. . .'

She paused.

'Than what?' he asked.

'Oh heavens,' she laughed suddenly, 'why ever should I be embarrassed! I've got a hundred and thirty marks in my savings account.'

He said slowly and proudly: 'Four hundred and seventy.'

'That's great!' said Lammchen. 'That makes a round six hundred marks. Sonny, what a pile of money!'

'I dunno. . .' he said 'It doesn't seem a lot to me. But living as a bachelor's very expensive.'

'And I had to give up seventy marks out of the hundred and twenty I'm paid, for board and lodging.'

'It takes a long time to save up that amount,' he said.

'An awful long time,' she said. 'It takes ages to grow.'

There was a pause.

'I don't believe we'll be able to get a flat in Ducherow straight away,' he said.

'Then we'll have to get a furnished room.'

'That way, we'll be able to save more for our furniture.'

'But I believe it's terribly expensive to rent furnished.'

'Let's work it out,' he suggested.

'Yes, let's see how we'll get by. And let's reckon as if we had nothing in the bank.'

'Oh yes, we mustn't break into that. That's got to grow. So, one hundred and eighty marks wages. . .'

'You'll get more as a married man.'

'Ah, I'm not so sure about that.' He had got very embarrassed. 'It's probably in the wage agreement, but my boss is so funny. . .'

'I wouldn't let it bother me whether he was funny or not.'

'Lammchen, let's reckon with a hundred and eighty to start with. If it's more so much the better, but let's work with what we're sure of.'

'All right,' she agreed. 'So, first, the deductions.'

'Yes,' he said. 'You can't change those. Taxes 6 marks and unemployment insurance 2 marks 70. Employee's insurance 4 marks, public health scheme 5 marks 40. Union dues 4 marks 50. . .'

'You can do without that union. . .'

Pinneberg said with some impatience: 'Oh, lay off. I've had enough of that from your father.'

'All right,' said Lammchen. 'That makes 22 marks 60 deductions. You don't need any fares, do you?'

'I don't, thank goodness.'

'So we're left with 157 basic. What would the rent be?'

'I don't know, actually. A room and a kitchen, furnished. Must be 40 marks.'

'Let's say 45,' was Lammchen's opinion. 'That leaves 112 marks 40. What do you think we need for food?'

'What would you say?'

'Mother always says she needs 1 mark 50 a day for each of us.'

'That's 90 marks a month,' he said.

'Then there'll be 22 marks 40 left over,' she said.

They looked at each other.

'And it doesn't leave us anything for heat,' said Lammchen swiftly, 'Or gas, or light or postage. There's nothing for clothes, or linen, or shoes. And you have to buy your own cutlery sometimes.'

'It'd be nice to go to the cinema once in a while. And go on an outing on Sundays. I do like to have the odd cigarette, too.'

'And we want to save something.'

'At least 20 marks a month.'

'Thirty.'

'But how?'

'Let's add it up again.'

'There's nothing to be done about the deductions.'

'And you can't get a room and a kitchen any cheaper.'

'Possibly five marks cheaper.'

'Well. . . we'll see. I would like to take a newspaper.'

'Of course. The food is the only thing we can cut down on. So, perhaps 10 marks less.'

They looked at each other again.

'We still won't manage. And saving's out of the question.'

'Tell me,' she said anxiously. 'Do you always have to wear starched shirts? I couldn't iron them.'

'Yes. The boss insists on it. A shirt costs sixty pfennigs to iron and a collar costs ten.'

'That's another five marks a month,' she calculated.

'And there's shoe repairs.'

'Oh, yes, that's dreadfully dear.'

A pause.

'Let's add it up again.'

After a while: 'So let's take another ten marks off the food. But I can't do it for under seventy.'

'How do other people manage?'

'I really don't know. Loads of other people have a lot less.'

'I don't understand it.'

'There must be a mistake somewhere. Let's add it up again.'

They added it up over and over again, but it always came out the same. They looked at each other. 'Do you know what?' said Lammchen suddenly, 'If I get married, surely I can cash my employee's insurance?'

'Oh great!' he said 'That'll put in a hundred and twenty marks at least.'

'What about your mother?' she asked. 'You've never told me anything about her.'

'There's nothing to tell,' he said shortly, 'I never write to her.'

'Oh,' she said. 'That's that, then.'

There was another silence.

A dead end had been reached, so they stood up, and stepped onto the balcony. The courtyard was almost completely dark now; the town itself had gone quiet. In the distance, a car hooted.

He was deep in thought. 'A haircut costs eighty pfennigs as well,' he said.

'Oh, stop it,' she begged. 'If other people manage, we can, too. It'll be all right.'

'Now listen, Lammchen,' he said. 'I won't give you any house-keeping money. At the beginning of the month we'll put all our money in a pot, and we can each take out what we need.'

'Yes,' she said. 'I've got a nice pot for that: blue earthenware. I'll show it you. And we'll be very economical. I might even learn to starch shirts.'

'And there's no sense in getting five-pfennig cigarettes,' he said, 'You can get perfectly decent ones for three.'

Suddenly she shrieked: 'Heavens! Sonny, we've forgotten the Shrimp! He'll cost money!'

He thought about it. 'But what costs are there for such a small child? After all there's the Confinement Grant, and the Nursing Mother's Grant and we'll be paying less tax. . . I don't think he'll cost anything at all for the first year or two.'

'I don't know,' she said doubtfully.

A white figure was standing in the doorway.

'Aren't you two going to bed at all tonight?' asked Mrs Morschel.
'You could still get three hours' sleep.'

'Yes, Mother,' said Lammchen.

'Go on, then,' said the old lady. 'I'll sleep with Father tonight.
Karl's not coming home. You can take him into bed with you,
your. . .' The door slammed, leaving whatever he was unsaid.

'I don't want to, actually,' said Pinneberg, rather offended. 'It's
awkward here, in your parents' place.'

'Oh God, Sonny,' she laughed. 'I believe Karl's right. You are a
bourgeois. . .'

'Not a bit of it,' he protested. 'If it doesn't bother your parents. . .'
He hesitated again. 'What if Dr Sesame were wrong; I've got nothing
on me.'

'In that case let's go back and sit on the kitchen chairs,' she
suggested. 'I'm aching all over.'

'Oh no, I'll come, Lammchen,' he said repentantly.

'Not if you don't want to. . .'

'I'm a sheep, Lammchen! I'm a sheep!'

'That makes two of us,' said she. 'We should get on well.'

'We will! You'll see!' he said.

PART ONE

THE SMALL TOWN

THE MARRIAGE BEGINS AS IT SHOULD, WITH A WEDDING TRIP, BUT – DO WE NEED A CASSEROLE?

The train which left Platz for Ducherow at 2.10 on that Saturday in August bearing Mr and Mrs Pinneberg in a third-class non-smoking compartment was also transporting in its luggage van a largish wicker trunk with Emma's belongings, a bag with Emma's bedding, but only hers ('how are we supposed to pay for his? – he can get it himself'), and a wooden egg-crate with Emma's china.

The train was quickly out of the large town of Platz; no one had come to the station; the last suburban houses were left behind, then came fields. For a while the train ran along beside the shimmering Strela, then came woodland with birch trees along the tracks.

The only other person in the compartment was a grumpy-looking man who could not make up his mind whether to read the newspaper, look at the scenery, or watch the young couple. He switched surprisingly from one pastime to the other, and always caught the two of them out just when they believed themselves completely safe from his gaze.

Pinneberg laid his right hand ostentatiously on his knee, where the ring gleamed reassuringly. After all, Grumpy-face wasn't seeing anything that wasn't sanctioned by law. But he was not looking at the ring just then, he was observing the scenery.

'The ring looks fine,' said Pinneberg contentedly. 'You wouldn't know it's only gilt.'

'You know it's funny wearing a ring; I can feel it all the time and I can't help looking at it.'

'That's because you're not used to it. People who have been married a long time don't notice it at all. They don't even know when they've lost it.'

'That'd never happen to me!' exclaimed Lammchen indignantly, 'I'll always know it's there, always, always!'

'Me too,' declared Pinneberg. 'Because it reminds me of you.'

'And me of you!'

Their heads moved closer together, closer and closer. And then pulled away: Grumpy-face was now giving them a perfectly bare-faced stare.

'He's not from Ducherow,' whispered Pinneberg. 'I'd know him.'

'D'you know everyone around here?'

'Anyone who's anyone, of course I do. From when I used to sell men's and women's wear at Bergmanns. That way you get to know everybody.'

'Why did you give that up? It's your line really, isn't it?'

'Had a row with the boss,' said Pinneberg, shortly.

Lammchen would have liked to inquire further, but she sensed another abyss, so she left it there. There was plenty of time for every-thing now they were properly married in a Registry Office.

His thoughts must have been running along similar lines, for he said: 'Your mother will have got back home a long time ago.'

'Yes,' she said. 'Mother's cross, that's why she didn't come to the station with us. When we were coming away from the Registry Office, she said: "What a mingy wedding".'

'She's better saving her money. I hate those sort of festive blow-outs where everyone makes dirty jokes.'

'Of course,' said Lammchen. 'It would just have been fun for Mother.'

'We didn't get married so your mother could have some fun,' he rejoined swiftly.

Pause.

'Hey,' Lammchen began again, 'I'm dying to see our flat.'

'Ah well, I hope you like it. There's not much choice in Ducherow.'

'Come on then, Hannes, describe it to me.'

'All right,' he said, and began once again to describe what he had often described before.

'As I told you, it's right out of town. In the depths of the country.'

'That's what I think's so nice. . .'

'But it's a real tenement block. Mothes the Builders put it out there thinking other people would come and build out there. But nobody's come.'

'Why not?'

'I dunno. Too lonely for people, twenty minutes out of town, no proper road.'

'About the flat,' she reminded him.

'Yes, well, we're right at the top, with a widow called Mrs Scharrenhofer.'

'What's she like then?'

'Ah, what can I say? She came on very refined, and I guess she has seen better days, but what with inflation. . . Anyway she did a lot of weeping when I was there.'

'Oh Lord!'

'She's not going to cry all the time. And anyway we're going to keep ourselves to ourselves, aren't we? We don't want to mix with other people. We've got each other and that's enough.'

'Of course. But what if she pesters us?'

'I don't think she will. She's a very refined old lady with snow white hair. And she's terribly anxious about her things. It's all good stuff and belonged to her late mother; and we have to remember to sit down slowly on the sofa – it has good old-fashioned springs and won't bear any sudden weight.'

'I only hope I remember,' said Lammchen doubtfully. 'If I'm really happy or if I'm sad and feel like bursting into tears I may well sit down and not give the good old-fashioned springs a thought.'

'You must,' said Pinneberg sternly. 'You've got to. And you mustn't wind up the clock under the glass case on the display cabinet. Nor must I. Only she can do that.'

'Then she can take her silly old clock out. I don't want a clock in my home that I can't wind up.'

'It's no big problem. We can simply say we're disturbed by the chime.'

'Let's do it this evening! Who knows, those grand sort of clocks may have to be wound up every night. So come on, tell me. What's it like when you come up the stairs and you get to the door of the flat, and then. . .'

'Then there's the hall, which we share. The first door on the left is our kitchen. That's to say. . . it's not really a proper kitchen; it must have been just an attic room once, under the sloping roof, but there's a gas cooker. . .'

'With two burners,' completed Lammchen, in a melancholy tone. 'How I'll cope with that is a mystery to me. Nobody can cook on two burners, it's impossible. Mother has four.'

'Of course it's possible with two.'

'You wait and see.'

'We want to eat very simply, and two burners are perfectly adequate.'

'Yes, I know. But you'd like some soup; that's one saucepan. Some meat: two saucepans. Vegetables: three. And potatoes: four. So while I've got two pots heating on the two burners, the other two will have gone cold. So how, if you please. . .?'

'Oh,' he said meditatively. 'I don't know. . .'

And then, in a fright: 'But then you'll need four saucepans!'

'I will indeed,' she said proudly. 'And that's not all. I have to have a casserole.'

'Oh no! I only bought one saucepan!'

Lammchen was adamant. 'So we have to buy four more.'

'But that can't be done on my salary, we'll have to take it out of our savings again!'

'It can't be helped, Sonny. Be reasonable. What must be, must be. We do need the saucepans.'

'I didn't think it was going to be like this,' he said sadly. 'I thought we'd get along nicely *and* save money, and here we are starting to spend it already.'

'But if it can't be helped!'

'A casserole is quite unnecessary!' he said heatedly. 'I never eat anything stewed. Never! Never! Just for the occasional bit of stewed meat, it would be crazy to lay out on a casserole.'

'Then what about roulades?' asked Lammchen. 'And pot roasts?'

'And there isn't any water in the kitchen, either,' he said despairingly. 'For water, you'll have to go in to Frau Scharrenhofer's kitchen.'

'Oh Lord!' she said yet again.

From a distance a marriage looks so extraordinarily easy: two people marry and have children. They live together, are as nice as possible to each other, and try to get on in life. Friendship, love, kindliness, food, drink, sleep, going to work, housekeeping, an outing on a Sunday, occasionally a visit to the cinema in the evening! And that's it.

But close up, the whole business dissolves into a thousand individual problems. The marriage itself recedes into the background; it is taken for granted and is simply the precondition for the rest. But what about the casserole? And should he tell Mrs Scharrenhofer this very evening to take the clock out of the room? That's the reality.

Both of them sensed it dimly. But those weren't yet urgent problems; all thought of casseroles was forgotten in the realization that they were now alone in the compartment. Grumpy-face had got out somewhere and they had not even noticed. Casserole and clock were thrown to the winds as they fell into each other's arms.

The train rattled along; and they kissed and kissed, pausing only to draw breath. Then the train began to slow down: Ducherow was approaching.

'Oh no, not already!' they cried together.

PINNEBERG TURNS MYSTERIOUS AND LAMMCHEN
HAS SOME RIDDLES TO SOLVE

'I've ordered a car,' said Pinneberg hastily. 'The walk to our place would be too much for you.'

'Why should it be? Don't we want to save money? Only last Sunday we walked around Platz for two hours!'

'But there's your things. . .'

'We could have got a porter to bring them along. Or someone from your firm. You've got workmen. . .'

'Oh no, I don't like that, it looks as if. . .'

'All right,' said Lammchen, submissively, 'As you like. . .'

'And one more thing,' he said hastily, as the train was already braking. 'Let's not act as if we're married. Let's pretend we've only just met.'

'But why?' asked Lammchen in astonishment. 'When we *are* married.'

'You see,' he explained with some embarrassment. 'It's the people here. We didn't send out any cards, we didn't put a notice in the paper, so if they saw we were married they might be offended, mightn't they?'

'I don't understand,' said Lammchen, utterly mystified. You'll have to explain again. Why should people be offended if we're married?'

'Yes, I'll explain it all to you. But not now. Now we have to. . . Are you taking your bag? Now, please, look as though you don't know me very well.'

Lammchen said nothing more, but kept casting dubious sidelong glances at him. He had suddenly become the perfect gentleman, helping his lady out of the carriage, then saying, with an embarrassed smile: 'This is the Central Station of Ducherow. We also have the narrow-gauge line to Maxfelde. This way, please.' And he went ahead, down the steps from the platform, really a little too fast for such a concerned husband, who had gone to the lengths of ordering a car in case the walk was too much for his wife. He kept two or three steps in front of her all the time, and went out through a side exit. There stood a car with its hood up.

The driver said: 'Good afternoon, Mr Pinneberg. Good afternoon, miss.'

Pinneberg murmured hastily, 'One moment please. Perhaps you could get in while I go and look after the luggage. . .' And he was off.

Lammchen stood and looked at the station square, with its small two-storey houses. Directly opposite was the Station Hotel.

'Is Kleinholz's round here?' she asked the driver.

'Where Mr Pinneberg works? No, miss, we'll be going by there shortly. It's right on the Market Place, beside the Town Hall.'

'I say,' said Lammchen. 'Couldn't we take the hood down? It's such a lovely day.'

'Sorry, miss,' said the driver. 'Mr Pinneberg expressly asked for the hood up. I don't normally have it up myself in this weather.'

'Ah well,' said Lammchen. 'If that was what Mr Pinneberg ordered.' And she got in.

She saw him coming, behind the porter who was pushing a cart with the trunk, the bed-bag and the crate. And because for the last five minutes she had been seeing her husband with quite new eyes, she was struck by the fact that he kept his right hand in his

trouser pocket. And that was really not his style; it was something
he never did; yet there he was with his right hand in his trouser
pocket.

They drove off.

'So,' he said, with a slightly embarrassed laugh. 'This way you get
to see the whole of Ducherow in passing. Ducherow is just one long
street.'

'Yes,' she said, 'you were going to explain to me why people might
be offended.'

'Later,' he said. 'It's difficult to talk now. The road-surface is awful
here.'

'All right, later,' she said, and was silent too. But then she noticed
something else; he had pressed his head right into the corner, so that
if anyone looked into the car they would not be able to recognize
him. 'There's your firm,' she said. '"Emil Kleinholz. Corn, animal
feed and fertilizers. Potatoes wholesale and retail." Oh, I can buy my
potatoes at your place.'

'No, no,' he said hastily. 'That's an old sign. We don't do potatoes
retail any more.'

'That's a pity,' she said. 'It would have been really fun coming into
your place and buying ten pounds of potatoes from you. I wouldn't
have acted married at all, you know!'

'Yes it is a pity,' he said. 'It would have been great fun.'

She tapped her foot and gave an indignant snort, but said nothing
further. A little later she asked pensively, 'Is there any water around
here?'

'What d'you mean?' he asked cautiously.

'To go swimming, of course,' snapped Lammchen. 'What else
would I mean?'

'Oh yes, there are a number of places where you can swim,' he said.

And they drove on. They had now left the main street –
Lammchen saw a sign reading 'Feldstrasse' – and there were detached
houses, all in their own gardens.

'Oh look, it's pretty here,' said she, happily. 'Masses of summer
flowers!'

The car was fairly bouncing along.

'Now we're in Green End,' said he.

'Green End?'

'Yes. Our road's called Green End.'

'This is a road? I thought the driver had got lost.'

On the left was a paddock, fortified with barbed-wire and occupied by a few cows and a horse. On the right was a field of pink clover in bloom.

'Do open the window now!' she begged.

'We're nearly there.'

The paddock marked the end of the levelled ground. There the town had planted its last memorial – and what a memorial! On the last piece of levelled ground stood Mothes the Builders' speculative apartment box, a lank and lofty affair, plastered brown and yellow in the front, its side walls bare, waiting for adjoining buildings.

'It's not exactly beautiful,' said Lammchen, looking up at it.

'But it's very nice inside,' he said encouragingly.

'Then let's go inside,' she said. 'And then of course it'll be lovely for the Shrimp. So healthy.'

Pinneberg and the driver picked up the wicker trunk, Lammchen took the egg-crate; the driver said: 'I'll go back for the bed-bag.'

On the ground floor where the shop was it smelled of cheese and potatoes; on the first floor it was mainly cheese, on the second floor cheese reigned supreme, and right at the top under the roof, the damp, mouldy potato-smell was there again.

'How did this smell get past the cheese? Can you tell me that?'

But Pinneberg was already opening the door.

'Let's go into our room first!'

They crossed the small hall, it was indeed small, with a wardrobe on the right and a chest on the left. The men could scarcely get by with the trunk.

'Here,' said Pinneberg, and flung open the door.

Lammchen stepped over the threshold.

'Goodness,' she said, in confused surprise. 'What's all this. . .?'

But then she threw down everything she was carrying onto a re-upholstered plush sofa, the springs of which groaned under the impact of the egg-crate, ran to the window – there were four big windows streaming light into the long room – tore it open and leaned out.

Down below her was the road, a field track of wheel-ruts worn into the sand, overgrown with grass, goose-foot and sow-thistles. And the clover field: now she could smell it, and nothing has such a glorious smell as flowering clover after the sun has been shining on it all day.

And next to the clover field were other fields, yellow and green, and a few strips of rye that were already cut to stubble. And then came a ribbon of deep green: meadows; and in between willows and poplars and elder there flowed the Strela, here quite a narrow little stream.

'On its way to Platz,' Lammchen thought. 'To my Platz where I worked so hard, and was so miserable and lonely, in a flat looking out onto a courtyard, nothing but walls and stones. . . Here you can see for ever.'

And then she saw in the window next to hers the face of her young man. He had just settled with the driver who had brought the bed-bag, and was now beaming at her, lost to himself with joy.

She called to him: 'Just look at all this. This is a place you can really live. . .'

She reached her right hand to him out of her window, and he took it with his left.

'The whole summer!' she called, and described a half-circle with the other arm.

'D'you see that little train. . .? That's the narrow-gauge railway to Maxfelde,' he said.

The driver appeared below. He must have been in the shop, for he hailed them with a bottle of beer. The man carefully wiped the rim with the palm of his hand, bent back his head, called 'Your good health!' and drank.

'Cheers!' called Pinneberg, dropping Lammchen's hand.

'Now then,' said Lammchen. 'Let's have a look at this chamber of horrors.'

And, like all such places, very horrid it was. To turn away from observing the clear simplicity of the countryside and see a room in which. . . Now Lammchen was certainly not spoilt, having perhaps once in her life seen simple, rectangular furniture in a shopwindow in Mainzerstrasse in Platz. But this!. . .

'Please, Sonny,' she said. 'Take me by the hand and lead me. I'm afraid I'll knock something over, or get stuck and not be able to go forward or back.'

'Oh, I don't think it's as bad as all that,' said he, a little hurt. 'I think there are some quite cosy corners here.'

'Yes, corners,' said she. 'But now tell me, what in heaven's name is this? No, don't say a word. Let's go on. I must examine it at close quarters.'

They set out on a tour of exploration, which most of the time they had to do in single file, Lammchen never relinquishing her Sonny's hand.

The room was a sort of ravine; not all that narrow, but extremely long, rather like a bridle path. Four-fifths of it was entirely filled with upholstered furniture, walnut tables, display cabinets, mirrored consoles, flower-stands, whatnots and a large parrot cage (without the parrot), while in the remaining fifth there was nothing but two beds and a wash-stand. But it was the partition between that and the rest of the room which had attracted Lammchen's attention. It had been erected to separate the living- from the sleeping-area, but it wasn't made of plaster-board, it didn't have a curtain or a folding screen. It was a kind of grape-vine trellis of slats extending from ceiling to floor with an arch to go through. Not ordinary plain slats, mark you, but beautifully-stained walnut, each with five parallel grooves carved down it. To stop it looking too naked, this trellis had been wound with paper and fabric flowers: roses, daffodils and bunches of violets. There were also those long green paper garlands that you get at beer festivals.

'Oh God!' said Lammchen, and sat down. She sat down just where she was standing, but there was no risk of landing on the floor, because there was something standing everywhere, and her bottom landed on the wicker seat of an ebony piano stool, just standing there without its piano.

Pinneberg stood there, speechless. He didn't know what to say. It had all quite appealed to him when he'd come to rent the place. The trellis had seemed distinctly gay.

Suddenly Lammchen's eyes began to fire sparks; her legs regained their strength, she stood up; she approached the flowered trellis; she ran her finger down one of the slats. The slat was as previously described: ridged, grooved, notched. Lammchen examined the finger.

'There!' She held it out to her young man. It was grey.

'A bit dusty,' he said cautiously.

'A bit!' Her eyes darted fire at him. 'Will you get me a charwoman? Five hours a day she'd need to be at it, at least!'

'But why? To do what?'

'And who's supposed to keep the place clean, may I ask? I could just about handle the ninety-three pieces of furniture with all their knobs and notches and pillars and shells, though it'd be a criminal waste of time. But this trellis will take three hours a day on its own. And then the paper flowers. . .'

She slapped a rose. The rose fell to the floor leaving in its wake a million grey dust-particles dancing in the sunshine.

'Are you going to get me a charwoman?' asked Lammchen, utterly unlike a lamb.

'What if you did it thoroughly once a week?'

'Don't be idiotic. And this is where the Shrimp is supposed to grow up? How many bruises is he going to get bumping into all the knobs and handles? Hm?'

'Perhaps by then we shall have a flat.'

'And what's going to happen in the meantime? Who's going to heat this place in winter? Under the roof? Two outside walls! Four windows! We could use up half a ton of briquettes a day and still have our teeth chattering!'

'But,' he said, rather offended, 'of course a furnished place is never the same as one of your own.'

'I know that. But you tell me: do *you* like it? D'you find it pleasant, would you like to live here? Just think of it, coming home and having to mind every step, and dustsheets all over the place. Ow! It's just as I thought; they're fastened down with pins.'

'But we won't find anything better.'

'I'll find something better. You bet I will. When can we give notice?'

'On the first of September. But. . .'

'To leave when?'

'The thirtieth of September. But. . .'

'Six weeks,' she groaned. 'Well, I'll survive it. I'm only sorry for the poor Shrimp, having to go through it all as well. I thought I was going to have a fine time taking him for walks out here. Cooking, polishing the furniture.'

'But we can't give notice straight after we've arrived!'

'Of course we can. Preferably today, this very minute!'

She stood there, all determination, aggressive, with red cheeks and flashing eyes, her head thrown back.

Pinneberg said slowly: 'You know, Lammchen, I'd thought you were quite different. Much gentler. . .'

She laughed, sprang over to him, ran her hand through his hair. 'Of course I'm different from what you thought I was. Did you really think I could be all sugar and spice when I've been going out to work since I left school, and had the sort of father and brother I've had, as well as that bitch of a boss and those workmates of mine?'

'Yes, I suppose. . .' said he, thinking about it.

The clock, the famous glass-covered clock on the mantelpiece above the stove, flanked by a hammering cupid and a glass oriole, struck seven, briskly.

'Quick march, Sonny! We'd better get down to the shop to buy the food for tonight and tomorrow. I can't wait to see this so-called kitchen.'

THE PINNEBERGS PAY A COURTESY CALL,
THERE IS SOME CRYING, AND THE ENGAGEMENT CLOCK
KEEPS ON STRIKING

Supper was over, a supper bought, prepared, conversed over and filled with plans by an utterly transformed Lammchen. There was bread and cold meats, and tea. Pinneberg had been in favour of beer, but Lammchen had declared. 'One: tea is cheaper. Two: beer isn't good for the Shrimp. Right up till he's born, we're not going to drink a drop of alcohol. And, as a general rule. . .'

'*We*,' thought Pinneberg, sadly, but he only asked: 'What, as a general rule?'

'As a general rule, this evening's feast is an exception. Twice a week at least all we'll have is fried potatoes and bread with margarine. Good butter – ? Perhaps on Sundays. Margarine has vitamins too.'

'But not the same ones. . .'

'Right, but either we want to get ahead, or we gradually use up what we've saved.'

'No, no,' he said hurriedly.

'So, now let's tidy the things away. I can wash up tomorrow morning early. Then I'll pack up the first consignment and we'll visit Mrs Scharrenhofer. It's only polite.'

'On the first evening?'

'Straight away. She must know at once. I'm surprised she hasn't put in an appearance by now.'

In the kitchen, which was really only an attic with a gas cooker, Lammchen said yet again, 'Oh well, six weeks will be soon over.'

Back in the room, a flurry of activity developed. She took off all the little covers and bits of crochet and carefully laid them in a very neat pile. 'Quick, Sonny, fetch a saucer from the kitchen. We don't want her to think we're keeping her pins.'

Finally: 'There we are.'

She laid the packet of covers over her arm and searched around with her eyes: 'And you take the clock, Sonny.'

He was still doubtful: 'Should I really?'

'You take the clock. I'll go ahead and open the doors.'

And she really did go ahead, quite without fear, first across the little hall, then into a room like a cupboard with brooms and other such clutter, then through the kitchen. . .

'Now that's a real kitchen, Sonny! And all I'm allowed to do here is fetch water!'

. . . then through a bedroom long and narrow as a roller-towel but containing two beds. . .

'And she's left her late husband's bed standing here. Better than letting us sleep in it.'

. . . and then into a little room, which was almost pitch-dark, so thick were the floor-length plush curtains hanging over the only window.

Mrs Pinneberg stopped in the doorway. 'Good evening,' she said, uncertainly, into the darkness. 'We only wanted to say good evening.'

'One moment,' said a tearful voice. 'Just one moment. I'll put the light on.'

Behind her, Pinneberg was doing something at a table and she heard a faint whirr from the precious clock. Doubtless he was moving it swiftly out of sight.

'All men are cowards,' thought Lammchen.

'I'm just putting the light on,' moaned the voice, still from the same corner. 'You must be the young people? I've got to straighten myself up a bit first. I always cry a little in the evenings. . .'

'Do you?' asked Lammchen. 'If we're disturbing you. . . We only wanted to. . .'

'No, no, I'll put the light on. Stay here, young folk. I'll tell you why I was crying, and I will put on the light. . .'

And now there really was light, or what old Mrs Scharrenhofer called light: a single dim bulb, high up near the ceiling, a murky twilight among satin and plush, a pallid, lifeless grey. And in the gloom stood a tall bony woman, the colour of lead, with a reddish long nose, moist eyes and thin grey-white hair in a grey alpaca dress.

'The young people!' she said, giving Lammchen a damp, bony hand. 'Young folk, in my home!'

Lammchen clutched her packet of covers closely to her. She so hoped the old lady's tear-clouded gaze would not light upon it. What a good thing her young man had got rid of the clock; perhaps they would be able to take it back unnoticed. Lammchen's courage was gone.

'But we really didn't want to disturb you,' said Lammchen.

'How could you disturb me? Nobody comes here any more. Now when my good man was still alive! But it's a good thing he isn't.'

'Was he very ill?' asked Lammchen, and was aghast at her silly question.

But the old lady hadn't heard it. 'Look!' she said. 'Young people, before the war, we had a comfortable fifty thousand marks. And now that money's all gone. How can it be all gone?' she asked anxiously. 'An old lady can't spend that much, can she?'

'Inflation,' said Pinneberg, cautiously.

'It can't have all gone,' said the old lady, unheeding.

'I sit here reckoning it up. I've written it all down. I sit here, reckoning. Here it says: a pound of butter: three thousand marks. . . can a pound of butter cost three thousand marks?'

'In the inflation. . .' began Lammchen, joining in.

'I'm going to tell you. I now know that my money's been stolen. Somebody who rented here stole it. I sit and wonder who. But I can't recall the names, so many people have lived here since the war. I sit and brood. I also realize it must have been someone really clever, because he falsified my housekeeping book so I wouldn't notice. He turned three into three thousand without me realizing.'

Lammchen looked despairingly at Pinneberg. Pinneberg didn't look up.

'Fifty thousand. . . how can fifty thousand have all gone? I've sat here and reckoned up everything I've bought in the years since my husband died: stockings and a few blouses. I had a lovely trousseau and I don't need much. I've written it all down and it doesn't even come to five thousand, I'm telling you.'

'But money has been devalued,' Lammchen tried again.

'He stole it,' said the old lady mournfully, and bright tear-drops flowed effortlessly from her eyes. 'I'll show you the books, I can see it now, the numbers are quite different later on, so many noughts.'

She stood up and went towards the mahogany secretaire.

'You don't need to do that,' said Pinneberg and Lammchen together.

At that moment, it happened: the clock outside, which Pinneberg had put down in the old lady's bedroom, struck a loud, brisk, silvery nine.

The old lady stopped in her tracks. Head raised, she peered into the darkness, listening with half-open mouth and trembling lip.

'What?' she asked nervously.

Lammchen seized Pinneberg's arm.

'That's my husband's clock: his engagement present. It's usually in the other room, surely?'

The clock had stopped striking.

'Mrs Scharrenhofer, we wanted to ask you,' Lammchen began.

But the old lady was not listening, perhaps she never listened to what other people said. She pushed the half-open door: there stood the clock, clearly visible even in the poor light. 'The young people have brought me my clock back,' whispered the old lady. 'My husband's engagement present. The young people don't like it here. They won't stay here either. No one stays. . .'

And as she spoke, the clock began to strike again, even faster and more glassily-sharp, stroke after stroke, ten times, fifteen times, twenty times, thirty times. . .

'That comes from moving it. It can't be moved any more,' whispered Pinneberg.

'Oh God, come away quickly!' begged Lammchen.

They stood up. But in the doorway stood the old lady, staring at the clock, and wouldn't let them by. 'It's striking,' she said. 'It's keeping on striking. And then it will never strike again. I'm hearing it for the last time. Everything's going. The money's gone, too. Whenever the clock struck, I always thought: my husband heard that. . .'

The clock stopped.

'Please, Mrs Scharrenhofer, I'm very sorry I touched your clock.'

'It's my fault,' sobbed Lammchen. 'It's all my fault. . .'

'Go, young people. Go away now. This had to be. Good night, young folk.'

The two of them squeezed past fearfully, timid as children.

Suddenly the old lady called loud and clear: 'Don't forget to go and register with the police on Monday. Otherwise I shall have trouble.'

THE VEIL OF MYSTERY IS RAISED:
BERGMANN AND KLEINHOLZ AND WHY PINNEBERG
MUST NOT BE MARRIED

They didn't rightly know how they got back to their own place, through the dark overstuffed rooms, clutching each other's hands like frightened children.

The room looked ghostly enough itself as they stood close to each other in the dark. Even the light seemed to have a grudging quality as though it was vying with the dimness at the old woman's next door.

'That was awful,' said Lammchen, drawing a deep breath.

'Yes,' he said. And then, after a while he repeated, 'Yes. She's mad, Lammchen. Pining about her money has turned her brain.'

'She is mad. And I. . .' The couple continued to clutch each other in the dark. 'I've got to be here all day on my own and she can come in whenever she likes! No! No!'

'Calm down, Lammchen. The other day she was quite different. Perhaps this was just the once.'

'Young people. . .' repeated Lammchen. 'It was so ugly the way she said it, as if she had some secret we couldn't know about. Oh, Sonny, Sonny, I don't want to end up like her! I couldn't be like her, could I?! I'm frightened.'

'You're Lammchen,' he said, and took her in his arms. She was so helpless; so tall and yet so helpless, and coming to him for protection. 'You're Lammchen and you'll stay Lammchen. How could you ever be like old Mrs Scharrenhofer?'

'You're right. And it wouldn't be good for the Shrimp for me to live here. He shouldn't have anything to be frightened of; he needs a happy mother to be happy himself.'

'Yes, yes,' he said, and stroked her and rocked her. 'Things will look after themselves; it'll turn out all right.'

'You say that. But you haven't promised me that we're going to move out. At once!'

'But how can we? Have we got the money to pay for two flats for a month and a half?'

'Oh, money!' said she. 'So I have to be frightened and the Shrimp stunted, all because of a bit of money!'

'Money,' he said. 'Wicked money, lovely money.'

He rocked her back and forth in his arms. He suddenly felt old and clever, and things that mattered once didn't matter any more. He could afford to be honest with her. 'I'm not particularly gifted at anything, Lammchen,' he said. 'I'm not going to rise very far. We're always going to have to struggle for money.'

'Oh you,' she said, in a sing-song voice, 'You.'

The white curtains moved gently against the windows in the wind. A soft light radiated through the room. An enchantment drew them towards the open window, arm in arm, and they leaned out.

The countryside was bathed in moonlight. Far to the right there was a tiny flickering dot of light; the last gas-lamp on Feldstrasse. But before them lay the countryside, beautifully divided up into patches of friendly brightness, and deep soft shade where the trees stood. It was so quiet that even up here they could hear the Strela rippling over the stones. And the night wind blew very gently on their foreheads.

'How beautiful it is,' she said. 'How peaceful!'

'Yes,' he said. 'It does you good. Just breathe in the air, it's not like your air in Platz.'

'My air in Platz! I'm not in Platz any more. I don't belong there any more. I'm in Green End, with Widow Scharrenhofer.'

'With her? No one else?'

'No one else. . .'

'Shall we go downstairs again?'

'Not now, Sonny, let's lie here a bit longer. I've got something to ask you.'

'Here it comes,' he thought.

But she didn't ask. She lay there in the window, the wind moving the fair hair on her forehead, laying it now this way, now that. He watched it.

'So peaceful. . .' said Lammchen.

'Yes,' he said. 'Come to bed, Lammchen.'

'Shan't we stay up a little longer? We can lie in tomorrow as it's Sunday. And I've got something to ask you.'

'Well, ask!'

That sounded irritable; he got himself a cigarette, lit it carefully, took a long drag and said again, but in a markedly gentler tone: 'Do ask, Lammchen.'

'Won't you tell me yourself?'

'But I don't know what you want to ask.'

'You know,' she said.

'I don't, really, Lammchen.'

'You know.'

'Lammchen, please be sensible. Ask me!'

'You know.'

'Well then, don't.' He was hurt.

'Sonny,' she said, 'Sonny, do you remember when we sat in Platz in the kitchen? On the day we got engaged? It was all dark, and there were such a lot of stars and we went out onto the kitchen balcony.'

'Yes,' he said crossly. 'I know all that. So. . .?'

'Don't you remember what we discussed?'

'Hey, listen, we gossiped on about a whole mass of things. How am I supposed to remember all that!'

'But we talked about something in particular. We even made a promise about it.'

'I dunno what it was,' he said shortly.

Before Mrs Emma Pinneberg, née Morschel, there lay this moonlit landscape, with the small gas lamp twinkling on the left. And straight opposite, still on this side of the Strela, was a cluster of trees, five or six of them. The Strela rippled and the night wind was very pleasant.

It was all very pleasant, and it would have been possible to let this evening be as it was: pleasant. But there was something that bored into Lammchen's mind like an intrusive voice that said: this cosiness is a fraud, it's all self-deception. You let things be pleasant and before you know what's happened you're up to your ears in trouble.

Lammchen turned her back to the landscape and said: 'No, we made a promise. We took each other's hands and promised that we would always be honest with each other, and have no secrets from each other.'

'Correction: you promised me.'

'You don't want to be honest?'

'Of course I do. But there are some things women don't need to know.'

'Oh,' said Lammchen, quite squashed. But she quickly recovered and hurried on: 'So your giving the driver five marks when the taxi-meter only said two marks forty, is that the sort of thing that we women don't need to know?'

'But he carried the trunk and the bed-bag upstairs!'

'For two marks sixty? And why did you go around with your right hand in your pocket so no one could see the ring? And why did the hood have to be on the car? And why didn't you go down with me to the shop earlier on? And why could people be offended if we were married? And why. . .?'

'Lammchen,' he said, 'Lammchen, I really don't want to. . .'

'It's ridiculous, Sonny,' she replied. 'You simply mustn't have any secrets from me, otherwise we'll start lying to each other, and we'll be just the same as everybody else.'

'That's all very well, Lammchen, but. . .'

'You can tell me everything, Sonny, everything! I'm not a gormless lamb, whatever you call me. I know I haven't anything to reproach you with.'

'Yes, yes, Lammchen; but you know it isn't as simple as that. I'd like to but it sounds so silly. . . so. . .'

'Is it something to do with a girl?' she asked resolutely.

'No, no. Well, actually, yes, but not in the way you think.'

'How, then? Just tell me, Sonny. I'm dying to know.'

'All right, Lammchen, if you must.' But then he hesitated again. 'Can't I tell you tomorrow?'

'Now! On the spot! How d'you think I'm going to get to sleep when I'm racking my brains over this? It's something to do with a girl but not to do with a girl. . . It sounds so mysterious.'

'Well then, listen. I've got to begin with Bergmann. You know I started off here at Bergmanns?'

'The outfitters? Yes, I know. And I do think drapery is much nicer than potatoes and fertilizers. Fertilizers – d'you sell actual manure as well?'

'Now Lammchen, if you're going to make fun of me. . .'

'I'm listening.' She had settled on the window seat and was looking alternately at her young man and the moonlit landscape. She was quite happy to look at it now, and very pleasant it looked too.

'All right; so at Bergmanns I was head salesman and got a hundred and seventy marks.'

'A hundred and seventy marks for a head salesman!'

'Will you be quiet! I was always the one to serve Mr Emil Kleinholz. He used up a lot of suits. He drinks, you see. He has to, for business reasons, with the farmers and the landowners. But he can't hold his drink. He falls down in the street and ruins his suits.'

'Shame! What does he look like?'

'Listen, will you! It was always me that had to serve him. Neither the boss nor the boss's wife could get him to order anything. If I wasn't there, they never had any luck with him, but I always sold him something. And all the time Kleinholz kept on at me about if I ever felt like a change and if I ever got fed up working for a Jewish firm, that he had a good clean Aryan business, and a good job as a book-keeper, and I'd earn more with him too... But I thought: you can talk away! I know when I'm well off, and old Bergmann is not at all bad and always fair to his employees.'

'So why did you leave him and go to Kleinholz?'

'It was over a complete trifle. You see, Lammchen, the custom here in Ducherow is that every morning the shops send their apprentices to get the mail from the post office. The other people in our line all do it: Sterns and Neuwirths, and Moses Minden. And the apprentices are strictly forbidden to show each other the mail. And the name of the sender has to be heavily crossed out straight away, so that our competitors don't know who we're buying from. But the apprentices were all at school together and they get nattering and forget the crossing out. And some of the businesses actually encourage them to nose around, Moses Minden in particular.'

'How petty everything is here!' said Lammchen.

'It's just as petty in big places. So what happened was that the Veterans' Association wanted to order three hundred windcheaters. And we four clothing businesses were all asked for a quote. The competition were nosing around to find where we were getting our designs from. And because we didn't trust the apprentices, I said to Bergmann: "I'll go myself, I'll get the post for the time being."'

'So? Did they find out?' asked Lammchen eagerly.

'No,' he said, highly affronted. 'Of course not. If an apprentice so much as squinted at my parcels from ten metres away, I threatened to give him a clip round the ear. *We* got the order.'

'Oh, come on Sonny, will you get to the point? When are we coming to the girl who isn't what I think? All that is no reason for you leaving Bergmanns.'

'I told you,' he said, embarrassed. 'It was all over a trifle. I fetched the mail myself for two weeks. And the boss's wife thought it was a very good arrangement, because there was never anything for me to do in the shop between eight and nine anyway, and in that time, while I was away, the apprentices could sweep the store-room. And so she simply declared, "Mr Pinneberg can get the mail every day", and I said, "No, that's not my job. A head salesman doesn't run round town with the parcels." And she said, "Oh yes you will!" and I said, "No, I won't" and in the end we both got into a temper, and I said to her: "You can't order me around. It was Mr Bergmann who employed me."'

'And what did he say?'

'What could he say? He couldn't put his wife in the wrong! He tried hard to persuade me, and in the end he said, very embarrassed, when I kept on saying No: "In that case, we're going to have to go our separate ways, Mr Pinneberg!" And I'd really got going by that time, so I said, "All right, I'll leave on the first day of next month." And he said, "You must think it over, Mr Pinneberg." And I would have thought it over, but by an unlucky chance Mr Kleinholz came into the shop that very day, and he noticed I was worked up, and got me to tell him all about it, and then he invited me to his house in the evening. We drank cognac and beer, and when I got home that night I had been taken on as book-keeper at a hundred and eighty marks. And knowing hardly anything about proper book-keeping at all.'

'Oh, Sonny. And your other boss: Bergmann? What did he say?'

'He was upset. He tried to talk me out of it. He kept saying: "Take it back, Pinneberg. Don't rush to your doom with your eyes open. How can you think of marrying that schicksa when you can see the memme's driving the father to drink, and the schicksa is worse than the memme?"'

'Did your boss really speak to you like that?'

'Oh yes, there are still a lot of real old-fashioned Jews around here. They're proud to be Jewish. I've often heard old Bergmann say: "Don't be so nasty, you're a Jew!"'

'I'm not so keen on Jews,' said Lammchen. 'What did he mean about the daughter?'

'Ah, you may well ask; that was the snag. I'd lived in Ducherow for four years and never knew that Kleinholz was dead set on marrying off his daughter. The mother is bad enough, carping all day and slopping around in crochet cardigans, but the daughter: what a cow! Called Marie.'

'And she's the one you were meant to marry, you poor boy?'

'I *am* meant to marry her, Lammchen! Kleinholz only employs unmarried men; there are three of us at the moment, but it's me they're gunning for the most.'

'So how old's this Marie?'

'Dunno,' he said shortly. 'Yes, I do. Thirty-two. Or thirty-three. Anyway it's neither here nor there because I'm not marrying her.'

'Ah heavens, you poor boy,' said Lammchen pityingly. 'Do people really do that? Twenty-two and thirty-three?'

'Of course they do,' he said sourly, 'quite frequently in fact. And if you ever want to make fun of me, just insist on me "telling you all" another time.'

'I'm not making fun. . . But you must admit, Sonny, it does have its funny side. Is she a good match then?'

'No, actually not,' said Pinneberg. 'The business isn't bringing in much any more. Old Kleinholz drinks too much, and then he buys too dear and sells too cheap. The son will get the business, and he's only ten. Marie will only get a few thousand marks if that, so that's why nobody's taking the bait.'

'So that was it,' said Lammchen. 'That was what you didn't want to tell me. And that was why you got married in dead secret with the car-hood up and your hand with the ring in your trouser pocket?'

'Yes, that's why. Oh God! Lammchen, if they found out that I was married, the women would turn him against me in a week, and I'd be out. And what then?'

'Then you'd go back to Bergmanns.'

'No chance! Look. . .' He swallowed, but carried on: '. . . Bergmann foresaw the Kleinholz job would go wrong and he told me so. He said: "Pinneberg, you'll come back to me! There's nowhere else in Ducherow for you but Bergmanns. Nowhere. You'll come back to me, Pinneberg, and I'll take you back. But I'll make you beg. You can hang around the Labour Exchange for a month at least and come begging to me for work. That sort of chutzpah has to be punished!" That's how he talked, and I can't go back to him. I can't and I won't.'

'Not even if he was right? You know yourself he was right.'

'Lammchen,' he said, pleadingly. 'Please, dear Lammchen, don't ask me to do it. Yes, of course he was right and I was a silly ass, and it wouldn't have done me any harm to carry the parcels. If you kept on asking me, I would go to him and he would take me. And then his wife would be there, and the other salesman, Mamlock, who's a fool, and they'd never let me forget it, and I'd never forgive you for it.'

'No, no, I won't ask you to do it, and we'll manage. But don't you believe it will come out, however careful we are?'

'It mustn't come out. It must not! I did everything so secretly, and now we're living out here, no one will ever see us together in town, and if we do ever meet on the street, we won't greet each other.'

Lammchen was quiet for a while, but finally she spoke: 'But we can't stay here, Sonny, you must see that?'

'Just try it, Lammchen,' he begged. 'Just for the fortnight till the first of the month. We can't give notice before then anyhow.'

She reflected for a while before she agreed. She glanced sideways at the bridle path track but could distinguish nothing. It was too dark. Then she sighed: 'Very well, I'll try, Sonny. But you know yourself that it can't go on. We could never be happy here, never.'

'Oh, thank you,' he said. 'Thank you. And the rest will work out all right; it must. I have to keep my job, at all costs.'

'At all costs,' she echoed.

And then they took one more look at the country, the quiet, moonlit country, and went to bed. They didn't have to close the curtains; there was no one to overlook them here. And as they were falling asleep, they seemed to catch the distant rippling of the Strela.

WHAT SHALL WE EAT? WHO MAY WE DANCE WITH? MUST WE GET MARRIED NOW?

On Monday morning the Pinnebergs were at the breakfast table, and Lammchen's eyes were fairly sparkling: 'Today's the day it all begins!' And with a glance at the chamber of horrors: 'I'm going to clear up this tip.' And, glancing into her cup: 'How do you find the coffee? Twenty-five per cent beans!'

'Well, since you ask. . .'

'Yes, Sonny, if we want to save. . .'

Whereupon Pinneberg pointed out to her how he had always managed to afford 'real' coffee every morning. And she explained to him that two people cost more than one. And he said he had always heard that it was cheaper to be married; that it was cheaper for two to eat at home than for one to eat out.

A long debate was setting in, when he said, 'Good grief, I've got to go! And fast!'

They said their goodbyes at the door. He was half-way down the stairs when she called, 'Sonny love, wait! What on earth are we going to eat today?'

'Don't mind,' echoed back the answer.

'Tell me, please tell me! I've no idea. . .'

'Neither have I!' And the door below slammed.

She rushed to the window. There he was on his way already, waving first with his hand then with a handkerchief. She stayed at the window until he had passed the lamp-post and finally disappeared behind a yellowish house-wall. And now, for the first time in her twenty-three years, Lammchen had a whole morning to herself, a flat to herself, and a shopping list to make out all on her own. She went to work.

Pinneberg, however, met the town clerk Kranz on the corner of Main Street and greeted him politely. Then something occurred to him. He had waved to him with his right hand, and on his right hand was the ring. He hoped Kranz hadn't seen it. Pinneberg took the ring off and placed it carefully in the 'secret compartment'

of his wallet; it stuck in his throat, but what must be, must
be. . .

Meanwhile, Emil Kleinholz, dispenser of Pinneberg's daily bread,
was up and about with his family. . . It was never a pleasant moment,
because they were all in a bad mood straight out of bed and apt to tell
each other home truths. But Monday morning was in general particularly bad, for on Sunday night Father was inclined to escapades, for
which the moment of awakening brought revenge.

For Mrs Emilie Kleinholz was not a gentle woman; in so far as one
can tame a man, she had tamed her Emil. And indeed on one or two
Sundays of late things had passed off very well. Emilie had quite
simply locked the front door on Sunday evening, treated her
husband to a flagon of beer with his dinner, and later gave him the
required lift with some cognac. Something like a family evening had
then ensued: the boy, who was a misery, moaned and groaned in a
corner, the women sat at the table sewing (for Marie's trousseau), and
Father read a newspaper, saying intermittently: 'Mother, let's have
another one.'

Whereupon Frau Kleinholz invariably said: 'Father, think of the
boy!' and then poured a little more out of the bottle, or not,
according to her husband's condition.

That was how this last Sunday had gone off, with everyone then
going to bed around ten.

Mrs Kleinholz woke at about eleven; it was dark in the room, and
she listened. She heard her daughter Marie next door whimpering in
her sleep, as she often did, the boy making the usual noises at the foot
of the paternal bed; only Father's snores were missing from the
chorus.

Mrs Kleinholz groped under her pillow; the front-door key was
there. Mrs Kleinholz put on the light; her husband was not there. She
got up. She went all through the house. She crossed the yard (the
lavatory was in the yard). Not a sign. Finally she discovered that an
office window was slightly open, and she had definitely shut it. She
was always very definite about that kind of thing.

Mrs Kleinholz was in a boiling, seething rage; quarter of a bottle of
cognac, a flagon of beer and all for nothing! She put on a few clothes,
threw her mauve quilted dressing-gown over the top, and went to

seek her husband. No doubt he was in Bruhn's pub at the corner, knocking back a drink.

Kleinholz Grain Merchants, on Market Place, was a good old-fashioned firm. Emil was the third generation to possess it. It had grown into a sound, respected concern with three hundred customers of many years' standing – farmers and estate-owners. When Emil Kleinholz said: 'Franz, the cotton-seed flour is good,' Franz didn't ask for a content-analysis, he bought it, and lo! it was good.

But that kind of business has one snag: it has to be watered with alcohol; it is by nature a thirsty business. An alcoholic business. Every cartload of potatoes, every consignment note, every settlement calls for beer, whisky, brandy. That doesn't matter if there's a kindly wife, a household that hangs together and is comfortable to be in, but it does matter if the wife nags.

Mrs Emilie Kleinholz had always nagged. She knew it was a mistake, but Emilie was jealous. She had married a handsome man, a prosperous man; when she was Miss Nobody with next to nothing, she had wrested him away from all the others. Now she bared her teeth over him; after thirty-four years of marriage she was still fighting for him as she did on the first day.

She slopped along in her slippers and dressing-gown to the corner, to Bruhn's. Her husband was not there. She could have asked politely whether he had been there, but that wasn't in her nature; she heaped reproaches on the barman: they were scoundrels to give drink to drunkards; she was going to lodge a complaint, it was incitement to drunkenness.

Old man Bruhn himself, with his big beard, led her out of the bar; she danced a jig with fury beside the huge man, but his was a firm and steady grip.

'There we are, young lady,' he said.

And there she was, outside. It was a typical small-town market place, with cobblestones, two-storied houses, some gabled, some flat-fronted, but all with curtains closed and all dark. Only the gas-lamps flickered as they swung. Should she go home now? What a fool that would make her look! Emil would mock her for days afterwards if she had gone out to look for him and not found him. She'd have to find him now. However good the booze was, and however drunken the company, she'd drag him away. However much fun he was having.

Fun! Suddenly she knew: there's dancing at the Tivoli this evening; that's where Emil will be.

That's where he is! There!

And just as she was, in her slippers and dressing-gown, she walked half-way across town and into the Tivoli. The treasurer of the Harmony Club wanted a mark entrance fee, but she only replied: 'Do you want a slap?'

The treasurer did not pursue it.

She stood in the dance-hall, a little constrained at first, looking around from behind a pillar, then exploding into rage. For there was her still handsome Emil, with his large golden beard, dancing with a little dark creature whom she didn't even know, if you could call that dancing, more like a drunken stagger. The master of ceremonies said: 'Madam! Please, Madam!'

Then he realized that this was a force of nature, a tornado, a volcanic eruption, against which human beings were powerless. And he stepped back. A path cleared through the dancing couples; she advanced between the walls of people towards the unsuspecting pair, as they stumbled and fumbled round the floor, the only couple who weren't in the know.

First came a rapid blow. He cried out 'Oh my sweetie!' without yet realizing. Then he realized. . .

She knew it was time to leave with dignity, with reserve. She gave him her arm: 'It's time, Emil. Come now.'

And he went with her. He trotted, humiliated, on her arm out of the hall; as undignified as a large dog who has just been beaten, he glanced back one more time at his nice little, gentle little dark girl, who worked in the frame factory in Stossel, who hadn't had much happiness in her life, and had been exceedingly pleased with her generous and dashing dancing-partner. He went away; she went away. And outside a car had suddenly appeared; the management of the Harmony Club knew enough to realize that on these occasions the best thing is to phone for a car as quickly as possible.

Emil Kleinholz fell asleep on the journey and he didn't wake up when his wife and the driver carried him indoors and put him to bed, in the hated marriage bed he had abandoned so full of the spirit of adventure exactly two hours before. He slept. And his wife put out the light and lay for a while in darkness, and then she put the light on again, and contemplated her husband, her handsome, dissipated, golden-blond husband. And she saw, through the livid bloated face, the face of long ago when he was courting her, always up to so many tricks, so full of fun and cheek, forever ready to make a grab at her breasts, but just as ready to have his ears boxed for it.

And in so far as her foolish little brain could think, she thought of the road from there to here: two children, a plain daughter and a bad-tempered ugly son. A business half in ruins, a husband gone to seed, and her? What about her?

Well, in the end all you can do is cry, which can be done in the dark, and that at least, when so much is going downhill, saves money on light. And then she thought of how much he must have squandered – yet again – in those two hours, and she put on the light and searched in his wallet and counted and reckoned. And once again in the darkness she resolved to be nice to him from now on, and she groaned, self-pitying: 'But it won't help. I'll just have to keep him on an even shorter lead!'

And then she cried again, and finally she went to sleep, as we always do finally go to sleep, after a toothache or childbirth, after a blazing row or after one of life's rare great joys.

Then came the first awakening at five o'clock, to quickly give the stableman the key to the oats bin; and then the second at six, when the girl knocked for the key to the larder. One more hour of sleep! One more hour of rest! And then the third, final awakening at quarter to seven, when the boy had to go to school. Her husband was still asleep. When she looked into the bedroom again at quarter to eight, he was awake and feeling sick.

'Serve you right for boozing,' she said and went away again. Then he came to the table for coffee, sombre, speechless, devastated. 'A herring, Marie,' was all he said.

'You should be ashamed of yourself, Father,' said Marie tartly, before fetching the herring. 'Carrying on like that.'

'God damn it!' he roared. 'It's time that girl was out of this house!' he roared again.

'You're quite right, Father,' his wife soothed him. 'What else are you feeding those three hungry mouths for?'

'Pinneberg's the best. He's the one,' said the man of the house.

'Of course. Just put the screws on him.'

'Leave it to me,' he said.

And then this man, upon whom Pinneberg depended for his daily bread, went over to his office, carrying in his hands the fate of Pinneberg, Lammchen and the as-yet-unborn Shrimp.

THE HARASSMENT BEGINS. THE NAZI LAUTERBACH,
THE DEMON SCHULZ AND THE HUSBAND-IN-SECRET ARE
ALL IN TROUBLE

Lauterbach was the first of the employees to arrive at the office, at five to eight. It wasn't out of a sense of duty, however, but out of boredom. This short, fat, flaxen-haired stump of a man with enormous hands had once been a farm bailiff, but, not liking the country, he had moved to town, to Emil Kleinholz's in Ducherow. There he had become a sort of expert in seeds and fertilizers. The farmers were not overjoyed to see him get into the cart when they were delivering potatoes; he saw at once if the load wasn't as specified, if white Silesians had been mixed in with the yellow Industrials. But he had his good side. Admittedly he never allowed himself to be bribed with brandy – he never drank brandy, because he had to protect the Aryan race from such decadent stimulants – so he never raised a glass and never took cigars. With a cry of 'You old crook' he would deal the farmers a cracking slap on the back and beat them down ten, fifteen, twenty per cent. But, and this was enough to placate them, he wore the swastika, he told them the best jokes about the Jews, he described the SA's latest recruitment drives in Buhrkow and Lensahn, in short he was a real German, trustworthy, and the sworn enemy of Jews, wogs, reparations, Social Democrats and Commies. And that made up for everything.

Lauterbach had only joined the Nazis out of boredom. It had turned out that Ducherow offered as little distraction as the country. He wasn't interested in girls, and since the cinema did not start until eight and church was over by eleven there was a long gap between the two.

The Nazis were not boring. He quickly joined the action, revealing himself as a young man with an unusually intelligent grasp of fighting, who used his hands (and whatever was in them) with an effectiveness that amounted almost to artistry. Lauterbach's lust for life was finally satisfied: almost every Sunday, and on occasional weekday evenings too, he was able to have a fight.

Lauterbach's home was the office. There he had colleagues, the boss, the boss's wife, workers, farmers: he could tell them all what had happened and what was going to happen. His talk spouted a continuous slow slush on the just and the unjust, enlivened by booms of laughter when he described how he had dealt with the friends of the USSR.

There wasn't anything of that nature to report today; however a new General Order had arrived for every SA squad leader – known to his troops as the 'Gruf' – the contents of which were now handed on to Pinneberg, who appeared punctually at eight. SA members now had new insignia! 'I think it's a stroke of genius! Up till now we've only had our troop numbers. You know, Pinneberg, arabic numerals embroidered on the right collar-tab. Now we've got two-colour braid on the collar. It's a stroke of genius. Now you can always tell even from behind what troop any SA man belongs to. Think of what it means in practice. Say we're in a fight, and somebody's working a man over, and I look at the collar. . .'

'Amazing,' agreed Pinneberg, sorting out delivery notes from Saturday. 'Was Munich 387 536 a load from several places?'

'The wagon of wheat? Yes. And just think, our Gruf now has a star on his left collar-tab.'

'What's a Gruf?' asked Pinneberg.

Schulz came, the third hungry mouth, at ten past eight. Schulz came and at a stroke all Nazi insignia and delivery notes for wheat were forgotten. The demon Schulz had arrived, the inspired but unreliable Schulz, Schulz who could reckon up 285.63 hundred-weight at 3.85 marks in his head quicker than Pinneberg could do it on paper, but who was a womanizer, an unscrupulous lecher, a philanderer, the only man talented enough to snatch a kiss in passing from Mariechen Kleinholz and not be married off to her on the spot.

Schulz came, he of the black pomaded curls, the sallow lined face and the big black sparkling eyes; Schulz the dandy of Ducherow, with his ironed-in creases and his black hat (fifty centimetres in diameter); Schulz with his beringed and nicotine-stained fingers; Schulz, king of hearts to all the servant girls, idol of the shop assistants, who waited for him after work in the evening and quarrelled over him at dances.

Schulz came.

Schulz said 'Mornin', carefully hung up his coat on a hanger, looked at his colleagues, first inquiringly, then pityingly, then contemptuously, and said, 'You haven't heard the news, of course?'

'You got off with some girl yesterday, as usual, so who was it?' asked Lauterbach.

'You don't know anything about anything. You sit here totting up delivery notes, doing the current account book while. . .'

'While what?'

'Emil. . . Emil and Emilie. . . yesterday evening at the Tivoli. . .'

'Did he take her with him? Wonders never cease!'

Schulz sat down.

'It's high time we got the clover samples out. Who'll do that, you or Lauterbach?'

'You.'

'I don't do the clover. That's our dear agricultural expert's business. The boss was shaking a leg with Frieda, that little dark-haired girl from the frame factory, I was two steps away, and the old lady pounced on him. Emilie in her dressing-gown, and probably nothing but her nightie on underneath. . .'

'In the Tivoli?'

'You must be kidding, Schulz!'

'As true as I'm sitting here. The Harmony Club were holding a family dance at the Tivoli. With a military band from Platz, very smart. The German army in their best. And suddenly our Emilie jumps on her Emil, biffs him one: 'You old boozer, you filthy pig. . .'

What price delivery notes, what price the day's work now? There's a sensation in the Kleinholz office.

Lauterbach begged: 'Tell us again, Schulz. Mrs Kleinholz comes into the ballroom. . . I can't imagine it. . . which door did she come in by then? When did you first see her?'

Schulz was flattered. 'What is there to add? You know it already. So she comes in, straight through the door from the lobby, bright red, you know the way she goes: bluish-purply-red. . . So she comes in. . .'

Emil Kleinholz entered. Into the office. The three started, sat on their chairs, rustled papers. Kleinholz stared at them, stood in front of them, gazing down at their bent heads.

'Nothing to do?' he rasped. 'Nothing to do? I'll lay one of you off. Now then, which one?'

The three did not look up.

'Rationalize. Have two working hard instead of three lazing around. What about you, Pinneberg? You're the youngest.'

Pinneberg did not reply.

'Of course you've all lost your tongues. . . It was a different story a few minutes ago. So what did my old lady look like, you old goat? Bluish-purply-red? Shall I throw you out? Shall I chuck you out on the spot?'

'The bastard was listening,' thought the three, turning inwardly pale with fright. 'Oh God, Oh God, what did I say?'

'We weren't talking about you at all, Mr Kleinholz,' said Schulz in a low tone, almost to himself.

'Well, and what about you?' Kleinholz turned to Lauterbach. But Lauterbach was not frightened like his two colleagues. Lauterbach was one of those rare employees who couldn't care less whether they had a job or not. 'Afraid? What have I got to be afraid of?' was doubtless what he said to himself. 'With these fists? I can do any job. I can be a groom or carry sacks. Book-keeper? I'm not dazzled by a title like that.'

So Lauterbach looked fearlessly into his boss's bloodshot eyes. 'Yes, Mr Kleinholz?'

Kleinholz dealt the counter-rail a reverberating blow. 'I'm laying off one of you band of brothers. You'll see. . . And the others needn't feel safe either – plenty more where you came from. You go to the foodstore, Lauterbach, and you and Kruse can put a hundred hundredweights of peanut-cake meal into sacks. Rufisque brand. No, wait, Schulz can go, he looks like death again today, it will do him good to lift some sacks.'

Schulz disappeared without a word, glad to have escaped.

'You go to the station, Pinneberg, and look sharp. Order four twenty-ton closed trucks for six tomorrow morning. We've got to get the wheat off to the mill. On your way.'

'Yes, Mr Kleinholz,' said Pinneberg, and was on his way, sharp. He was not in a very cheerful frame of mind, though he realized Emil's talk was mainly the effect of his hangover. All the same. . .

As he was going back to Kleinholz's from the goods-yard, he saw a figure on the opposite pavement: a particular figure, a girl, a woman, his wife.

So he slowly crossed the street onto her side of the road. Lammchen was walking in his direction, a string shopping-bag in her hand. She had not noticed him. She went up to the shop window of Brechts the Butchers, and stopped to look at the display. He went right close up to her, casting a wary eye up and down the street. There was no sign of danger.

'So what's the grub for tonight, young lady?' he whispered over her shoulder and moved smartly on. Ten paces down the street he looked back just once and saw that her face had lit up with joy. Oh dear, supposing Mrs Brecht had seen that; she knew him because he always bought his sausage off her. He'd been careless again, but how could he help it with a wife like that. Well, she didn't seem to have bought any pots yet; they were going to have to be so careful with money. . .

Back at the office, he found the boss sitting alone. No Lauterbach. No Schulz. Bad, thought Pinneberg, very bad. But the boss paid no attention to him. With one hand he was supporting his forehead and with the other he was slowly struggling up and down the columns of figures in the accounts book, as though he was spelling them out to himself.

Pinneberg took stock. 'The typewriter's the best bet,' he thought. 'When you're typing people are less likely to disturb you.'

He was wrong. He had barely written 'Gentlemen, we are taking the liberty of sending you herewith a sample of this year's harvest of red clover, guaranteed fibre-free, fertility: ninety-five per-cent, purity: ninety-nine per cent. . .'. . . when a hand descended on his shoulder and the boss said: 'You, Pinneberg, one moment. . .'

'Yes, Mr Kleinholz?' asked Pinneberg, dropping his fingers from the keys.

'You're writing about the red clover. You can leave that to Lauterbach. . .'

'Oh. . .'

'Is that all set with the railway trucks?'

'Yes, it's all set, Mr Kleinholz.'

'Then it'll have to be all hands to the wheel this afternoon to get the wheat in the sacks. My two females will have to help. Tie the sacks.'

'Yes, Mr Kleinholz.'

'Marie is handy at that kind of thing. She's handy at most things. . . She's no beauty but she's handy.'

'Certainly, Mr Kleinholz.'

They sat there, facing one another. Something like a pause had ensued in the conversation. Mr Kleinholz's last words had been productive in intent; like the developer in photography they were intended to reveal what was on the plate.

The boss sat humped before him, in green loden and top boots. Anxious and oppressed, Pinneberg sat and stared at him.

'Yes, Pinneberg,' the boss began again, in quite a sentimental tone. 'Have you considered it? What do you think?'

Pinneberg cast fearfully about for a way out but could see none.

'What about, Mr Kleinholz?' he asked feebly.

'About cutting the staff,' said the dispenser of his daily bread, after a long pause. 'Who would you lay off if you were me?'

Pinneberg went hot under the collar. What a bastard. What a swine. Hassling me.

'I can't say, Mr Kleinholz,' he declared uneasily. 'I can't speak against my colleagues.'

Mr Kleinholz was enjoying himself.

'You wouldn't fire yourself, if you were me?' he asked.

'If I were you. . .? Me?. . . How can I?. . .'

'Well,' said Emil Kleinholz and stood up. 'I'm sure you'll think it over. I'd have to give you a month's notice, wouldn't I? That would be from September 1st to October 1st, wouldn't it?'

Kleinholz left the office to tell Mother how he'd put the squeeze on Pinneberg. Possibly Mother would let him have a drink. He felt just like one.

PEA SOUP IS PREPARED AND A LETTER IS WRITTEN, BUT THE WATER IS TOO THIN

First thing in the morning, stopping only to hang the bedding out of the window to air, Lammchen went shopping. Why hadn't he told her what they should have for dinner? *She* didn't know! And she had no idea what he liked.

The possibilities proved less numerous on reflection and Lammchen's forward-planning spirit finally homed in on pea soup. It was easy and cheap and could be eaten twice running.

'Lord, it must be so easy for girls who've had proper cooking lessons. My mother always chased me away from the stove. "Get your clumsy fingers out of here."'

What did she need? There was water. And a pot. How much peas? Half a pound's bound to be enough for two: peas swell so. Salt? Soup vegetables? A bit of fat? Well, perhaps we need that in any case. How much meat? And what sort of meat? Beef of course. Half a pound must be enough. Peas are very nourishing, and it's unhealthy to eat too much meat. Then potatoes of course.

Lammchen went shopping. It was great to stroll along the street on a weekday morning when everybody was in their offices. The air was still fresh, though the sun was hot already.

A large yellow post-van hooted slowly across the market place. Her young man could be behind those windows over there. But he was elsewhere, and ten minutes later he was inquiring over her shoulder what their grub for dinner was. The butcher's wife must have noticed something, she's a funny type, and she asked thirty pfennigs a pound for soup bones. Surely that sort of thing was thrown in, just bare white bones without a scrap of meat. She would write and ask mother. No, better not, better manage on her own. But she ought to write to his mother. And she began composing the letter on the way home.

Mrs Scharrenhofer was evidently a nightbird. In the kitchen, when Lammchen went for the water, she saw no sign that anything had been cooked or was going to be cooked; it was all cold and shiny, and no sound came through from the room behind. She put her peas on, wondering whether to add the salt now. No, better to wait to the end when it would be easier to know how much.

Now for the cleaning. It was hard, much harder than she had ever imagined; oh, those horrible paper roses, those garlands, bleached and poisonous green, and faded upholstered furniture, corners, knobs, balustrades! She had to be ready by half past eleven, to write the letter. Sonny had between twelve and two off for lunch, but he was unlikely to be back before quarter to one as he had to go and register at the town hall.

At quarter to twelve she sat down at a little walnut table with the yellow letter-writing paper dating from her girlhood in front of her.

First the address: 'Mrs Marie Pinneberg – Berlin NW 40 – Spenerstrasse 92 II.'

A person surely had to write to his mother, tell her when he got married, especially if he was the only son, the only child indeed. Even if you didn't get along with her, even if you disapproved of her way of life, as a son you ought to write.

'Mother ought to be ashamed of herself,' Pinneberg declared.

'But Sonny, she's been a widow twenty years.'

'That makes no difference. And it hasn't always been the same man.'

'Hannes, you had other girls besides me.'

'That's completely different.'

'Well in that case, what might the Shrimp say if he compared his birth-date with the date when we got married?'

'We don't know when his birth-date will be.'

'We do. The beginning of March.'

'How d'you know that?'

'Never you mind, Sonny. I know. And I am going to write to your mother. It's only right.'

'Do what you like, but I don't want to hear any more about it.'

'"Dear Madam," – That sounds silly, doesn't it? People don't write like that. "Dear Mrs Pinneberg" – but that's my name, and it doesn't sound right either. Hannes is bound to read the letter.'

'Oh, who cares,' thought Lammchen. 'Either she's like what Hannes says, in which case it doesn't matter what I write, or she's a nice woman, in which case I'd want to write as I feel. So. . .'

"Dear Mother!

I am your new daughter-in-law Emma, called Lammchen, and Hannes and I got married the day before yesterday, on Saturday. We are happy and contented, and would be very pleased if you would share in our happiness. Things are going well for us, except that unfortunately Hannes had to give up selling clothes and works in a fertilizer business which we don't like so much. With best wishes from your Lammchen. . ."'

And there she left a space. 'And you *are* going to add your name, Sonny!'

And because there was still a half an hour to go, she took out her book, which she had bought at Wickel's a fortnight ago: *The Sacred Miracle of Motherhood.*

She read, frowning: 'Happy, sun-filled days are here. The little child has come, a heaven-sent compensation for human imperfections.'

She tried to understand, but the sense kept eluding her. It seemed dreadfully difficult, and its relevance to the Shrimp was hard to see. But then came some poetry, which she read slowly, several times:

> 'Voice of a child,
> Voice of unknowingness
> But knowing like Solomon
> Wisdom in joyfulness,
> Meaning in birdsong.'

Lammchen didn't quite understand that either. But it was so happy; she leaned back; there were times now when her body felt so heavy, her womb so rich; she repeated with closed eyes: 'Knowing like Solomon wisdom in joyfulness, meaning in birdsong.'

'A baby must be about the happiest thing there is,' was her feeling. 'The Shrimp will be happy! Meaning in birdsong. . .'

'Lunch!' called Sonny from the hall. How had he got there? She must have slept a little; lately there had been times when she was very tired.

'That lunch of mine,' she thought, slowly rising to her feet.

'Isn't the table laid yet?' he asked.

'In a moment, Sonny love,' she said, and rushed to the kitchen. 'May I bring the pot to the table? I'll use the tureen if you like.'

'What is there, then?'

'Pea soup.'

'Fine. Bring the pot. I'll lay the table.'

Lammchen filled the plates. She looked rather worried. 'Isn't it rather thin?' she asked anxiously.

'It'll be all right,' he said, carving the meat on the little serving dish.

She tried the soup. 'Heavens, it's thin!' she exclaimed involuntarily. Followed by: 'Oh Lord, the salt!'

He too laid down his spoon. Across the table, over the plates and the heavy enamelled pot, their glances met.

'And it was meant to be so good,' wailed Lammchen. 'I had the right quantities: half a pound of peas, half a pound of meat, a whole pound of bones. It *ought* to be good soup!'

He had stood up, and was stirring reflectively in the pot with the enamel ladle. 'Now and again you do come across a pea husk. How much water did you put in Lammchen?'

'It must be the peas. They haven't swelled up at all.' 'How much water?' he repeated.

'The pot full.'

'Five litres – and a half a pound of peas. I believe, Lammchen', he said with an air of detection, 'that it's the water. The water is too thin.'

Lammchen was cast down. 'Do you mean I put in too much? Five litres. It was meant to be enough for two days.'

'Five litres – I believe it's more than enough for two days.' He tried once again. 'No, I'm sorry Lammchen, it's really only hot water.'

'Oh, my poor Sonny. Are you dreadfully hungry? What shall I

make? Shall I run down quickly and get some eggs, and make egg and fried potatoes? I'm sure I can do that.'

'Let's get going then!' he said. 'I'll run down for the eggs.' And he was off.

When he came back to her in the kitchen her eyes were streaming, but not from the onions she had been cutting up for the potatoes.

'Lammchen,' he said, 'It's not a tragedy!'

She threw both arms around his neck. 'Sonny love, supposing I turn into a useless housewife! I want to make everything so nice for you. And if the Shrimp doesn't get proper food he won't thrive.'

'D'you mean now, or later?' he asked, laughing. 'D'you think you'll never learn?'

'There you are! You still aren't taking me seriously.'

'As for the soup, I was just thinking about it on the stairs. The only thing wrong with it is too much water. If you put it on again and let it boil a long time, the extra water will boil away, and we'll have some really good pea soup.'

'Great!' she said, beaming. 'You're right. I'll do it this very afternoon, so we can have another plate of it for dinner.'

They moved with their fried potatoes and two fried eggs each into the living-room. 'Does it taste nice? Does it taste the way you expect it to? I hope it's not too late for you? Can you lie down for a moment? You look so tired, Sonny love.'

'No, not because it's too late. Today I can't sleep. Kleinholz is a man who. . .'

He had considered at length whether to tell her anything about it.

But they had promised each other on Saturday night that there would be no more secrets. And so he told her. And it was such a relief to be able to say everything that was on his mind.

'What do I do now?' he asked. 'If I don't say anything, he'll certainly give me the sack on the first. What if I simply told him the truth? Supposing I tell him I'm married; he can't just put me out on the street.'

But on this matter Lammchen was entirely her father's child: an employee could not expect anything from an employer. 'He couldn't care less,' she said angrily. 'There used to be a few honest ones, possibly. But now with so many people unemployed and getting by somehow or other, they think, oh well, it doesn't matter about my people either.'

'Kleinholz isn't bad really,' said Pinneberg. 'He just doesn't think. He ought to have it explained to him. That we're expecting the Shrimp and so. . .'

Lammchen was outraged. 'You'd tell *him* that, when he's trying to blackmail you. No, Sonny, you must never, never do that.'

'But what am I to do then? I have to tell him something.'

'If I were you,' said Lammchen thoughtfully, 'I'd talk to your colleagues. Perhaps he's threatened them like you. If you all stick together he can't sack you all.'

'It might work,' he said. 'Provided nobody pulled a fast one. Lauterbach doesn't cheat, he's too stupid for that, but Schulz. . .'

Lammchen believed in the solidarity of all workers: 'Your colleagues won't land you in it! It'll turn out all right, Sonny love. I always believe nothing bad can happen to us. Why should it? We're hard-working, we're thrifty, we're not bad people, we want our Shrimp, we want him very much – why should anything bad happen to us? It wouldn't make sense!'

KLEINHOLZ MAKES TROUBLE, KUBE MAKES TROUBLE,
THE OFFICE WORKERS MAKE A PACT AND THERE ARE
STILL NO PEAS

The granary at Kleinholz's was a poky old place. There wasn't even a proper sacking machine. Everything still had to be weighed out on scales and then the sacks were despatched from a skylight down a chute into the lorry.

And once again it was the typical Kleinholz performance of sacking up sixteen hundred hundredweight of grain in one day. No division of labour, no organization. The wheat had been lying there a week or two, they could have begun the work ages ago, but no: it all had to be done in one afternoon!

The granary loft was teeming with people; everyone Kleinholz had been able to drum up on the spur of the moment was helping. A couple of women were sweeping the wheat back into a heap; three scales were in use: Schulz on one, Lauterbach on the other, Pinneberg on the third.

Emil was dashing around, in an even worse humour than the morning, as Emilie was keeping him totally dry, for which reason she and Marie had not been allowed up to the loft. Rage at being henpecked had won out entirely over fatherly concern for Marie's future. 'I don't want you cows anywhere near me.'

'Have you added the weight of the sack, Mr Lauterbach? The right weight? What a nitwit. A two-hundredweight sack weighs three pounds, not two pounds! Exactly two hundredweight and three pounds is the correct weight. And nobody give any more. I can't afford to give presents. Schulz, you heart-throb, I'm checking yours.'

Two men were dragging a sack to the slide when it burst, and a flood of red-brown wheat rustled onto the floor.

'Who tied that sack? You, Schmidt? Good God, man, you should be able to deal with old bags, you're not a bloody virgin. And stop staring, Pinneberg. Your scales are uneven. Didn't I tell you we aren't giving any over. Idiot.'

This time Pinneberg did stare at his boss, and very angrily.

'And don't go looking like that. If you don't like it here, you're welcome to leave. Schulz, you old goat, leave the Marheinecke girl alone. He's even chasing the women in my granary!'

Schulz muttered something.

'Hold your tongue. You pinched her bottom. How many sacks have you got to now?'

'Twenty-three.'

'We're making no headway! No headway at all! I tell you none of you's coming down from the floor until the eight hundred sacks are ready. There'll be no breaks. I'll see that it's done, even if you're still here at eleven o'clock at night. . .'

It was oppressively hot; above them the August sun beat down in all its strength on the roof-tiles. The men wore only their vest and trousers, the women little more. There was a smell of dry dust, sweat, hay, the fresh shiny jute of the wheat sacks, but above all of sweat, sweat, sweat. A thick miasma of physicality, a stench of tawdry sensuality gradually permeated the loft. And all the while Kleinholz's voice rang out like a continuously-droning gong.

'Lederer, kindly handle your shovel correctly! Man, how can you handle a shovel like that! Hold the sack open properly, you fat sow, it must have a mouth. That's how you do it. . .'

Pinneberg was operating his scales. Letting down the bar had become quite mechanical. 'A bit more, Mrs Friebe. Just a little. Now that's too much. Take a handful out. Right. Next! Get ready, Hinrichsen, you're next. Or we'll still be here at midnight.'

Meanwhile thoughts drifted through Pinneberg's brain in snatches: 'Lammchen's lucky. Fresh air. White curtains blowing. Just shut your trap, will you? D'you have to keep barking all the time like a dog? And this is what people live in fear and trembling of losing? No thanks.'

And off went the gong again. 'Hurry up, Kube. What did that heap come to? Ninety-eight hundredweight. It was a hundred. That was the wheat from Nickelsdorf. It was a hundred. What have you done with the two hundredweight, Schulz? I'll weigh it again. Go on, put the sack back on the scales.'

Kube, who'd worked in grain stores since way back, voiced his opinion: 'The wheat's shrunk in the heat. It was bloody dry when we brought it from Nickels farm.'

'So I buy dry wheat now, do I? Shut your gob; you can't talk. Did you take it home to Mother? Shrunk, did you say? I say it was pinched. Everyone steals round here.'

'You didn't ought to have said that, sir,' said Kube. 'Accusing me of stealing. I'll report it to the union. You didn't ought to. Now we'll see.'

He looked his boss straight in the eye, salt-and-pepper whiskers bristling.

'Good stuff!' Pinneberg rejoiced inwardly. 'His union! If we could only do that! What does ours do? Nowt.'

Kleinholz was far from being struck dumb. Kleinholz was used to that sort of thing. 'Did I say you'd been stealing? I never said anything of the sort. Mice steal too. We've plenty of mouse food here. We must put down sea onions or spread diphtheria, Kube.'

'You said, Mr Kleinholz, that I'd stolen wheat. All the people in the granary are my witness. I'm going to the union and filing a complaint against you, Mr Kleinholz.'

'I didn't say anything. I didn't say a word to you. Hey, Mr Schulz, did I say anything to Kube about stealing? '

'I didn't hear anything, Mr Kleinholz.'

'You see, Kube. And you, Mr Pinneberg, did you hear anything?'

'No. Nothing,' said Pinneberg hesitantly, weeping tears of blood inside.

'So,' said Kleinholz. 'You and your endless trouble-making, Kube. You're out to be a shop steward.'

'Just go easy, Mr Kleinholz,' warned Kube. 'You're at it again. You know the score. You've ended up in court with old Kube three times before, and I'll do it a fourth time. I'm not frightened, Mr Kleinholz.'

'You're blethering,' said Kleinholz furiously. 'You're old, Kube. You don't know what you're saying any more. I'm sorry for you.'

But Kleinholz had had enough. And it really was too hot up here, running up and down shouting all the time. He was going downstairs for a break.

'I'm going to the office, Pinneberg. Mind they keep going. No breaks, you understand? You'll answer to me, Pinneberg!'

He disappeared down the steps from the loft and at once lively conversation broke out. There was no lack of subject-matter; Kleinholz had seen to that.

'Well, we all know why he's so out of sorts today.'

'Wet his whistle and he'll soon act differently.'

'Break!' shouted old Kube. 'Break!'

Emil couldn't yet be across the courtyard.

'Please, Kube,' said the twenty-three-year-old Pinneberg to the sixty-three-year-old Kube. 'Please don't make any trouble. Mr Kleinholz expressly forbade it.'

'It's in the collective agreement, Mr Pinneberg,' said Kube with the walrus-whiskers. 'Breaks are statutory. The boss can't take them away from us.'

'But I shall get into the worst trouble. . .'

'What do I care?' snorted Kube. 'When you didn't even hear him accusing me of thieving!'

'If you were in my position, Kube. . .'

'I know, I know. If everyone thought like you, young man, we'd all be slaving in chains and begging the employers on our knees for every bit of bread. Ah well, you're young, you've got a lot of time ahead of you, and you'll find out how far crawling to them will get you. Take a break!'

But all the workmen had long been taking a break. The three clerks were on their own.

'The gentlemen could carry on filling the sacks,' said one workman.

'Get into Emil's good books,' said another, 'then perhaps he'll let them have a sniff of the cognac.'

'Or a sniff of Mariechen.'

'All three of them?' A bellow of laughter.

'She'll have all three. She's not choosy.'

One began to sing: 'Sweet Marie, my little pussy,' followed by most of the others.

'I do hope there's no trouble!' said Pinneberg.

'I'm not going to put up with it any longer,' said Schulz. 'Why should I take it when he calls me a goat in front of everybody? What I should do is get Marie pregnant and then drop her.' He gave a sombre and malicious grin.

'We ought to lie in wait for him one night when he's drunk and do him over,' said the doughty Lauterbach. 'That'd help.'

'But then none of us does anything,' said Pinneberg. 'The workers are right. We're always shit-scared.'

'You may be. I'm not,' said Lauterbach.

'Nor am I,' said Schulz. 'I'm sick of the whole outfit.'

'Well then, let's do something,' suggested Pinneberg. 'Did he have a talk with you this morning?'

The three looked at each other: testing, mistrustful, embarrassed.

'Let me tell you something,' declared Pinneberg, who'd realized he had nothing to lose. 'This morning he started on to me about what a good girl Marie was, and then he said I ought to state my intentions, what about I didn't know, then whether I would volunteer for redundancy because I was the youngest. It was all about Marie.'

'I had it too. He said my being a Nazi gave him a lot of trouble.'

'With me it was because I go out with a girl now and then.'

Pinneberg took a deep breath. 'Well?'

'What d'you mean: well?'

'What are you going to say on the first of the month?'

'What about?'

'Whether you want Marie?'

'Out of the question!'

'I'd rather be on the dole!'

'So.'

'What d'you mean: so?'

'We could come to an agreement.'

'What about?'

'For instance: we all give our word of honour to say "No" to Marie.'

'But he won't say anything about her, Emil isn't such a fool as that.'

'Marie isn't grounds for dismissal.'

'Well then, let's agree that if he dismisses one of us, we all go. Give our word of honour on it.'

The three looked thoughtful, each weighing up his chances of being dismissed, and whether it was worth giving his word of honour.

'He wouldn't dismiss us all,' urged Pinneberg.

'Pinneberg's right there,' confirmed Lauterbach. 'He couldn't do that just now. I'll give my word.'

'Me too,' said Pinneberg. 'And you Schulz?'

'Oh, why not? Count me in.'

'Break over!' roared Kube. 'Will the gentlemen stir themselves, please!'

'So that's agreed?'

'Word of honour!'

'Word of honour!'

'Lord, how pleased Lammchen will be,' thought her young man. 'Another month's security.'

They went back to their scales.

It was getting on for eleven when Pinneberg got home. Curled up in the corner of the sofa he found Lammchen, asleep. She had the face of a child who has cried itself to sleep. Her eyelids were still wet.

'Goodness, is that you? At last. I was so frightened.'

'Why were you frightened? What could happen to me? I had to work after hours. I get that pleasure every so often.'

'And I was so scared! Are you hungry?'

'I should say so. D'you know there's a funny smell in here?'

'Funny?' snuffled Lammchen. 'My pea soup!'

They rushed in to the kitchen, to be met by a stinking barrier of smoke.

'Open the window! Quick, open all the windows! Create a through-draught!'

'Find the gas tap. Turn the gas off first.'

At last, breathing somewhat purer air, they both looked into the big cooking-pot.

'My beautiful pea-soup,' whispered Lammchen.

'More like coal.'

'The beautiful meat!'

They stared into the pot, the bottom and sides of which were covered with a blackish, sticky, stinking mass.

'I put it on at around five,' explained Lammchen. 'I thought you would come at about seven. The water was meant to boil away in that time. And then you didn't come, and I got so frightened and didn't give a thought to the silly old pot.'

'It's done for too,' said Pinneberg sadly.

'Perhaps I could get it off,' mused Lammchen. 'With one of those wire brushes.'

'All costs money,' said Pinneberg shortly. 'When I think of the money we've squandered already these last few days. And now all these pots and wire brushes, and the meal – I could have had lunch for three weeks in a restaurant for that. Yes, you may cry, but it's true. . .'

She was sobbing now. 'I try so hard, Sonny. But when I'm so worried about you I can't think about the food. And couldn't you have come even half an hour earlier? That wouldn't have been too late to turn off the gas.'

'Never mind,' said Pinneberg, putting the lid back on the pot. 'Put it down to experience. I. . .' (making a heroic effort) 'I make mistakes sometimes too. So don't cry. And now give me something to eat. I'm starving.'

Saturday, that fateful Saturday the thirtieth of August, dawned bright and deep-blue. Over their morning coffee Lammchen repeated: 'So you've definitely got tomorrow off. Tomorrow we'll go to Maxfelde on the little train.'

'Tomorrow is Lauterbach's turn at the stables,' said Pinneberg. 'Tomorrow we'll be off. I promise.'

'And then we'll take a rowing-boat and row across the Maxsee and up the Maxe.' She laughed. 'Goodness what funny names! I keep thinking you're pulling my leg!'

'I'd love to. But I've got to go to work. 'Bye, wife!'

''Bye, husband.'

Then Lauterbach came up to Pinneberg. 'Listen, Pinneberg, we're going on a recruitment march tomorrow and my Gruf has told me I have to be there. Would you look after the stables for me?'

'Dreadfully sorry, Lauterbach. Tomorrow is out. Any other time willingly.'

'Do me a favour, man.'

'No, I really cannot. You know I'm always willing to help but just this time it's out. Try Schulz.'

'No, Schulz can't either. He's in trouble with some girl, about maintenance. So be a sport.'

'Not this time.'

'But you never have anything planned.'

'This time I have.'

'You're just being mean. I'm sure you haven't.'

'I do this time.'

'I'll work two Sundays for you Pinneberg.'

'No, I can't. And now shut up about it. I'm not doing it.'

'Well, all right, if you're going to be like that. And it was a special order from my Gruf!' Lauterbach was wildly hurt.

That was how it began, and how it went on.

Two hours later Kleinholz and Pinneberg were alone in the office.

The flies kept up a summery buzzing and humming. The boss was bright red, he'd certainly had a few glasses already and was in a good mood.

So it was in quite a peaceable way that he asked, 'Will you do stable-duty tomorrow for Lauterbach, Pinneberg? He's asked me for the day off.'

Pinneberg looked up. 'Dreadfully sorry, Mr Kleinholz. Tomorrow I can't. I've already told Lauterbach.'

'You can put it off. You've never had anything important on before.'

'This time unfortunately I have, Mr Kleinholz.'

Mr Kleinholz looked searchingly at his book-keeper. 'Listen, Pinneberg. Don't make trouble. I gave Lauterbach leave. I can't take it back.'

Pinneberg didn't answer.

'Look here, Pinneberg,' Emil Kleinholz explained, in a friendly man-to-man way, 'Lauterbach is a fool. But he is also a Nazi and his Group Leader is Rothsprack the miller. I don't want to get into his bad books, because he always helps us out when we need to get something milled in a hurry.'

'But I really can't do it, Mr Kleinholz,' insisted Pinneberg.

'Schulz might have stood in,' pondered Kleinholz, 'but then he can't either. He's got a family funeral, and he's due to inherit. So he has to go. You see why: otherwise the relations will take everything.'

'What a scoundrel!' thought Pinneberg. 'Him and his women.'

'Yes, Mr Kleinholz. . .' he began.

But Kleinholz had got up. 'As for me, I'd do it willingly, I'm not like that, as you know.'

'You're not like that, Mr Kleinholz,' confirmed Pinneberg.

'But I'm afraid tomorrow, Pinneberg, I simply can't. I have to go into the country and make sure that we get in the clover orders. We haven't sold a thing yet this year.'

He looked expectantly at Pinneberg.

'I must go on a Sunday, Pinneberg, because I'm sure of finding the farmers at home.'

Pinneberg nodded. 'Supposing old Kube distributed the feed for once, Mr Kleinholz!'

Kleinholz was indignant. 'Old Kube! I, give the key to the granary to old Kube! He's been here since Father's day, but he's never held the key. No, no, Mr Pinneberg, you see you're the only man for the job. You work tomorrow.'

'But I can't, Mr Kleinholz!'

Kleinholz was astounded. 'But I've just explained. No one's got the time but you.'

'But I haven't got the time, Mr Kleinholz!'

'Mr Pinneberg, you can't ask me to stand in for you tomorrow just for a whim. What do you have on tomorrow?'

'I have. . .' he began. 'I must. . .' he continued, then fell silent. On the spur of the moment, he couldn't think of anything to say.

'There you are you see. I can't let my clover business go to rack and ruin just because you don't feel like it. Mr Pinneberg! Be reasonable.'

'I am reasonable, Mr Kleinholz. But I definitely can't.'

Mr Kleinholz got up and walked backwards to the door, keeping a sorrowful eye on his book-keeper. 'I was wrong about you, Mr Pinneberg,' he said. 'Very wrong.'

And slammed the door.

Lammchen was naturally of the same opinion as her young man.

'Why ever should you? And I think it was awfully mean of the others to drop you in it like that. In your place I'd have told the boss that Schulz was lying about the funeral.'

'You don't do things like that to your colleagues.'

Lammchen regretted her thought. 'No, of course not. You're quite right. But I'd tell Schulz a thing or two. I'd tell him.'

'I will tell him, Lammchen. I will.'

And there they were, the two of them, on the little train to Maxfelde. The train was jam-packed, despite the fact that it left Ducherow at the early hour of six a.m. And Maxfelde itself, with the Maxsee and the Maxe was a disappointment – noisy, crowded and dusty. Thousands of people had come from Platz and there were hundreds of cars and tents on the beach. Nor was there any chance of a rowing-boat; the few there were had been taken hours ago.

Pinneberg and his Emma were newly married; they yearned for solitude. All this hurly-burly appalled them.

'So let's move on,' suggested Pinneberg. 'It's all woods and water and mountains round here. . .'

'But where to?'

'I don't mind. Just away from here. We'll find somewhere.'

And they did find somewhere. At first the woodland path was fairly wide and there were crowds of people walking along it, but then Lammchen said that it smelled of fungus here under the beeches and she lured him away from the path. They ran ever deeper into the green, and suddenly they were in a meadow between two wooded slopes. They climbed up the other side holding each other's hands, and when they were at the top they came to a fire-break which cut ever deeper through the loneliest depths of the forest, uphill and downhill, and they wandered along it.

Above them the sun rose, slowly, gradually, and now and then the sea-wind from the far-distant Baltic gusted into the tops of the beeches, stirring them into a glorious burst of rustling. That sea-wind had been in Platz too, where Lammchen's home had been in the far-distant past, and she told her young man about the only summer holiday of her life, when she had spent nine days in Upper Bavaria with three other young girls.

And he grew talkative too and talked about how he had always been alone, how he didn't like his mother, and how she had never bothered about him and he had been in the way of her and her lovers. Also, she had a dreadful profession, she was. . . it took him a long while to bring out the confession that she was a hostess in a nightclub.

That set Lammchen thinking, and she almost regretted that letter, because a hostess in a nightclub was indeed something quite different, though Lammchen wasn't at all clear what the function of a hostess was since she had never been in a nightclub, and what she had heard about such ladies didn't seem to fit the age of her young man's mother. In short, it would most probably have been better to put 'Dear Madam'. But now was of course not the moment to talk about it to Pinneberg.

They walked for a long while in silence, hand in hand. But just as the silence was growing too heavy and they felt a distance coming between them, Lammchen said: 'My darling Sonny, aren't we so. . . so happy!' and raised her lips to his.

Suddenly the wood lightened in front of them and they stepped out into the brilliant sunshine of a huge clearing. Directly opposite was a high sandy hill and at the top a crowd of people were busying themselves around a curious contraption. Suddenly the contraption rose up, and sailed through the air.

'A glider!' shouted Pinneberg. 'Lammchen, a glider!'

He was greatly excited, and tried to explain to her how the thing could go higher and higher without an engine. But as he wasn't very clear about it himself, Lammchen didn't understand much, but she said 'Yes' and 'of course' very dutifully.

Then they sat down at the edge of the wood, breakfasted copiously from their picnic, and drank the thermos dry. The big, white, circling bird sank, and rose again and finally settled on the ground a long way off. The people who had been on the hill top rushed after it; it had gone a fair way, and by the time the couple had finished their breakfast and Pinneberg had lighted his cigarette, they were only just beginning to drag the plane back.

'Now they're going to drag it up the hill again,' Pinneberg explained.

'What a performance though! Why doesn't it go on its own?'

'Because it doesn't have an engine, Lammchen. It's a glider.'

'Haven't they the money for an engine? Are they that expensive? It looks like a lot of bother to me.'

'But Lammchen. . .' and he wanted to explain it again.

But Lammchen wrapped herself tightly in his arms saying: 'Oh, isn't it great that we've got each other, Sonny my darling!'

And at that moment, it happened.

Along the sandy road which ran beside the wood a car had come creeping as though on carpet slippers, and by the time the two had noticed it, and broken apart in embarrassment, it was almost upon them. In principle they should have been seeing the faces of the passengers in profile; in fact, these were all turned towards them. And they were astonished faces, stern and indignant faces.

Lammchen didn't understand it; the stupid way those people stared as though they had never seen a couple kissing before, and especially the conduct of her young man, who sprang up, babbling something incomprehensible, and made a deep bow towards the car.

But at that point all the faces suddenly reverted, as if on a secret command, to the profile position; no one acknowledged Pinneberg's magnificent bow, and with a shrill hoot the car accelerated and disappeared among the bushes and trees. They caught one more flash of its red paint, and then it was gone. Gone.

Sonny was left standing, as white as a corpse, his hands in his pockets, murmuring: 'We're done for, Lammchen. Tomorrow he'll throw me out.'

'Who will? Who?'

'Kleinholz of course! Ah God, you don't know, do you? That was the Kleinholzes.'

'Oh God,' echoed Lammchen, and drew a deep breath. 'Now that's what I call bad luck.'

And then she took her young man like a big son in her arms and comforted him as best she could.

HOW PINNEBERG WRESTLES WITH THE ANGEL AND
MARIECHEN KLEINHOLZ, BUT IT'S STILL TOO LATE

Hard on the footsteps of every Sunday comes Monday, however firmly one may believe at eleven o'clock on Sunday morning that it's light-years away.

But it comes, it comes ineluctably, and the common round begins again. At the corner of Market Place, where Pinneberg always met Kranz, the town clerk, he looked round, and lo, there was Kranz approaching, and when the two men were almost level, they raised their hats, and greeted each other.

After they had passed each other, Pinneberg held out his right hand; the wedding-ring sparkled golden in the sun. Slowly Pinneberg twisted the ring off his finger, slowly he reached for his wallet, and then swiftly and defiantly he put the ring on again. Standing tall, with his wedding-ring on his finger, he went to meet his fate.

His fate wasn't on time. Even the punctual Lauterbach wasn't there on that particular Monday, and not one of the Kleinholzes had shown up.

Must be in the stable, thought Pinneberg, and busied himself in
the courtyard. There stood the red car, being washed. 'If only you'd
broken down at ten yesterday morning,' thought Pinneberg, and said
aloud, 'Boss not up yet?'

'All asleep still, Mr Pinneberg.'

'Who fed the horses yesterday?'

'Old Kube did, Mr Pinneberg, Kube.'

'Aha,' said Pinneberg, and went back into the office.

There he found Schulz had just dawdled in, when it had already
turned eight-fifteen, yellowish green in complexion and jaundiced in
humour. 'Where's Lauterbach?' he asked crossly. 'Is the swine
playing sick, today when we've got so much work on?'

'Looks like it,' said Pinneberg. 'Lauterbach never comes in late.
Had a good Sunday, Schulz?'

'Damnable!' Schulz burst out. 'Damnable! Damnable!' He sank
into brooding silence, then began, wildly: 'You remember,
Pinneberg, I told you once, but you won't remember, eight or
nine months ago I went to Helldorf to a dance, a real knees-up
with the local yokels. And this girl now says I'm the father of
her child and have got to fork out. I won't do it. I'll accuse her of
perjury.'

'How will you do that?' asked Pinneberg, and thought: 'He's got
his troubles too.'

'I spent the whole of yesterday in Helldorf finding out who else
she. . . But those stupid peasants all stick together. She can go ahead
and perjure herself – if she dares!'

'Supposing she does dare?'

'I'll tell the judge what for. Would you believe it, Pinneberg, now
tell me honestly: I danced with her twice, and then I said: "Would
you care to come outside, my dear, it's so smoky in here." And then
and there. . . We only missed one dance. You see what I mean. And
it's only me who could be the father? It's crazy.'

'If you can't prove anything.'

'I'll say she's perjuring herself, and the judge will see the point.
How could I pay, anyway? You know yourself, on our salary.'

'Today's hiring and firing day,' said Pinneberg quietly and
casually.

But Schulz didn't hear. He only groaned: 'And alcohol always makes me so sick. . .!'

At twenty past eight, Lauterbach entered.

Oh Lauterbach! Oh Ernst! Oh poor Ernst Lauterbach!

A black eye: one. Left hand in bandages: two. Cuts all over the face: three, four, five. A sort of black silk hood over the back of the head, and a pervasive smell of chloroform: six, seven. And that nose: that swollen, bloody nose! Eight! And that lower lip, partially split, thick, negroid: nine! Knockout Lauterbach! General conclusion: Ernst Lauterbach had spent Sunday out among the local inhabitants, recruiting for his political ideas with zeal and dedication.

His two colleagues danced excitedly around him.

'Oh boy, oh boy, you have been mauled around.'

'Oh Ern, Ern, you never learn.'

Lauterbach sat down, very stiffly and carefully. 'What you can see is nothing at all. You should see my back.'

'Why on earth. . .?'

'That's the way I am! I could very well have stayed at home today, but I thought of you, when there's so much to do.'

'And today is hiring and firing day,' said Pinneberg.

'And the one who isn't there will be thrown to the dogs.'

'Listen, we're not having any of that. We've given our word of honour.'

Emil Kleinholz entered.

On that morning Kleinholz was unfortunately sober, so sober indeed that he smelled the beer and spirits emanating from Schulz as he came through the doorway. He struck the tone for the day at once: 'Workless again, gentlemen? I'm glad it's hiring and firing day; I'm going to make one of you redundant.' He grinned. 'Not much work about, is there?'

He surveyed the three triumphantly as they crept shamefacedly to their places. Kleinholz swiftly fired a second volley: 'Well, my dear Schulz, you look capable of sleeping off your hangover in the office at my expense. A well-watered family funeral was it? So what shall we. . .?' He thought. Then he had it. 'You know what? You can climb up on the trailer behind the truck and go to the wheat mill. And make sure you work the brake properly – it's an uphill, downhill ride

– I'll tell the driver to keep an eye on you, and give you a clout if you forget to brake.'

Kleinholz laughed. He had made a joke, and so he laughed. Because of course that bit about the clout wasn't meant to be taken seriously, even if he did mean it. Schulz got up to go.

'Are you going without the paperwork? Pinneberg, make out the delivery notes for Schulz. The man can't write today; he's got the shakes.'

Pinneberg scrawled away, glad to have something to do.

Then he gave Schulz the papers: 'Here you are, Schulz.'

'One moment more, Mr Schulz,' said Emil. 'You can't be back before twelve, and I can only fire you up to twelve o'clock according to our contract. You know I'm still not sure which of you three I'm going to fire, I'll have to see. . . So I'll fire you now provisionally, to give you something to think about on the way, and if you work the brakes properly I almost believe you'll sober up, Schulz!'

Schulz stood and moved his lips soundlessly. He had, as has been observed before, a lined, sallow face, and he hadn't been looking too good that morning to start with, but now, what an ashen heap of misery he was!

'Get off now!' said Kleinholz. 'And report to me when you come back. Then I'll tell you whether I'll withdraw my dismissal or not.'

So Schulz got off. The door closed, and slowly, with a trembling hand, on which the wedding-ring glittered, Pinneberg pushed away his blotting-pad. 'Will it be my turn next or Lauterbach's?'

At the first word he saw it was going to be Lauterbach. Kleinholz took a different tone with Lauterbach: Lauterbach was stupid but strong, and if you pushed him too far he simply lashed out. You couldn't needle Lauterbach too much; you had to take another tack. But Emil knew how to do that too.

'Just look at you, Mr Lauterbach. What a wretched sight. Black eye. Poppy nose. Mouth you can barely open to speak, and your arm. . . yet you're going to give me a full day's work? And want a full day's pay, I'll bet.'

'My work's all right,' said Lauterbach.

'Easy does it, Mr Lauterbach, easy does it. You know, politics is all right, and National Socialist is quite possibly very much all right, we'll see at the next elections and act accordingly, but I don't see why I in particular should bear the cost. . .'

'I can work,' said Lauterbach.

'Well maybe,' said Emil mildly. 'We shall see. I don't think you'll be doing the work I've got on today. . . You're a sick man.'

'I'll do any ——ing work,' said Lauterbach.

'If you say so, Mr Lauterbach! But I don't think that's quite true. The Brommen woman has let me down today, and we've got to winnow the winter barley again, and I thought of asking you to turn the fan. . .'

That was the height of meanness even for Emil. For working the fan was not a clerk's job in the first place, and secondly you needed two very sound, strong arms to do it.

'There you are,' said Kleinholz. 'It's as I thought. You're unfit for duty. Just go home, Mr Lauterbach, but I'll dock your pay. What you've got is not an illness.'

'I'll work,' raged Lauterbach defiantly. 'I'll turn the fan. Never you fear, Mr Kleinholz!'

'Well, as you like, I'll come up to you before twelve, Lauterbach, and tell you if I'm going to fire you.'

Lauterbach muttered something unintelligible and cleared off.

Now the two of them were alone. Now he'll start on me, thought Pinneberg. But to his surprise Kleinholz said quite affably: 'Nothing to choose between them, those colleagues of yours: about as different as a heap of dung and a heap of manure.'

Pinneberg did not reply.

'You look quite festive today. I can't give you any dirty work, can I? Make me up a statement for the Hoenow estate account, as of the 31st August. And be careful when you come to the straw deliveries. They delivered oat straw instead of rye straw that one time, and there's a query against that load.'

'I know about that, Mr Kleinholz,' said Pinneberg. 'That was the load that went to the racing-stables in Karlshorst.'

'Good man,' said Emil. 'You get things right, Pinneberg. If only all my people were like you! Good, that's what you'll do then. Good morning.'

And he was away.

Oh Lammchen! rejoiced Pinneberg. Oh my Lammchen! We're safe, we can stop worrying about my job and the Shrimp.

He got up and fetched the folder with the specialist's report, the straw-wagon having been examined by a specialist on the occasion in question.

'So what was the balance at 31st March? Debit. Three thousand, seven hundred and sixty-five marks, fifty-five. So. . .'

He looked up, thunderstruck. 'And I, stupid fool that I am, gave my word of honour and agreed with the others that we'd all give notice if one of us was sacked. I put them up to it myself; what an idiot, what a dumb clot! I mustn't do that. He'd simply throw us all out!'

He jumped to his feet; he paced up and down.

It was Pinneberg's moment of truth, in which he wrestled with his angel.

He thought that he would certainly not get another job in Ducherow. Nor, as things stood at present, anywhere else in the world either. He thought of how he had been unemployed for three months before he went to Bergmanns, and how dreadful that had been when he was on his own; but now there were two of them and a third on the way! He thought of his colleagues whom deep down he couldn't stand, and both of whom could much more readily bear to be sacked than he. He thought that it was far from certain they would keep their word if he was sacked. He reflected that if he gave notice and Kleinholz let him go, he would not be entitled to unemployment benefit for quite a long time, as a penalty for having given up a job. He thought of Lammchen, of old Bergmann the rag-trade Jew, of Marie Kleinholz, and suddenly of his mother. Then he thought of a picture out of the *Miracles of Motherhood* showing an embryo in the third month; that was how far the Shrimp had developed already, a naked mole, gruesome to contemplate. He thought about that for quite a long time.

He paced to and fro, getting very heated.

'What should I do? I can't simply. . . And the others certainly wouldn't! So?. . . But I don't want to be a rat. I don't want to be ashamed of myself. If only Lammchen were here! If only I could ask her! Lammchen is so upright; she always knows what you can do without having anything on your conscience.'

He rushed to the window of the office; he stared at Market Place. If only she would come by. Now! She was due to pass this way early today, as she said she wanted to get some meat. 'Dear Lammchen, kind Lammchen, please come by now.'

The door opened, and Marie Kleinholz came in.

It was an old prerogative of the women of the house of Kleinholz to be allowed, on Monday morning, when nobody visited the office, to lay out their washing on the big office table. And it was further the right of these ladies to demand of the clerks that they should find that table cleared. This, however, in the excitement of the day, had not been done.

'The table!' said Marie Kleinholz sharply.

Pinneberg sprang into action. 'One moment! So sorry; it'll be ready at once.'

He threw samples of wheat into cupboard drawers, stacked ring-binders on the window-sill, was temporarily at a loss where to put the corn-tester.

'Hurry along, man,' said Marie, trying to pick a quarrel. 'I'm standing here with my washing.'

'Just one moment,' said Pinneberg very gently.

'A moment, a moment,' she nagged. 'It could have been done long ago. But if you must watch out for tarts at the window. . .'

Pinneberg preferred not to answer. Marie flung her load of washing with panache onto the now empty table. 'It's filthy! Only just got this stuff clean and straight away it's dirty again. Where've you put the duster?'

'Dunno,' said Pinneberg with the beginnings of ill-humour, and pretended to look for it.

'Every Saturday evening I hang a fresh duster here, and by Monday it's gone. Somebody must be stealing them.'

'That's a bit much,' said Pinneberg crossly.

'What d'you mean a bit much? No one's accusing you. Did I say anything about you stealing dusters? I just said somebody. Some man. I don't believe girls like that ever pick up a duster; far too common for them.'

'Listen, Miss Kleinholz,' began Pinneberg, then thought better of it. 'Oh never mind!' he said, and sat down to work in his place.

'Yes, you'd better be quiet. Canoodling with a girl like that on the public road. . .'

She waited a while to see if her dart had struck. Then: 'All I saw was the canoodling, I don't know what else may have happened. I'm only talking about what I could swear to. . .'

She was silent again. Pinneberg thought desperately: 'I must hold my tongue. She hasn't got a lot of washing there. Then she's bound to wander off. . .'

Marie took up the thread of her chatter again. 'Awfully common she looked. All got up.'

Pause.

'Father says he saw her in the "Palm Grotto", she was a waitress.'

There was another pause.

'Lots of men like girls to be common; it turns them on, Father says.'

Another pause.

'I'm sorry for you, Mr Pinneberg.'

'And I'm sorry for you,' said Pinneberg.

A fairly long pause. Marie was rather taken aback. Finally: 'If you get cheeky with me, Mr Pinneberg, I'll tell Father. He'll throw you out on the spot.'

'What do you mean: cheeky?' said Pinneberg. 'I said exactly the same to you as you said to me.'

Silence now reigned. It look as though it had set in for good. The sprinkler rattled every so often when Marie Kleinholz shook it over the washing; the steel pen tapped the ink bottle.

Suddenly Marie gave a cry. She rushed triumphantly to the window. 'There she is, the silly cow! Goodness, she's plastered with make-up. It's enough to make you sick.'

Pinneberg stood up and looked out. The person going by outside was Emma Pinneberg with the string shopping-bag, his Lammchen, the most wonderful thing in the world to him. And what Marie had been saying about 'make-up' was a lie, that he knew.

He stood up and stared after Lammchen until she had gone round the corner and disappeared into Bahnhofstrasse. He turned round and went towards Miss Kleinholz. His face was disturbing to look at, very white and threaded with lines on the forehead, but strangely alive about the eyes.

'Listen to me, Miss Kleinholz,' he said, sticking his hands firmly in his pockets as a precaution. He swallowed and began again. 'Listen, Miss Kleinholz. If you ever say anything like that again, I'll hit you right in your ugly mug.'

She tried to say something, her thin lips twitched, her little bird-like head jerked towards him.

'You keep your mouth shut,' he said coarsely. 'That's my wife, do you understand!' And now his hand did leave his pocket, and the gleaming wedding-ring was held right under her nose. 'And you can count yourself lucky if you ever in your life turn out half such a decent woman as she is.'

With that, Pinneberg turned on his heel, he had said everything he had to say and he felt wonderfully relieved. Consequences? What consequences? They could do what they liked, all of them! Pinneberg turned on his heel, and walked back to his seat. For a long time Marie said nothing at all. He squinted over at her. She wasn't looking at him. She was pressing her poor, small head with the thin ash-blond hair against the window. But the other woman had gone; she could not see her any more.

And then she sat down on a chair, laid her head on the edge of the table and began to cry, real heartbreaking sobs.

'Oh God,' said Pinneberg, a little (but only a little) ashamed of his brutality, 'it wasn't meant as badly as that, Miss Kleinholz.'

But she was weeping floods of tears; it must have been doing her good in some way, and in between she stammered something to the effect that she couldn't help being like she was, that she'd always thought him a thoroughly decent man, quite different from his colleagues, and was he really married, ah, not in church then, and he shouldn't be afraid of her telling her father, because she wouldn't, and whether his girl was from here, she didn't look like it, and what she'd said before she'd said only to annoy him, she looked very nice.

So it went on, and would have gone on a fair while longer, had not the sharp voice of Mrs Kleinholz rung out: 'What are you doing with the washing, Marie? We've got to get on with the mangling!'

With a horrified 'Oh God!' Marie Kleinholz sprang up from table and chair, grabbed her washing and dashed out. Pinneberg, however, remained seated, feeling actually quite satisfied. He whistled to himself, calculating zealously and glancing up every so often to see whether Lammchen might not be coming back. But perhaps she had already passed.

And so it turned eleven, then half-past eleven, then quarter to twelve, and Pinneberg was already singing his 'Hosanna, praise be to my Lammchen, we're safe for another month', and everything might yet have gone well. But at five to twelve, father Kleinholz came into the office, surveyed his book-keeper, went and stared out of the window and spoke, in a kindly tone: 'I've been humming and hawing, humming and hawing, Pinneberg. I'd prefer to keep you and let one of the others go. But the fact that you wished the Sunday stable duty on to me simply so that you could go and amuse yourself with your women, that I can't forgive, and that's why I'm going to give you notice.'

'Mr Kleinholz!' began Pinneberg in the firm and manly resolve of explaining his case in such detail that it would take them way beyond the latest possible time for giving him notice, which was twelve o'clock. 'Mr Kleinholz, I. . .'

But at that moment Emil Kleinholz cried out furiously: 'Damn it, there's that woman again! I'm giving you notice till 31st October, Mr Pinneberg!'

And before Johannes Pinneberg could say a word, Emil had gone, slamming the door thunderously behind him. Just then Pinneberg saw his Lammchen disappearing around the corner of Market Place. He sighed deeply and looked at the clock. Three minutes to twelve. At two minutes to twelve Pinneberg was to be seen dashing across the courtyard to the seed-corn store. There he rushed up to Lauterbach and said breathlessly: 'Lauterbach, get over to Kleinholz and give notice. Remember you gave your word of honour. He's just given me notice.'

Ernst Lauterbach, however, slowly let go the handle of the winnow, looked in astonishment at Pinneberg and spoke: 'First, it's one minute to twelve, and after twelve I can't give notice; second, I'd have to talk to Schulz first, and he is not here. And third, I just heard

from Mariechen that you're married, and if that's true you've not
been as frank with us as your colleagues. And fourth. . .'

But Pinneberg never learned what the fourth thing was; for the
clock in the tower struck slowly twelve times and then it was too late.
Pinneberg had been given notice, and there was nothing more to be
done.

MR FRIEDRICHS, THE SALMON AND MR BERGMANN,
ALL IN VAIN: THERE IS NOTHING FOR PINNEBERG

Three weeks later – it was a cold, overcast, rainy September day, very
windy – three weeks later Pinneberg slowly closed the outer door of
the local office of the Clerical, Office and Professional Employees
Association of Germany. He stopped for a moment at the top of the
steps, and gazed absently at a notice calling for the solidarity of all
white-collar workers. He sighed deeply and went slowly down the
steps.

The fat man with the splendid gold teeth had conclusively proved
to him that there was nothing to be done for him, that his lot was to
be unemployed. 'You know yourself, Mr Pinneberg, what it's like in
the clothing sector here in Ducherow. No vacancies.' A pause, then
more emphatically: 'And there will be no vacancies.'

'But the Association's got offices all over the place,' said Pinneberg
timidly. 'Perhaps you could get in touch with one of them. I've got
such good references. Perhaps somewhere,' he gestured plaintively
into the beyond, 'Perhaps somewhere there is something to be done.'

'Out of the question!' declared Mr Friedrichs definitely. 'If a
vacancy did occur, which it won't because everyone who's got a job
sticks to it like glue, but if it did there'd be all those local members
waiting for it. It wouldn't be fair to put someone from outside in
before them.'

'But if the man from outside needed work more than they did?'

'No, no, that would be highly unfair. Today, everyone needs
work.'

Pinneberg didn't pursue the question of what was fair. 'What else
is there?' he asked obstinately.

'What else. . .' Mr Friedrichs shrugged his shoulders. 'There's nothing else. You're not a fully qualified book-keeper, although you will have picked up a bit at Kleinholz's. Now there's a funny place. . . is it true that he gets drunk every night and brings loose women into the house?'

'I don't know,' said Pinneberg shortly, 'I don't work nights.'

'Come on, Mr Pinneberg,' said Mr Friedrichs rather crossly. 'The Association is against that sort of thing: inadequately trained staff moving from one branch to another. The Association can't support it; it undermines the status of the members.'

'Oh dear,' was all Pinneberg said. Then, still obstinate: 'But you've got to find something for me, by the first, Mr Friedrichs. I'm married.'

'By the first! In precisely eight days' time. It's quite out of the question, Pinneberg, how can I? You must know that, Mr Pinneberg. You're a reasonable man.'

Pinneberg had no faith in reason. 'We're expecting a baby, Mr Friedrichs,' he said quietly.

Friedrichs turned his eyes up to the applicant. Then he said in a kindly, comforting tone: 'Ah well, children are a blessing. So they say. You will get the dole after all. There are so many people managing on less than that. It will be all right, you'll see.'

'But I must. . .'

Mr Friedrichs realized he had to do something. 'Now listen, Pinneberg. I can see you're in a spot. Look at this: I'm writing your name on my notepad: Pinneberg, Johannes, twenty-three years old. Salesman, address. . . What's your address?'

'Green End.'

'Oh! Way out there! And your membership number? Good. . .' Mr Friedrichs looked thoughtfully at the note. 'I'm putting it here, next to my inkwell, you see, so it's always in front of me. And so if anything comes up, you'll be the first I'll think of.'

Pinneberg started to say something. 'I'm giving you special treatment, Mr Pinneberg. Actually it's not fair on the other members, but I'll answer for that. I'm doing it because you're in a spot!'

Mr Friedrichs looked at the note with narrowed eyes, took a red pencil and added a thick, red exclamation-mark for good measure. 'There you are,' he said, satisfied, and laid it beside the inkwell.

Pinneberg sighed, and resigned himself to leaving. 'You will think of me, Mr Friedrichs, won't you?'

'I've got the note. I've got it here. Good day Mr Pinneberg.'

Pinneberg stood on the street wondering what to do next. He ought really to go back to the office at Kleinholz's. He only had a couple of hours off to look for a job. But he hated the thought, particularly being with his dear colleagues, who hadn't resigned, weren't even giving it a thought, but still asked sympathetically: 'Still no job, Pinneberg? Get up a bit of steam then. The children are crying for bread, the honeymoon's over.'

'Stuff it. . .' said Pinneberg emphatically, and set off for the town park.

It was cold, windy, and empty. Desolate flower-beds! Puddles everywhere! And too windy even to get a cigarette alight! Just as well, soon there'd be no more smoking anyhow. What an idiot! No one ought to have to give up smoking six weeks after getting married.

Then there was the wind. When you got to the place where the town park met the fields, it fairly jumped out at you. It shook you, your coat flapped, you had to grab at your hat to hold it on. The fields were thoroughly autumnal: wet, dripping, cheerless, in a mess. . . So, go home. There was a silly saying round here: 'It's a good thing houses are hollow, so people can live inside.'

So, home to Green End. But when Green End was at an end, there'd be somewhere else. Somewhere cheaper, well, four walls at any rate, a roof over their heads, warmth. A woman, oh yes, a woman! It was so lovely to lie in bed with another person snuffling next to you in the night. So lovely to read the newspaper with some-one sitting in the corner of the sofa, sewing and darning. So lovely to come home and hear someone say: 'Hello, Sonny, love. How was it today? Was it all right?' It was lovely to have someone to work for and care for. . . well, to care for, even when you hadn't any work. It was lovely to have someone who allowed you to comfort them.

Suddenly Pinneberg had to laugh. That salmon. That quarter of a salmon. Poor Lämmchen. How unhappy she had been! To comfort someone, that was the thing.

One evening they were just sitting down to dinner when Lammchen declared that she couldn't eat anything, that she was nauseated by everything. But today she had seen a smoked salmon in the delicatessen, so juicy and rosy pink: if only she had that!

'Why didn't you get it?'

'What! Just think what it would cost.'

So they'd talked about it and talked about it, and of course it would be idiotic, it was far too expensive. But if Lammchen couldn't eat anything else! Right away – supper was put off for half an hour – he was going to town for it right away.

Certainly not! Lammchen would go herself. What was he thinking of? Walking was very healthy, and anyway, did he imagine she'd want to stay here worrying in case he bought a piece off the wrong salmon? She had to see the woman in the shop slicing off the pieces, one by one. She had to go herself.

'All right. You go.'

'And how much?'

'An eighth. No. It's only once we're lashing out, bring a quarter.'

He watched her set out: she had a beautiful long sturdy stride, and in that blue dress she was dazzling. He followed her with his eyes, leaning out of the window until she had disappeared, and then he wandered up and down. He reckoned that by the time he had wound his way round the room fifty times she would be back in sight. He ran to the window. Yes, he'd got it right. Lammchen was just coming into the house; she didn't look up. Only two or three minutes more. He stood and waited. He thought he heard the hall door open. But Lammchen did not come.

What in the world was the matter? He'd seen her come into the house, but she wasn't here.

He opened the door onto the hall, and there, next to the outer door, stood Lammchen, pressed against the wall with a frightened face streaming with tears, holding out a wax-paper wrapper shining with grease-marks but with nothing in it.

'Oh gosh, Lammchen, what's the matter? Did the salmon fall out of the paper?'

'I ate it,' she sobbed. 'I ate it all, by myself.'

'Like that, out of the paper? Without any bread? The whole quarter? But Lammchen!'

'I ate it,' she sobbed. 'All by myself.'

'Now come on here, Lammchen; tell me what happened. Come in. It's nothing to cry about. Start from the beginning. So you bought the salmon. . .'

'Yes, and I had such a craving for it. I couldn't watch while she was slicing it and weighing it. I was barely outside, but I went into the nearest doorway and quickly took out a slice and it was gone.'

'And then?'

'Yes, Sonny,' she sobbed. 'That's what I did all the way home, whenever a doorway came up. I couldn't stop myself and went in. When I started I wasn't going to cheat you out of any; I divided it up very carefully, half and half. . . But then I thought, one slice won't matter to him, and I kept on eating yours, but I did leave one piece for you, and I brought it upstairs, right up here to the hall, as far as this door. . .'

'But then you ate it?'

'Yes, then I ate it, and it was so wicked of me, because there's no salmon at all for you, Sonny love. But it's not because I'm wicked myself,' breaking out in new sobs, 'it's my condition. I've never been greedy. And I'm so unhappy in case the Shrimp turns out greedy now. And. . . shall I run quickly back into town and get some salmon for you. I'll bring it back, I truly, truthfully will.'

He rocked her in his arms. 'Oh, you great big baby, you silly little girl, if it's nothing more dreadful than that. . .'

And he comforted her and calmed her and wiped away her tears, and gradually they got to kissing, and then it was evening and then it was night. . .

Pinneberg had left the windy town park. He was on his way through the streets of Ducherow towards a precise goal. He had not turned off into Feldstrasse and he was not going back to Kleinholz's office. He had taken a great decision and was marching towards it. Pinneberg had discovered that his pride was idiotic. He now realized that nothing mattered but keeping Lammchen out of hardship and making the Shrimp happy. What did Pinneberg matter? Pinneberg wasn't important, he could easily humble himself, provided all went well for them.

He marched straight into Bergmann's shop, and straight into the little dark birdcage which was simply partitioned off from the shop. And there indeed sat the boss, taking a letter out of the letter press. That was the way things were still done at Bergmanns.

'Well, if it isn't Pinneberg!' said Bergmann. 'Life still treating you well?'

'Mr Bergmann,' said Pinneberg breathlessly. 'I was a prize idiot to leave you. I'm very sorry, Mr Bergmann, and I would like the job back.'

'Hold on,' shouted Bergmann. 'Don't talk rubbish, Mr Pinneberg. I didn't hear what you've just said, Mr Pinneberg. There's no need to apologize to me, I'm not taking you back.'

'Mr Bergmann!'

'Don't speak! Don't beg! Afterwards you'll only be ashamed that you begged and it was all for nothing. I'm not taking you back.'

'Mr Bergmann, you said at the time you were going to keep me in suspense for a month before taking me on again. . .'

'I did say that, Mr Pinneberg, you're right, and I'm sorry I said a thing like that. I said it out of anger because you're such a decent chap, and so helpful, except for that business with the post, and then you go and work for that drunken womanizer. I said it out of anger.'

'Mr Bergmann,' Pinneberg began again. 'I'm married now, and we're having a baby. Kleinholz has sacked me. What shall I do? You know what it's like here in Ducherow. There's no work here in Ducherow. Take me back. You know I earn my money.'

'I know, I know,' he said, shaking his head.

'Take me on again, Mr Bergmann. Please.'

The little ugly Jew, whose Maker had been less than generous in his creation, shook his head. 'I'm not taking you back, Mr Pinneberg. And why? Because I can't!'

'Oh, Mr Bergmann!'

'Marriage is no easy matter, Mr Pinneberg. You've started early. Do you have a good wife?'

'Oh, Mr Bergmann!'

'I see you do. I see you do. May she stay so. Listen, Pinneberg: I'm telling you the simple truth. I'd like to have you back, but I can't; my wife won't have it. She was incensed by what you said – "you can't order me around" – and she refuses to forgive you. I'm not allowed to take you back on. I'm very sorry. It can't be done.'

There was a pause. A long pause. Little Bergmann turned the letter press, took his letter out and looked at it.

'Yes, Mr Pinneberg,' he said slowly.

'Supposing I went to your wife,' whispered Pinneberg. 'I would go to her, Mr Bergmann.'

'And would that do any good? No, it wouldn't do any good. Do you know what she would do? She'd let you plead with her. She'd say to come back, she'll think about it. But she wouldn't take you on, and in the end I would still have to tell you there was nothing doing. Women are like that, Mr Pinneberg. Ah well, you're young, you don't know anything about all that. How long have you been married?'

'A good four weeks.'

'A good four weeks. Still counting in weeks. You're going to be a good husband, that's clear. You need not be ashamed to ask for something, it hurts nobody. If people just stay friends. Stay friends with your wife. Always think to yourself: she's only a woman and she doesn't understand. I'm sorry, Mr Pinneberg.'

Pinneberg went slowly away.

A LETTER COMES AND LAMMCHEN RUNS THROUGH THE TOWN IN HER APRON TO GO AND CRY AT KLEINHOLZ'S

It was 26 September, a Friday, and on this Friday Pinneberg was still in the office as usual. Lammchen, however, was cleaning. And as she dusted around, there was a knock on the door. She said 'Come in', and in came the postman and said, 'Does Mrs Pinneberg live here?'

'That's me.'

'Here's a letter for you. You ought to have your name on the door. I'm not psychic.'

And with that, the Heavenly Messenger was on his way.

Lammchen stood there with the letter in her hand, a large pale mauve envelope, with large spidery writing on it. It was the first letter that Lammchen had had since she was married. She and the Platz people didn't write.

This wasn't a letter from Platz in any case, it was from Berlin. And on turning it over Lammchen saw that there was even the name of the sender on it: a female sender.

'Mia Pinneberg, Berlin NW 40, Spenerstrasse 92 II.'

'Sonny's mother. Mia, not Maria,' thought Lammchen. 'She took her time.'

But she didn't open the letter. She laid it on the table while she continued with the cleaning, looking across at it occasionally. It was sitting there, and would continue to sit there till her young man came. She would read it with him, together – that would be best.

Suddenly, she put aside the duster. She had a premonition that this was a momentous occasion; she was certain of it. She ran quickly into Mrs Scharrenhofer's kitchen, and rinsed her hands under the tap. Mrs Scharrenhofer said something or other to her, and she answered 'Yes' mechanically, but she hadn't heard a thing. She was in front of the mirror already, fixing her hair so that she looked a bit smarter.

And then she sat down in the corner with the forbidden thump (the springs went 'Ha-Yup'), took up the letter and opened it.

And read it.

It took her a while to understand.

She read it a second time.

But then she got up, her legs were trembling a little, but that didn't matter, they would get her as far as Kleinholz's. She simply had to speak to Sonny.

Heavens, she ought not to be getting so excited, it was bad for the Shrimp.

'Any kind of over-excitement must be strenuously avoided,' *The Miracles of Motherhood* had warned.

'But how on earth can I avoid it? And do I want to?'

A dozy mood reigned in Kleinholz's office. The three book-keepers were sitting around, and Emil was sitting around too. There wasn't really anything to do that day. But whereas the book-keepers had to look as if they were doing something, and doing it with feverish zeal,

Emil just sat around and wondered whether Emilie was going to pour another drink. He'd been lucky twice this morning already.

The door of this bored office suddenly flew open and a young woman burst in with flashing eyes, streaming hair and attractively-flushed cheeks, but wearing (oh, shame!) a kitchen apron. And she shouted: 'Sonny, come out at once! I have to speak to you immediately.'

Then, seeing how taken aback they all looked, she said, suddenly quite self-possessed: 'Please excuse me, Mr Kleinholz. My name is Pinneberg, and I have to speak to my husband urgently.'

And suddenly this self-possessed young woman gave a loud sob and cried: 'Sonny, oh! Sonny love, do come quickly. I. . .'

Emil growled something, Lauterbach squeaked like the fool he was, Schulz smirked, and Pinneberg was madly embarrassed. With a helpless gesture of apology he moved towards the door.

In the yard entrance which led to the office, the broad entrance where all the lorries rolled through with their sacks of wheat and potates, Lammchen flung herself, still sobbing, around her husband's neck. 'Oh Sonny, Sonny, I'm so wildly happy! We've got a job. There, read!'

Having no idea what was going on, he was utterly bemused. Then he read:

My dear daughter-in-law, called Lammchen,

I expect the boy is just as big a fool as ever, and you're going to have a lot of trouble with him. What madness after I gave him such a good education to be working in 'fertilizers'! He must come here at once and take up a job I've found for him in Mandels Department Store starting on 1st October. To begin with, you'll live with me.

Kind regards from your Mama.

PS: I wanted to write to you a month ago, but I didn't get round to it. Now you must send me a telegram to say when you're coming.

'Oh Sonny, Sonny darling, I'm so happy!'

'Yes, my little girl. Yes, my sweetheart. So am I. Though I don't know what she means by "education". . . well, I won't say any more. I'll go straight away and send a telegram.'

It was a little while before they were able to tear themselves apart.

Then Pinneberg stepped back into the office, very stiff, quite silent, swelling with pride.

'What's new in the job market?' asked Lauterbach.

And Pinneberg said casually: I've got a position as chief salesman in Mandels Department Store in Berlin. Three hundred and fifty marks salary.'

'Mandel?' asked Lauterbach. 'Jews, of course.'

'Mandel?' asked Emil Kleinholz. 'Watch out that it's a respectable firm. In your place I'd look into it first.'

'I had a girlfriend like that once,' said Schulz thoughtfully. 'Always howled when she was the least bit excited. Is your wife always so hysterical, Pinneberg?'

PART TWO

BERLIN

A taxi-cab drove slowly up Invalidenstrasse, struggling through the mêlée of pedestrians and trams until it reached the less crowded square in front of Berlin's Stettin Station. Then it sped, hooting as though released, up on to the station forecourt where it came to a stop.

A lady got out. 'How much?' she asked the driver.

'Two marks sixty, lady,' said the driver.

The lady had begun delving in her little handbag, but now she withdrew her hand. 'Two-sixty for such a short journey. Oh no, dear, I'm not a millionairess. My son will pay. Wait.'

'Can't, lady,' said the driver.

'What d'you mean, can't? I'm not paying, so you'll have to wait till my son arrives. The ten past four from Stettin.'

'Not allowed to,' said the driver. 'We're not allowed to stop in the forecourt.'

'Then wait over there, dearie. We'll come over and get in.'

The taxi-driver cocked his head to one side and screwed up his eyes at her. 'Oh, I believe you'll come, lady. As sure as the next pay-cut. But I tell yer what: get the money back from yer son. That's easier for you, isn't it?'

'What's going on here?' asked a policeman. 'Move along, driver.'

'Lady wants me to wait, officer.'

'Move along.'

'She won't pay.'

'Please pay, lady. You can't do that here, other people have to get away too.'

'I don't want to. I'm coming straight back.'

'I want my money, yer made-up old. . .'

'I'll report you, driver.'

'Move along, dumb-head, or I'll bang your Bugatti.'

'Oh come on, Madam, please do pay. You can see how it is. . .' In his desperation the policeman did a kind of dancing-school bow, clicking his heels together.

The lady beamed. 'But of course I'll pay. If the man can't wait I don't want to do anything against the law. What a fuss! Goodness, constable, we women ought to deal with these things. Everything would go so smoothly. . .'

Station hall. Steps. A machine for platform tickets. 'Shall I take one? That's another twenty pfennigs. But then there are a couple of exits and I'd miss them. I'll get it back from him. I must buy some decent butter on the way back. Tinned sardines. Tomatoes. Jachmann's sending the wine. Flowers for the young woman? No, better not, it all costs money and it'll just spoil her.' Mrs Mia Pinneberg wandered up and down the platform. She had a soft, fleshy face, with remarkably pale blue eyes, so pale they looked faded. She was blonde, very blonde, with dark pencilled eyebrows, and because she was meeting them at the station she had put on a touch of make-up. Just a touch, in honour of the occasion. She wasn't usually out and about at this hour of the day.

'Bless the lad,' she thought, quite touched; she knew she ought to feel touched or this business of meeting them would be nothing but a bore. 'I wonder if he's still so gormless. Must be. Whoever would marry a girl from Ducherow? And I could have really made something out of him, he would have been so useful. . . His wife. . . well, she can be useful too, if she's a good little cleaner. Come to think of it, especially if she's a good little cleaner. Jachmann's always saying I spend too much on the housekeeping. Maybe this way I could get rid of Mrs Möller. We'll see. Thank the Lord, here's the train.'

'Hello,' she beamed. 'You look wonderful, son. The coal trade seems a healthy business. You're not in the coal trade? Well, why write and say you were then? Yes, it's all right to give me a kiss. My lipstick is kiss-proof. And you, Lammchen. You're not what I expected at all.'

She held Lammchen at arms' length.

'Really, Mama?' asked Lammchen, smiling. 'What did you expect?'

'Oh, you know, a country girl, with a name like Emma, and he calls you Lammchen. . . I hear you're all supposed to be still in flannel underwear in Pomerania. Hans, how on earth can you call this girl a little lamb? She's a Valkyrie, high-bosomed and proud-hearted. . . Oh, now don't go blushing for heaven's sake, or I'll start thinking about Ducherow again.'

'I'm not blushing,' laughed Lammchen. 'Why shouldn't I have a high bosom? And I am proud. Especially today. Berlin! Mandel! And a mother-in-law like you. But I don't have anything in flannel.'

'Yes, speaking of flannel, what about your things? You'd better get them sent on. Or do you have furniture?'

'We haven't got any furniture yet, Mama. We haven't got as far as that yet.'

'There's no hurry. I've got a furnished room for you that's fit for a king. I tell you: luxurious. Money's better than furniture. I hope you've got plenty of money.'

'Where from?' growled Pinneberg. 'Where are we supposed to get money? What does Mandel pay?'

'Who's Mandel?'

'You know, Mandels the Department Store. Where I've got the job.'

'Did I write something about Mandels? I'd quite forgotten. You must discuss it with Jachmann this evening. He knows all about it.'

'Jachmann. . .?'

'Let's get a cab. I've got a little party this evening, and I'll be too late otherwise. Go on, Hans, there's the baggage counter. Don't let them deliver your things before eleven. I don't like people ringing the bell earlier than that.'

The two women were alone together for a moment.

'You like to sleep late, Mama?' asked Lammchen.

'Of course. Don't you? Every sensible person likes to sleep late. I hope you aren't up and creeping round the flat at eight o'clock in the morning.'

'I like to sleep late of course. But he has to be up and into work in good time.'

'He? Who? Oh, him! You call him Sonny, don't you? I call him Hans. He's really called Johannes, that's what old Pinneberg wanted, he was like that. But that's no reason for you to get up so early. It's just a superstition men have. They can make their coffee and butter their rolls perfectly well on their own. But just ask him to be a little bit quiet. He used to be dreadfully inconsiderate.'

'Not to me!' said Lammchen decisively. 'To me he's always been the most considerate person in the world.'

'How long have you been married. . .? Don't speak too soon, Lammchen! Goodness, I'll have to find something else to call you. All settled, son? So let's get a cab.'

'92 Spenerstrasse,' said Pinneberg to the driver. Then, as they were sitting down: 'You're giving a party today, Mama? Surely not. . .?' He paused.

'What's the matter?,' his mother cajoled him. 'Are you embarrassed? A party in your honour, you meant to say, didn't you? No, my son. Firstly I don't have the money for that sort of thing, and secondly it's business, not a party. Just business!'

'So you don't go out in the evenings any more to. . .' Once again he couldn't finish the question.

'Oh heavens, Lammchen!' his mother cried despairingly. 'What do I do with him? Now he's embarrassed again. He wants to ask whether I still go to the bar. He'll still be asking me that when I'm eighty. No, no, son, I stopped going there years ago. I'm sure he's told you that I go to a bar, that I'm a hostess. Well, hasn't he? Speak up!'

'Well, he did say something. . .' said Lammchen, hesitantly.

'There you are!' cried Mama Pinneberg triumphantly. 'D'you know, my son Hans has been running around half his life gloating over his mother's immorality. He's downright proud of his misery. He'd be even more happily unhappy if he was illegitimate. But you're out of luck there, son, you're legitimate, and I was faithful to Pinneberg too, more fool I.'

'Oh! d'you mind, Mama!' protested Pinneberg.

'Goodness, what fun!' thought Lammchen. 'It's all so much better than I'd thought. She's not at all bad.'

'Now listen, Lammchen. If I only had another name for you. About the bar, it wasn't like that at all. In the first place it's at least ten years ago. Then, it was a very big bar, with four or five girls and a man who mixed the cocktails. And because they were always cheating with the spirits, and writing out the bills wrong, and the bottles never agreed in the morning, I took the job as a favour to the owner. I was a sort of supervisor, a manager. . .'

'Oh Sonny, how could you have. . .'

'I'll tell you how he could. He spied through the curtain at the entrance. . .'

'I didn't spy!'

'Oh yes, you did, Hans, and don't pretend you didn't. And of course, if I knew the customers well, I sometimes had a glass of champagne with them.'

'Spirits,' said Pinneberg darkly.

'I like a liqueur now and again. And so does your wife, I'm sure.'

'My wife doesn't drink alcohol.'

'Very clever of you, Lammchen. Your skin won't get so flabby. And it's better for the stomach, too. Liqueurs make me so fat, too; it's ghastly.'

'What sort of business party have you got on today?' asked Pinneberg.

'Look at him, Lammchen. A real examining magistrate. He was like that at fifteen. "Which gentleman did you have coffee with? There was a cigar stub in the ashtray." What a son!'

'You started about the party, Mama!'

'Oh did I! Well, I'm not interested, now. One look at your expression and it puts me right off. Anyway you're excused.'

'But what is all this?' asked Lammchen bewildered. 'We were all so happy just now.'

'The brat is always bringing up these disgusting stories about the bar!' raged Frau Pinneberg senior. 'It's been going on for years and years.'

'You brought it up, not me!' said Pinneberg angrily.

Lammchen looked from one to the other. She hadn't heard her young man use that tone before.

'And who is Jachmann?' asked Pinneberg, unmoved by these emotional outbursts, and his voice wasn't nice at all.

'Jachmann?' asked Mia Pinneberg, her pale eyes flashing dangerously. 'Jachmann is my current lover, I sleep with him. He's also your current surrogate father, Hans my son, and you will show him some respect.' She gave a snort. 'Heavens, there's my delicatessen! Stop, driver. Wait.'

And she was out of the car.

'See that, Lammchen,' said Johannes Pinneberg, deeply satisfied.

'That is my mother. I wanted you to see her as she is at once. That is how she is.'

'But how could you, Sonny!' said Lammchen, and for the first time she felt really cross with him.

A GENUINE FRENCH BED, FIT FOR A KING BUT TOO DEAR.
JACHMANN DOESN'T KNOW ANYTHING ABOUT A JOB AND
LAMMCHEN LEARNS TO BEG

'There,' said Mrs Pinneberg triumphantly, opening a door. 'This is your room. . .'

She switched on the light and the glow of a red bulb mingled with the dying September day. She'd said it was fit for a king, and regal it certainly was. The bed was on a dais; it was broad, and made of gilded wood, with cherubs. Red silk eiderdowns, some sort of white fleece on the step. A canopy above. A ceremonial bed, a bed of state. . .

'Oh God!' cried Lammchen, repeating her reaction to her first new home. Then she said quietly: 'But it's much too fine for us. We're simple people.'

'It's genuine,' said Mrs Pinneberg proudly. 'Louis Seize or rococo, I can't remember which, you'll have to ask Jachmann, he gave it to me.'

'He gives her beds,' thought Pinneberg.

'I've always let it up till now,' continued Mrs Mia Pinneberg. 'It looks splendid, but actually it's not all that comfortable. To foreigners mostly. I used to get two hundred a month for it with that little room over there. But no one could pay that today. We'll let you have it for a hundred.'

'I can't possibly give you a hundred marks rent, Mama,' declared Pinneberg.

'Why not? A hundred marks isn't much for such an elegant room. And you can share our telephone.'

'I don't need a telephone. I don't need a grand room,' said Pinneberg crossly. 'I don't even know yet what I'm going to be earning, and you say a hundred marks rent.'

'Very well, let's have coffee,' said Mrs Pinneberg, switching out the light. 'If you don't know what you're pay's going to be, you may very well be able to afford a hundred marks. We'll put your things down here right away. And listen, Lammchen, my domestic, Mrs Möller left me in the lurch today of all days, so could you please help with the preparations? You wouldn't mind?'

'I'll do it with pleasure, Mama,' said Lammchen. 'I only hope I can do it properly though. I'm not much of a housewife.'

After a while the picture in the kitchen was as follows: Mrs Pinneberg senior was sitting on a rather dilapidated cane chair, chain-smoking. At the sink stood the two young Pinnebergs, doing the washing-up. She washed, he dried. There was an endless amount to wash up; saucepans with remains of food in them were standing everywhere, regiments of cups, squadrons of wine-glasses, plates, cutlery, cutlery and more cutlery. No one could have washed up for a fortnight.

Mrs Mia Pinneberg entertained them: 'Now this is typical of Mrs Möller. I never come into the kitchen in the normal way and this is how she leaves it! I can't think why I keep pouring my precious money down her throat; I'm going to throw her out tomorrow. Hans, my son, be careful not to leave any fluff in the wine-glasses. Jachmann's so fussy, he just smashes any glass he finds like that. And when we've finished the washing-up, let's make the supper. That'll be easy: nice rolls, and there should be a large piece of left-over roast veal lying around somewhere. Thank the Lord, there comes Jachmann; he'll lend a hand as well.'

The door opened and Mr Holger Jachmann came in.

'Who have we here?' he asked in amazement, staring at the two washers-up.

Jachmann was a giant of a man, quite, quite different from how the young Pinnebergs had imagined him. A tall, fair, broad-shouldered fellow with blue eyes and a strong, cheerful, honest face, and still not wearing a jacket or a waistcoat even though winter was coming on.

He stopped, taken aback, in the doorway, and said, 'Who have we here? Did that old bag of a Möller finally overdose on our brandy?'

'Charming, Jachmann,' said Mrs Pinneberg, remaining firmly ensconced in her chair. 'You stand there and stare. I ought to make a note of how many times you stand and stare. Considering I told you quite distinctly that I was expecting my son and daughter-in-law.'

'Not a word did you breathe to me about it, Pinneberg, not a word,' swore the giant. 'It's the first time I've heard you had a son. And now there's a daughter-in-law as well. Madam. . .' Lammchen, standing by the sink with wet hands, received the first kiss on the hand of her life. 'Madam, I'm delighted to meet you. Are you always going to wash up here? Allow me!' He took a pot out of her hand. 'Now this looks to me like a hopeless case. Pinneberg must have been trying to cook shoe-leather in it. If I remember right and the late Möller hasn't taken it with her to the grave, there was some Vim in the kitchen cupboard. Thank you, young man, we'll christen our friendship with a drink afterwards.'

'What are you talking about, Jachmann?' Mrs Pinneberg piped up from the background. 'First you start flirting, then you claim I never told you about my son. Not only did I tell you about my son, but you personally fixed him up with a job in Mandels, to start on the first of October, which is tomorrow. Typical.'

'I certainly did not,' grinned Jachmann. 'I never find jobs for people with times as they are, Pinneberg. It only comes to grief.'

'Oh God, what a man!' exclaimed Mrs Pinneberg. 'You said it was all sewn up, and I was to send for him.'

'You've got it wrong, Pinneberg, it's all in your mind. I may have spoken about it, as a possibility, I do have a vague memory of something like that, but you certainly never mentioned a son. It's your damned vanity. Son – I never heard you speak the word.'

'Well!' said Mrs Pinneberg indignantly.

'And as for it being all sewn up, I'm very precise about the deals I make, I'm the most orderly person in the world, really pedantic, so it can't possibly be. I was with Lehmann the day before yesterday – he's the head of Personnel at Mandels, and he'd certainly have said something about it. No, Pinneberg, you've been building castles in the air again.'

The two young Pinnebergs had long ceased washing up; they stood looking from one to the other. At Mama, whom the gigantic Jachmann addressed simply as Pinneberg, and at the giant himself, who simply denied all knowledge. And now considered the whole matter closed, completely closed.

But Johannes Pinneberg was to be reckoned with. He couldn't care less about Jachmann, he didn't like the man, and anyway what he was saying was a lot of blah. But he took two steps towards his mother and said, very pale, and a little halting in his speech, but very clearly:

'Mama, does this mean that you got us to come here from Ducherow, and pay out all that money for the journey, for a fantasy? Just because you'd like to have rented your princely bed for a hundred marks. . .'

'Sonny,' cried Lammchen.

But her young man continued ever more resolutely: 'And just because you needed someone to do the washing-up. We're poor people, Lammchen and I, I probably don't even get the dole here, so what. . . what?' Suddenly he began to swallow hard. 'What in the world are we going to do now?' He stared round the kitchen.

'Now, now, now,' said Mama. 'Don't let's have any crying. You can always go back to Ducherow. You heard, and Lammchen, you heard too: I'm not to blame for this. It's him, Jachmann, made another of his mess-ups. If you listen to him you'd think he had everything sewn up, that he was the most orderly person under the sun, but in reality. . . Look at him standing there: I bet he's forgotten that the Stoschussens are bringing three Dutchmen this evening, and that he was meant to get Mullensiefen along, and Claire and Nina. And you were meant to bring the écarté cards as well. . .'

'Listen to her,' said the giant triumphantly. 'That's Pinneberg all over. She told me about the three Dutchmen, and she told me to order the girls. But she didn't say a word to me about Mullensiefen. What do we need him for, anyway? There's nothing he can do that I can't do standing on my head.'

'And the écarté cards, my treasure?' asked Mrs Pinneberg threateningly.

'Got them! Got them! They're in my overcoat. At least, that's where they should be if I had it on. . . I'll have a quick look in the hall. . .'

'Mr Jachmann!' said Lammchen suddenly, stepping into his way. 'Listen a moment. It won't seem important to you that we haven't a job. I'm sure you can always find a way out, because you're much cleverer than we are. . .'

'Hear that, Pinneberg?' cried Jachmann, highly gratified.

'But we're very ordinary people, and we're so unhappy when Sonny has no job. So I beg you, if you can, please do it, do find us a job.'

'Little lady!' said the big man emphatically. 'I'll do it. I'll find your young man there a job. What's it to be? How much d'you need to live on?'

'But you know all about it,' piped up Mrs Pinneberg. 'Salesman at Mandels. Menswear.'

'Mandels? D'you really want to work in a sweatshop like that?' He looked searchingly at him. 'Besides I'm sure he wouldn't get more than five hundred a month.'

'You're mad,' said Mrs Pinneberg. 'Five hundred for a salesman! Two hundred. Two hundred and fifty at the most.'

Even Pinneberg nodded agreement.

'Oh, in that case!' said the giant with relief. 'Let's leave all that nonsense. No, what I'll do is talk to old Manasse, and we'll get you a nice little shop in the old West End, something really unique, out of the ordinary. I'll set you up, young lady, I'll set you up properly.'

'Now give over,' said Mrs Pinneberg crossly. 'I've had enough of you setting people up.'

And Lammchen said: 'All we need is a job, Mr Jachmann, just a job at the standard wage.'

'Well, if it's no more than that! I've sorted that kind of thing out hundreds of times. So, Mandels it is. I'll simply go to old Lehmann; he's so dim he's happy to do you a favour.'

'But you mustn't forget, Mr Jachmann. It has to be at once.'

'I'll speak to him tomorrow. Your husband will begin the day after. Word of honour.'

'Thank you, Mr Jachmann. Thank you very much.'

'That's all right, young lady. That's quite all right. And now I really must look for those damned écarté cards. . . I could have sworn I put my overcoat on when I left home. And then I must have hung it up, but God knows where. It's always the same routine in autumn: I'm not used to the thing, I don't think about it and I leave it hanging somewhere. Then in spring, I'm always putting on other people's coats. . .'

Jachmann disappeared into the hall.

'And the man says he never forgets anything,' said Mrs Pinneberg comfortingly.

JACHMANN LIES, MISS SEMMLER LIES, MR LEHMANN LIES AND PINNEBERG ALSO LIES, BUT AT LEAST HE GETS A JOB (FATHER INCLUDED)

Mr Jachmann had been waiting for Pinneberg outside Mandels' window-display of Boys' and Young Men's Clothing.

'Ah, there you are. Don't look so worried. It's all set up. I talked my head off to old Lehmann, and now he's wild about you. Did we disturb you much last night?'

'A little bit,' said Pinneberg hesitantly. 'We're not used to it yet. And perhaps it was the journey too. Do I have to go in to Mr Lehmann now?'

'Oh, let the stupid fellow wait. He'll be happy to have you. I had to spin him a line of course. Who's hiring anybody these days? If he wants to know anything about you, you don't know anything.'

'Perhaps you should tell me what you said. I ought to be in the know.'

'Nonsense! Why should you? You're incapable of lying, anybody can see that. No, you don't know anything. Come over to the café for a while. . .'

'No, I'd really rather not. . .' said Pinneberg tenaciously. 'I'd like to get something definite. It's so important for my wife and me. . .'

'Important! Two hundred marks salary. . . No, no, don't give me that sort of look, I didn't mean to be nasty. Listen, Pinneberg,' said the great Jachmann, resting his hand quite gently on the little man's shoulder. 'I'm not just standing here giving you a lot of eyewash, Pinneberg. . .' He looked intently at him. 'Does it worry you my being friends with your mother?'

'No, no,' said Pinneberg very slowly, wishing he was somewhere else.

'Look here,' said Jachmann, and his voice sounded genuinely nice. 'I'm like that. I have to talk about everything! A lot of people would have gone all stuck up and not said anything but thought to themselves: what the hell are those kids to do with me! There, I can see it worries you. Don't let it. And tell your wife too. . . No, you needn't. She's not like you, I saw that at once. . . And when Pinneberg and I have a scrap, don't think anything of it. It's part of our relationship and we'd be bored without it. . . And as for her wanting a hundred marks from you for her moth-eaten room, that's rubbish, just don't give it her, she'd only squander it. And you mustn't get into a stew about the evening parties. They happen and they'll go on happening until there are no suckers left. . . And another thing, Pinneberg. . .' And now the big blusterer was really lovable, and despite all his initial dislike, Pinneberg found himself charmed and carried away. . . 'Another thing, Pinneberg. Don't tell your mother yet that you're expecting a baby. That your wife is, I mean. That's the worst thing in her opinion, worse than rats and bugs, she can't have had a very positive experience with you. Don't say anything. Deny it. There's time yet. I'll break it to her slowly. . . He doesn't grab the soap in the bath yet, does he?'

'What do you mean, the soap?' asked Pinneberg, baffled. 'Well. . .' said Jachmann, grinning. 'When the son reaches out at bathtime, and steals the mother's soap out of the tub, he's on his way. . . Taxi! Hey, taxi!' bellowed the giant suddenly. 'I ought to have been at Alexanderplatz half-an-hour ago, the chaps are going to tear me off a strip.' From the car window he shouted again: 'Second courtyard, right-hand side. Don't say anything. Cheers and good luck. Kiss on the hand to the young lady. Good hunting. . .!'

Second courtyard, right-hand side. Everywhere was Mandels. Heavens, what a large store. No shop where Pinneberg had worked to date was one-tenth as large as this. Not one-hundredth perhaps. And he promised himself to graft all he was able, to make out well at the job, to be long-suffering and not lose his temper. 'Oh Lammchen, oh Shrimp!'

Second courtyard, right-hand side. There on the ground floor: 'Mandels, Personnel office.' And another gigantic notice: 'No vacancies. Applications futile'. A third notice: 'Enter without knocking.' Pinneberg entered without knocking.

A counter. Behind it five typewriters. Behind the five typewriters, five girls, some younger, some older. All five looked up, then down, and continued to bang away on their machines; no one had seen that someone had come in. Pinneberg stood for a while and waited. Then he said to a girl in a green blouse who was the nearest to him: 'Please. Miss. . .'

'Whatcha want?' said Green-blouse, looking as indignant as if he had made an urgent, and improper, suggestion. . .

'I'd like to speak to Mr Lehmann.'

'Notice outside!'

'Excuse me?'

'Notice outside!!'

'I don't understand, Miss.'

Green-Blouse was highly annoyed: 'Read the notice outside. No vacancies.'

'I've read it. But I've got an appointment with Mr Lehmann. He's expecting me.'

The young lady – Pinneberg thought she looked quite ladylike, quite nice really (did she speak like that to her boss as well as her colleagues?) – the young lady looked crossly at him. 'Form!' she said. Then, getting quite worked up: 'You have to fill in a form!'

Pinneberg followed her glance. On a desk in the corner lay a block of forms; a pencil was hanging on a chain.

'Mr/Mrs/Miss. . . would like to speak to Mr/Mrs/Miss. . .
Purpose of interview (be specific). . .'

Pinneberg put down his name first, then Lehmann's, but he hesitated about the purpose of the visit, about which one had to be so specific. He wavered between 'acquaintance' and 'job'. But the strict young lady wouldn't be likely to pass either of those, and so he wrote 'Jachmann'.

'There you are, Miss.'

'Put it down there.'

The slip lay on the counter, the typewriters hammered on. Pinneberg waited.

After a while he said gently: 'Miss, I believe Mr Lehmann is waiting for me.'

No answer.

'Miss, please!'

The lady made an abrupt and indeterminate noise like a snake – 'sssss'.

'What if they're all like this here?' thought Pinneberg dejectedly. And continued to wait.

After a while a messenger in a grey uniform came in.

'Form!' said the young girl.

The messenger took the form, read it, surveyed Pinneberg and vanished.

This time Pinneberg did not have long to wait. The messenger came back, said quite politely: 'Mr Lehmann will see you!' and led him through the barrier, across a passage and into a room.

It wasn't Lehmann's room yet. But it was his anteroom.

There sat a not-so-young lady with a yellowish complexion. 'That's his private secretary', thought Pinneberg, awed. And the lady said with a melancholy, long-suffering demeanour: 'Take a seat, please. Mr Lehmann is still engaged.'

Pinneberg took a seat. The anteroom had a lot of filing-cabinets in it, the roll-top fronts were all up and the spring folders were grouped in batches: blue, yellow, green, red. Every folder had a label, on which he read a name: Fichte, Filchner, Fischer.

'Those are the names of employees,' he thought. 'Personnel files.' Some of these life-stories were very thin, some medium-thick; there were no really thick life-stories. The not-so-young spinster with the yellow complexion went back and forth. She picked up a carbon-copy, looked at it with a long-suffering expression, sighed, punched holes in it. She took out a file, put the carbon-copy in it. Was it the sack or a wage-rise? Did the letter say that Miss Bier must be friendlier to the customers?

'Maybe, oh, maybe, tomorrow. . .' thought Pinneberg, 'this spinster with the yellowish face is going to put in a personnel file labelled Johannes Pinneberg, maybe this afternoon even. Oh I do hope so.' The telephone buzzed. The spinster took a file and put the letter in it. The telephone buzzed. She clamped the letters down, and put back the file into its compartment. The telephone buzzed. The spinster lifted the receiver, and said, in her long-suffering, sour voice: 'Personnel department. Yes, Mr Lehmann is here. Who wants to speak to him? Director Kussnick? Yes, please bring Director Kussnick to the phone. Then I'll put him through to Mr Lehmann.'

A short pause. The spinster bent right over the telephone to listen; she seemed to see the person on the other end of the line, a delicate pink coloured her pale cheeks. Her voice was still melancholy, but a tiny bit sharp, as she said: 'I'm sorry, I'm not allowed to put you through to Mr Lehmann until the caller is on the line.'

A pause while she listened. Then, a tiny bit sharper: 'You can only put Director Kussnick through when Mr Lehmann is on the line?' Pause. Proudly: 'I can only put Mr Lehmann through when Director Kussnick is on the line.' Now the dialogue speeded up and the tone grew sharper:

'You were the one who called!'

'No, I have my orders.'

. . .

'I've no time for this sort of thing.'

. . .

'No, Mr Kussnick must be on the line.'

. . .

'Please. Otherwise I shall hang up.'

. . .

'No. It has happened to me too many times already. Later, your boss will be speaking on another line. Mr Lehmann can't wait.'

. . .

Gentler: 'Yes, I told you, Mr Lehmann is here. I'll put you through straight away.' Pause. Then quite another voice, long-suffering, soft: 'Director Kussnick. . .? I'm putting you through to Mr Lehmann.' Pressing a button and whispering: 'Mr Lehmann, Director Kussnick is on the line. What?' She listened with her whole body. Then, stricken: 'Certainly, Mr Lehmann.' Pressing the button: 'Director Kussnick? I've just heard that Mr Lehmann has gone to a meeting. No, I can't reach him. He's not in the building. No, sir, I didn't say that Mr Lehmann was here. Your secretary must have got it wrong. No, I can't say when Mr Lehmann is coming back. No, I didn't say anything of the kind, your secretary is mistaken. Goodbye.'

She rang off, still long-suffering but with a touch of pink in her yellow, melancholy face. It seemed to Pinneberg there was something a bit more spirited in her demeanour as she resumed her task of putting papers in personnel files.

'Seemed to do her good, that little row,' thought Pinneberg. 'She's pleased her colleague in Kussnick's office is going to get some stick, provided she's sitting pretty herself.'

The telephone buzzed. Twice. Sharply. The file flew from her hand onto the ground, the spinster was hanging on the line. 'Yes, Mr Lehmann? Yes, straight away.' And, to Pinneberg: 'Mr Lehmann will see you now.'

She opened the brown padded door in front of him.

'A good thing I saw all that,' thought Pinneberg as he went through the door. 'Look really humble. Say as little as possible. Yes, sir, no, sir, three bags full, sir.'

It was a gigantic room, with one wall almost all window. In front of the window stood a mammoth desk with nothing on it but a telephone. And a mammoth yellow pencil. Not one sheet of paper, nothing. At one side of the desk stood a chair – empty. On the other side a small wicker chair and on it, that must be Mr Lehmann, an elongated man with a yellow face criss-crossed with lines, a little black beard, and a sickly-looking bald patch. Very dark, round, piercing eyes.

Pinneberg stood in front of the desk; spiritually he was, so to speak, standing to attention, and he had sunk his head between his shoulders so as not to appear too tall. For it was only for form's sake that Mr Lehmann was sitting on a wicker chair; to indicate the gulf between them he ought to have been sitting on the uppermost rung of a step-ladder.

'Good morning,' said Mr Pinneberg in a quiet, polite tone, and bowed.

Mr Lehmann said nothing. But he picked up the mammoth pencil, and set it in a perpendicular position.

Pinneberg waited.

'What do you want?' snapped Mr Lehmann.

To Pinneberg it was a body-blow; one below the belt.

'I. . . I thought. . . Mr Jachmann. . .' His breath ran out.

Mr Lehmann observed him. 'I'm not interested in Mr Jachmann. I'm asking what *you* want.'

'I am applying,' said Pinneberg, very slowly, so that his breath wouldn't fail him again, 'for a position as salesman.'

Mr Lehmann put the pen in a horizontal position.

'We're not taking on anyone,' he said definitively. And waited.

Mr Lehmann was a very patient man. He continued to wait. Finally he said, standing the pencil upright again: 'Anything else?'

'Perhaps later. . .?' stammered Pinneberg.

'In times like these!' replied Mr Lehmann dismissively.

Silence.

'So I can go,' thought Pinneberg. 'Unexpected and unwanted. Again. Oh, poor Lammchen!' He was about to say goodbye when Mr Lehmann said: 'Show me your references.'

Pinneberg spread them out, with a trembling hand, genuinely frightened. He didn't know what Mr Lehmann was playing at, but Mandels department store had almost a thousand employees and Mr Lehmann was the personnel officer, and so a big man. Perhaps he was simply playing games.

So Pinneberg spread out his references, trembling; his apprenticeship certificate, then references from Wendheim, Bergmann, Kleinholz.

They were all very good. Mr Lehmann read them very slowly and impassively. Then he looked up and seemed to be reflecting. Perhaps, perhaps. . .

Mr Lehmann spoke: 'We don't stock fertilizers.'

So, it was out! And of course he looked a fool; all he could do was stammer: 'I thought. . . really I'm in menswear. . . that was just a temporary job.'

Lehmann was enjoying himself. It was so choice that he repeated it: 'No we don't stock fertilizers. Or potatoes,' he added.

He could have mentioned corn, or seeds, all of which were on Emil Kleinholz's letterhead, but the potatoes were quite unsatisfactory enough. He growled: 'Where's your employee's insurance card?'

'What is all this?' thought Pinneberg. 'What does he want my card for? Is it just to torment me?' And he handed over the green card. Mr Lehmann examined it at length, looked at the stamps, nodded.

'And your income-tax card.'

Pinneberg handed that over as well, and it too was carefully examined. Then there was a pause, calculated to set Pinneberg's feelings see-sawing between hope and despair.

'Well,' said Mr Lehmann finally, laying his hand on the papers. 'We're not taking on any new staff. We can't. We're laying off old staff. '

So that was that. The last word. But Mr Lehmann's hand was still lying on the papers; he had even laid the mammoth yellow pencil on them.

'However. . .' said Mr Lehmann. 'However we are allowed to take on staff from our branches. Particularly competent staff. Are you competent?'

Pinneberg whispered something. But it wasn't a protest, and it satisfied Mr Lehmann.

'You, Mr Pinneberg, will be taken on from our branch in Breslau. You come from Breslau, don't you?'

Another whisper, but again it satisfied Mr Lehmann.

'In the gentlemen's clothing department, where you will be working, there isn't anyone from Breslau, you understand.'

Pinneberg uttered a murmur.

'Good. Then you'll start tomorrow morning. Report at eight-thirty to Miss Semmler next door. You'll then sign the contract and the company's rules and regulations, and Miss Semmler will tell you what to do. Good morning.'

'Good morning,' responded Pinneberg, and bowed. He went backwards to the door. He had his hand on the door handle when Mr Lehmann whispered, loud enough to be heard across the room: 'My best to your father. Tell your father I've taken you on. Tell Holger that I'd be free on Wednesday evening. Good morning, Mr Pinneberg.'

And without those last words Pinneberg would never have known that Mr Lehmann was capable of a smile, rather a pinched one, but a smile nonetheless.

PINNEBERG WALKS THROUGH THE LITTLE TIERGARTEN, IS AFRAID AND CANNOT BE HAPPY

Pinneberg was outside on the street again. He felt tired, as tired as if he had been working to the limit of his endurance all day, as if he had been in mortal danger and only just escaped, as if he had had a shock. After having been stretched to screaming pitch, his nerves sagged, and would take no more. Slowly he started to wander home.

It was a real autumn day. In Ducherow there would have been a lot of wind, blowing continuously from the same direction. Here in Berlin it came from all directions, round the corners this way and that, with hurrying clouds which no one looked up at, and now and then a little sun. The pavement was wet and dry, but it was soon going to be wet all over again before it had got completely dry.

So now Pinneberg had a father, a real live father. And since that father was called Jachmann, and he was called Pinneberg, that made him illegitimate. But being illegitimate had undoubtedly helped him with Lehmann, who looked a complete lecher, and he could just imagine how Jachmann had portrayed this fictitious youthful folly to him. And, because of Jachmann's monstrous invention, he had been lucky again, he had become the man from the branch in Breslau and had snapped up a job. References: useless. Competence: useless. Good appearance: useless. Humility: useless. Everything useless, except the intervention of a type like Jachmann!

And what sort of a type was he?

What had been going on in the flat last night? They'd been laughing, bellowing, boozing. Lammchen and her young man had lain in their princely bed and pretended not to hear. They hadn't spoken about it: after all she was his mother, but the place wasn't kosher, certainly not.

How did Pinneberg know? He had been round the back; the lavatory was round the back, and to get to it you had to go through that Berlin-style living-room, since the Pinnebergs slept at the front. And really cosy it had looked in that living-room with just the mushroom-shaped lamp on, and the whole company sitting on the two big divans. The ladies, very young, very elegant, very high-society, and those Dutchmen – Dutchmen were supposed to be blond and fat, but these were dark, tall and thin. And all of them were sitting around drinking wine and smoking. And Holger Jachmann, who was walking up and down in his shirt sleeves as usual, was just at that moment saying: 'Nina, will you stop being all refined and making a fuss; I hate that.' And he didn't sound nearly as friendly and jovial as he usually did.

And in the midst of it all was Mrs Mia Pinneberg. Not that she stuck out too much, she'd made herself up wonderfully, so that she only looked slightly, ever so slightly older than the young girls. She'd undoubtedly been a part of whatever was going on, but what had been going on till four in the morning? True there had been long periods during which nothing was heard but a faint murmur in the distance, and then suddenly there would be another fifteen minutes of noisy merriment. Cards. They must have been playing cards for money, with two painted young girls, Claire and Nina, and three Dutchmen, for whom Mullensiefen was meant to have been invited, but in the end Jachmann's arts had sufficed. Wasn't that clear enough, Pinneberg? Though of course it might have been something quite different. . .

What sort of thing? If Pinneberg knew anybody, he knew his mother. She had good reason to get mad if he so much as mentioned the bar. And that business was different from how she said it was. It wasn't ten years ago, it was five, and he hadn't looked through a curtain, he had sat at a table, and three tables along sat Mrs Mia Pinneberg. But she hadn't seen him, she was too far gone for that. Manager in a bar! She needed managing herself. At first she hadn't been able to deny it and spun some story about a birthday party. Later on, the drunkenness and necking at that birthday party was all forgotten, gone, denied, and all that had happened was that he'd looked through a curtain and his managerial mother had stood respectably behind the bar. That was what it had been like then – so what was to be expected now?

It was all too clear.

And here he was back in the Little Tiergarten. Pinneberg had known it since childhood. It had never been particularly pretty, no comparison with its larger brother on the other side of the Spree, just a makeshift bit of green. But on this first of October, half wet and half dry, half cloudy, half sunny, with the wind blowing out of all corners and a lot of ugly brownish-yellow leaves, it looked particularly desolate. It wasn't empty, far from it. Masses of people were there, clothed in grey, and sallow-faced. Unemployed people, waiting for something, they didn't themselves know what, for who waited for work any more. . .? They were just standing around, without any plans; it was equally unpleasant at home, so why shouldn't they stand around? There was no sense in going home now, since they always ended up there anyway, however reluctantly, and there was plenty of time for that.

Pinneberg, however, ought to go home. He ought to go home quickly, as Lammchen would be waiting for him. But he lingered among the unemployed, went a few steps, then stopped again. Externally, he didn't belong to them, his outer shell was smart. He was wearing the reddish-brown winter ulster that Bergmann had let him have for thirty-eight marks, and the hard black hat, also one of Bergmanns', no longer completely in fashion, the brim's too wide, so shall we say three marks twenty, Pinneberg?

Externally then, Pinneberg did not belong to the unemployed, but internally. . .

He had just been to see Lehmann, the head of Personnel at Mandels department store; he had gone to get a job and he'd got one, it was a simple commercial transaction. But as a result of this transaction Pinneberg had the feeling, despite the fact that he was about to become a wage-earner again, that he was much closer to these non-earners than to people who earned a great deal. He was one of them, any day he could find himself standing here among them, and there was nothing he could do about it. He had no protection.

He was one of millions. Ministers made speeches to him, enjoined him to tighten his belt, to make sacrifices, to feel German, to put his money in the savings-bank and to vote for the constitutional party.

Sometimes he did, sometimes he didn't, according to the circumstances, but he didn't believe what they said. Not in the least.

His innermost conviction was: they all want something *from* me, but not *for* me. It's all the same to them whether I live or die. They couldn't care less whether I can afford to go to the cinema or not, whether Lammchen can get proper food or has too much excitement, whether the Shrimp is happy or miserable. Nobody gives a damn.

And all these people standing round in the Little Tiergarten, and a real zoo it was, full of proletarian animals rendered harmless by lack of food and lack of hope, they shared the same fate. Three months' unemployment and – goodbye, reddish-brown overcoat! Goodbye to any prospects for the future! Jachmann and Lehmann could have a quarrel on Wednesday evening, and suddenly I'll be worthless again. Goodbye.

These are my only comrades, these men here, though to them I'm stuck up, a proletarian in a suit with a starched white collar. But that's temporary. Only I know how little it means. Today, yes, today, I can earn a few bob, tomorrow, tomorrow, I'll be out of a job. . .

Perhaps he was still too new to living with Lammchen, but standing here looking at these people, he scarcely thought about her. And he wouldn't be able to tell her any of this. She wouldn't understand. However gentle she was, she was much tougher than him. She wouldn't stand here. She'd been in the Socialist Party, and the Anti-Fascist League but only because her father was in them, she actually belonged in the Communist Party. She had a few simple ideas: that most people are only bad because they have been made bad, that you shouldn't judge anybody because you never know what you would do yourself, that the rich and the powerful think ordinary people don't have the same feelings as they do – that's what Lammchen instinctively believed, though she hadn't thought it out. Lammchen's heart was with the Communists.

And that is why he couldn't tell her. Now he had to go to her and announce that he has a job, and they have reason to be happy. And he really is happy. But behind that happiness lies the fear: will it last?

No, of course it won't last. So, how long will it last?'

KESSLER REVEALS HIMSELF. HOW PINNEBERG STAYS
ON TOP AND HEILBUTT SAVES THE DAY

It was the thirty-first of October, nine-thirty in the morning.
Pinneberg was in the Gentlemen's Clothing Department of
Mandels, arranging grey striped trousers.

'Sixteen fifty. . . sixteen fifty. . . sixteen fifty. . . eighteen ninety. . .
where the hell are the trousers at seventeen seventy-five? We did have
trousers for seventeen seventy-five. That clot Kessler's gone and lost
them again. Where are the trousers. . .?'

A little further into the department, the apprentices Beerbaum and
Maiwald were brushing coats. Maiwald was a sportsman, and even an
apprenticeship in Clothing can be treated as sport. Maiwald's latest
record was one hundred and nine coats impeccably brushed in one
hour, though excessive zeal had resulted in the breakage of a bakelite
button, for which Jänecke, the under-manager, reprimanded him
severely.

The manager, Kröpelin, would certainly not have said anything.
Kröpelin understood that things like that were bound to happen
from time to time. But Jänecke could only become manager if
Kröpelin had ceased to occupy that role, so he had to be sharp,
zealous, and always thinking of the good of the firm.

The apprentices counted loudly: 'Eighty-seven, eighty-eight,
eighty-nine, ninety. . .'

Jänecke wasn't in sight. Kröpelin hadn't appeared yet either. They
must be advising the buyer about winter coats; they badly needed new
stock, there was not a single blue trench-coat left in the stockroom.

Pinneberg was looking for the trousers at seventeen seventy-five.
He could ask Kessler, Kessler was doing something only ten metres
away, but he didn't like him. For Kessler had remarked, audibly,
when Pinneberg arrived: 'Breslau? That old dodge, he's been put in
by Lehmann for sure.'

Pinneberg continued sorting. Very quiet today for a Friday. Only
one customer had been in so far and he'd bought a boiler-suit. Of
course Kessler made that sale, he'd pushed himself forward,

although it had been Heilbutt's turn. Heilbutt, the senior salesman, was a gentleman and let that sort of thing pass, he sold quite enough anyway, and above all Heilbutt knew that when a difficult case came along, Kessler would run to him for help. That was enough for Heilbutt. It wouldn't be enough for Pinneberg, but Pinneberg was not Heilbutt. Pinneberg bared his teeth sometimes, Heilbutt was much too dignified to do anything of the kind.

Heilbutt was standing at the back beside the cash desk doing a calculation. Pinneberg studied him, wondering whether he should ask him where the missing trousers might be. It would be a good excuse for starting up a conversation with him, but Pinneberg thought better of it. He'd tried a few times to converse with Heilbutt, who had always been impeccably polite, but somehow the conversation had petered out.

Pinneberg didn't want to push things with Heilbutt because he admired him. It had to come spontaneously, and he was sure it would. All the while he dreamt about inviting Heilbutt to the flat in Spenerstrasse, preferably today. He wanted to show Heilbutt to his Lammchen, but above all he wanted to show his Lammchen to Heilbutt. He wanted to prove that he was no ordinary one-dimensional salesman, that he had Lammchen. Which of the others had anyone like that?

Slowly the shop came to life. Only a moment ago they had been standing around in complete boredom, only doing things for show, and suddenly they were selling. Wendt was at work, Lasch was selling, Heilbutt was selling. Kessler hadn't waited his turn, but had gone in when it should have been Pinneberg. But soon Pinneberg had his buyer too, a student. But he was out of luck: the student, a young man with duelling scars, briskly demanded a blue trench-coat.

The thought shot through Pinneberg's head: 'None in stock. And he's not the type to be talked out of it. Kessler's going to laugh if I fall on my face. I've got to work it. . .'

He had already manoeuvred the student in front of a mirror: 'A blue trench-coat: certainly. One moment. Can we just slip on this ulster first?

'I don't want an ulster,' declared the student.

'No, of course not. Just on account of the size. Put it on, sir. Look, exceptionally smart, isn't it?'

'Yes,' said the student. 'Doesn't look at all bad. And now show me a blue trench-coat.'

'Sixty-nine marks fifty,' said Pinneberg casually, then, feeling his way: 'One of our special offers. Last winter this ulster cost ninety. Woven lining. Pure wool. . .'

'Good,' said the student. 'That was about what I wanted to pay, but I wanted a trench-coat. Please show me. . .'

Slowly and hesitantly, Pinneberg took off the handsome Marengo ulster. 'I don't believe anything else would suit you as well. Blue trench-coats have gone out of fashion. People have seen too much of them.'

'Just show me one!' said the student vehemently. Then, in a gentler tone, 'Or don't you want to sell me a trench-coat?'

'But of course, of course, of course, anything you like.' And he smiled, just as the student had smiled at his last question. 'But. . .' he cast around feverishly. No, no more tricks. It's worth a try. 'But I can't sell you a blue trench-coat.' Pause. 'We don't stock blue trench-coats any more.'

'Why didn't you tell me so straight away?!' said the student, part amazed, part annoyed.

'Because I wanted to convince you how perfectly that ulster suited you. It really looks good on you. You see,' he continued, in a lower tone, and with a deprecating smile, 'I only wanted to show you how much better it is than a blue trench-coat. That was just a fad, but this ulster. . .'

Pinneberg looked lovingly at it, stroked the sleeves, hung it up again on the hanger, and went to put it back on the rail.

'Wait a minute!' said the student. 'I could try it again. . . It doesn't look too bad. . .'

'No, it doesn't look at all bad,' said Pinneberg, and helped the gentleman back into the coat. 'An ulster looks downright distinguished. Or could I perhaps show the gentleman another ulster? Or a light-coloured trench-coat?'

He could see that the mouse was already almost in the trap. It was already sniffing at the bacon. Now he could take his chance.

'So you do have light-coloured trench-coats,' grumbled the student.

'Yes, we do have something there. . .,' said Pinneberg, and went to another rail.

On that rail hung a yellowish-green trench-coat, it had already been marked down twice. Its brothers from the same makers, in the same colour and the same cut, had long found their buyers. This coat seemed fated never to leave Mandels. It had the effect of making the wearer look a funny shape, and wrongly or insufficiently dressed.

'We have something here. . .,' said Pinneberg. He threw the coat over his arm. 'There you are, a light-coloured trench-coat. Thirty-five marks.'

The student put his arms in the sleeves. 'Thirty-five?' he asked in surprise.

'Yes,' replied Pinneberg in a disparaging tone. 'These trench-coats aren't very expensive.'

The student examined himself in the mirror. And once again, the coat worked its spell: a good-looking young man transformed into a scarecrow. 'Take the thing off!' he cried. 'It's hideous.'

'It's a trench-coat,' said Pinneberg seriously.

And then Pinneberg made out the bill for sixty-nine fifty, gave it to the gentleman, and made his bow. 'Thank you kindly.'

'No, thank *you*,' laughed the student, doubtless thinking about the yellow trenchcoat.

'Well, that's that,' thought Pinneberg. He quickly surveyed the department. The others were still with their original customers or had moved on to new ones. Only Kessler and he were free. So the next turn was Kessler's. Pinneberg was not going to push in front. But then, just as he was looking at Kessler, something strange happened; Kessler began shrinking back, step by step, towards the rails at the back. It was just as if he wanted to hide. Looking towards the entrance, Pinneberg saw the reason for this cowardly retreat: first came one lady, then another, both in their thirties, followed by another, older, lady, the mother or mother-in-law, and finally by a gentleman: moustache, pale blue eyes, bald as an egg. 'You miserable coward,' thought Pinneberg indignantly, 'A case like that, and you run away. Typical. Now watch me!'

And he said, bowing low: 'Ladies. Gentlemen! How can I help you?' allowing his gaze to rest an exactly equal length of time upon all the four faces, so that none got short measure.

One of the ladies said crossly: 'My husband would like an evening suit. Please, Franz, you tell the salesman what you'd like.'

'I would like. . .' began the gentleman.

'But they don't seem to have anything really high-class,' said the second lady in her thirties.

'I told you not to go to Mandels,' said the older one. 'Obermeyers is the place for that.'

'. . .to have an evening suit,' concluded the gentleman with the pale blue, bulging eyes.

'A dinner-jacket?' inquired Pinneberg cautiously. He tried to distribute the question equally among the three ladies, without neglecting the gentleman, because even worms like him were capable of upsetting a sale.

'A dinner-jacket!' exclaimed the ladies indignantly.

The straw-blonde said: 'My husband has of course already got a dinner-jacket. We want an evening suit.'

'A dark jacket,' said the gentleman.

'With striped trousers,' said the dark-haired lady, who was apparently the sister-in-law of the blonde lady, her status as the man's sister conferring even older rights over him than the wife's.

'Very good,' said Pinneberg.

'We'd already have found exactly the right thing at Obermeyers,' said the older lady.

Pinneberg produced a jacket. 'Oh no, nothing like that,' said the wife.

'What could you expect here?'

'Well, we can have a look at any rate. It costs nothing to look. Let me see something else, young man.'

'Try that on, Franz!'

'Oh, Else, for pity's sake! That jacket. . .'

'What do you think, mother?'

'I shan't say anything. Don't ask me. I shan't say anything. Afterwards you'll say it was me who chose it.'

'If the gentleman could please straighten his shoulders a little?'

'Don't straighten your shoulders on any account, Franz! My husband is always round-shouldered, it has to fit him as he is.'

'Turn round, Franz.'

'No, I think this one's out of the question.'

'Please, Franz, move around a bit. You're standing there as stiff as a poker.'

'Perhaps this one would be better.'

'I don't know why you're going through all this at Mandels anyway.'

'Do you want my husband to run around in the same jacket all the time? If we're not going to be served here. . .'

'If we could perhaps try on this jacket. . .'

'Please, Franz.'

'No, I don't want that one. I don't like it.'

'Why don't you like it? I think it's very nice!'

'Fifty-five marks.'

'I don't like it. The shoulders are too padded.'

'You're so round-shouldered, you need it.'

'The Saligers got a lovely evening suit for forty marks. And here, just for the jacket. . .'

'The suit has to be impressive, you understand, young man. If we're going to pay out a hundred marks, we might as well get it made to measure.'

'Now do please show us a suitable jacket.'

'How do you like this one, Madam?'

'That material seems a bit light.'

'Madam notices everything. It does make up rather light. What about this one?'

'That's a bit better. Is it pure wool?'

'Pure wool, madam. And a quilted lining, as you see.'

'I like that one.'

'Oh, Else, how can you? What do you say, Franz?'

'You can see they've got nothing here. No one goes to Mandels.'

'Just try on this one, Franz.'

'No, I'm not trying on anything more. You're just making me look a fright.'

'Now what are you saying? Did you want an evening suit or did I?'

'It was you!'

'No, you wanted one.'

'You said that Saliger had one and that I was making myself a laughing-stock with my everlasting dinner-jacket.'

'Would Madam kindly look at this one? Very discreet. Very distinguished.' Pinneberg had decided to place his bet on the straw-blond, Elsa.

'That one's really quite nice. How much does it cost?'

'Well, this one is sixty. But it's very exclusive. Not for the ordinary customer.'

'Very expensive.'

'Else, you'd fall for anything. He's shown us that one already.'

'My dear child, I know that as well as you do. Now Franz, please, try it on once more.'

'No,' said the bald head angrily. 'I don't want a suit. It's you who said I wanted one.'

'Please, Franz. . .'

'In this time we could have got ten suits at Obermeyers.'

'Come on, Franz, try on the jacket.'

'He's had it on already.'

'Not this one!'

'Yes, he has.'

'If you're going to quarrel, I'm off.'

'I'm off too. Else always wants her own way at any price.'

Pandemonium. Snide remarks, and jackets, were thrown hither and thither.

'At Obermeyers. . .'

'Mother, *please!*'

'Well, let's go to Obermeyers then.'

'Just don't say I dragged you there!'

'You did.'

'No, I. . .'

Pinneberg was unable to get a word in edgeways. In his extremity he looked all around him, and his eyes met Heilbutt's in a mute cry for help.

And at the same moment he did something desperate. He said to the egg-headed man: 'Your jacket, sir!'

And he helped the man into the disputed sixty-mark jacket,
then, almost before it was on his back, said 'Oh, I'm sorry, my
mistake,' Then he cried out, in astonished pleasure: 'How well
that suits you!'

'Yes, Else, if you like it. . .'

'I always said that jacket. . .'

'What do you say, Franz?'

'What's the price?'

'Sixty, Madam.'

'Sixty for that? It's madness. Sixty, in these times? And especially at
a shop like Mandels. . .'

A quiet but firm voice next to Pinneberg said: 'You've found what
you were looking for? Ah, our smartest evening jacket.'

Silence.

The ladies looked at Mr Heilbutt. Mr Heilbutt stood there: tall,
dark, brown-haired, elegant.

'A fine-quality garment,' said Mr Heilbutt after a pause. And then
he bowed and passed on his mysterious way somewhere behind the
coat stands; perhaps it was Mr Mandel himself, passing through the
shop.

'Well, you have a right to expect something for sixty marks,' said
the discontented voice of the old lady, but not quite as discontented
as before.

'Do you like it too, Franz?' asked the blonde Else. 'You're the one
it's for, after all.'

'I suppose so. . .,' said Franz.

'Now, the trousers to go with it. . .,' began the sister-in-law.

Buying the trousers wasn't nearly such a performance. Agreement
was reached quickly; even to the extent of choosing an expensive pair.
The total on the cash register amounted to over ninety-five marks.
The old lady said once more: 'I tell you, at Obermeyers. . .', but no
one was listening.

Pinneberg bowed again at the cash desk, an extra bow. Then he
returned to his post, as proud as a general after a victory in the field
and as worn-out as a soldier. Next to the trousers stood Heilbutt,
looking across at him.

'Thank you,' said Pinneberg. 'You saved the day, Heilbutt.'

'It wasn't me, Pinneberg,' said Heilbutt. 'You wouldn't have lost that sale. Not you. You're a born salesman, Pinneberg.'

ON THE THREE TYPES OF SALESMAN AND WHICH TYPE IS PREFERRED BY UNDER-MANAGER JÄNECKE. INVITATION TO A SNACK

Pinneberg's heart swelled with happiness. 'D' you really think so, Heilbutt? D'you really think I'm a born salesman?'

'But you know that yourself, Pinneberg. You enjoy selling.'

'I enjoy dealing with people,' said Pinneberg. 'I like working out who they are and what angle you have to take to make them buy.' He took a deep breath. 'I very seldom lose a sale.'

'I've noticed that, Pinneberg.'

'Except that there are impossible ones who don't really want to buy, just haggle and talk.'

'No one sells anything to them.'

'You do,' said Pinneberg. 'You do.'

'Perhaps. No. Well perhaps I do sometimes, because people are frightened of me.'

'You're so terribly imposing, Heilbutt. People don't have the nerve to put on airs, however much they'd like to.' He laughed. 'I wouldn't look imposing to a flea. I have to get under people's skins and guess what they want. Which is why I know how furious they're going to be at having bought that expensive suit. They'll all be angry with each other but no one will know exactly why they did it.'

'So why did they buy it, in your opinion, Pinneberg?'

Pinneberg couldn't think; he racked his brains. 'Now I don't know either. . . They were all talking at once. . .'

Heilbutt smiled.

'There you are you see, you're laughing, Heilbutt, you're laughing at me. But I know why it was, it was because you impressed them so.'

'Nonsense,' said Heilbutt. 'Complete nonsense, Pinneberg. You know nobody buys anything for that reason. All I may have done is speeded things up a bit. . .'

'A lot!'

'No, the deciding factor was that you never got offended. Some of our colleagues. . .' and Heilbutt's dark eyes swept the room until they lighted on the person he was seeking. . . 'get offended straight away. If they say: this is a very exclusive model, and the customers says: but I don't like it, then they snap back with: well, tastes differ, or else they're so hurt they say nothing at all. You're not like that, Pinneberg. . .'

'What's this, gentlemen?' said the under-manager, Mr Jänecke, 'A little chin-wag? Been busy selling already? Have to keep busy. Times are hard and it takes a lot of sales to make up a salesman's salary.'

'We were just talking, Mr Jänecke,' said Heilbutt, discreetly restraining Pinneberg by the elbow, 'about the different types of salesmen there are. We found there were three: the imposing, who sell by inspiring respect, the good guessers, who sell by finding what people want, and the others, who sell purely by chance. What's your opinion, Mr Jänecke?'

'Very interesting as a theory, gentlemen,' said Mr Jänecke, smiling. 'I only know one kind of salesman. The kind who has big figures on his sales record at the end of the day. I know there are still some with low figures, but they aren't going to be here much longer if I can help it.'

And with that Mr Jänecke hurried off to spur on someone else, and Heilbutt looked after him and said not at all quietly: 'Swine.'

Pinneberg thought it was splendid, just to say 'Swine' like that, regardless of the consequences, but it also struck him as a bit risky. Heilbutt was just about to go away, saying, with a nod of the head: 'Well, Pinneberg. . .' when he suddenly asked him: 'Would you do me a great favour, Heilbutt?'

Heilbutt was rather taken aback: 'Eh? Of course, Pinneberg.'

'Would you visit us some time?' He was even more taken aback. 'I've told my wife so much about you, and she'd love to meet you. If you had the time one day. Just for a snack.'

Heilbutt smiled again, but it was a delightful smile, out of the corner of his eyes. 'Of course, Pinneberg. I had no idea you'd like that. I shall be glad to come some time.'

Pinneberg asked hurriedly: 'Would it. . . would it be all right for this evening?'

'This evening?' Heilbutt thought about it. 'I'll just have a look.' He took a leather-bound notebook out of his pocket. 'Wait a bit. Tomorrow there's a lecture on Greek sculpture at the Adult Education Centre. You know about that. . .'

Pinneberg nodded.

'And the day after tomorrow it's my naturist evening. You know I belong to a naturist club. . . And the next evening I've promised to see my girlfriend. So far as I can see, Pinneberg, I'm free tonight.'

'Excellent!' exclaimed Pinneberg, quite breathless with joy. 'That suits me down to the ground. If you want to take down my address; it's 92 Spenerstrasse, second floor.'

'Mr and Mrs Pinneberg,' noted Heilbutt. '92 Spenerstrasse. Second floor. The best station for me would be Bellevue. What time?'

'Would eight o'clock do? I'm leaving earlier. I'm free at four, but I've got something to do.'

'Well, eight o'clock it is, Pinneberg. I'll come a bit earlier so the downstairs door isn't locked.'

PINNEBERG RECEIVES HIS WAGES, BEHAVES
BADLY TO A SALESMAN AND BECOMES THE OWNER OF A
DRESSING-TABLE

Pinneberg stood in front of the door of Mandels department store, one hand clutching the wage-packet in his pocket. He had been working there a month, but all that time he had no idea how much pay he was going to get. When Mr Lehmann had hired him, he had been so pleased to get the job that he hadn't asked.

He hadn't asked his colleagues either.

'If I'd been in Breslau I'd know what Mandels paid,' he had replied when Lammchen had once pressed for clarity on this point.

'Well, go to the Association.'

'They're only polite when they want money off you.'

'But they must know, Sonny.'

'We'll see at the end of the month, Lammchen. They can't pay under the agreed rate. And the agreed rate for Berlin can't be bad.'

So now he had his agreed wage for Berlin, which couldn't be bad.

It was exactly a hundred and seventy marks net! Eighty marks less than Lammchen had expected, sixty marks less than his most pessimistic calculations.

Robbers! Do they ever once worry their heads about how we're going to manage? All they ever think is that other people manage with less. And we have to creep and crawl to get it. One hundred and seventy marks net. No joke in Berlin. Mama will have to wait a bit for the rent. A hundred marks, she's batty, Jachmann was right there. The question was, how he and Lammchen were ever going to get any household goods. They would have to give something to Mama; she was very persistent.

A hundred and seventy marks, and he had had such a lovely plan. He had wanted to give Lammchen a surprise.

It had begun one evening with Lammchen pointing at an empty corner in the regal bedroom and saying: 'A dressing-table would go nicely in there.'

'Do we need one?' he had asked, surprised. He'd thought no further than beds, a leather armchair, and an oak desk.

'Of course not. It'd just be nice. I'd love to do my hair at a dressing-table. Oh, don't look like that, Sonny love. It's only a dream.'

And that's how it began. Lammchen needed to go on walks in her condition. And now they had something to go and see: dressing-tables. They went on long voyages of discovery, there were some districts and side streets which were one mass of carpenters' shops and little furniture factories. There they stopped and said, 'Take a look at that one!'

'All that grain in the wood looks fussy to me.'

'D'you think so?'

In the end they acquired favourites, the chief of which stood in the shop of a certain Himmlisch in Frankfurter Allee. The speciality of the Himmlisch establishment was bedrooms. They seemed to attach some importance to this fact, since their sign read: 'Himmlisch for Beds. Modern bedroom-suites a speciality.'

There had been a bedroom-suite in their window for weeks, not very expensive, seven hundred and ninety-five marks inclusive of mattresses and genuine marble tops. But, in line with the current fashion for chilly night-time excursions, without chamber-pot cupboards. One of the pieces was a dressing-table in Caucasian walnut. . .

They always stood for a long time looking at it. It was a good hour-and-a-half's walk away. Lammchen stood there, and finally said: 'Ah, Sonny, if one could only buy a thing like that. I think I'd weep for joy.'

Pinneberg thought a moment 'The people who could buy it,' he remarked wisely, 'wouldn't weep for joy. But it would be great to be able to.'

'It would,' confirmed Lammchen, 'It would be wonderful.'

And then they turned for home. They always walked arm in arm, with his arm through hers, so that he could feel her breast, now growing fuller. It gave him a pleasant sense of home in these vast streets thronged with strangers. But it was in the course of walking home this way that Pinneberg had come on the idea of surprising Lammchen. They had to begin buying furniture some day, and when they had one piece the rest would surely follow. That was the reason why he had got off at four today. Today was the thirty-first of October, pay day. He hadn't let out a word of it to Lammchen; he was simply going to have it sent and then behave as though he knew nothing about it.

But a hundred and seventy marks! It was out of the question. Quite simply out of the question.

However, you don't say goodbye to your dreams as easily as that. Pinneberg didn't feel up to just going along home with his hundred and seventy marks. He would have to be cheerful when he arrived. Lammchen had been reckoning on two hundred and fifty. He started in the direction of Frankfurter Allee. To say goodbye. And then never go to the window again. There was no point in it. For people like them a dressing-table was out of the question, all they might be able to stretch to was a pair of iron bedsteads.

He arrived at the shop window with the bedroom-suite in it, and there, to one side, stood the dressing-table. It had a rectangular mirror with a delicate greenish hue in a brown frame. The dressing-table itself was rectangular, too, with a set of drawers to right and left. It was really rather mysterious how one could fall in love with a thing like that when there were thousands of others like it or almost like it, but this was the one, the only one.

Pinneberg looked at it, at length. He stepped back, then forward; it was just as beautiful either way. The mirror was a good one too. It would be lovely to see Lammchen sitting in front of it in the morning in her red and white bathrobe. . . It would have been lovely.

Pinneberg sighed sorrowfully and turned away. Nothing. Nothing. Not for you and people like you. Other people manage it, goodness knows how, but not you. Go home, little man, and fritter away your money on whatever you like – and can afford – but not on things like that.

At the next street corner he looked back once more. Himmlisch's shop-window gleamed as heavenly as its name. He could still make out the dressing-table.

He did a sudden about-turn. Without hesitation, without giving the piece of furniture another glance, he quick-marched up to the shop door. . .

And while he was doing it, a great deal went through his head.

'What does it matter in the end?'

And: 'You've got to start somewhere. Why should we always have nothing?'

Then quite determinedly: 'I want it and I'm going to do it. Just once in my life I want to have been like that, and hang the consequences.' A little bit further down the line, and that is the mood in which a man steals, fights and kills. And it was in this mood that Pinneberg bought a dressing-table. To him it was all the same.

'May I help you, sir?' asked the elderly salesman, a dark man with a few streaks of hair plastered over his skull like anchovies on a plate.

'You've got a bedroom-suite in the window,' barked Pinneberg, seething with anger. He sounded very aggressive. 'Caucasian walnut.'

'Yes, indeed,' said the salesman. 'Seven hundred and ninety-five. A bargain. The last of a series. We can't produce them at that price any more. If we were to do it again, it would cost at least eleven hundred.'

'How come?' asked Pinneberg scornfully. 'Wages keep on falling.'

'Taxes, sir. And import duty. Can you imagine the import duty you pay on Caucasian walnut! It's tripled in the last three months.'

'For something that's so cheap, it's been standing a long time in your shop window.'

'Money,' said the salesman. 'Who's got money today, sir?' He laughed mournfully. 'I haven't.'

'Nor have I,' said Pinneberg brutally. 'And I don't want to buy the bedroom-suite. I'll never get so much money together in my whole life. I want to buy the dressing-table.'

'A dressing-table? If you'd just like to step upstairs. The single items of furniture are on the first floor.'

'That one!' shouted Pinneberg, pointing indignantly. 'I want to buy that dressing-table.'

'The one in the set? Out of the bedroom-suite?' said the salesman, as the penny gradually began to drop. 'I'm very sorry, sir, but we can't sell off individual items out of the set. Because then we couldn't sell the suite. But we do have some very nice dressing-tables.'

Pinneberg made as if to leave.

'Almost exactly the same,' said the salesman hurriedly. 'If you'd like to take a look at them, just a look.'

Pinneberg snorted. He glanced around. 'This is a furniture factory, isn't it?'

'Yes?' said the salesman nervously.

'So,' said Pinneberg. 'If you've got a factory, why don't you make another dressing-table like it? I want that one, understand. So make a copy. Or don't sell it to me, I don't mind. There are lots of other shops where you get decent service.'

And while Pinneberg was saying all that, and getting more and more worked up, he was inwardly aware of being a swine, that he was behaving as badly as his worst customers. That he was treating the confused and anxious old gentleman atrociously. But he could not help it, he was in a rage against the world, and everyone in it. It was the elderly salesman's misfortune that he was the only one available on whom Pinneberg could vent his wrath.

'One moment please,' stammered the old man. 'I'll ask the manager.'

He vanished and Pinneberg stared after him with sorrow and scorn. 'Why am I being like this?' he thought. 'I ought to have brought Lammchen along, Lammchen is never like this.'

'Why is she never like that?' he reflected. 'Things aren't easy for her either.'

The salesman came back. 'You can have the dressing-table,' he said briefly. His tone had changed considerably. 'The price will be a hundred and twenty-five marks.'

Pinneberg thought: 'A hundred and twenty-five! That's crazy. These fellows here are having me on. The whole suite only costs seven hundred and ninety-five.'

'I think that's too expensive,' he said.

'It's not expensive at all,' said the salesman. 'A first-class crystal mirror like that costs fifty marks on its own.'

'And what would it be if I paid by instalments. . .?'

Now money had reared its head, the wind had all gone out of Pinneberg's sails. He had become very small and the salesman very large.

'Instalments are not possible in this case,' said the salesman in a superior tone, looking Pinneberg up and down. 'It was only done as a favour, in the expectation that later on you would patronise. . .'

'I can't go back now,' thought Pinneberg desperately. 'I came on so important. If I hadn't done, I could go back. It's crazy. What will Lammchen say?'

And aloud he said. 'Right, I'll take the dressing-table. But you must send it to my house today.'

'Today? It's too late to do that. The staff are off in quarter of an hour.'

'I can still go back,' said something inside Pinneberg's head. 'I could go back, if I hadn't made such a fuss.'

'It has to be today,' he persisted. 'It's a present. Any later and it would be pointless.'

And as he said it he reflected that Heilbutt was coming, and it would be fine for his friend to see what a present he was giving his wife.

'Just a moment, please,' said the salesman and vanished again.

'The best that could happen,' thought Pinneberg, 'would be if he said that it was too late to do it today, and then I could say I was sorry but it would be no good. I must be ready to leave the shop quickly.' And he positioned himself near the door.

'The manager says he will lend you a handcart and the apprentice.

You will have to give the apprentice a tip because it's after working hours.'

'Well. . .' said Pinneberg, hesitating.

'It's not heavy,' said the salesman comfortingly. 'If you push a bit from behind, the apprentice will be able to pull it. And be careful with the mirror. We'll wrap it in a cloth. . .'

'All right, done,' said Pinneberg. 'A hundred and twenty-five marks.'

LAMMCHEN HAS A VISITOR AND LOOKS AT HERSELF IN
THE MIRROR. NO ONE MENTIONS MONEY ALL EVENING

Lammchen was sitting in the regal bedroom darning socks. Darning is by its nature one of the most depressing occupations in the world: nothing brings home to women so clearly the crazy futility of what they do. Because once a thing really goes into holes, there's no point anyway, you have to keep on doing it wash after wash. Most women get unhappy while darning.

But Lammchen was not unhappy. Lammchen scarcely noticed what her hands were up to. Lammchen was doing some calculations. He'll bring in two hundred and fifty, they'll give fifty to Mama, though actually that was much too much, considering she did five or six hours' work for her every day. A hundred and thirty has to do for everything else, that leaves sixty. . .

Lammchen leaned back slightly for a moment, to rest the small of her back. She got a lot of pain there now. . . She'd seen layettes in the Kadewe department store for sixty marks, and for eighty, and for a hundred. That was crazy, of course. She was going to make a lot of it herself. It was a pity that there was no sewing-machine in the house, but sewing-machines weren't in Mrs Mia Pinneberg's line.

She wanted to discuss all that with Pinneberg straight away this evening and go shopping tomorrow; she wouldn't be happy till she had everything laid in. She knew very well he had some other plans, she had noticed he wanted to buy something; he was thinking about her shabby winter coat no doubt, but there was time for that, time for everything but the layette, which had to be there, ready.

Mrs Emma Pinneberg let fall her young man's woollen sock and listened. Then she felt her belly, very gently. She laid a finger here, and there. There it was! The Shrimp had just moved, there. It was the fifth time she had felt him move in the last few days. Lammchen glanced scornfully in the direction of *The Sacred Miracles of Motherhood* lying on a nearby table. 'Rubbish,' she said aloud, and meant it. She was thinking of a particular passage, a mixture of erudition and sentiment, which went: 'Exactly half way through pregnancy the baby first begins to move in the womb. The expectant mother thrills to the delicate tapping of her unborn child with never-ceasing wonder.'

'Rubbish,' thought Lammchen again. 'Delicate tapping. When it first happened I thought I was being pinched by something that couldn't get out. Delicate tapping, what rubbish!' But she smiled all the same. It didn't matter what it felt like, it was still wonderful, it was beautiful. It showed the Shrimp was really there, and now she must make him feel that he was expected, and expected with joy, that everything was ready for him. . .

Lammchen started to darn again.

The door opened a crack, and Mrs Marie Pinneberg's somewhat tousled head looked in. 'Hans not there yet?' she asked, for the fifth or sixth time.

'No, not yet,' said Lammchen shortly. This was getting on her nerves.

'It's nearly half past seven. He wouldn't have. . .?'

'Wouldn't have what?' asked Lammchen sharply.

But the older woman had her wits about her. 'I wouldn't dream of saying, my dear daughter-in-law!' she replied with a laugh. 'You of course have got a model husband, who never stays out on pay-night for a drink.'

'Sonny never has a drink,' declared Lammchen.

'Exactly. Just as I said. Your husband wouldn't do a thing like that.'

'He wouldn't.'

'No, of course not.'

'No.'

The head withdrew. Lammchen was alone again.

'The old cow,' she thought angrily. 'She's always after us, stirring things up. And all she's worried about is her rent really. Well, if she's reckoning on a hundred. . .'

Lammchen started to darn once more.

The bell rang outside. 'Sonny,' thought Lammchen. 'Has he forgotten his key? No, it'll be someone for Mother, she can answer it herself.'

But she didn't go, and there was another ring. With a sigh, Lammchen went into the hall. Her mother-in-law's face peered round the door of the Berlin-style living-room, already half in her war-paint. 'If it's someone for me, Emma, show them into the little room. I'll be ready in a moment.'

'Of course it's someone for you, Mama,' said Lammchen. The head disappeared, and Lammchen opened the door just as the bell rang for the third time. There stood a dark man in a light-grey over-coat, with his hat in his hand, smiling. 'Mrs Pinneberg?' he inquired.

'Just coming,' said Lammchen. 'Why don't you take off your coat in the meantime. And step into this room here.'

The gentleman seemed a little bemused, as though there was something he didn't quite understand. 'Mr Pinneberg isn't in?' he asked, as he went into the little room.

'It's years since Mr Pinneberg. . .' she was going to say 'died' and then she realized: 'Oh, you want Mr Pinneberg. He isn't here yet. I'm expecting him any moment.'

'That's funny,' said the gentleman, seeming pleased rather than offended. 'He left Mandels at four today, having just invited me round for this evening. My name is Heilbutt.'

'Oh heavens! You're Mr Heilbutt!' said Lammchen, and then said no more, thunderstruck. 'What about supper?' she thought. 'Left at four. Where can he have got to? What have I got in the house? And any minute Mama's going to come barging in. . .'

'Yes, I'm Heilbutt,' said the gentleman, who was obviously a very patient man.

'Goodness, Mr Heilbutt, whatever must you think of me?' said Lammchen. 'It's no good me telling you anything but the truth. So first I thought you wanted my mother-in-law who is also called Pinneberg. . .'

'Right,' said Heilbutt smiling merrily.

'And second, Sonny didn't say anything about wanting to invite you today. That's why I was so taken aback.'

'Not very,' said Mr Heilbutt reassuringly.

'And third, I don't understand how he could have left at four – and why leave at four anyhow? – and not be here yet.'

'He had something he wanted to do.'

'Oh dear, I'm afraid he's trying to buy me a winter coat.'

Heilbutt reflected for a moment: 'I don't think so,' he said. 'He'd get that with the employee's discount at Mandels.'

'So what. . .?'

The door opened, and Mrs Mia Pinneberg sailed up to Heilbutt with a joyous smile. 'You must be Mr Siebold, who rang up about my advert today. May I, Emma. . .?'

But Emma didn't budge. 'This is Mr Heilbutt, Mama, a colleague of Hannes. He's come to see me.'

Mrs Mia Pinneberg beamed. 'Oh, of course, excuse me. I'm pleased to meet you, Mr Heilbutt. You work in ready-to-wear as well?'

'I'm a salesman,' said Heilbutt.

There was the sound of a door shutting outside. 'That must be Sonny,' said Lammchen.

And it was him, on the landing holding one end of a dressing-table, the other end of which was being carried by the apprentice from 'Himmlisch for Beds'. 'Good evening, Mama. Good evening, Heilbutt. I'm glad you're here already. Evening, Lammchen. Yes, you may well stare. This is our dressing-table. We nearly got run over by a bus on Alexanderplatz. I tell you, I was sweating blood all the way home. Would someone open the door to our bedroom?'

'But Sonny!'

'Did you bring that thing here yourself, Pinneberg?'

'In person,' beamed Pinneberg. He continued in English: 'I myself with this – how do you call him?' – lapsing back into German – 'apprentice?'

'A dressing-table!' exclaimed Mrs Pinneberg, highly amused. 'You must be well-heeled, you two. Whoever needs a dressing-table now we all have our hair cut like little boys?'

But Pinneberg hadn't heard. He felt that he had won the right to own the thing by pushing and shoving it through the hurly-burly of the Berlin streets, and no budgetary considerations were going to cloud his hour of glory.

'Over there in the corner, young man,' he said to the wretched-looking apprentice. 'Sideways on a bit. That way the light is better. We must put a lamp in over it. There we are, young man, now let's go down and get the mirror. You'll have to excuse me one moment longer. . . This is my wife, Heilbutt,' he said, smiling broadly, 'I hope you like her?'

'I can shift the mirror meself, guv,' said the apprentice.

'I like her immensely,' responded Heilbutt.

'But Sonny!' laughed Lammchen.

'He's off his head today,' declared Mrs Mia Pinneberg.

'Certainly not. It's too expensive for you to fall up the stairs with!' And, in a mysterious undertone. 'The mirror is real engraved crystal; it costs fifty marks all on its own.'

He disappeared with the youth, leaving the others looking at each other.

'Well, I won't disturb you any longer,' said Mrs Pinneberg. 'You'll have to see to the supper, Lammchen. If you need any help, just let me know.'

'Oh dear, whatever shall I do about supper?' cried Lammchen despairingly.

'Well, as I said,' said her mother-in-law, departing, 'I'll gladly help.'

'Please don't worry about it,' said Heilbutt, laying his hand on Lammchen's arm. 'I didn't come for the food.'

The door opened again, and Pinneberg reappeared with the boy.

'Now wait, and you'll see it in its full beauty. Lift it a bit, son. Have you got the screws? Wait everybody. . .' He sweated, and screwed in the screws, and talked non-stop: 'A little bit more light here. That's right, it's got to be really bright. Please, Heilbutt, do me a favour and don't go near it yet. Lammchen's got to be the first to see herself in the mirror. I haven't looked in it either. I've kept the cover over it. Here, son, there's something for you. All right? Get off then. It'll still be open downstairs. 'Bye. Lammchen, there's something I want you to do. You needn't be embarrassed with Heilbutt. Isn't that right, Heilbutt?'

'Of course. Not with me.'

'So. Put on your bathrobe. Just over your clothes. Please. Please. I've kept thinking of how you'd look in the mirror in your bathrobe. I'd like it to be the first sight I see in it. Please Lammchen. . .'

'Sonny, Sonny,' said Lammchen, but of course she was moved by so much enthusiasm. 'You see, Mr Heilbutt, there's nothing to be done.' And she took a bathrobe out of the wardrobe.

'Speaking for myself,' said Heilbutt, 'I love to see things like that. And your husband's quite right. Every mirror ought to start off by reflecting something particularly pretty. . .'

'Oh, stop it,' said Lammchen, waving off the compliment.

'But it's true. . .'

'Lammchen,' said Pinneberg, looking in turn at Lammchen herself and at her reflection. 'I've dreamed about this. To think it's come true! D'you know, Heilbutt, the big bosses up there can bully us and under-pay us and treat us like trash. . .'

'Which is all we are,' said Heilbutt. 'We don't matter at all.'

'Of course,' said Pinneberg. 'I always knew that. But they can't take this away from me. Let them go to hell and take all their speeches with them. But standing here looking at my wife in her bathrobe in the mirror, they can't take that away from me.'

'Have I been sitting in state long enough?' asked Lammchen. 'Is it a good mirror? Does it give a good reflection?' asked Pinneberg. Then, to Heilbutt by way of explanation: 'Some mirrors make you look greenish, like a drowned corpse, not that I've ever seen one. Some make you look broad, some make you look dusty. But this mirror is a good one, isn't it, Lammchen?'

There was a knock, the door opened a crack, and Mrs Pinneberg's head appeared: 'Have you got a moment, Hans?'

'Soon, Mama.'

'Well, make it really soon, please. I have to speak to you urgently.' The door shut again.

'Mama will be after the rent,' explained Lammchen.

Pinneberg looked surprisingly sombre. 'Mama can go to. . .' he said.

'But Sonny!'

'She should stop fussing,' he said crossly. 'She'll get her money.'

'Well, of course Mama will think we've got a lot of money because of the dressing-table. And you do get good wages at Mandels, don't you, Mr Heilbutt?'

'Well. . .' said Heilbutt hesitantly, 'It depends on what you mean by good. But I suppose a dressing-table like that costs at least sixty marks. . .'

'Sixty. . . you're off your chump, Heilbutt,' said Pinneberg excitedly. And then, seeing Lammchen was watching him. 'I'm sorry, Heilbutt, you can't be expected to know. . .' Then, very loudly: 'And now I proclaim that nobody's going to talk about money for the whole evening. We're all going to go into the kitchen and see what we can find for supper. I, for one, am hungry.'

'Right you are, Sonny love,' said Lammchen, looking at him very hard. 'Just as you like.'

And they went into the kitchen.

CONJUGAL HABITS OF THE PINNEBERGS. MOTHER AND SON. JACHMANN TO THE RESCUE AS USUAL

It was night. The Pinnebergs were going to bed, their visitor had gone. Pinneberg got undressed slowly and thoughtfully, glancing over now and then at Lammchen, who was out of her clothes in a trice. He sighed deeply, and then asked, with surprising cheerfulness: 'How did you like Heilbutt?'

'Oh, I did like him,' but Pinneberg saw from her tone that she didn't mean to talk about Heilbutt. He sighed again deeply.

Lammchen had got into her nightie, and was now perched on the edge of the bed, slipping off her stockings. She laid them over the dressing-table. Pinneberg noted with regret that she had no sense of where she was laying them.

But Lammchen didn't get into bed. 'What did you say to Mama about the rent?' she asked suddenly. Pinneberg was rather embarrassed: 'About the rent? Oh, nothing. I told her I had no money at present.'

Pause.

Then Lammchen sighed. She swung herself into bed, pulled up the cover, and said: 'Aren't you going to give her anything?'

'I don't know. Yes. Just not yet.'

Lammchen was silent.

Now Pinneberg was in his nightshirt. Since the light-switch was near the door and could not be operated from the bed, it was part of Pinneberg's marital duties to switch off the light before climbing into bed. It was, however, Lammchen's wish to kiss goodnight with the light on as she liked to be able to see him. So Pinneberg had to go right round to her side of the regal bed to deliver the goodnight kiss, then go back to the door and turn out the light before getting into bed himself.

The goodnight kiss itself was divided into two parts: his and hers. His part was fairly constant: three kisses on the lips. Hers fluctuated greatly, either she took his head between her hands and smothered him with kisses, or she put her arms around his neck and held him very tight to give him one lingering kiss. Or she laid his head on her breast and stroked his hair.

He generally made a manly attempt to hide how tedious he found this extended billing and cooing, and was not quite sure how far she saw through him, or whether she simply didn't notice his coolness.

This evening he wished the whole goodnight business were over, and for a moment he even contemplated 'forgetting' it. But that would certainly only complicate matters. So he went around the bed with as indifferent an air as possible, yawned loudly and said: 'Fearfully tired, old girl. Got to work hard again tomorrow. Good night.' And swiftly gave her the three kisses.

'Good night, my Sonny,' said Lammchen, and kissed him hard, once. 'You sleep well too.'

Her lips tasted particularly soft and full, yet cool, and for a moment he would have had no objection to continuing. But life was complicated enough already, he controlled himself, turned around, clicked the switch and swung himself into bed. 'Good night, Lammchen', he said once more.

'Good night,' she said.

At first it was, as always, pitch-dark in the room, then very gradually the two windows became visible as grey patches, and at the same time the noises became clearer. Now they could hear the city railway, the shunting of an engine, then the sound of a bus going down Paulstrasse. Suddenly, almost on top of them, a roar of laughter, which made them both jump, followed by shouts, catcalls and giggles.

'Jachmann's on form tonight,' commented Pinneberg involuntarily.

'They got a whole case of wine from Kempinski today. Fifty bottles,' explained Lammchen.

'How they booze!' said he. 'What a waste of money. . .'

He was sorry the remark had slipped out: it could provide an opening for Lammchen. But she remained silent.

It was a long time later that she said quietly: 'Sonny, darling?'

'Yes?'

'D'you know what sort of an advertisement Mama had put in the paper?'

'An advertisement? No idea.'

'When Heilbutt came, she thought it was for her, and asked if he was the man who'd phoned about the advertisement.'

'I don't understand, I've no idea. What sort of advertisement could it be?'

'I don't know. She wouldn't be going to let our room, would she?'

'She can't do it without telling us. No, I don't think so. She's glad to have us.'

'Even if we don't pay any rent?'

'Please, Lammchen. We're going to pay.'

'But what can it be? D'you think it's got to do with these parties?'

'How? You don't advertise a party.'

'I don't understand.'

'Nor do I. Good night then, Lammchen.'

'Good night, Sonny.'

There was silence. Lammchen lay facing the window and Pinneberg facing the door. It was now of course quite out of the question for him to get to sleep, firstly because of the stimulating kiss of just now, and the fact that there was a woman tossing from side to side a foot away from him and breathing fitfully. And secondly because of the dressing-table. He would have done better to confess earlier.

'Listen, Sonny,' said Lammchen very quietly and gently.

'Yes,' he said, with an anxious feeling.

'May I come over to you a moment?'

Pause. Silence. A moment of surprise.

Then he said: 'Please do, Lammchen. Of course.' And turned onto his side.

This was the fourth or fifth time in their marriage that Lammchen had made such a request to her husband. And it did not constitute a hidden invitation to love-making on Lammchen's part. Although love-making was usually what resulted, due to Pinneberg's rather obvious, down-to-earth and typically male interpretation of the request.

For Lammchen it was actually a continuation of the goodnight kiss, a need to cuddle up to him, a longing for tenderness. Lammchen only wanted to hold her young man for a while in her arms. There was a wild, wide, noisy and hostile world out there, which knew nothing of them and cared less. It was so good to lie one against the other, like a little warm island!

And so they lay now, in each other's arms, face to face, a small warm patch in the middle of thousands of miles of darkness – and you had to lie very close when there was only one of those modern four-foot-square eiderdowns to cover the two of you, otherwise draughts got in on every side.

At first, there was something strange about the warmth of each other's bodies, but that was soon gone, and they were one. And now it was he who pressed himself closer and closer to her.

'Sonny,' said Lammchen, 'My Sonny, my only. . .'

'You, you. Oh, Lammchen. . .'

He kissed her, but it wasn't duty kisses any more. Oh, how good it was now to kiss that mouth that seemed to bloom under his lips, and become ever softer and fuller and riper. . .

But suddenly Pinneberg stopped kissing, and he even put a distance between his body and hers, so that only their shoulders touched.

'Lammchen,' he said, with great honesty. 'I have been a frightful idiot.'

'Have you?' she said, and thought for a while before she said: 'What did the dressing-table cost then? But you needn't talk about it if you don't want to. It's all right. You wanted to please me.'

'You sweet girl!' he said. And suddenly they were together again. But then he made up his mind, and the gap was there again, and he said 'It cost a hundred and twenty-five marks.'

Silence.

Lammchen said nothing.

'It does sound a bit much,' he said very apologetically, 'but you must bear in mind that the mirror alone cost at least fifty marks.'

'True,' said Lammchen. 'The mirror is a good one. It's rather beyond our means, and we aren't really going to need a dressing-table in the next five or ten years, but it was I who put the idea into your head. And it is nice to have it. And you are a kind old, silly old chap. But you mustn't be cross if I go around in my shabby old blue winter coat for another year, because we have to look after the Shrimp first. . .'

'You're so kind,' he said, and the kissing began anew. They were pressed very close, and the explanation might well have got no further that evening. But suddenly a veritable tornado of sounds burst from the Berlin-style living-room next door: laughter, shouts and screams, a male voice speaking very fast, and above it all the complaining peevish tones of Mrs Mia Pinneberg.

'They're three-quarters gone already,' said Pinneberg, very much disturbed.

'Mama isn't in a very good mood,' remarked Lammchen.

'Mama is always quarrelsome when she's drunk,' he said.

'Can't you give her the rent, at least something?' asked Lammchen.

'All I have,' said Pinneberg resolutely, 'is forty-two marks.'

'What?!!!' asked Lammchen, sitting up. Relinquishing the cosy amorous stuffiness under the bedclothes, she sat up straight as an arrow. 'What have you got left from your wages?'

'Forty-two marks,' said Pinneberg in a very small voice. 'Listen to me, Lammchen.' But Lammchen wasn't listening. This time the shock was too great. 'Forty-two,' she whispered, as she reckoned. 'One hundred and twenty-five. So you got a hundred and sixty-seven marks salary? That's not possible!'

'A hundred and seventy. I gave three marks to the boy.'
Lammchen stumbled over those three marks: 'Which boy? Why?'

'You know. The apprentice.'

'Oh yes. A hundred and seventy. And you go and buy. . .? Oh
God, what will happen now, what shall we live on?'

'Lammchen,' he pleaded. 'I know. I was so stupid. But it will never,
never happen again. And we are going to get maternity benefit.'

'And that'll soon be gone if we handle it this way. And there's the
Shrimp. We have to buy things for him. You may not mind if he goes
around in rags. I do. I don't care how rough we live, we can take it, but
the Shrimp's not going to have a hard time, not for his first five or six
years, not if I can help it. And then you go and do a thing like that.'

Pinneberg sat up too. Lammchen's voice was so changed, she was
talking as though he, her Sonny, had ceased to exist, as though he was
just anybody. And even if most of the time he was just a junior
salesman, with the early-inculcated sense that he was nothing special,
a little animal that you could let live or die, it really didn't matter,
someone who – even in his moments of deepest love for Lammchen
– felt transient, impermanent, not worth making any trouble over;
this time, at this moment, he was very definitely there. He, Johannes
Pinneberg, knew that what was at stake here was the only thing that
gave his life worth and meaning. He had to hold onto that. He had to
fight for that; no one was going to do him out of that.

And he said: 'Lammchen, my darling Lammchen. I said I'd been
an idiot. I did everything all wrong. But that's how I am. And you
mustn't speak to me that way, because I was always like that. You
have to stick with me, and speak to me like your Sonny and not just
someone to quarrel with. . .'

'Sonny, love, I. . .'

But he went on talking, this was his hour, and everything had been
leading up to this from the very beginning. He wasn't going to give
way, so he kept on speaking: 'Lammchen, you must really forgive me.
You know, right from the bottom of your heart, so that you don't
think about it any more, so that you can laugh about your silly
husband when you see the dressing-table.'

'Sonny, my darling Sonny. . .'

'No!' he said, and sprang out of bed. 'Now I must put the light on.

I have to see your face, and see how you look when you rea̶
me, so that I know later. . .'

And the light went on, and he hurried back to her but didn't g̶
into bed. He bent over her, and looked at her. . .

Their two faces were hot, flushed, their eyes very wide. Their hair
mingled, their lips touched, in the open front of her nightdress her
white breasts were so wonderfully firm, with their bluish veins. . .

'How lucky I am,' he felt. 'Oh what happiness. . .'

'Oh my Sonny,' she thought. 'My Sonny, my big, foolish, beloved
Sonny, to think I've got you inside me, in my womb. . .'

And suddenly her face became radiant, brighter and brighter as he
looked at her, it seemed to grow, as though the sun was rising over
the landscape of that face.

'Lammchen!' he called to her, beckoning her, as she receded ever
further from him into her bliss, 'Lammchen!'

And she took his hand, and placed it against her belly: 'There, feel,
the Shrimp's just moved, he was knocking. . . Can you feel it? He's
done it again.'

He heard nothing at all, but borne along by her maternal joy, he
bent over her. He gently laid his cheek on her full, taut belly, which
was yet so soft. . . And suddenly it felt like the most wonderful
cushion in the world. No, that was stupid, it was like a wave. Her
belly rose and fell, an immeasurable sea of happiness flowed over
him. . . was it summer? It must be, the corn was ripe. What a happy
child, with ash-blond tousled hair, and his mother's blue eyes. What
a good smell there was here in the field: earth, mother, love. Love,
enjoyed so many times but always fresh. . . The prickly ears of wheat
tickled his cheeks, and beyond he saw the beautiful inward sweep of
her thighs and the little dark wood. . . And moving up as though her
arms had lifted him, he rested on her motherly breast, seeing her eyes
so wide and so beaming. . . Oh! all you people in small, cramped
rooms, that's one thing they can't take away from you. . .

'Everything is all right,' whispered Lammchen. 'It's all, all right,
my Sonny.'

'Yes,' he said, slipping swiftly in beside her and bending his face
over hers. 'Yes,' he said. 'I'm happier than I've ever been in my life.
Lammchen, my love. . .'

bony finger rapped at the door.

...ked a voice.

...said Pinneberg proudly. 'You're not disturbing

...chen's shoulder to prevent her from slipping
...side of the bed.

...g came slowly in and surveyed the scene.

'I hope I'm not ...sturbing you. I saw the light was still on. But of course I didn't think you were already in bed. Are you sure I'm not disturbing you?' And with that she sat down.

'Of course you aren't. We don't mind a bit. Anyway we're married.'

Mrs Mia Pinneberg sat there breathing heavily. Despite her face-paint, she was visibly flushed. No doubt she had drunk a little too much.

'Good Lord!' murmured Mrs Pinneberg, causing Pinneberg to reflect that Lammchen's nighties were excessively revealing, 'what a bosom she's got. You don't see it in the daytime. You're not expecting, are you?'

'Oh no,' said Pinneberg, bestowing an expert glance on the cleavage. 'She's always had that; ever since she was a little girl.'

'Sonny!' said Lammchen warningly.

'You see what it's like, Emma,' said Mrs Pinneberg with tearful indignation. 'Your husband's making fun of me. And that lot over there do it too. I'm going to be away for at least five minutes now, and I am the hostess, but do you think one of them is going to ask after me? They're all after those silly cows Claire and Nina. And Holger has changed altogether these last few weeks. No one bothers about me.'

She gave a slight sob.

'Oh Mama!' said Lammchen, rather embarrassed. She felt sorry for her, and would like to have got out of bed to go to her, but her young man held her fast.

'Leave her alone, Lammchen,' he said pitilessly. 'You've had one too many, Mama. Never mind, you'll soon get over that.'

'It's always the same thing when she's had one too many,' he explained, quite unmoved. 'First she cries, then she starts an argument, then she cries again. I've seen it ever since I was a schoolboy.'

'Please, Sonny, don't be like that,' whispered Lammchen. 'You shouldn't. . .'

And Mrs Pinneberg said: 'You just try harking back to your schooldays! I could tell your wife how the policeman came about the indecent games you'd been having with the girls in the sand-pit. . .'

'Go ahead!' said Pinneberg. 'My wife knows all about it. We're coming up to the quarrel, you see, Lammchen. Now she's going to start.'

'I won't hear any more of this,' said Lammchen with flaming cheeks. 'We've all got things to be ashamed of as I know only too well. Nobody protected me either. But that's no way for a son to speak to his mother.'

'Calm down,' said Pinneberg. 'It's not me who drags up these nasty stories. It's Mama.'

'And what about my rent?' asked Mrs Pinneberg in a sudden rage, as she got onto what was really on her mind. 'Today is the thirty-first, everywhere else you'd have had to pay in advance, and I haven't had a penny.'

'You'll get it,' said Pinneberg, 'not today or tomorrow, but you will get it. Sometime.'

'I must have it today. I've got to pay for the wine. Nobody thinks of where I'm to get my money from.'

'Don't be stupid, Mama. You don't have to pay for the wine tonight. You're just talking. And kindly remember that Lammchen does all your work for you.'

'I want my money,' said Mrs Pinneberg, exhausted. 'I'm sure Lammchen doesn't mind doing me the odd little favour. I made the tea for you today, and am I asking to be paid for that?'

'You're off your head, Mama,' said Pinneberg. 'What's the comparison between clearing up the whole flat every day and brewing a cup of tea?'

'There's no difference,' said Mrs Pinneberg. 'A favour's a favour.' Looking very pale, she rose unsteadily to her feet. 'I'll be back in a moment,' she whispered, and staggered out.

'Now, let's put the light out quick,' said Pinneberg. 'It's a damn

nuisance that we can't lock the door. Nothing works in this pigsty.'
He cuddled up to her again. 'Oh Lammchen, if only the old woman
hadn't come in just when we'd got going so beautifully.'

'I can't bear it,' whispered Lammchen, and he could feel that her
whole body was trembling. 'I can't bear to hear you speak to Mama
like that. She is your mother, Sonny love.'

'More's the pity,' said her young man, unmoved. 'More's the pity.
And it's because I know her so well, that I know what a cow she is.
You're still taken in by her, Lammchen, because in the daytime,
when she's sober, she's witty. She makes jokes and understands a
joke. But that's all cunning. She doesn't like anybody really. And
how long d'you think things will stay happy with Jachmann? He'll
get wise and realize she's just using him. And she'll soon be too old to
be just a bed-partner.'

'Sonny,' she said, very seriously. 'I never want to hear you speak
like that about Mama again. You may be right, and I may be just a
sentimental household drudge, but I don't want to hear it ever again.
It makes me think the Shrimp might talk about me that way one
day.'

'About you?' queried Pinneberg, and his tone said it all. 'The
Shrimp might talk that way about you? But you're you! You're
Lammchen! You're. . . Oh, God damn it, there she is at the door
again. We're sleeping now, Mama!'

'Kids!' said a voice, which, very surprisingly, was Jachmann's. He
too was tipsy. 'Kids, pardon me a minute.'

'We certainly will,' said Pinneberg. 'Just get out, Mr Jachmann.'

'Only a minute, young lady, and I'm going. You're married and
we're married. Not officially, but otherwise genuinely, including the
rows. . . shouldn't we help each other?'

'Out!' was all Pinneberg replied.

'You're a charming woman,' said Jachmann, and sat down heavily
on the bed.

'I'm afraid this is me,' said Pinneberg.

'Doesn't matter,' said Jachmann. 'I know my way here, I'll simply
go round the bed.'

'You're meant to be going out,' protested Pinneberg somewhat
helplessly.

'And I will,' said Jachmann, looking for the narrow passage between the wash-stand and the cupboard. 'I've only come about the rent.'

'Oh God!' sighed the Pinnebergs together.

'Is that you, young lady?' boomed Jachmann 'Oh, do put on the light. Say "Oh God" again.' He made his way towards the bed by the window, struggling through the pitfalls with which the room was littered.

'You know your mother's been grousing non-stop because she hasn't had her rent. Tonight she messed up the whole evening for us. And now she's in there crying. So I thought to myself: Jachmann, you've been earning good money recently. You'd have given it to your old lady anyway, so why not give it to the kids. They'll give it to her, so it'll come to the same thing. And then we'll have peace.'

'No, Mr Jachmann, that's too kind of you,' began Pinneberg.

'Kind. . . Oh damnation, whatever's this here? Oh, it's a new bit of furniture! A mirror! Well, I need my peace and quiet. Come here, young lady, here's the money.'

'I'm very sorry, Mr Jachmann,' said Pinneberg merrily. 'I'm afraid you went round the houses for nothing. That bed's empty. My wife is with me.'

'Dammit,' muttered the giant, as a lachrymose voice arose outside: 'Holger, where are you, Holger?'

'Quick, hide, she's coming in!' whispered Pinneberg.

Crash, bang, and the door opened. 'Is Jachmann in here?' Mrs Pinneberg put the light on. Two pairs of eyes looked rather anxiously around, but he wasn't there. Doubtless he was hiding behind the other bed.

'Where can he have got to this time? He sometimes rushes out onto the street just because he's too hot. . . Oh!'

Pinneberg and Lammchen followed Mama's glance in dismay. But it wasn't Holger that she had discovered, but some banknotes, lying loose on Lammchen's red silk padded quilt.

'Yes, Mama,' said Lammchen, who was the calmer of the two. 'We've just been talking it over. That's the rent for the next few weeks. Please take it.'

Mrs Mia Pinneberg took the money. 'Three hundred marks,' she gasped. 'Well, I'm glad you changed your minds. That'll do for October and November, and then there'll be a small amount for the gas and the electric light. We'll work that out some other time. Well that's that. . . thank you. . . good night.' She had talked herself out of the door, anxiously guarding her treasure.

Jachmann's beaming face emerged from behind the other bed. 'What a woman!' he said. 'What a woman! Three hundred marks for October and November: she's done very nicely thank you. Well, excuse me, kids, now I must go to her. First I'm very curious to see whether she mentions the money. And second she'll be very worked up, so good night.'

And out he went, too.

KESSLER REVEALS ALL AND GETS A BOX ON THE EARS. THE PINNEBERGS STILL HAVE TO MOVE OUT

It was morning, a dreary grey November morning, all was still very quiet at Mandels. Pinneberg had just arrived. He was the first, or almost the first, in the department. Someone seemed to be doing something round the back.

Pinneberg was out of sorts, oppressed, it must be the weather. He took a roll of Melton cloth and began measuring it. Rumm – rumm – rumm.

The person round the back rustled nearer, not directly towards him as Heilbutt would do, but stopping here and there. It must be Kessler, and Kessler must have something to say to him; one of his eternal pinpricks, his cowardly little attacks. Unfortunately, they annoyed Pinneberg afresh every time: he got really wild, so angry he would have liked to wallop Kessler. It had been going on ever since he had made the remark about him having been brought in by Lehmann.

'Morning,' said Kessler.

'Morning,' said Pinneberg, without looking up.

'Still very dark today,' said Kessler.

Pinneberg did not reply. Rumm, rumm, went the cloth.

'You're keen to earn your beer,' said Kessler, with a rather embarrassed smile.

'I don't drink beer,' replied Pinneberg.

Kessler seemed to be working himself up for something, or perhaps simply searching for a way to begin. Pinneberg was very nervous; he knew the man had some object in mind, and that it couldn't be friendly.

Kessler asked: 'You live in Spenerstrasse, don't you Pinneberg?'

'How do you know that?'

'I heard you did.'

'Oh yes.'

'Because I live in Paulstrasse. It's funny that we've never met on the tram.'

'The fellow's got something on his mind,' thought Pinneberg. 'I just wish he'd come out with it! What a swine.'

'And you're married,' said Kessler. 'It's not easy being married these days. D'you have children?'

'I dunno,' cried Pinneberg furiously. 'Why don't you find something to do instead of just standing around here?'

'You don't know! That's a good one,' said Kessler. Now he had the bit between his teeth and was openly insolent. 'Might be true though. Pretty good when a father of a family says he doesn't know.'

'Now you listen, Mr Kessler. . .!' began Pinneberg, raising the measuring ruler slightly.

'Why?' asked Kessler. 'It was you who said it. Or didn't you say it? As long as Mrs Mia is in the know too. . .'

'What?' shouted Pinneberg. The few people who had since come in stared in their direction. 'What?' he asked, involuntarily lowering his voice. 'What d'you want with me? I'll give you a punch on the jaw, you stupid fool, always picking a quarrel.'

'So that's the discreet introduction to high-class company?' sneered Kessler. 'You'd better not come on so strong with me, man. I'd like to see what Mr Jänecke would say if I showed him the advertisement. A man who allows his wife to put in such dirty adverts. Filthy. . .'

Pinneberg was no sportsman. He couldn't get over the counter in one bound, he had to go round it to grab the man, all the way round.

'. . . a disgrace to our profession! Don't start a fight in here.'

But Pinneberg was now on top of him. He was, as stated, no

sportsman; he tried to box Kessler's ears, the other hit back, and now they grappled at each other ineptly.

'You just wait, you bastard,' panted Pinneberg.

The people came running from the other counters.

'You can't do that!'

'If Jänecke sees you, you'll both be out on your ears.'

'All we need now is for the customers to come in.'

Suddenly, Pinneberg felt himself grabbed from behind, held fast, and pulled off his opponent.

'Let me go!' he shouted. 'I must get at that. . .'

But it was Heilbutt, and Heilbutt said quite coolly: 'Don't be silly, Pinneberg. I'm much stronger than you are, and I'm not letting you go.'

A little way off Kessler was already straightening his tie. He wasn't particularly agitated. If you're a born stirrer, you get quite a few clips round the ear in life. 'I'd like to know why he's getting so excited?' he remarked to the onlookers. 'When he lets his old woman advertise openly in the newspaper!'

'Heilbutt!' begged Pinneberg, straining at his chains.

But Heilbutt had no intention of letting him go.

He said: 'Come on, out with it, Kessler! What sort of an advert is it? Show it here!'

'You can't order me about,' declared Kessler. 'You're no better than me even if you do call yourself Senior Salesman.'

But now a general murmur of annoyance arose: 'Come on, out with it, mate.'

'You can't go back on it now.'

'All right then, I'll read it,' said Kessler, and unfolded the newspaper. 'But it's embarrassing.'

He hesitated again, to raise the tension.

'Come on, man.'

'He's always got to be stirring.'

Kessler said: 'It's in the small ads. I'm surprised the police don't follow it up. It can't go on much longer.'

'Just read, will you!'

Kessler read. He did it very nicely. He must have been rehearsing that morning: 'Unlucky in love? I can introduce you to a charming circle of uninhibited ladies. Satisfaction guaranteed. Mrs Mia Pinneberg, Spenerstrasse 92-II.'

Kessler relished his triumph. 'Satisfaction guaranteed. Now what do you say?' And he explained 'I'd never have breathed a word about it, but he told me explicitly that he lived in Spenerstrasse.'

'Well, that's a turn-up for the books!'

'We could take a lesson from him.'

'I didn't. . .' stammered Pinneberg, who had gone as white as a sheet.

'Give me the page,' said Heilbutt suddenly, sounding as angry as it was possible for him to be angry. 'Where? Ah, here. . . Mrs Mia Pinneberg. . . Your wife isn't called Mia, is she, Pinneberg?. . . Your wife's called. . .?'

'Emma,' said Pinneberg in a flat voice.

'Well that's another box on the ears for you, Kessler,' said Heilbutt. 'It wasn't Pinneberg's wife for a start. I also think it was in very bad taste. . .'

'Cut it out, will you?' protested Kessler. 'That's something I just can't stand.'

'It's also perfectly clear,' Heilbutt continued, 'that our colleague Pinneberg here knew nothing whatever about it. You live with a relation, don't you?'

'Yes,' whispered Pinneberg.

'There you are,' said Heilbutt. 'I couldn't answer for all my relations. Nothing you can do about it.'

'Well you can be grateful to me all the same,' said Kessler, striving to regain his cool in the face of a discomfiting atmosphere of disapproval. 'I pointed this disgusting business out to you. Though it's funny you didn't notice it. . .'

'That's enough,' declared Heilbutt, to general assent. 'And now, gentlemen, I think we ought to be doing something. Mr Jänecke could come along at any moment. And I think the decent thing would be not to talk about this any more. Not the way for colleagues to behave, is it?

They nodded and withdrew.

'Now listen to me, Kessler,' said Heilbutt, taking him by the shoulder. The two of them disappeared behind the rack with the ulsters. They talked a long while, mostly in whispers with occasional lively protestations from Kessler, but finally he went very quiet.

'Well, that's that,' said Heilbutt returning to Pinneberg. 'He won't give you any more trouble. But I'm sorry I was a bit familiar with you just now. We're friends enough to do that though, aren't we?'

'If it's all right by you, it's all right by me.'

'Good. Kessler will leave you in peace. I've brought him down a peg.'

'I'm very grateful to you, Heilbutt,' said Pinneberg, 'It's all been such a shock, I feel stunned.'

'It's your mother, isn't it?' asked Heilbutt.

'Yes,' said Pinneberg. 'I never thought very much of her. But not something like that. . . no.'

'I don't see it quite that way,' said Heilbutt, 'It doesn't look so terrible to me.'

'But in any case I'm moving out.'

'I would do that. And as quickly as possible. If only because the others know about it now. It's quite possible they'd call, just out of curiosity.'

Pinneberg winced. 'God forbid. When I'm away I don't know what goes on. They play cards as well. I always thought it was something to do with the cards, I was so worried sometimes. Well now, Lammchen will have to find us somewhere to live, and quickly.'

LAMMCHEN SEARCHES, NO ONE WANTS CHILDREN
AND SHE FAINTS, BUT IT PAYS OFF

Lammchen was looking for somewhere to live. It involved going up a lot of stairs, and that wasn't as easy as it had been six months before. Then a staircase was as easy as anything to go up and down. You could dance to the top, no trouble at all, hop, step, hop. . . But now she frequently had to stop on a landing; her forehead was covered in sweat, she wiped that off, but then those pains in the small of her back started. She could put up with the pain itself if only it wasn't doing any harm to the Shrimp!

She walked, climbed stairs, inquired, and went on. A flat must turn up soon, it was more than she could stand seeing her young man turning white and trembling whenever Mrs Mia Pinneberg came into the room. She had made him promise to keep quiet to his mother about the whole thing, they were just going to leave secretly; one morning they would simply be gone. But he was beginning to find it such a strain. He would so like to have made a scene, to storm about. She couldn't for her part understand why, but she understood very well that her young man was like that. . .

Anyone else would have smelled a rat long ago, but in this respect Mrs Mia Pinneberg was touchingly naïve. She breezed into the room where they were sitting, crying gaily: 'Whatever are you doing, sitting here like chickens in the rain? You're supposed to be young! When I was your age. . .'

'Yes, Mama,' said Lammchen.

'Cheer up! Cheer up! Life's bad enough already, you can't let it get you down. I wanted to ask if you'd help me with the washing-up, Emma? I've got a shameful pile of it lying there.'

'Sorry, Mama, I've got to do some sewing,' said Lammchen, who knew her husband would throw a tantrum if she helped.

'Oh well, we'll leave the washing-up for another day. You'll feel more like it tomorrow. What's all this sewing you're doing? Just don't injure your eyes. Sewing's not worth it any more. You can get things cheaper and better ready-made.'

'Yes, Mama,' replied Lammchen meekly, and Mrs Pinneberg sailed off, having cheered the young people up a little.

But Lammchen didn't help with the washing-up the next day either, she was out and about looking for somewhere to live, day after day. It was urgent; her young man was burning to leave.

Oh! those landladies! There was one sort who, when Lammchen inquired after the furnished room with the use of the kitchen, stared straight at her middle, saying: 'Expecting, aren't yer? Na, if we wanted kids bawling round the 'ouse, we'd 'ave our own. Then we could 'ave a choir of 'em.'

And, bang! The door was shut.

And sometimes, when it was more or less settled and Lammchen was just thinking to herself, 'Tomorrow morning Sonny is going to be able to wake up carefree', Lammchen would say – because they didn't want to be thrown out after two or three weeks – 'Oh, and we're expecting a baby.' Then the landlady's face would drop, and she would say, 'Oh no, dear, I'm very sorry, I like you very much, but my husband. . .'

On to the next one! Keep going, Lammchen, it's a wide world and Berlin's a big city. There must be some nice people, too. Surely it's a blessing to be expecting a baby, this is the era of the child. . .

'Oh, and we're expecting a baby.'

'Oh, that's no big problem. Can't do without them, can we? The only trouble is that children do a lot of damage in a flat, all that washing when the baby's little, the steam, the vapour, and we do have such nice furniture. And then a child scratches the polish so. I'd be glad to have you, but. . . I'll have to charge at least eighty marks instead of fifty. Well, let's say seventy. . .'

'No, thank you,' said Lammchen, and went on.

Oh, but she did see some lovely places: bright, sunny, properly furnished rooms, with clean colourful curtains, and fresh bright wallpaper. . . and she thought so lovingly of the Shrimp.

Then some elderly woman would appear and look at the younger woman with a friendly eye when she whispered something to her about the expected baby – and indeed, for anyone with eyes in their head it was a pleasure to look at her. And then the elderly woman would say to her, glancing thoughtfully at the blue, very shabby coat: 'But you know, I can't really charge less than a hundred and twenty marks. The landlord gets eighty, and I only have my little pension, and I've got to live too.'

'Oh why, oh why,' thought Lammchen, 'don't we have just a little bit more money? If only we didn't have to watch the pennies so! It would all be so simple, life would look so different, and we'd just be able to look forward to the Shrimp without worrying about a thing.'

Oh! why not? And the sleek cars roared by, and there were delicatessens, and people who earned so much they didn't know how to spend it all. No, Lammchen didn't understand it. In the evening her young man was often home before her, waiting for her in their room.

'Nothing?' he would ask.

'Not yet,' she would reply. 'But don't lose heart. I've got the

feeling I'll definitely find something tomorrow. Oh Lord, my feet are
so cold!'

But she was only saying that to head him off and keep him busy. It
was true that she had cold feet, and they were wet too, but she was
only saying that to distract him from the disappointment of not
having a flat yet. Because what he did then was take her shoes and
stockings off and rub her feet with a towel to warm them.

'There you are,' he said, satisfied. 'Now they're warm again, put
your slippers on.'

'Lovely,' she said. 'And tomorrow I'm sure to find something.'

'Don't overdo it,' he said. 'A day here or there won't matter. I'm
not losing heart yet.'

'No, no,' she said. 'I know that.'

But it was she that was soon going to lose heart. All this walking,
walking, and what use was it? For the money they could lay out, there
simply wasn't anything decent to be had.

Recently she'd been going ever further east and north, where there
were endless frightful blocks of flats, overcrowded, malodorous,
noisy. And working-class women had opened the door to her and
said: 'Of course, you can look round, but you won't take it. Not good
enough for you.'

And she would go and look at the room with the stains on the
wall. . . 'Yes, we did have bugs, but we got rid of them with prussic
acid.' The wobbly iron bedstead. . . 'You can have a bedside rug if
you like that sort of thing, but it only makes more work. . .' A
wooden table, two chairs, a few hooks on the wall and that was it. 'A
child? As many as you like. A few more shouting around the place
won't make any difference to me, I've got five already.'

'Yes, I don't know' said Lammchen uncertainly. 'Perhaps I'll come
back.'

'No, you won't', said the woman. 'I know what it's like. I had a
parlour once, and it's not easy to settle for less.'

No, it wasn't easy. That was rock-bottom, that was giving up
everything you'd wanted out of life; a grimy wooden table with him
on one side, her on the other, and the child whining in the bed.

'Never!' said Lammchen. Or, if she was tired, or had pains, she
added very quietly: 'At least not yet.'

No, it wasn't easy to settle for that, the woman was right, and it turned out to be a good thing for Lammchen that it wasn't because things did in fact turn out quite differently. . .

One afternoon she was standing in a little shop in Spenerstrasse where they sold soap; she was buying a packet of Persil, half a pound of soft soap, and a packet of bleaching soda. Suddenly she felt ill, everything went black, she just managed to grasp at the counter and hold herself up.

'Emil!' shouted the woman to her husband.

Then Lammchen was given a chair and a cup of hot coffee, she started to be able to see again, and whispered apologetically: 'I've done so much walking.'

'You shouldn't. A bit of walking's healthy in your condition, but not too much.'

'But I have to!' cried Lammchen despairingly. 'I've got to find somewhere to live.'

And suddenly she was talkative; she told the couple who owned the shop everything about her fruitless search. She had to talk to someone, just once. With Sonny she had to be brave all the time.

The woman was tall and thin with a sallow wrinkled face and black hair. She looked rather severe. He was a thick-set, red-faced fellow, looming in the background in shirtsleeves, corpulent.

'Yes,' he said, 'Yes, young woman, they feed the birds in winter so they don't starve, but the likes of us. . .'

'Nonsense,' said the wife. 'Don't talk rubbish. Think. Have you any ideas?'

'Ideas?' he asked. 'Talk about the privileges of being a white-collar worker: don't make me laugh. Privileged to take shit.'

'I'm sure the young woman knows all about that without needing you to tell her. Especially not in that sort of language,' growled the woman. 'Come on, think! Don't you know?'

'Oh, don't keep on at me: just say what you mean. What am I meant to know?'

'Emil Puttbreese of course.'

'Oh, I'm meant to be thinking of somewhere for the lady to live. Why didn't you say so?'

'How are things at Puttbreese's? Is it still free?'

'Is Puttbreese planning to let? What?'

'Where he used to store the furniture. You know.'

'That's the first I ever heard of it. Now supposing he does want to let that poky place, this young woman's never going to get to it up the step-ladder. Not in her condition.'

'Rubbish,' said the wife. 'Listen to me, young woman. You go and lie down for a couple of hours, then come down to me around four and we'll go to Puttbreese together.'

'Thank you very, very much,' said Lammchen.

'If the young lady rents Puttbreese's place,' said the shirt-sleeved Emil, 'I'll eat my hat. My best hat, worth one mark eighty-five.'

'Rubbish,' said the soap-shop lady.

And then Lammchen went and lay down. 'Puttbreese,' she thought. 'Puttbreese. As soon as I heard the name I knew something was going to come of it.'

And then she fell asleep, quite satisfied with her little fainting-fit.

AN EXTRAORDINARY HOME. MR PUTTBREESE PULLS
AND MR JACHMANN HELPS

When Pinneberg came home that evening, he was surprised by the sudden flash of a torch and a voice crying: 'Stop! Hands up!' 'What's going on?' he asked grumpily; he wasn't in a very good mood these days. 'Where d'you get the torch?'

'We'll need it,' called Lammchen cheerfully. 'There's no light on the stairs in our new palace.'

'We've got somewhere?' he asked breathlessly. 'Oh Lammchen, have we really got somewhere?'

'Yes, we have!' rejoiced Lammchen. 'We've got a proper home!' She paused. 'If you want it, that is, I didn't actually agree to rent it yet.'

'Oh no!' he said, aghast. 'Supposing someone else has gone and rented it in the meantime?'

'They won't,' she soothed him. 'I've got an option till tonight. We'll go round there as soon as we've finished. Just eat up.'

During the meal he kept questioning her, but she didn't give him any proper answers. 'No, you have to see it for yourself. Oh Sonny, I do hope you feel like I do.'

'So let's go,' he said, getting up while he was still chewing.

They went up Spenerstrasse, arms enlaced, then into the Alt-Moabit district.

'A flat,' he murmured. 'A real honest-to-goodness home, just for us.'

'It isn't exactly a real flat' said Lammchen apologetically. 'Please don't be shocked.'

'You're an expert torturer, you know!'

In front of them was a cinema, and they went through a wide doorway next to the cinema and came onto a courtyard. There are two sorts of courtyards; this was the other sort, more of a factory store-yard. A dim gas-lamp illuminated a large double door like the door of a garage. 'Karl Puttbreese Furniture Store' was written upon it.

Lammchen pointed somewhere into the dark courtyard. 'That's our toilet,' she said.

'Where?' he asked. 'Where?'

'There,' she said, pointing again. 'The little door at the back.'

'I think you're having me on.'

'And this is our entrance,' said Lammchen, and opened up the garage door with 'Puttbreese' on it.

'What. . .?' said Pinneberg.

They entered a large storage shed, stuffed full of old furniture. Overhead the feeble light of the little torch was lost in a murky tangle of beams and spiders' webs.

'I hope,' said Pinneberg, taking a deep breath, 'this isn't our living-room.'

'This is Mr Puttbreese's store. He's a carpenter, and he deals in old furniture on the side,' explained Lammchen. 'Wait and I'll show you everything. See the black wall at the back, that doesn't quite go up to the roof? We have to go up there.'

'Oh yes,' said he.

'That's the cinema. You saw the cinema, didn't you?'

'I did,' he said, guardedly.

'Oh Sonny, don't pull such a face. You'll see. So that's the cinema, and we go up on top of it.'

As they approached, the lamp picked out a small wooden staircase, as steep as a ladder, going up the wall. On closer inspection it turned out to be very much more of a ladder than a staircase.

'Are you going up there?' said Pinneberg doubtfully. 'In your condition?'

'I'll show you,' said she, and was already on the way up. 'You have to hold on really tight. Now we're nearly there.'

The roof was just above their heads. They went into a sort of vaulted tunnel, with Puttbreese's furniture stacked in the dimness to their left.

'Keep close on my footsteps or you may fall back down again.'

And now Lammchen opened a door, a real door up here in the roof, and put on the light, real electric light, and said: 'Here we are.'

'Yes, here we are,' said Pinneberg, and looked around. And then he said: 'Oh, there is something here!'

'See,' said Lammchen.

It was two rooms, or rather one, for the door between the two had been taken out. They were very low, with thick beams in the whitewashed ceiling. The room in which they were standing was the bedroom, with two beds, a cupboard, a chair and a wash-stand. That was all. No window.

But in the other room there was a handsome round table and a gigantic black oilcloth-covered sofa with white buttons, and a desk and a sewing-table. All old mahogany furniture. There was also a carpet on the floor. It looked wonderfully homelike, especially with the pretty white curtains at the windows. There were three windows, all very small with four panes.

'Where's the kitchen?' he asked.

'Here,' she said, and opened the iron stove which had two ovens. And the water?'

'All there, my Sonny.' And there turned out to be a tap and a sink between the desk and the stove.

'And what does it cost?' he asked, still doubtful.

'Forty marks,' she said. 'That's to say: nothing.'

'What d'you mean, nothing?'

'Listen and I'll explain,' she said. 'Have you grasped why there's that ladder and why the rooms are in such a funny place?'

'No idea,' he said. 'A mad builder? There must be plenty of them.'

'Mad nothing!' she cried enthusiastically. 'This was once a real flat up here with a kitchen and a toilet and a landing and everything. And there was a proper staircase up to it.'

'So where did all that go?'

'It was when they put in the cinema. The auditorium goes right up to the wall of our bedroom. The rest of the flat was removed to make way for it. These two rooms were left over and nobody knew what to do with them. They were quite forgotten till Puttbreese found them. And he put the ladder up from his store-room down there, and because he needs money he wants to rent them.'

'And why does the flat cost nothing, but also costs forty marks?'

'Because of course he can't rent it, the building inspectors wouldn't allow it because of the fire risk and the danger to life and limb.'

'I don't know how you're going to get up here in a couple of months' time.'

'Leave that to me. The main thing is whether you want it.'

'It's all right, so far as I can see.'

'Oh, you nitwit! Nitwit! Nitwit! All right. . .! We'd be on our own here. No one will stick their nose into our business ever again. It's marvellous.'

'Well then, girl, let's rent it. You're the one who's going to do the work, and if you don't mind the inconvenience it's all right by me.'

'It's all right by me,' she said. 'Let's go.'

'Young man,' said Puttbreese the carpenter, twinkling his small bloodshot eyes at Pinneberg, 'I'm naturally not taking any money for that makeshift place. You know what I mean.'

'Yes,' said Pinneberg.

'You know what I mean!' he repeated, louder.

'Yes?' asked Pinneberg, encouragingly.

'Good God,' said Lammchen. 'Just put twenty marks on the table.'

'That's right,' said the master-carpenter. 'The young lady's got the message. That'll be half of November. And don't you worry about

the bulge, young lady. When it gets too big for you to go up the
ladder, we'll put in a hoist with a chair on it, and we'll pull you up
slowly. That'll be a pleasure for me.'

'Ah well!' laughed Lammchen. 'That's one worry less.'

'And when are we moving in?' asked the master-carpenter.

The couple looked at each other.

'Today,' said Pinneberg.

'Today,' said Lammchen.

'But how?'

'Tell me,' said Lammchen, turning to Mr Puttbreese. 'Could you
perhaps lend us a hand-cart? And would you perhaps help us push?
It's only two trunks and a dressing-table.'

'A dressing-table! That's a good one. I'd have bet on a pram. But
you never know what you're going to come by. Right?'

'Quite right,' said Lammchen.

'Well, all right, you're on,' said the master-carpenter. 'It'll cost you
a beer and a whisky. Well let's get moving then.'

They got moving with a hand-cart.

Afterwards in the bar it wasn't easy to make Mr Puttbreese
understand that the move had to take place in the greatest secrecy.

'I see,' said the master-carpenter finally. 'You want to do a
moonlight flit. That's none of my business. But I can tell you, you've
got to lay my money on the table every month in advance, sharp.
And if you don't, never fear I'll move you for free: out onto the
street.'

And his little red eyes blinked, as he laughed a booming laugh.

But then it all went off splendidly. Lammchen packed with pixie-
like speed, Pinneberg stood at the door holding onto the handle
just to be on the safe side, for there were festivities under way again
in the dining-room, and the master-carpenter sat on the regal bed
and kept repeating in admiration: 'A golden bed, I must tell my old
woman about that. It must be as exciting as being in bed with a
virgin.'

And then the time had come for the men to pick up the dressing-
table. Puttbreese used only one hand, the other was holding the
mirror, and by the time they got back upstairs, the trunks were
already closed, the wardrobe yawned empty, the drawers pulled out.

'So let's go,' said Pinneberg.

Puttbreese took one end of both trunks, Lammchen and Sonny took one end each. On top lay a small suitcase, Lammchen's smart bag, and the egg-crate with the china.

'Quick march!' said Puttbreese.

Lammchen cast one backward glance at the room. It had been her first room in Berlin, and it was hard to leave it. Oh no! she'd left the light on.

'One moment!' called Lammchen, 'The light!' and she let go her handle of the trunk.

First, her smart bag slipped off, it hit the floor with a not very loud crack, the suitcase made a little more noise, but the egg-crate. . .

'Young woman,' said Puttbreese's deep bass, 'if they didn't hear that they deserve to lose their money.'

The Pinnebergs stood like sinners caught in the act, their eyes fixed on the door of the Berlin-style room. And, right enough, the door opened, and in it, with laughing, reddened face, stood Holger Jachmann. The Pinnebergs stared at him. Jachmann's face changed, he drew the door shut behind him, and took a step towards the group. 'Aha,' he said.

'Mr Jachmann,' said Lammchen quietly, in a pleading voice. 'Mr Jachmann, we're moving! Please. . . you know why!'

Jachmann's face had changed again, he looked thoughtfully at the young woman, there was a vertical line down his forehead and his mouth had half opened.

He took another step, and said, very quietly: 'You shouldn't be lifting cases in your condition.'

He took hold of the basketwork trunk with one hand, the suitcase with the other.

'Off we go.'

'Mr Jachmann,' said Lammchen again.

But Jachmann did not speak another word. He carried the luggage silently down the stairs, put it onto the cart in silence, and received the Pinnebergs' handshakes in silence. Then he watched them disappearing into the grey foggy street: a cart with their few things, a rather shabbily-dressed pregnant woman, a young nobody in pseudo-smart clothes, and a fat drunken animal in a blue work-shirt.

Mr Jachmann stuck out his upper lip and thought hard a̶
There he stood, dinner-jacketed, elegant, spruce after his long
bath of that afternoon. Then he sighed deeply and then went slow̶
up the stairs one by one. He shut the landing door, which was still
standing open, looked briefly into the deserted room, shook his head,
clicked off the light and went into the Berlin-style living-room.

'Where have you been off to again?' Mrs Pinneberg greeted him,
from within the circle of guests. 'With the young people again? I
could get jealous, if I was the jealous type.'

'Give me a brandy,' said Jachmann, and drank it down.

'By the way, the young people send you their love. They've just
moved out.'

'Moved out?' queried Mrs Pinneberg.

And then she said a great many things, very angrily, very fast.

A BUDGET IS DRAWN UP AND THERE IS NOT ENOUGH
MEAT. PINNEBERG FINDS HIS LAMMCHEN COMICAL

Late one dark afternoon Lammchen sat in her flat with a notebook in
front of her, some loose sheets of paper, a pen holder, a pencil and a
ruler. She wrote and added up, crossed something out and added
something on. As she did so, she sighed, shook her head, sighed
again, thought 'It's not possible', and carried on reckoning.

The room was really cosy with its low-beamed ceiling and the
warm red-brown mahogany furniture. It was not a modern room at
all, and the master-carpenter had thought it quite in keeping to have
a piece of embroidery with black and white pearls saying 'Be true
even unto death' hanging on the wall. Lammchen too was quite in
keeping, with her gentle face and her straight nose, in her
voluminous blue dress with the little machine-lace collar. It was
pleasantly warm in the room; the wet December wind occasionally
buffeted the panes, but that only made everything more home-like.

Lammchen had finished what she was writing; she read it all
through once more. It read as follows, with much underlining, and
small and large letters:

udget for Johannes and Lammchen Pinneberg
ded under any circumstances!!!!

173

out it.
eep

ГS

thly wage   200 marks

ITURE

Food

Butter and margarine	10	
Eggs	4	
Vegetables	8	
Meat	12	
Sausages and cheese	5	
Bread	10	
Other groceries	5	
Fish	3	
Fruit	5	62

b. Other

Insurance and taxes	31.75	
Association dues	5.10	
Rent	40	
Travel	9	
Electric light	3	
Fire	5	
Clothes including underwear	10	
Shoe repairs	4	
Washing, ironing, starching	3	
Cleaning materials	5	
Cigarettes	3	
Outings	3	
Flowers	1.15	
Replacements	8	
The unexpected	3	134

Total expenditure	196 marks
Amount remaining	4 marks

The undersigned solemnly agree that they will not, under any
circumstances or on any pretext, take out money from the kitty for
any but the above purposes, or in excess of the amount stated. Berlin,
30 November.

Lammchen hesitated a moment, thinking, 'Sonny's going to get a shock', then she took the pen and put her name at the bottom. She put everything tidily together and laid it in a compartment of the desk. Out of the middle section of the desk she took out a pot-bellied blue vase and shook out the contents onto the table: a few banknotes, a little silver, some coppers. She counted it: all it would come to was a hundred marks. She sighed gently, put the money in another compartment, and put the empty vase back in its place.

Then she went to the door, switched off the electric light, and settled comfortably in the big wicker chair in the window, her hands over her belly, her legs spread. A red glow shone through the translucent opening of the oven and danced gently to and fro on the ceiling, stopped, trembling, for a long while, then started to dance again. It was so lovely to sit in your own home, alone in the darkness, waiting for your husband; perhaps the baby would move inside. She felt so big, so wide, so overflowing. It reminded her of the sea, the sea rose and fell too, flowing out all the time. She didn't know the purpose of that either, but it was good that it was so.

Lammchen slept, her mouth half open, her head leaning on one shoulder, a swift happy nap, which lifted her and comforted her, so that she was immediately awake and alert the moment her Sonny switched on the light. 'How's things?' he said. 'You sitting in the dark, Lammchen? Has the Shrimp shown signs of life?'

'No, not yet. Hello, husband.'

'Hello, wife.' And they gave each other a kiss.

He laid the table and she prepared the food. She said rather hesitantly. 'There's cod with mustard sauce today. It was so nice and cheap.'

'Very good,' said he. 'I like fish now and then.'

'You're in a good mood,' she said. 'Did it go well today? How's the Christmas trade?'

'So-so, starting up a bit. People are scared to buy.'

'Did you sell well?'

'Yes, I was lucky today. I sold over five hundred marks' worth.'

'You must be the best salesman they have.' 'No, Lammchen. Heilbutt is better. And Wendt is at least as good. But there's going to be an innovation.'

'What? It can't be anything good.'

'There's a new organizer coming. He's going to reorganize the whole business, find ways of economizing, that sort of thing.'

'They can't economize any more on your wages.'

'There's no telling how they think. He'll find something. Lasch heard he's getting three thousand marks a month.'

'What?' asked Lammchen. 'Three thousand marks, and Mandels call that economizing?'

'Yes. He's going to have to cut Mandels' costs by that amount. He'll find something.'

'But how?'

'They're saying that every salesman is going to have it laid down how much they have to sell, and if they don't they're sacked.'

'That's mean! What if the customers don't come, or they don't have any money, or they don't like what's for sale? That sort of thing oughtn't to be allowed.'

'Not only is it allowed,' said Pinneberg. 'They're all mad about it. They say it's clever, it'll save money, because they'll find out who's no good. It's all rubbish. Lasch for example, he's a bit nervous. He was just saying today that if they measured him by his sales-pad, he'd always be afraid he wouldn't make it and he'd be so nervous he wouldn't sell anything!'

'And anyway what does it matter,' said Lammchen, flaring up, 'If he really doesn't sell very much and isn't so good at the job? What sort of people are they to take away a person's job and their wages and their happiness just like that? What are the weaker meant to do: disappear? Measuring a person by how many pairs of trousers he can sell!'

'You're getting very worked up, Lammchen!'

'I am. That sort of thing makes me very angry!'

'But what they would say is that they don't pay a person for being nice, but for selling a lot of trousers.'

'Of course that's not true.' said Lammchen. 'That's not true, Sonny. Of course they want to have decent people. But what they're doing now, to the workers for some time and now to us, is creating nothing but wild beasts, and – I tell you, Sonny – they've got something coming to them.'

'Of course they have,' said Pinneberg. 'Most of the people at our place are Nazis already.'

'Well you can keep that,' said Lammchen. 'I know what we'll be voting.'

'Oh yes, what? Communist?'

'Of course.'

'Let's think it over,' said Pinneberg. 'I always feel I want to, but then I can't quite bring myself to do it. We've got a job at the moment anyhow; we don't have to yet.'

Lammchen looked thoughtfully at her husband. 'Well, all right, Sonny,' she said. 'Let's talk about it again before the next election.'

And with that they both got up from the remains of the cod and Lammchen washed up quickly and he dried.

'Did you see Puttbreese about the rent?' asked Lammchen suddenly. 'All paid up,' he said.

'Then I'll put the rest of the money away at once.'

'Very good,' he said and opened the desk, took out the blue vase, reached into his pocket, took the money out of his wallet, looked into the blue vase and said in astonishment: 'There's no more money left in it.'

'No,' said Lammchen firmly, and looked at her husband.

'But how can that be?' he asked, amazed. 'There ought to be money left in there! Our money can't be all used up.'

'Oh yes, it is,' said Lammchen. 'Our money's gone. Our savings have all gone, so has the insurance. All of it. From now on we have to manage on your salary!'

He became more and more confused. It just couldn't be that Lammchen, his Lammchen, was cheating him. 'But I saw money in the pot yesterday or the day before. I'm certain there was a fifty-mark note left in there and a load of little notes.'

'It was a hundred,' said Lammchen.

'And where's it gone?' he asked.

'It's gone,' she said.

'But. . .' Suddenly he was vexed. 'Damn it, what have you bought with it? Just tell me.'

'Nothing,' she replied. Then, as she saw he was about to get really angry: 'Don't you get it, Sonny? I've put it aside, in a safe place. It no longer exists for us. Now we have to get by on your wages.'

'But why put it aside? All we have to do is say we're not going to use it.'

'It wouldn't work.'

'That's your story.'

'Listen, Sonny. We always wanted to get by on your wages. We even wanted to save out of them, and where are our savings? Even the extra money we got has gone.'

'How did it happen?' said he, becoming thoughtful. 'We haven't lived extravagantly.'

'First of all there was our engagement, when we were travelling back and forth all the time, and we went out a lot.'

'And that disgusting old Sesame and his fifteen marks. I'll never forgive him for that.'

'And our wedding,' said she. 'That cost money too.'

'And the things we bought to start off with. The pots and the cutlery, the broom and the bed linen, and my eiderdown.'

'We went on a lot of excursions too.'

'Then there was the move to Berlin.'

'Yes and there was. . .' she stopped.

'The dressing-table,' he said courageously.

'And the Shrimp's layette.'

'And we bought his cot.'

'And we've still got a hundred marks left!' she concluded, beaming.

'Well, there you are,' he said, highly gratified also. 'We bought a whole lot of things. I don't know what you're bleating about.'

'That's all very well,' she said in an altered tone. 'We have bought all kinds of things. But we ought to have been able to do most of that without dipping into our reserves. You see, Sonny, it was very nice of you not to give me housekeeping money but just let me take what I needed out of the blue pot. But it made me reckless. I sometimes dipped in when it wasn't really necessary, like last month I got the veal cutlets and the bottle of Moselle to celebrate moving in here.'

'The Moselle cost a mark. We must have some fun. . .'

'We'll have to take more advantage of free amusements.'

'There aren't any,' he said. 'Anything that's fun costs money. You want to go out into the country: hand over the money! Listen to music: where's your money? Everything costs something, you can't do anything without it.'

'I thought maybe museums. . .' She broke off suddenly. 'I know you can't go to museums all the time and we don't know anything about it and never seem to find the right thing to look at. But anyway, now we have to manage, and I've written down everything we need in the month. May I show it to you?'

'You can show it to me if you like.'

'You're really not cross?'

'Why should I be? You're very probably right. I can't handle money.'

'Nor can I. That's why we've got to learn.'

And then she showed him her page, and his brow cleared as he began to read. '"Standard budget", that's good, Lammchen. I'll keep to this standard budget under all circumstances. I swear.'

'Don't swear too soon,' she warned. At first, he read quickly. 'Food: yes, we have to have all that. Have you tried it out?'

'Yes, I've been writing it down for a long time.'

'Meat: twelve marks seems an awful lot to me.'

'Sonny love, that's only forty pfennigs' worth of meat for both of us per day, and that's a whole lot less than you've been getting recently. We have to have a meatless day at least twice a week.'

'What do we eat then?' he asked anxiously.

'All kinds of things. Lentils. Macaroni. Barley broth and plums.'

'Oh God!' he said. Then, seeing her react, he added: 'No, I understand, Lammchen. Just don't tell me beforehand if you're going to cook one of those things, or I won't look forward to coming home.'

She made a little face, then decided to meet him half way.

'All right,' she said. 'I'll do it as little as possible. But if it isn't so nice every time, don't get scratchy at once will you? I always get into a mood when you're in a mood, and what is there to live for if we're both scratchy?'

'Come on here then pussy-cat,' he tempted her. 'Big pussy-cat, fine pussy-cat. Come on, purr a bit.'

She allowed herself to be stroked, luxuriously. Then she slipped

away from him. 'No, not now, Sonny love. I want you to look at it all
first, or I won't be happy. And anyway. . .'

'What d'you mean "anyway"?' he asked, surprised.

'No, nothing. It just slipped out. Later. There's plenty of time yet.'

That really alarmed him. 'What do you mean? Don't you want to
any more?'

'Sonny!' she said. 'Oh Sonny, don't be stupid. Of course you know
I want to!'

'Then what did you mean just now?' he persisted.

'I meant something quite different,' she said defensively. 'In the
book,' she glanced at the desk, 'it says that towards the end you
shouldn't. That the mother doesn't want it and that it isn't good for
the baby. . . But. . .' she paused. . . 'for now, I still want to.'

'How long is that meant to go on?' he asked suspiciously.

'Oh, I don't know. Six weeks, eight weeks.'

Casting a withering glance at her, he took the book from the desk.

'Oh don't!' she cried. 'It's a long time yet.'

But he had already found the place. 'At least three months!' he
said, crushed.

'Well that's as may be,' she said. 'I think it's coming later for me
than other people. I haven't felt like that at all yet. Now shut the silly
old book.'

But he went on reading, with raised eyebrows, his forehead
furrowed in amazement.

'And you have to go on abstaining afterwards!' he said, astonished.
'Eight more weeks during breast-feeding. So let's say ten weeks and
eight weeks: eighteen weeks. Look here, what did we get married for?'

She looked at him with a smile, but did not reply, until he, too,
began to smile. 'Lord!' he said. 'The world's quite a different place,
isn't it? We never thought of all this. The Shrimp's starting out well,'
he grinned, 'a friendly child: pushing his father away from the
feeding-trough.'

She laughed. 'You've got a lot more to learn yet.'

'There's nothing like being forewarned.' He beamed. 'Starting from
now, Emma Pinneberg, we're going to feast before we have to fast.'

'That's fine by me,' she said. 'Just read to the end of the budget.
Then we'll start feasting.'

'Right,' he said. 'What's this? Cleaning materials?'

'That's things like soap and toothpaste and your razor blades and cleaning spirit. Haircuts are in there too.'

'Well done, for including the haircuts. Ten marks for clothing and underclothes. . . we aren't going to get any new clothes for a while it seems.'

'Well, the eight marks for replacements covers clothes as well, but then there's shoes. I thought a new suit for you every two years at the most, and every three years a winter coat for one of us.'

'Very generous,' he said. 'Three marks for cigarettes, that's very nice of you.'

'Three a day at a pfennig each,' she said. 'You'll be gasping sometimes.'

'I'll manage. What's this, three marks a month for outings? Where will you go for three marks? To the cinema?'

'Nowhere at all to start with,' she replied. 'Oh, Sonny, I had this idea. I'd like once in my life to go out properly, like rich people do. Without thinking about the cost.'

'For three marks?'

'We'll put them away each month. And when there's a tidy sum in there, like twenty or thirty marks, then we can really go out for once.'

He stared at her searchingly. His face was a little sad, as he asked: 'Once a year?'

But this time she didn't notice. 'I'm willing to wait a year. The more we've got in the kitty the better. And then we'll lash out, really go on the town.'

'That's funny,' he said. 'I never thought something like that would give you pleasure.'

'Why d'you think it's funny?' she asked. 'It's the most natural thing in the world. I've never had that experience in my whole life. You have, when you were a bachelor.'

'Of course you're right,' he said slowly, and fell silent. Then suddenly he banged on the table, crying furiously. 'Oh, God damn it!'

'What is it? What's the matter, Sonny?'

'Oh nothing,' he said, relapsing into quiet gloom again. 'It just suddenly makes you so angry, the way things are set up.'

'You mean, for some people? Forget about them. What good does it do them? And now sign, Sonny, to say you're going to keep our agreement.'

He took the pen and signed.

THE PERFUMED CHRISTMAS-TREE AND THE MOTHER OF TWO. HEILBUTT THINKS WE'RE BRAVE. ARE WE?

Christmas had come and gone, a quiet little Christmas with a pine-tree in a pot, a tie, a shirt and some spats for Sonny, a maternity girdle and a bottle of eau-de-Cologne for Lammchen.

'I don't want you to get a sagging tummy,' he explained. 'I want to keep my pretty wife.'

'Next year the Shrimp will see the tree,' said Lammchen.

It turned out a very strong-smelling tree, and the eau-de-Cologne was used up on Christmas Eve.

Everything gets more complicated when you're poor. Lammchen had a plans for the potted pine tree. She wanted to let it grow and re-pot it in the spring. The Shrimp would see it the next year and it would grow ever bigger and more beautiful, competing with the Shrimp in growth from Christmas to Christmas, their first and only Christmas tree. That was what was meant to happen.

Before the holiday Lammchen had put the pine tree on the cinema roof. God knows how the cat got at it, Lammchen hadn't even known there were cats around here. But there were: she found traces of them on the earth in the pot, when they came to decorate it, and the traces were very smelly. Lammchen removed what there was to remove, she washed, and she scrubbed, but it was all to no avail. No sooner was the official part of the festivities over, the exchange of kisses, the deep look into each other's eyes, the opening of the presents, than Sonny said, 'Have you noticed the odd smell in here?'

Lammchen put him in the picture. He laughed and said: 'Nothing simpler!' then opened the eau-de-Cologne bottle and sprinkled some on the pot.

Oh, he did a lot of sprinkling that evening, which stunned the cat for a while, but then it awakened, victorious to ever-renewed life.

The bottle emptied and the cat still stank. Finally, before Christmas Eve was at an end, they put the tree outside the door. The smell had proved invincible.

And on the first day of the holiday, very early, Pinneberg went out and stole a little pile of garden earth. They re-potted the tree. But firstly it still stank, and secondly they found out that it wasn't a proper tree, grown in its pot, but a useless replanted one that had been shorn of all its roots so it would fit the pot. A nine days' wonder.

Pinneberg was in the mood to find that quite typical. 'People like us always get the duds,' he said.

'No, not always,' said Lammchen.

'What d'you mean?'

'Well, I got you, didn't I?'

All in all December was a good month. Despite the Christmas festivities, the Pinneberg household did not overstep its budget. They were as happy as sandboys. 'There you are! We can do it. And it was Christmas!'

And they made plans about what they were going to do with all their savings in the months to come.

But January turned out dark, miserable and anxiety-ridden. In December, Mr Spannfuss, Mandels' new organizer, had been merely looking around. In January he got going. The sales-quota for every salesman in Gentlemen's Outfitting was set at twenty times his monthly wage. Mr Spannfuss gave an elegant little speech. The arrangement was solely in the interests of the employees; everyone now had the mathematical certainty that he was being judged by his worth alone. 'Flattery, creeping to the bosses, all those things so destructive to the morale of a business, will be no more!' cried Mr Spannfuss. 'Give me your sales-pad, and I'll know what sort of a man you are!'

The employees listened with serious faces, one or two very good friends may perhaps have risked a remark to each other, but nothing was said out loud.

Nonetheless there was muttered resentment when Kessler bought two sales off Wendt at the end of January. Wendt had already fulfilled his quota by the twenty-fifth, but Kessler was still 300 marks short on the twenty-ninth.

When Wendt sold two suits one after the other on the thirtieth,

Kessler offered him five marks per sale if Wendt allowed him to put them down on his own sales-pad. Wendt agreed to the proposal.

All this was not known till later; Mr Spannfuss was the first to hear of it. How, remained unclear. Mr Wendt was asked to resign for taking advantage of his colleague's misfortune, whereas Mr Kessler got off with a warning. A very severe warning, he told everyone.

Pinneberg, for his part, achieved his January quota with ease. 'They know what they can do with their silly ideas,' he said, confidently.

In February it was generally expected that the sales quota would be reduced, since there were only twenty-four selling-days in February, whereas there had been twenty-seven in January, as well as the stock-taking sale. A few brave spirits mentioned this to Mr Spannfuss but he refused. 'Gentlemen, you may or may not be aware of it, but your whole being, your energy, your will to achieve, is now calibrated at that times-twenty figure. Any reduction in the quota would bring about a reduction in your efficiency, which you would yourselves regret. I have the greatest confidence that each and every one of you will reach the quota and even exceed it.'

And he looked sharply and meaningfully at them all and went on his way. But the consequences of these measures were not quite so moral as their idealistic author had imagined. On the principle of 'The devil take the hindmost!' the employees laid siege to the customers. Many a customer was rather surprised, as he wandered through Mandels Gentlemen's Outfitting Department, to see pale, desperately smiling faces popping up all round him: 'Can I help you, sir?'

It was all rather like a red-light district, and every salesman was only too pleased when he snatched a colleague's customer.

Pinneberg could not remain aloof, he had to join in with the rest of them.

Lammchen learned that month to greet her husband with a smile that wasn't so bright that it would annoy him if he was in a bad mood. She learned to wait quietly until he spoke, because a word could throw him into a sudden rage in which he ranted on about these slave-drivers, who turned people into animals, and who deserved a bomb up the backside.

Around the twentieth he became very sombre indeed. Infected by

the others, he had lost his self-confi...
he had lost the knack.

In bed she took him in her arms a...
nerves were at breaking point, he cried
saying over and over again: 'Sonny, even
you mustn't give up hope. Don't let th...
never, never complain, I swear.'

The next day he was calm, though still ...
him a few days later that Heilbutt had hel...
hundred marks off his takings. Heilbutt, the ...adn't
allowed himself to be touched by the collective ...ia, who carried
on as if there was no such thing as sales quotas, who even made fun of
Spannfuss.

Pinneberg livened up as he told her the story, his face lightening
into gaiety.

'Now, Mr Heilbutt,' Spannfuss had said with a smile. 'I hear you
are a man of superior intellect. May I ask whether you've considered
how economies are to be effected in this business?'

'Yes,' said Heilbutt, fixing his dark, almond-shaped eyes on the
dictator. 'I have considered that question.'

'And what conclusion did you come to?'

'That every employee earning more than four hundred marks
ought to be made redundant.'

Mr Spannfuss turned on his heel and left. The whole of
Gentlemen's Outfitting, however, rejoiced.

Lammchen understood what was the matter. It wasn't just
worries at work; he wouldn't normally have let it get to him so
easily; the real trouble was that he had to do without her. She had
got so heavy, so shapeless and fat that when she got into bed she had
to settle her belly down as well. It had to be manoeuvred carefully
into position, otherwise it got in her way and she couldn't get to
sleep.

Sonny had got used to her, she could always tell when he got
restless, and now he could no longer have her it happened much
more frequently. She was often tempted to say: 'Go out and find a
girl', and the reason that she didn't was not because she'd have been
jealous of him or the girl, but because of the money. Just simply the

...nd it wouldn't have helped, finally. Because she ...s something else: she wasn't just living for her young ...ore, her unborn child had a claim on her too. Well, all ...Sonny told her a bit about his troubles, she listened to him and ...ood by him but, if she was absolutely honest, she kept a slight distance. She wasn't going to let it disturb the Shrimp. Nothing must be allowed to disturb the Shrimp.

So she went to bed. The light was still on and her young man was pottering at something. She preferred to be lying down, the small of her back was so painful. And, as she lay there, she pulled up her nightie and lay almost naked looking at her belly.

Then – she seldom had very long to wait – she saw something move, and started. It took her breath away.

'Gosh, Sonny!' she called. 'The Shrimp kicked me again. He's going mad.'

Yes, he was alive in there, and seemingly quite merry. He was a lively child, he kicked and punched. Once it might have been tummy-rumbles, now it was unmistakeable.

'Look at that, Sonny,' she cried. 'You can see it quite plainly.'

'Can you?' he asked, and approached hesitantly.

They both waited, and then she cried: 'There! There!' and then realized that he wasn't looking that way at all but at her breasts.

Then she was shocked at herself for having unintentionally tormented him once again, pulled down her nightie, and murmured: 'Shame on me, Sonny.'

'Oh no,' he said. 'I'm a silly fool too.' and he found something to occupy him in the semi-darkness.

It kept on happening. However ashamed she felt afterwards, she just couldn't stop herself from watching the Shrimp thumping and kicking about. She would have preferred to be alone, but they had only these two rooms with the door removed in between, and they had to share each other's every mood.

Once, and only once, Heilbutt came to visit them in their ship's cabin. It was now impossible to conceal that she was expecting a baby, and it turned out that Sonny had never told his friend about it. Lammchen was surprised.

But Heilbutt took it all in his stride, joked a bit, inquired what it was like. He was a bachelor, and his worries in that direction had never gone beyond hoping his girlfriend took precautions every time. And so far, touch wood, it had worked. Thank Heaven. Heilbutt was interested, sympathetic, raised his teacup and said 'Here's to the Shrimp!' And then, as he set the cup down, he said: 'You're a brave pair.'

In the evening, as the couple were lying in bed, and the light was already out, Pinneberg said: 'Did you hear what Heilbutt said, that we're brave.'

'Yes,' said Lammchen.

And then they were both silent.

But Lammchen reflected long about whether they were really brave, or whether it wasn't rather that everything would be quite hopeless without the prospect of the Shrimp. For what else was there in life for them to look forward to? She wanted to talk about it with Sonny some time, but not just at the moment.

SONNY HAS TO HAVE HIS LUNCH AND FRIEDA IS GIVEN AN OBJECT-LESSON. WHAT IF I NEVER SEE HER AGAIN?

Pinneberg was coming home from Mandels. It was Saturday afternoon; he'd got Mr Kröpelin to let him off, he was restless.

'You go on home,' said Mr Kröpelin, understanding fellow that he was. 'Good luck to your wife.'

'Thank you very much,' replied Pinneberg. 'I don't know for sure it'll be today. I'm just so restless.'

'Well, go home, Pinneberg,' said Kröpelin.

Spring was early this year; although it was still only mid-March, the twigs were already green and the air was soft. 'I hope it will soon be over for Lammchen,' he thought. 'Then we can get out a bit. This waiting's dreadful. I wish this Mr Shrimp would get a move on.'

He went slowly up Calvinstrasse, his coat open to the light breeze. 'Everything is so much easier when the weather is good. How I wish it would start!'

He crossed the Alt-Moabit district and a few steps further on a man offered him a sprig of lily-of-the-valley, but though he'd have liked to take it, the budget did not permit. Then he was back at the yard. The garage door was standing open and Puttbreese was busy with his furniture.

'Now then, young man,' he said, blinking with his red-rimmed eyes out of the darkness into the sunshine. 'Are you a father yet?'

'Not yet,' said Pinneberg. 'Soon.'

'They take their time, these women, 'said Puttbreese, reeking of spirits. 'It's bloody stupid when you think about it. Mad. You think about it, young man. It's only a moment, not even a moment: wham bam! and then you've got this millstone round your neck for the rest of your life.'

'That's right,' said Pinneberg. 'Well, enjoy your lunch. I'm off to have mine.'

'Nice though, wasn't it, young man?' remarked Mr Puttbreese. 'And I'm not saying you called a halt once you'd done it: wham bam and that's your lot. No, not the way we are.'

And he thumped himself on the chest. Pinneberg retreated up the ladder into the darkness.

Lammchen came towards him, smiling. Every time he came home now, it was with the feeling that something must have happened, but it never had. The limit had surely been reached, her body looked weird, tight as a drum, her once white skin threaded with innumerable ugly blue and red veins.

'Hello, wife,' said Pinneberg and gave her a kiss. 'Kröpelin has let me off. I'm free.'

'Hello, husband,' said she. 'That's great. Don't start smoking. We can eat straight away.'

'Really?' he said. 'I'm gasping for a cigarette. Could it wait a moment?'

'Of course,' she said, settling in her chair. 'How was it?'

'Same old thing. And here?'

'The same.'

Pinneberg sighed. 'He's taking his time.'

'It's nearly over, Sonny love.'

'It seems silly,' he said, after a pause, 'that we don't know anyone to ask. How will you know that you're in labour? You might think it was just a belly-ache.'

'Oh, I think you know.'

He'd finished his cigarette, and they began lunch.

'Well!' exclaimed Pinneberg. 'Chops! This is a Sunday lunch.'

'Pork's very cheap at the moment,' she replied apologetically. 'I cooked enough for tomorrow, so that you. . . that we have more time for ourselves.'

'I thought,' he said, 'that we'd go on a leisurely stroll down to the Castle Park. It's so beautiful there now.'

'Tomorrow morning, Sonny, tomorrow morning.'

They were washing up. Lammchen was standing with a plate in her hand when she suddenly opened her mouth and groaned. Her face went very pale, then grey, then very red.

'What is it, Lammchen?' he asked, frightened, leading her to her chair.

'The pains,' was all she whispered, without attending to him at all, sitting doubled up with the plate still in her hand.

He stood there, quite at a loss, looking at the window, at the door, wanting to run away, stroking her. Ought he to get a doctor? Gently he took away the plate.

Lammchen righted herself, her colour came back, she mopped her face.

'Lammchen,' he whispered. 'My Lammchen. . .'

'Yes,' she said and smiled. 'It's time to go. Last time there was an hour between the pains and this time it was only forty minutes. I thought we'd have time to finish the washing up.'

'And you didn't say anything to me, and you let me have a cigarette!'

'We've got time. When it's about to happen they come every minute.'

'You ought to have told me,' he persisted.

'Then you wouldn't have eaten anything. You're always so low when you come in from work.'

'Let's go then.'

'Yes,' she said, glancing round the room one more time, her face

lighted with a strange, fleeting smile. 'Yes, you'll have to wash up on
your own now. And you will keep our little nest clean, won't you? It's
a bit of extra work, but I do like thinking about this place when I'm
away.'

'Lammchen,' was all he said. 'Lammchen!'

'Yes, let's go,' she said. 'The best is if you go down first. I hope the
pains don't come on when I'm on the ladder.'

'But you said forty minutes at the most,' he began reproachfully.

'How can you know?' she asked. 'Perhaps he's in a hurry. I wish
he'd wait just a bit and then he'd be a Sunday boy.'

And they climbed down.

It all passed off well. There was no Puttbreese either. 'Thank
heaven,' said Sonny. 'His drunken jabber would have been the last
straw.'

And now they were out in the Alt-Moabit district, the trams
jingled, the buses drove by. They strolled very slowly through the
warm March sunshine. Some of the men stared really nastily at
Lammchen, some looked shocked, some appeared to leer. The
women looked at them quite differently, with a serious, concerned
air, as though sharing in her ordeal.

Pinneberg was deep in thought, he struggled with himself, then
took a decision. 'Definitely,' said he.

'What's that, Sonny love?'

'No, I'll tell you afterwards, right at the end. I've made a
resolution.'

'Very good,' said she. 'But you don't need to make any resolutions.
You're fine as you are.'

They only had to cross the Little Tiergarten, and then they were
there, they could see the hospital gates over the other side. But they
only got as far as a bench. Five or six women were sitting on it. They
were immediately in the picture.

Lammchen sat doubled up with her eyes closed. Pinneberg
stood by, helpless and rather embarrassed, with her little bag in his
hand.

A fat, shapeless woman said in a deep voice: 'Cheer up girl, if you
can't get any further they'll fetch you with a stretcher.'

A young woman remarked: 'With her build, she'll be all right. She'll just put on weight.'

The others cast her an unfriendly glance.

'It's a good thing to be well-covered in these hard times. No need to be jealous.'

'I didn't mean it like that, 'said the young woman defensively, but no one was listening.

A dark woman with a pointed nose observed reflectively: 'That's the way it is. The men have the pleasure and we have the pain.'

An older woman with a sallow face called a fat thirteen-year old girl to her side, saying: 'Take a look at that, that's what'll happen to you if you get in with men. Take a good look, Frieda, it's for your own good. Get like that, and father'll throw you out.'

Lammchen had recovered. Seeing the circle of women's faces around her as she came to, she tried to smile.

'It'll be coming on again soon,' she said. 'Let's go on at once, Sonny. Do you mind it very much?'

'Oh God,' was all he said.

And the Pinnebergs went on, one step at a time.

'Tell me, Lammchen,' said Sonny hesitantly.

'What is it? Do ask.'

'You don't ever think like that old girl, that it's only for my pleasure?'

'That's rubbish!' was all Lammchen replied, but she said it with such fervour that he was perfectly satisfied. And now they were at the hospital gates, where there was a fat porter. 'Delivery? Reception's on the left.'

'Can't we go in straight away,' asked Sonny anxiously. 'The pains have already started. Into bed, I mean?'

'Good God!' said the porter. 'It won't happen that quick.'

Slowly they climbed the few steps to Reception. 'We had a woman recently, thought she was going to have it here in the hall, and then lay in there for a fortnight, and then went back home again, and it went on another fortnight. Some women can't count.'

The door to Reception opened. A nurse was sitting there, but no one seemed at all excited that the Pinnebergs had arrived and were in the process of founding a real family, which after all wasn't such a common thing as it used to be.

It seemed to be very usual here. 'Delivery?' asked the nurse. 'I don't know. I'm not sure we've got a bed free. We may have to send you somewhere else. How often are the pains coming? Can you still walk?'

'Now listen!' cried Pinneberg, who was beginning to get very angry.

But the nurse was already phoning. Then she hung up. 'There'll be a bed tomorrow. But you'll be all right till then.'

'I beg your pardon!' cried Pinneberg, incensed. 'My wife is having pains every quarter of an hour already. She can't do without a bed till tomorrow.'

The nurse laughed, she laughed at him to his face. 'Your first, isn't it?' she asked Lammchen, and Lammchen nodded. 'Well, of course you'll go to the Delivery Room first, and then. . .' taking pity on Pinneberg, she turned to him to explain: 'then by the time the baby has arrived a bed is sure to be free.' In a different tone: 'And now be quick, young man, go and get the paperwork done, and then pick your wife up here.'

Mercifully the paperwork didn't take long. 'No, you don't need to pay anything. Just sign here that you surrender your right to benefit. Then we get the money from the insurance. Good. All done.'

Lammchen had just been through another attack.

'Well, yes, it is starting, slowly,' said the nurse. 'But not before ten or eleven tonight I wouldn't think.'

'As long as that?' said Lammchen, looking pensively at the nurse.

Her expression had changed a great deal, Pinneberg thought, as though she had moved a long way away from other people, even from him, and was thrown back on her own resources. 'As long as that?' she asked.

'Yes,' said the nurse. 'Of course it could go quicker. You're strong. With some women it's over in two hours. Others are still in labour twenty-four hours later.'

'Twenty-four hours,' said Lammchen, feeling very much on her own. 'Come along then, Sonny.'

They stood up and tottered off. It turned out that the maternity block was the very last of the buildings, and they had to drag along an endless distance to get to it. He would have liked to talk to Lammchen, to take her mind off things. She was going along so silently, with a closed face, and her worried frown; she must be thinking about those twenty-four hours.

'You know, Lammchen,' he began, wanting to explain that he thought such torture was altogether too cruel. But he didn't; instead he said, 'I wanted to entertain you a bit. But I can't think of anything. All I can do is think of This.'

'You needn't say anything, Sonny,' she said. 'And you needn't worry either. This time it's really true to say that what other women can do, I can do too.'

'I suppose so,' he said. 'But all the same. . .'

And then they arrived at the maternity block.

A tall blonde nurse was in the corridor at the time, and turned around when she saw them coming, and perhaps she liked the look of Lammchen (all nice people liked Lammchen) as she put her arm round her shoulders and said brightly: 'You've come to visit us, I see? Well, you're in the right place, dear.' And then she asked the question which seemed to be standard here: 'Your first, isn't it?'

And then she said to Pinneberg: 'Now I'm going to take your wife away. No, don't look so horrified, you'll have a chance to say goodbye to her. And you must take all her things away with you. Nothing stays here. You can bring them back in a week when your wife goes home.'

And with that she bore Lammchen away. Lammchen nodded to him once more, over her shoulder, and then disappeared into the meshes of this baby-production plant, manned by professionals who knew what to do. And Pinneberg was left outside.

Then he had to give their details all over again, to a grey-haired, severe-looking sister. 'I hope Lammchen doesn't get her,' thought Pinneberg. 'She's bound to be nasty to her if she doesn't do things right.' He tried to curry favour with her by behaving very humbly, and then was terribly ashamed not to know Lammchen's date of birth. The sister remarked, 'Typical. No man ever knows.'

It would have been so nice not to be like the others.

'Now you can say goodbye to your wife.'

He entered a long, narrow room, filled with all kinds of machines whose use he could not conceive of, and there sat Lammchen in a long white nightie, smiling at him. She looked like a little girl, rosy, with her hair hanging loose, and seemed a little ashamed.

'Say goodbye now,' said the sister, fiddling around with something by the door.

The first thing he noticed as he stood by Lammchen was the pretty little blue garlands of flowers printed on her nightie. They made it look so cheerful. But when she put her arm around his neck and drew his head down to her, he saw that they weren't flowers but letters, which spelled out, all over the nightie, 'Berlin City Hospitals'.

The second thing he noticed was that there was a very nasty smell around the place, just like. . .

Then Lammchen said: 'Well, Sonny, maybe this evening, certainly by tomorrow morning. I'm so looking forward to the Shrimp.'

And he whispered: 'I can tell you what I swore, Lammchen. I will never, in my life, smoke on a Saturday ever again if everything turns out well.'

And she said: 'Oh Sonny, Sonny. . .'

Then the sister called: 'Come on, Mr Pinneberg!' And to Lammchen she said: 'Has the enema worked?'

Lammchen blushed and nodded, and Pinneberg realized for the first time that she had been sitting on a commode while he said good-bye, and he too blushed, though he thought he was a fool for doing so.

'You can ring in any time during the night, Mr Pinneberg,' said the sister. 'Here are your wife's things.'

He went slowly away, feeling unhappy, because it was the first time in their marriage that he had handed her over entirely to other people, and because she was experiencing something that he couldn't share. 'Perhaps a midwife would have been better. Then at least I could have been there.'

The Little Tiergarten. No, the women were no longer on the bench; he wouldn't have minded, in fact, he would have been glad to talk to one of them. And Puttbreese turned out not to be around, so he couldn't talk to him either; he had to return alone to the silence of his ship's cabin.

There he stood, in shirt-sleeves and Lammchen's apron, finishing
the washing-up, when suddenly he said aloud, very slowly. 'What if I
never see her again? Things can happen. They quite often do.'

MUCH TOO LITTLE WASHING-UP! CREATION OF THE
SHRIMP. LAMMCHEN WILL SCREAM TOO

It isn't easy to stand around thinking 'perhaps I shall never see her
again' in an empty flat. It wasn't easy for Pinneberg, anyhow. Well,
there was the washing-up to be getting on with first, and that was
something to keep him going. He went at it slowly and thoroughly,
attacking every pot with Vim and a brush. Nobody was going to
accuse him of not doing a good job. His thoughts went no further
than the nightie with the garlands of letters printed in blue on it,
and Lammchen looking flushed and childlike, and what more was
there?

There was more.

The washing-up was over. What now? It occurred to him that he
had long been intending to draught-proof the door with strips of felt
but had never got around to it. The strips of felt and the drawing-
pins had been lying around since the beginning of the winter, and
now it was March. He went to work. He fitted the strip carefully,
fixed it roughly and tested whether the door would shut. It shut, so
then he fastened the strips, positioning the tacks with great care. He
could take as long as he liked; it would be useless to ring before seven.
Actually he needn't ring, he could go there. Save a groschen and
possibly find out more. He might even be able to see her.

Or he might never see her again.

All that was left now was to put her clothes away, they smelled of
her, it was so nice, he had always loved her smell. Of course he hadn't
been kind enough to her; he had been grousy too often, and he had
never really given a thought to what might be worrying her. Things
like that. Of course all men thought of things like that when it might
be too late. Typical, like the sister had said. It really was typical. Such
regrets were useless.

Five-fifteen. It was little more than an hour since he had left the hospital and already there was nothing more for him to do. He threw himself down on the big oilcloth-covered sofa and lay still for a long time, his face buried in his hands. Yes, he was small and wretched, he shouted and struggled and elbowed to keep his place in life, but did he deserve a place? He was a nothing. And she had to go through this torment because of him. If he had never. . . if he had not been. . . if he had only. . .

He lay there, not exactly thinking, but being taken over by thoughts which he could not control.

In Berlin NW, however remote from it you may lie in your half-a-ship's cabin, on your oilcloth-covered sofa in a flat facing a garden, the noise of the big city still reaches you. The only difference is that here all the individual noises melt into one big sound. It swells and dies down, it is very loud and then it's almost gone, as though the wind had swallowed it up.

Pinneberg lay there, the noise reached him and lifted him, then dropped him slowly again, he felt the cool oilcloth coming up to his face, lifting him up and down but never letting him go, like sea-swell. That too goes on and on, to what purpose?. . .

Lensahn was the name of the place, and there were cheap day-trips to it from Ducherow at weekends. On one Saturday afternoon at two, Pinneberg set off. It was early summer, May or June. No, it was June. Bergmann had declared a holiday.

Lensahn is not very far from Platz. And so it happened that the village was full of people, radios blared out of every inn garden, and they were rampaging like wild things on the beach.

But proper sandy beaches tempt you to go on and on. Pinneberg took off his shoes and socks and strolled off into the blue. He had no idea where he was going, whether he would get to another place, but what did that matter?

He walked for a couple of hours, until there were no more people to be seen, then he sat down on the beach and smoked a cigarette.

He got up and went on. What a beach it was, with its bays and headlands, sometimes it looked as if there was nothing behind the next tongue of land, as if you would walk straight into the sea.

But it went on, curving ever so gently inland. A great bay, filled with blue, white-crested water, rimmed in the far distance by another tongue of dunes.

Beyond that there could surely be nothing.

But no, there was a bay, as usual. And something else: a person, coming towards him. He screwed up his eyes, it was only a tiny black dot, but it was definitely a person. What were people doing out here? Why didn't they stop in Lensahn?

As they came nearer to each other, he saw it was a girl, wandering barefoot towards him: broad-shouldered, long, thin-legged, wearing a pink silk blouse and a pleated white skirt.

Evening was approaching and the sky was reddish.

'Good evening,' said Pinneberg, and stopped and looked at her.

'Good evening,' said Emma Morschel, and stopped and looked at him.

'Don't go that way,' he said, pointing in the direction he had come. 'It's nothing but jazz, and half of them are drunk.'

'Oh yes?' she said. 'Well, don't go that way either,' she pointed in the direction she had come. 'Wiek is just the same.'

'What shall we do?' he asked, and laughed.

'What is there to do?' she asked.

'Let's have our tea,' he suggested.

'That's all right by me,' she said.

They plodded into the dunes and sat in a hollow like a large friendly hand, where the wind skimmed their heads as it brushed over the dunes. They exchanged hard-boiled eggs and sausage sandwiches; he had coffee in his thermos, she had cocoa.

They chatted a bit and laughed. But chiefly they ate, copiously and long. They also agreed wholeheartedly that people were a pain.

'Oh dear, I don't want to go to Lensahn,' she said.

'Nor I to Wiek,' said he.

'So what shall we do?'

'Let's have a swim first.'

The sun had gone down, but it was still light. They ran into the gentle surf, splashed each other and laughed. They were well-behaved people: each had brought a swimsuit and a towel (or rather, Pinneberg had brought his landlady's towel).

Later they sat and didn't know what to do.

'Shall we go?' she said.

'Yes, it's getting cold.'

And they remained seated, saying nothing, nothing at all.

'Shall we go back to Wiek or Lensahn?' she asked, after a long interval.

'I don't mind,' he said.

'Nor do I,' said she.

Another long silence. The sea becomes a presence at such moments, it intervenes in the conversation, it gets louder and louder.

'So let's go,' she said again.

Very cautiously and gently he put his arm round her. He was trembling, so was she. The water became very loud.

He bent his head over hers; her eyes were dark caves with a light in them.

His lips settled on hers; they parted willingly, came towards him, opened.

'Oh!' he said, and breathed out, deeply.

Then his hand dropped gently from her shoulder, moved down until he felt her breast under the soft silk, full and firm. She made a little movement.

'Please. . .' he said softly.

And the breast came back into his hand.

And suddenly she said: 'Yes. Yes. Yes.'

It was a cry of joy. It came out from deep within her breast. She flung her arms around his neck, she pressed herself against him. He felt her coming towards him.

She had said 'Yes' three times.

They did not even know each other's names. They had never seen each other before.

The sea was there, and above them the sky, which Lammchen saw very clearly, grew darker and darker, and the stars came out one by one.

No, they didn't know anything about each other, they only felt that they were young, and that it was so good to love. They didn't think about the Shrimp.

But now he was on his way. . .

The roar of the city returned. It had been glorious, it had stayed glorious, he had won the jackpot, the girl in the dunes had become the best wife in the world. But he hadn't become the best husband.

Pinneberg stood up slowly. He put on the light, and looked at the clock. It was seven. She was over there, three streets away. It was happening there, now.

He put on his coat and ran over. The porter asked: 'Where are you off to, now?'

'The maternity block. I. . .' But there was no need for explanations.

'Straight ahead. The last building.'

'Thank you,' said Pinneberg.

He threaded his way between the buildings. In every window there was a light. Under every light stood four, six, eight beds. There they lay. Hundreds, thousands, dying slowly, or quickly. Some got better, only to die later on: life was a sad story.

It was dark in the corridor of the maternity block. No one in the sister's office. He stood indecisively. A nurse came along: 'Yes?'

He explained that his name was Pinneberg, and that he would like to know. . .

'Pinneberg?' said the nurse. 'One moment please. . .'

She went through a door, the door was padded. Immediately behind it was another door, that too was padded. She shut it. Pinneberg stood and waited.

Then a nurse burst through the padded door, a different nurse, dark, stocky, energetic.

'Mr Pinneberg? It's all going fine. No, it's not time yet. Perhaps you could call around twelve. No, everything's all right.'

At that moment a yell sounded from behind the padded door, no not a yell a shriek, a wail, a series of agonized cries wrenched out of the depths of somebody's being. It was inhuman, no human voice sounded like that. Then it ebbed away.

Pinneberg had gone as white as a sheet. The nurse looked at him. 'Is that,' he stammered, 'is that my wife?' 'No,' said the sister. 'That's not your wife. She hasn't reached that stage yet.'

'Must she. . .,' asked Pinneberg, with trembling lips. 'Will my wife cry like that. . .?'

The nurse looked at him again. Perhaps she was thinking that it was a good thing for him to know; men today weren't all that nice to their wives. 'Yes,' she said. 'The first one is usually hard.'

Pinneberg stood and listened. But the building was quiet.

'Around twelve then,' said the nurse, and went.

'Thank you, nurse,' he said, still listening.

PINNEBERG PAYS A CALL AND IS EXPOSED
TO THE CHARMS OF NUDITY

In the end he had to go. The screaming didn't come back, or was absorbed by the padded double-doors. So now he knew: Lammchen was going to scream like that. It was to be expected after all. You paid for everything. Why not for that?'

Pinneberg stood indecisively on the street. The street lights were on already. The UFA cinema was festively bright, everything was going on as usual and would go on, with or without Lammchen, with or without the Pinnebergs. It wasn't so easy to get that clear in your brain, almost impossible.

Was it possible to go home with such thoughts? The flat was empty, so terribly empty, precisely because everything in it reminded him of Lammchen. There were the two beds, each evening they'd held each other's hands across the gap between them, that had been lovely. That wasn't going to happen tonight. Perhaps it would never happen again. But where was he to go?'

Have a drink? No, that wouldn't do. It cost money, and then he had to call at eleven or twelve, and it would be shameful if he was drunk. It would be shameful to get drunk while Lammchen was going through this ordeal. He wasn't going to shirk his part of it, he would at least think of Lammchen screaming as she screamed.

But where was he to go? Walk the streets for four hours? He couldn't do that. He walked past the cinema which had their flat above it, he walked past the end of Spenerstrasse, where his mother lived. No, all that was out of the question.

He walked slowly on. There were the law-courts, and there were the cells. Perhaps there were other tormented souls behind those lightless barred windows. You ought to know about such things; perhaps life would be easier if you did. But you were so terribly ignorant. You went on your way, thinking your own thoughts, horribly alone, and on an evening like this you didn't know where to go.

Suddenly he knew. He looked at his watch. He would have to go by tram or the street door of the flats would be closed before he got there.

He travelled a stretch on one tram, then changed onto another and went a bit further. Now he was looking forward to his visit, with every kilometre further away from the hospital, Lammchen and the baby she had to bear receded further into a state of semi-unreality.

No, he was no hero, in any respect, either on the attack or in his self-torturing; he was a totally ordinary young man. He did his duty; he would have considered it a disgrace to get drunk. But a visit to a friend: that was all right, you could even look forward to it. That wasn't a disgrace.

Chance was on his side: 'Yes, Mr Heilbutt is at home.'

Heilbutt was eating his dinner, and he would of course not have been Heilbutt if he had been in the least surprised by this late visit. 'Pinneberg. How nice of you to come. Have you had dinner yet? No, of course you haven't. It's not eight yet. Come and have some.'

He asked no questions. Pinneberg was annoyed that he didn't, but he didn't.

'What a good idea of yours to come. Look around. It's just the usual sort of den, hideous really but I don't mind. It doesn't worry me. It's nothing to do with me.'

He paused.

'Do you see the nude photos? Yes, I've got quite a collection. Thereby hangs a tale. Whenever I move in anywhere, and put the pictures up on the wall, the landlady is always horrified. Some want me to move out on the spot.'

He paused again. He looked around him. 'Yes, there's always trouble to start with,' said Heilbutt. 'These landladies are mostly incredibly narrow-minded. But then I convince them. One simply has to reflect that in itself nudity is the only decent state. That's how I convince them.' Another pause. 'My landlady here, for example, Mrs Witt. She was in such a state! "Put them in the chest of drawers," she said, "excite yourself with them as much as you like, but not in front of me. . .".'

Heilbutt stared earnestly at Pinneberg: 'I convinced her. You must realize, Pinneberg, that I'm a born naturist, so I said to Mrs Witt: "All right, sleep on it, and if tomorrow morning you s till want me to take the pictures down, I will. Coffee at seven please." So at seven o'clock in the morning she knocks at the door with the coffee tray, and I'm standing here, completely naked doing my morning exercises. I say to her: "Mrs Witt, look at me, look closely at me. Does it disturb you? Does it excite you? Natural nakedness is without shame, and you aren't ashamed either." She's convinced. She's stopped grumbling about them. She thinks I'm right.'

Heilbutt stared into space: 'People only need to know, Pinneberg; it hasn't been properly explained to them. You should do it too, Pinneberg, and your wife. It would be good for you both, Pinneberg.'

'My wife. . .' began Pinneberg.

But Heilbutt was unstoppable. Heilbutt, so dark, so reserved, so distinguished, had his hobby-horse like everyone else. 'Take these nudes for instance. There's not a collection like it anywhere in Berlin. There are companies that send nude photos by post,' he curled his lip, 'dozens of them, but they're no good, ugly models with ugly bodies. These that you see here were all privately taken. There are ladies here,' Heilbutt's voice grew solemn, 'from the highest society. They subscribe to our principles.' Raising his voice: 'We are free people, Pinneberg.'

'Yes, I should think so,' replied Pinneberg, embarrassed.

'Do you imagine,' whispered Heilbutt, bending very near, 'that I could stand this eternal selling, and the silly people who work with us, and the odious bosses,' he gestured towards the window, 'and all that out there, the nasty mess that Germany's in, if I didn't have this? It'd be enough to make you despair, but I know it's going to be different one day. That helps, Pinneberg. That helps. You ought to try it too, you and your wife.' But he didn't wait for an answer. He stood up and called out of the door: 'Mrs Witt, you can clear away now.'

'Books,' said Heilbutt, coming back, 'sport, theatre, girls, politics, everything the people at work do; they're just a drug; they're not the real thing. The real thing. . .'

'But. . .' began Pinneberg, but got no further as Mrs Witt came in with a tray.

'Look who's here, Mrs Witt,' said Heilbutt. 'This is my friend Pinneberg. I want to take him to our meeting this evening.'

Mrs Witt was a small round elderly lady. 'You do that, Mr Heilbutt,' she said. 'It'll be fun for the young gentleman. You needn't be nervous,' she reassured Pinneberg. 'You don't have to undress if you don't want to. I didn't undress when Mr Heilbutt took me.'

'I. . .' began Pinneberg.

'It is funny though,' Mrs Witt told him, 'when all of them are going around naked and talking to you quite naked, elderly gentlemen with beards and glasses, and you have your clothes on. Very embarrassing it is, too.'

'You see,' said Heilbutt. 'And we aren't embarrassed.'

'Well, it must be quite nice for the young gentlemen,' said plump, elderly Mrs Witt. 'I don't quite see what there is in it for the girls, but it must be a good way for the men to pick up a lady-friend. They don't have to buy a pig in a poke.'

'That's your opinion, Mrs Witt,' said Heilbutt shortly, visibly annoyed. 'If you could clear away, please.'

'You don't like me saying that, Mr Heilbutt,' pushing the dinner things together,' but it's the truth, some of them were going into the cubicles together quite openly.'

'You don't understand, Mrs Witt,' said Heilbutt. 'Good evening, Mrs Witt.'

'Good evening, gentlemen,' said Mrs Witt, going off with her tray, but stopping a moment in the doorway to say: 'Of course I don't understand it. But it's cheaper than going to the pub.' And with that she was off, leaving Heilbutt staring angrily at the brown varnished door.

'You can't blame the woman,' he said, blaming her deeply. 'She doesn't know any better. Of course, Pinneberg, of course people strike up relationships, but that happens everywhere when young people get together. It has nothing to do with our movement.' He

broke off. 'You'll see for yourself. You've got time, haven't you.
You'll come with me?'

'I'm not sure,' said Pinneberg, embarrassed. 'I have to make a
phone call first. My wife is in hospital.'

'Oh,' said Heilbutt sympathetically. Then he realized: 'Is it
happening?'

'Yes,' said Pinneberg. 'I took her in this afternoon. It'll probably be
tonight. And Heilbutt. . .' he wanted to say more, about his
unhappiness, his fears, but he couldn't bring himself to do it.

'You can telephone from the baths,' said Heilbutt. 'You don't
think your wife would have anything against it?'

'No, I don't think so. It just seems so strange, when she's lying
there in the maternity ward, the delivery room it's called, where they
give birth, and it seems to be so hard. I heard one of them shrieking,
it was awful.'

'Well, yes, no doubt it hurts,' said Heilbutt with an outsider's
sang-froid. 'But it always goes off all right. You'll both be happy to
have it behind you. And, as I said, you don't have to undress.'

WHAT PINNEBERG THINKS OF NATURISM AND
MRS NOTHNAGEL'S FEELINGS ABOUT IT

For an inexperienced man like Pinneberg an invitation like
Heilbutt's was dangerous in all sorts of ways. Not that he had ever
been particularly shy in sexual matters, on the contrary. He had
grown up in Berlin and, as Mrs Pinneberg had not long ago
reminded him, there had been those games with schoolgirls in the
sand-pit that had given such offence at the time. And then when you
grow up in the clothing business where the jokes and the models are
as free as the supply of clothes, you don't have many romantic ideas
left. Girls are girls, and men are men, and however different they are,
they all like to do it. And if they behave as if they don't, then they
have reasons which are actually nothing to do with the matter: they
want to get married, or the boss doesn't like it, or because they've got
silly ideas of some kind.

So that wasn't the source of the danger. The source of the danger

was precisely that he knew too well w
illusions about it. It was all very well
of the sort ever entered people's
Something of the sort *did* enter peop

Pinneberg had only to paint the
young girls and women running ab
and he knew what went on.

But – and this was Pinneberg's gr
have any sensations in that quarter
Lammchen. He had behind him the
disenchantments and revelations, and at least a dozen girlfriends, not
counting escapades. And then he had met Lammchen, and the joyful
and pleasant experience that had happened for the first time in the
dunes between Wiek and Lensahn had for a long time stayed just
that: something that made life happier.

Then they had got married, and they had often done what comes
so easily and naturally in marriage, and it had always been good and
pleasant and liberating, just as it had always been, but then again not
as it had always been. For out of it a commitment had emerged;
whether because Lammchen was such a wonderful woman, or
whether from the habit of marriage, but the mysteries and the
illusions had returned. And now he was on a pilgrimage to the baths
with his friend Heilbutt (whom he admired but now found just a
trifle absurd), he knew very clearly that he didn't want to feel
anything that wasn't connected with Lammchen. He belonged to
her, as she belonged to him, and he did not want any pleasure that
had not its origin and fulfilment in her; he just didn't want it.

It was on the tip of his tongue to say to Heilbutt: 'You know,
Heilbutt, I'd rather go to the hospital. I'm a bit worried.'

Just an excuse, so that he didn't look too foolish. But then, before
he could snatch a pause in Heilbutt's stream of talk, everything was
all mixed up again: his flat, the delivery room, the swimming-pool
with naked women, the nude photos, what little pointed breasts
some girls had! He used to think that was nice, but since he had
known Lammchen's full, soft bosom. . . well, it was the same story,
wasn't it, everything that she was was good, so now he was really
going to tell Heilbutt. . .

d Heilbutt.

ked up at the building and said. 'Oh, it's a normal
ght. . .'

ught we had our own. No, we aren't that rich yet.'

berg's heart was beating nineteen to the dozen, he was
lly frightened. Nothing frightening presented itself for the
moment however. A grey female sat at the ticket office and said:
'Good evening, Joachim. You're in thirty-seven.' And gave him a key
with a number.

'Thank you,' said Heilbutt. Fancy him being called Joachim,
thought Pinneberg.

'And the gentleman?' asked the female, motioning her head
towards Pinneberg.

'A guest,' replied Heilbutt. 'So you don't want to swim?'

'No,' said Pinneberg, embarrassed. 'I'd rather not today.'

'Just as you like,' said Heilbutt, smiling. 'Take a look at everything
and perhaps you'll come for a key later.'

And then the two of them went down the corridor between the
cubicles, and from the pool, invisible from here, there came the usual
laughing and splashing and cries, and there was the usual tepid
watery swimming-pool smell. It was all so normal that Pinneberg was
beginning to feel much calmer when a cubicle door open a crack and
he saw something rosy and wanted to look away. And then the
cubicle door opened and a young female person dressed in nothing at
all appeared in the doorway and said: 'Oh, there you are at last,
Achim, I thought you weren't coming again.'

'Oh no,' said Heilbutt. 'Allow me to introduce my friend
Pinneberg. Mr Pinneberg: Miss Emma Coutureau.'

Miss Coutureau inclined her head, and extended her hand to
Pinneberg like a princess. And he looked away, looked round, didn't
know where to look.

'I'm pleased to meet you,' said Miss Coutureau, who remained
stark naked. 'I'm sure you'll see we've got the right idea.'

But then Pinneberg spied a way out: a telephone booth. 'I have
to make a quick call. Excuse me,' he murmured, and dashed
off.

Heilbutt called after him: 'We're in cubicle thirty-seven.'

Pinneberg took a lot of time getting through. [...] too early to be phoning, it was only nine, but it was [...] there for the moment.

'Maybe you don't feel any desire?' he reflected. 'Perhap[...] would be to be naked too.'

And then he put in a coin and asked for Moabit 8650.

Oh God, how long it all takes! His heart began hammering agai[...] Perhaps I shall never see her again.

The nurse said: 'One moment please. I'll find out. Who's calling? Pallenberg?'

'No, Pinneberg, nurse, Pinneberg.'

'Pallenberg, that's what I said. One moment please.'

'Nurse, Pinne. . .'

But she'd already gone. And perhaps there was a Mrs Pallenberg in the maternity ward, and he might be given the wrong information, and think it had all gone off well when in reality. . .

'Are you still there, Mr Pinneberg?'

Thank heaven, a different nurse. Perhaps the one who was looking after Lammchen.

'No, it's not time yet. It could last another three or four hours. Perhaps you could call again around midnight?'

'Is it going all right? Is everything as it should be?'

'Yes, completely normal. Ring us again at midnight, Mr Pinneberg.'

He hung up. Now he had to go out again. Heilbutt was waiting for him in cubicle thirty-seven. How ever had he been mad enough to come here?

Pinneberg knocked at thirty-seven, and Heilbutt called, 'Come in'. They were sitting side by side on the little bench, and appeared really only to have been chatting; perhaps it was all in his mind, perhaps he, like Mrs Witt, was too corrupted for these things.

'So let's go,' said the naked Heilbutt, stretching. 'It's cramped in here. You've got me really warmed up, Emma.'

'And you me!' laughed Miss Coutureau.

Pinneberg followed behind them, and once again decided that it was purely and simply embarrassing.

'What news of your wife?' called Heilbutt over his shoulder, then

rs Pinneberg is in the hospital. She's

berg. 'It could last another three or

e to see everything,' said Heilbutt,

chance to get thoroughly cross with

rea. 'Not many here' was his first impression. But then he realized there were actually lots of them. A whole crowd were gathered on the diving-boards, all incredibly naked, and one by one they stepped forward and executed a leap off the board and into the pool.

'I think it would be best if you stayed here,' said Heilbutt, 'and if you want to know anything, you need only wave to me.'

And with that the two went off, leaving Pinneberg perfectly safe and unmolested in his corner. He watched what was happening on the diving-board. Heilbutt appeared to be something of a leading light, everyone greeted him, smiled and beamed at him; the shouts of 'Joachim!' reached as far as Pinneberg.

True, there were some tall, good-looking young men among them, and some very young girls, with firm sturdy bodies, but they were very much in the minority. The main contingent were dignified older gentlemen and stout women. Pinneberg could very well imagine them listening to a military band and drinking coffee; in this place they looked utterly incongruous.

'Excuse me,' said a whispering, very polite voice behind him. 'Are you a guest too?'

Pinneberg started and looked round. A very stocky lady was standing behind him, mercifully with all her clothes on, horn-rimmed glasses balancing on her hooked nose.

'Yes, I'm a guest,' he said.

'So am I,' said the lady, and introduced herself: 'My name is Nothnagel.'

'Pinneberg,' said he.

'Very interesting, isn't it?' she asked. 'So unusual.'

'Very interesting,' confirmed Pinneberg.

'Were you introduced by a. . .' she paused, and then asked, terribly discreetly,. . . 'by a girlfriend?'

'No, a man friend.'

'Oh, a man. I was introduced by a man friend too. And may I ask whether you've decided yet?' asked the lady.

'About what?'

'About joining? Whether you want to become a member?'

'No, I haven't decided.'

'Neither have I. This is the third time I've been, would you believe it? and I haven't been able to decide. At my age, it isn't so simple.'

She gave him a timid, questioning glance. Pinneberg said: 'It isn't at all easy.'

She was pleased. 'There you are, that's just what I keep saying to Max. Max is my friend. There he is, no, now you can't see him any more. . .'

But he could see Max, who turned out to be a good-looking forty-year old, tanned, upstanding and dark-haired, the very model of a go-getting businessman.

'Yes, I keep saying to Max, it's not as easy as you think, not at all, above all not for a woman.' She again looked appealingly at Pinneberg, so that he felt obliged to say: 'Yes, it's terribly difficult.'

'You see! Max is always saying: look at it from the business angle, it'll be an advantage to you to join. He's right it's benefited his business a great deal already, being a member.'

'Oh yes?' said Pinneberg politely, genuinely curious.

'Well, I can't see any reason why I shouldn't talk to you about it. Max has a carpet and curtain agency. Now business is getting worse and worse, and so he joined up here. Wherever he hears there's a big club, he joins it, and sells to the other members. Of course he gives them a respectable discount, and he says there's still enough left for him. But it's easy for Max: he's so good-looking and knows such good jokes and is such good company always. For me it's much more difficult.'

She sighed deeply.

'Are you in business too?' asked Pinneberg, looking at the poor, foolish, grey creature.

'Yes,' she said, looking confidentially up at him. 'I'm in business too, but I don't have much luck. I had a chocolate shop, it was a good business in a good situation, but I didn't have the gift for it. I had bad luck all the time. I wanted to make it look really nice once upon a time, so I got a window-dresser, fifteen marks I paid him, and he did the window for me. There were two hundred marks' worth of goods in there. I was so busy and hopeful, I thought it was bound to work, and in my enthusiasm I forgot to pull down the blinds, and the sun – it was summer – shone into the shop window. And well, I really don't know how to tell you, by the time I noticed it, all the goods had melted and run into each other. All spoiled. I sold them for ten pfennigs a pound to children. Imagine that, the most expensive chocolates, ten pfennigs a pound. What a waste!' She looked mournfully at Pinneberg, who was moved by the sad, yet ridiculous tale, and had quite forgotten about the goings-on in the baths.

'Didn't you have anyone who could have helped you a bit?' he asked.

'No, nobody. Max came later. He got me an agency in trusses, girdles and bras. It ought to have been a very good agency, but I don't sell anything. Hardly anything.'

'Well, that sort of business is difficult today,' said Pinneberg.

'Isn't it!' she agreed gratefully. 'I run about all day, upstairs and downstairs, and sometimes I don't even sell five marks' worth. 'Now,' and she tried to smile, 'that isn't so bad. People really don't have the money. But if only some of them weren't so nasty! You see,' she said warily, 'I'm Jewish. Have you noticed?'

'No. . . not particularly,' said Pinneberg, awkwardly. . .

'You see!' she said. 'People do notice. That's what I'm always saying to Max, they do notice. And I just wish that anti-semites would have a notice on their door, so that one doesn't need to bother them in the first place. It always comes like a bolt from the blue. "Take your indecent stuff out of here, you filthy old Jewess", someone said to me yesterday.'

'What a swine!' said Pinneberg, incensed.

'I have sometimes thought of leaving the Jewish faith, I'm not really practising, I eat pork and everything. But I don't feel I can do that now, when everyone has it in for the Jews.'

'You're right there!' agreed Pinneberg. 'I shouldn't do that.'

'So Max thought I ought to join up here, and I'd be able to sell a lot. He's right, too, you can see that most of the women – I'm not talking about the young girls – could do with a girdle or a bra. I know exactly what every woman here needs, I've been standing here three evenings running. Max keeps on saying: "Make up your mind, Elsa. It's money for jam." And yet I can't. Can you understand that?'

'Oh, I understand. I'm not going to decide either.'

'So you mean I shouldn't do it, in spite of the business opportunity?'

'It's difficult for me to say,' said Pinneberg, looking thoughtfully at her. 'You must know how necessary it is, and whether it's really worth it.'

'Max would be very cross if I said no. He's been so impatient with me lately, I'm afraid. . .'

But Pinneberg was suddenly alarmed in case she was going to unburden that chapter of her life onto him as well. She was a sad little grey creature to be sure, and it was far from clear what she could do with her life: in fact, as she talked he had found himself hoping desperately that he would not die soon and leave Lammchen in just such an agonizing plight. But he was quite sad enough already, and he suddenly cut her short quite rudely by saying: 'I've got to make a telephone call. Excuse me!'

And she said very politely: 'Oh please do, I didn't want to detain you.'

And Pinneberg went.

PINNEBERG IS TREATED TO A BEER, GOES TO STEAL SOME FLOWERS AND ENDS UP LYING TO HIS LAMMCHEN

Pinneberg hadn't said goodbye to Heilbutt, he didn't care whether he minded or not. He simply couldn't listen to any more of that depressed and depressing chat. He fled. He tramped all the long way from the outermost eastern district of Berlin to Alt-Moabit which was in the north-west. He might just as well walk, there was plenty of time till twelve, he could save the fare. Sometimes he thought fleetingly of

Lammchen, then of the Nothnagel woman, and then Jänecke, who would soon be head of department, because Mr Kröpelin was not in Mr Spannfuss's good books, but mostly he thought of nothing. You could just walk, and look in the shops, and the buses drove by, and the illuminated advertisements were so pretty, and once it occurred to him: what was it that Bergmann had said? 'She's only a woman. They don't understand.' What did he know, he'd never met Lammchen!

So he walked, and when he got to Alt-Moabit, it was eleven-thirty. He looked round to find the cheapest place to phone from, but then just hurried into the nearest pub and ordered a beer. He resolved to drink it very slowly and smoke two cigarettes at the same time. And then to make his phone call. By that time the half an hour till midnight would be over.

But before the beer was even on the table, he had jumped up and rushed into the telephone box. The coin was already in his hand, how it had got there he didn't know, and he asked for Moabit 8650.

A man's voice came on first, and Pinneberg asked for the maternity ward. There was a long wait, and a woman's voice asked: 'Hello? Is that Mr Pinneberg?'

'Yes. Nurse, tell me. . .'

'Twenty minutes ago. Everything went perfectly smoothly. Mother and child both doing well. Congratulations.'

'Oh, that's wonderful, nurse, thank you, nurse, thank you.'

Suddenly Pinneberg was in high good humour, the nightmare had gone, he was happy. 'Now tell me, nurse, is it a boy or a girl?'

'Sorry,' said the nurse at the other end of the line. 'I'm sorry, Mr Pinneberg, we're not allowed to.'

You could have knocked Pinneberg down with a feather. 'But why not, nurse? I'm the father, you can tell me.'

'I'm not allowed to, Mr Pinneberg. The mother has to tell the father herself.'

'Oh, I see,' said Pinneberg, feeling quite abashed by so much forethought.

'May I come over straight away?'

'Good heavens, no! The doctor's with your wife at the moment. Tomorrow morning at eight.'

And with that, after a hasty 'Goodnight, Mr Pinneberg', the nurse rang off. Johannes Pinneberg, however, stepped like a man in a dream out of the telephone kiosk, and without any idea where he was, marched right through the pub towards the street, and would have gone on if the waiter had not taken him by the arm and said: 'Listen here, young man, you haven't paid for your beer.'

At that Pinneberg woke up and said very politely 'Oh, please excuse me', sat down at his table, took a swig from the glass, and seeing the waiter still casting a baleful look at him said, 'Please excuse me. I've just heard on the phone that I'm a father.'

'Goodness me!' said the waiter. 'That's enough to scare the pants off anybody. Boy or girl?'

'Boy,' claimed Pinneberg boldly. He could hardly reveal he didn't know.

'It would be,' said the waiter. 'They cost the most. You can't get away from it.' He looked again at Pinneberg, sitting huddled in his chair and said, still uncomprehending: 'Well, just to cut the damages a bit, I'll stand you the beer.' Then Pinneberg came to himself and said: 'Not at all! Not at all!' laid down a mark and said: 'It's fine. It's just fine!' and rushed out.

The waiter stared after him, recognition finally dawning: 'He's pleased. The dimwit is actually pleased! He's got a shock coming.'

It was a three minutes' walk home, but Pinneberg went on past the cinema, past where he lived, deep in thought. He was thinking how he was going to get some flowers before eight in the morning. What do you do, when there's nowhere to buy flowers, and you have no garden to pick them from? You go out and steal them! And what better place to steal them than the public flower beds of Berlin, to which you, as a citizen, had a certain right?

And so began Pinneberg's wanderings through the hours of night: to the Grosser Stern, to Lützowplatz, to Nollendorfplatz, to Viktoria-Luise-Platz, to Prager Platz. At each of the squares he stopped and stared thoughtfully at the beds. Though it was already the middle of March not one of them had been planted out yet: quite a scandal really.

Such flowers as there were didn't add up to much. A few crocuses or a scattering of snowdrops in the grass. Was that fit for Lammchen? Pinneberg was very dissatisfied with the city of Berlin.

He continued his wanderings, through Nikolsburger Platz and on to Hindenburgpark. Then to Fehrbelliner Platz, Olivaer Platz and Savignyplatz. Nothing. Not a flower for this day of days. Finally, however, he raised his eyes from the ground and saw a clump of bushes covered with shining yellow blossom. Sprays as golden as the sun, without a green leaf; nothing but yellow flowers on the bare twigs. He didn't stop to think. He didn't even look to see whether anyone was watching. Waking from his dream, he climbed over the iron railing, went over the lawn and picked a whole armful of those golden branches. And he went back over the lawn and the railing, quite unmolested, and walked all the way home with the brilliant sprays in his hand. A kindly star must have been shining over him in his ecstasy, for he passed dozens of policemen before he climbed the ladder to his little home in Alt-Moabit. Stopping only to thrust the twigs into a can of water, he flung himself into bed with a deep sigh, and fell asleep the moment he lay down.

He had naturally forgotten to put on the alarm, but he just as naturally woke on the dot of seven, lit the fire and made his coffee, heating up his shaving water at the same time. He put on fresh underwear, made himself as clean and spruce as possible, then, whistling with all his might, at ten to eight he grabbed his flowers and marched out.

Behind his joy there had been the slight fear that the porter would object to letting him into the hospital so early, but no such obstacle arose. He simply said: 'Maternity block', and the porter answered automatically: 'Last building straight ahead!' Pinneberg smiled and the porter smiled back. It was a different sort of smile, but Pinneberg didn't notice.

He floated with his gleaming yellow bush down the asphalt path between the hospital blocks, and all the sick and dying people in them didn't concern him one jot.

Then he met a nurse again, and the nurse said: 'This way, please!' and he went through a white door and into a long room, and for a moment he had the sense of many women's faces looking at him. And then he saw them no more, for directly in front of him was Lammchen, not in a bed, but on a stretcher, with a soft melting smile all over her face, and she whispered in a faraway voice, 'Oh my Sonny!'

He bent over her very gently, and laid the stolen twigs on the coverlet, whispering 'Oh Lammchen! It's so good to see you again. Just to see you again.' She slowly reached up to him, letting fall the nightie with the funny blue rings of letters from her tired white arms. They found their way round his neck and she whispered: 'The Shrimp's here. He's really here. It's a he, Sonny.'

He suddenly noticed that he was crying, in jerky sobs, and he said angrily: 'Why haven't these women given you a bed? I'm going to kick up an almighty fuss right now.'

'There's no bed free yet,' whispered Lammchen. 'I shall get one in an hour or two.' She too was crying. 'Darling Sonny, are you very happy? You mustn't cry. It's all over now.'

'Was it bad?' he asked. 'Was it very bad? Did it make you scream?'

'It's over,' she whispered. 'I'm beginning to forget about it already. But we won't let it happen again for a while, will we? Not for quite a while.'

A nurse said from the door: 'Mr Pinneberg, come along now if you want to see your son.' And Lammchen smiled and said: 'Say hello to our Shrimp.'

He followed the nurse into a long narrow room. There were more nurses standing there looking at him, and he was not at all embarrassed that he had been crying and was still sobbing a little.

'Well young man, how does it feel to be a father?' asked a fat nurse with a deep bass voice.

'You can't ask him that yet!' said another nurse. Why! it was that golden-blonde one who had put her arm round Lammchen so kindly yesterday. 'He doesn't know, he hasn't even seen his son.'

Pinneberg nodded and laughed.

Then the door opened into a side room, and the nurse who had called him was standing on the threshold with a white bundle in her arms, and in the bundle was a very old, very red, very ugly, wrinkled face, with a pointed pear-shaped head, and it was squealing: sharply, piercingly, plaintively.

Then Pinneberg was suddenly wide awake, and all his sins came back to him, from the very earliest days: the masturbation, the little girls, that dose of clap, and how on four or five occasions he had been completely drunk.

And while the nurses were smiling at the ancient little wizened dwarf, the fear rose higher and higher. Lammchen can't have taken a proper look at him. Finally he could restrain himself no longer, and asked fearfully: 'Tell me nurse, does he really look all right? Do all new-born babies look like that?'

'Oh lord!' exclaimed the dark nurse with the bass voice. 'Now he doesn't like the look of his son! You're much too handsome for your father, little lad.'

But Pinneberg was still afraid. 'Please, nurse, was any other child born here tonight? Yes? Please show it to me, so I know how they look.'

'Would you believe it,' said the blonde nurse. 'He's got the nicest babe in the whole ward and he doesn't like him. Come here, have a look at this, young man.' And she opened the door to the side room, and went in with Pinneberg, and there, sure enough, were sixty to eighty cots with dwarfs and gnomes in them, old and wrinkled, pale or red. Pinneberg looked anxiously at them, half reassured.

'But my little boy has got such a pointed head,' he said at last, hesitantly. 'Please, nurse, that's not water on the brain, is it?'

'Water on the brain?' said the nurse, and began to laugh. 'You fathers are the limit! That's how it's meant to be: a baby's head gets pressed together when he's born, it grows out later. Now you go to your wife, but don't stay too long.'

Casting one more glance at his son, Pinneberg went to Lammchen, who beamed at him, and whispered. 'Isn't our Shrimp sweet? Isn't he beautiful?"

'Yes, he is sweet,' he whispered. 'He is beautiful!'

THE LORDS OF CREATION HAVE CHILDREN
AND LAMMCHEN EMBRACES PUTTBREESE

It was a Wednesday at the end of March. Holding a suitcase, Pinneberg walked slowly, step by step, up through Alt-Moabit, and turned into the Little Tiergarten. He ought by rights at this time to be on his way to Mandels department store, but he'd taken another day off to fetch Lammchen from the hospital. In the Little Tiergarten he put down the case once again; there was plenty of time still, he didn't have to be there till eight. He'd been up since half-past four; the room was in wonderful order, he had even waxed and polished the floor and changed the beds. It was right that everything should be bright and clean, now that a new life, a different life, was to begin. There would be a child at home. All must be sunshine from now on.

It was pretty in the Little Tiergarten now, the trees were turning green, the shrubs were green already: spring was coming early this year. Later it would be nicer still when Lammchen could take the Shrimp into the Big Tiergarten. It was farther away, but not so depressing as here, where despite the early hour unemployed people were already sitting around. Lammchen took that sort of thing so much to heart.

Up with the suitcase and onwards! Through the main door and past the fat porter, who at the word 'Maternity' answered quite automatically: 'Straight ahead, last building.'

A few taxis drove by with men sitting in them: fathers, presumably, better off than he, who could afford to pick up their wives by car.

Maternity Block. He'd been right: that was where the cars were stopping. Should he get one? He stood there with his suitcase, not knowing what to do, it wasn't a long walk home, but perhaps it was the proper thing to do, perhaps the nurses would think it was dreadful of him not to have a car.

Pinneberg stood and watched a taxi turning awkwardly into the small square, and the man called to the driver: 'It'll be a little while.'

'No,' said Pinneberg to himself, 'No, it can't be done. But it isn't right; it isn't right at all.'

He went into the hall, put down his case and waited. The men who had arrived by car had already disappeared; they were no doubt long since with their wives. Pinneberg stood and waited. If he spoke to a nurse, she said hurriedly, 'I'll be with you in an instant!' and ran off.

A feeling of bitterness began to rise up in Pinneberg. He knew he must be wrong, the nurses could have no idea who came with a car and who without. Or was that really so? Why otherwise should he have been left standing here? Was he less important than the others? Was his Lammchen less important? Oh no, what a lot of nonsense, he was an idiot to think like that, of course they didn't make exceptions! But his pleasure was gone. He stood staring gloomily into space. Thus it began and thus it would go on; it was perfectly fruitless to believe that a new, brighter, sunnier life was beginning, things would be exactly as before. He and Lammchen were used to it, but wasn't there going to be anything better for the Shrimp?

'Nurse, please!'

'In a moment. I've just got to. . .'

And she was off. Gone. Well, it didn't matter, he'd got a day off, which he would like to have spent with Lammchen. He could wait until ten or eleven. What he wanted was neither here nor there; it was of no consequence.

'Mr Pinneberg! You are Mr Pinneberg, aren't you? The case, please. Where's the key? Good. The best thing would be if you went over to the Administration Block straight away and got the papers. Meantime your wife can get dressed.'

'All right,' said Pinneberg, took his form and set off.

'They're going to give me a lot of hassle,' he thought, in his ill-temper. But he was mistaken, everything went quite smoothly. He got his papers, signed something, and was ready.

And then it was back to the corridor. The cars were still waiting. Suddenly he caught sight of Lammchen, still only partially dressed, running from one door to the next. She beamed, and waved to him: 'Hello, Sonny love!'

And she was away. 'Hello, Sonny love!' Well it was still the same old Lammchen, anyway, however rotten life might be, she still beamed and waved and called 'Hello Sonny'. And she couldn't be feeling too good either, only two days ago she'd fainted when she got up.

So he stood, and waited. There were now several men waiting, that was evidently the way it was – he hadn't been signalled out for neglect. Silly of them to have their cars wait so long, though; he wouldn't want to throw his money away like that. The fathers talked among themselves:

'It's a good thing I've got my mother-in-law at home just now. She'll do all the work for my wife,' said one man.

'We've got a maid. A woman can't do it all, with a tiny baby, and so soon after giving birth.'

'Permit me to disagree,' said a fat man with glasses, emphatically. 'It's nothing for a healthy woman to give birth. It's good for her. I said to my wife: of course I could get you some help, but it would only make you sluggish. You'll get better quicker, the more you have to do.'

'I'm not sure. . .' said another, hesitantly.

'No question! No question!' insisted the spectacle-wearer. 'I've heard that in the country they have children and then go straight out and harvest hay the next day. Any other way just makes them soft. I'm very against these hospitals. My wife's been here nine days and the doctors still didn't want to let her go. "I beg your pardon, Doctor," I said. "She's my wife, and I decide. How do you think my Germanic ancestors treated their women?" He went as red as a beetroot! You can be sure his ancestors weren't Germanic.'

'Was it a difficult birth?'

'Difficult! My dear Sir! I tell you the doctors were with my wife for five hours, they fetched the consultant at two in the morning.'

'My wife tore so badly, I can tell you they had to put in seventeen stitches.'

'My wife's rather narrow too. This is the third, but she's still narrow. Well, it does have its advantages of course. But the doctors said: "Dear lady, this time it went off all right, but next time. . ."'

Another man asked: 'Did you get a lot of printed matter to do with the baby?'

'Terrible. Nothing but a nuisance. Prospectuses for prams, baby food, stout.'

'Yes, I got a token for three bottles of stout.'

'It's supposed to be wonderful for the woman. It creates more milk.'

'I wouldn't give my wife any. It's alcoholic, isn't it?'

'What d'you mean? Stout's not alcoholic.'

'Of course it is.'

'Have you read the doctors' testimonials for it in the prospectus?'

'Oh, who pays attention to testimonials any more? My wife isn't having any stout.'

'I'm going to get my three bottles, and if my wife doesn't want them, I'll drink them. Saves buying a pint.'

The wives started coming.

A door opened here, another opened there, and they came out with oblong white parcels in their arms, three women, five women, seven women, all with a similar parcel, and all with similar rather soft melting smiles on their pale faces.

The men were silent.

They looked towards their wives. Their expressions, so confident a moment ago, became uncertain, they took a small step forward and stopped again. They had become strangers once again. All they had eyes for was their wives, and the oblong parcel in their arms. They were all very embarrassed. Then suddenly they were very loudly and noisily concerned about them. 'Well, hello. No, let me. You look wonderful! Completely recovered. Do you think I could carry him? Oh well, whatever you think. But I will take the case. Where is the case? Why's it so light? Oh, of course, you've got it all on. How's the walking going? A bit unsteady, eh? I've got a car outside. We'll fetch it. That'll be a surprise for the little chap, going by car, he's never tried it. He won't notice. Don't say that. You hear so much these days about repressed childhood memories from the very earliest time, perhaps he'll enjoy it. . .'

And meanwhile Pinneberg was standing beside his Lammchen, and all he said was: 'You're here again! I've got you back!'

'My Sonny,' she said, 'Are you happy? Were they a bad ten days? Well, it's all over and done with now. Oh, I'm so looking forward to our little home!'

'It's all ready, all in order,' said he, glowing. 'You'll see. D'you want to walk, or shall I get a cab?'

'Why a cab? I'm looking forward to walking in the fresh air. We've got time. You've got the day off, haven't you?'

'Yes, I've got today off.'

'Well then, let's go slowly. Take my arm.'

Pinneberg took her arm and they went out onto the little square in front of the Maternity Block where the cars were already clattering into action. And they went slowly, slowly, to the entrance, the cars whizzed by them, and they went step by step. 'It doesn't matter,' thought Pinneberg, 'I heard you talk. I know quite well it doesn't matter not having any money.'

Then they passed the porter, and the porter didn't even have time to say goodbye to them, as he had two people standing in front of him: a young man and a woman. It was plain from her figure what they wanted. And they heard the porter say: 'Go to Reception first, please.'

'They're just beginning,' said Pinneberg dreamily, 'And we've come through.'

It seemed quite odd that everything was going on here as before; fathers coming and waiting and ringing up and getting nervous, and then fetching their wives, every day, every hour, it was really odd. And then he looked down at Lammchen and said: 'How slim you've got! Like a pine-tree.'

'Thank heaven,' said Lammchen. 'Thank heaven. You can't imagine what it's like being without that tummy.'

'Oh, yes, I can,' he said seriously.

They stepped out through the entrance into the March sunshine and the March wind. Lammchen stopped momentarily, and looked up at the sky with the white cotton-wool clouds scurrying across, at the green of the Little Tiergarten, and at the traffic in the street. She didn't speak.

'What is it, Lammchen?' he asked.

'You know. . .' she began. And broke off. 'Oh no, nothing.'

But he persisted. 'Tell me. It was something.'

'Oh, it's silly. It's being out again. When you're in there, you don't need to worry about a thing. And now everything depends on us.' She hesitated. 'We're still very young. And we've got nobody.'

'We've got each other. And the baby,' he said.

'I know that. But you do understand?'

'Yes, I understand. It worries me too. And things aren't so easy now at Mandels. But it'll work out.'

'Of course it will.'

And then they crossed the road arm in arm and went slowly, step by step, across the Little Tiergarten. Pinneberg said: 'Give me the baby for a bit.'

'No, no, I can carry him. Why ever shouldn't I?'

'It's no trouble. Let me.'

'No. No. If you like we can sit on a bench for a little while.'

They did so, then set slowly off again.

'He's not moving at all,' said Pinneberg.

'He'll be asleep. He had a feed just before we left.'

'When does he have his next feed?'

'Every four hours.'

And then they were in Mr Puttbreese's furniture store, and the master-carpenter was there himself, watching the threesome arrive.

'Well, did it go off all right, young lady?' he asked, blinking. 'Did the old stork give you a nasty peck?'

'I'm all right, thank you,' said Lammchen.

'Now, how are we to going manage this?' asked the master-carpenter nodding towards the ladder. 'How do we get up there with the little chap? It is a boy?'

'Of course.'

'But how are we going to get up?'

'We'll manage,' said Lammchen, looking rather dubiously towards the ladder. 'I'm getting well very quickly.'

'I'll tell you what, young woman, put your arms round my neck and I'll carry you piggy-back up the ladder. Give your son to your husband. He'll get him up there safe and sound.'

'Actually it's quite impossible. . .' began Pinneberg.

'What d'you mean, impossible?' asked the master-carpenter. 'The flat, do you mean? Have you got a better one? Could you pay for a better one? If it's impossible you can move out any day. That's fine by me.'

'I didn't mean it that way,' said Pinneberg, chastened, 'but you've got to admit it's a bit difficult.'

'If you mean it's difficult for your wife to put her arms round my neck, then you're right, it is difficult,' said Puttbreese crossly.

'Come on, let's go!' said Lammchen.

And before Pinneberg could think twice about it, he was carrying the long firm parcel and Lammchen had put her arms round the neck of the tipsy old carpenter, and he gripped her gently round the thighs and said, 'If I pinch let me know and I'll let you down at once, young woman.'

'Oh yes? Half way up the ladder?' laughed Lammchen.

And clutching the ladder like grim death with one hand, his other arm round the parcel, Pinneberg clambered up behind them, one rung at a time.

Then they were in their room, alone. Puttbreese had vanished, they could hear him hammering in his storeroom, but they were here by themselves. The door was shut.

Pinneberg stood there with the warm, motionless parcel in his arms. It was bright in the room, a few splashes of sunshine lay on the polished floor.

Lammchen had flung off her coat onto the bed. With light soundless steps she moved around, and Pinneberg watched her.

She went to and fro, delicately straightening a picture-frame, patting the armchair, stroking the bed, bending momentarily over the two primulas at the window, all very softly and light-footedly. She went to the cupboard, opened the door, looked inside, shut the door. At the sink she turned on the tap and let the water run a minute, then turned the tap off again.

And suddenly she had her arm round Pinneberg's neck. 'I'm happy,' she whispered. 'I'm very happy.'

'I'm happy too,' he whispered.

They stood for a while like that, quite still, she with her arm round his neck, he holding the child. They looked out of the windows, shaded already by the green of the treetops.

'This is lovely,' said Lammchen.

'It is,' said he.

'Are you still holding the baby?' she asked. 'Lay him on my bed. I'll go and do his cot.'

She quickly put on the little woollen blanket and spread the sheet. Then she cautiously opened the parcel. 'He's asleep,' she whispered. And he too bent over the package, and there lay the Shrimp, their son. His face was rather red, he had a worried expression, and the hairs on his head had got rather lighter.

'I'm not sure,' she said doubtfully. 'I think I ought to put a dry nappy on him before he goes in the cot. He's bound to be wet.'

'D'you have to disturb him?'

'He'll get sore! I'd rather put a dry nappy on him. Wait, the r
showed me how.'

She laid a couple of squares of cloth in a triangle, and then unpeeled the parcel, very slowly. Oh heavens, how small his limbs were, they looked wasted, and his head was so enormous! Pinneberg was disturbed, there was something gruesome about the baby, but he knew he mustn't avert his eyes. That was no way to start out with your own son.

Lammchen was fiddling hurriedly with the nappy, talking under her breath: 'How was it now? Oh, why am I so clumsy?'

The little creature had opened its eyes. Eyes of a tired, faded blue. It opened its mouth and began to cry, or rather to scream, a helpless, complaining, piercing wail.

'There, he's awake!' said Pinneberg reproachfully. 'He must be cold.'

'I'll be done in a minute!' she said, trying to get the nappy firmly around him.

'Do be quick!' he urged her.

'Um. It won't do like that. There mustn't be any wrinkles or he'll get sore. How ever did it go. . .?' She tried again.

He looked on, frowning. Lammchen was very clumsy. So what you did was pull the corner through, that was easy enough, then from the other side. . .

'Let me!' he said impatiently. 'You'll never do it.'

'Oh, please do,' she said, with relief. 'If you can.'

He took hold of the nappy. It looked so easy, the tiny limbs could scarcely move. So, you laid him on it, you took hold of the two points and pulled the other one through. . .

'It's full of creases,' said Lammchen.

'Just wait, will you,' he said impatiently, and fiddled quicker. The Shrimp screamed! The small bright room re-echoed with his screeching; his little voice was extremely loud and piercing. He was getting bright red. He's got to draw breath some time, thought Pinneberg, and he couldn't refrain from looking at him, which did not assist his efforts.

'Shall I have another go?' asked Lammchen gently.

'Please!' said he. 'If you think you can manage it.'

And suddenly she had got it; it all happened quite smoothly, in the twinkling of an eye.

'We're just nervous,' she said. 'But it's easy to learn.'

In his cot the Shrimp began to screech again, staring up at the ceiling. Now he had got into his stride he looked set to continue.

'What do we do?' whispered Pinneberg.

'Nothing at all,' said Lammchen. 'Let him cry. In two hours he'll get his feed, and then he'll stop all on his own.'

'But we can't let him cry for two hours.'

'Yes we can. It's better if we do. It's good for him.'

'What about us?' Pinneberg wanted to ask. But he didn't. He went to the window and stared out. Behind his back, his son cried. Once again, things were rather different from what he had imagined. He had wanted to have a cosy breakfast with Lammchen; he'd actually laid on some nice things for it, but while the Shrimp was bawling like that. . . the whole room was full of it. He rested his head against the panes.

Lammchen was standing behind him.

'Could we walk up and down with him for a bit, or rock him?' asked Pinneberg. 'I believe I've heard that's what you do with crying babies.'

'You just start doing that!' exclaimed Lammchen indignantly. 'Then we'd never be able to do anything else but walk up and down and rock him.'

'But perhaps just for today, as it's his first day with us,' begged Pinneberg. 'We ought to make it nice for him.'

'I'm telling you,' said Lammchen emphatically. 'We're not going to start that. The nurse told me the best thing was to let him bawl himself out; the first few nights he'll cry all through the night. Probably. . .' she corrected herself, glancing at her husband. 'It can work out differently. But on no account are we to pick him up. The bawling can't hurt him. And then he realizes that crying gets him nowhere.'

'I don't know,' said Pinneberg. 'It seems a bit heartless to me.'

'But Sonny love, it's only the first two or three nights, and then everyone benefits when he begins to sleep through.' Her voice took on a seductive tone: 'The nurse said that was the only right way. But not three out of a hundred parents manage it. It would be great if we were ones that did!'

'Perhaps you're right,' he said. 'I can understand that he has to learn to sleep through the night. But during the day, like now, I could easily carry him.'

'Under no circumstances,' said Lammchen. 'Absolutely not. He doesn't know the difference between night and day.'

'You don't need to speak so loudly, that must disturb him too.'

'He can't hear anything yet!' said Lammchen triumphantly. 'In the first weeks we can make as much noise as we like.'

'I don't know about that,' said Pinneberg, quite horrified by Lammchen's views.

But things did settle down, and after a while the Shrimp stopped crying and lay still. They breakfasted as nicely as he had intended, and from time to time Pinneberg stood up and went nearer to the cot and looked at the child who was lying there with open eyes. He crept up on tiptoe. In vain Lammchen explained to him again that the child wouldn't be disturbed by anything yet, he still went on tiptoe. Then he sat down again and said to Lammchen:

'It's really nice, you know. We've got something to look forward to every day.'

'Certainly we do,' said Lammchen.

'The way he'll develop,' he said. 'When he'll first learn to speak. When do children learn to speak actually?'

'Some as early as a year.'

'Do you call that early? I'm already looking forward to telling him a story. When will he learn to walk?'

'Oh Sonny, it all happens gradually. First of all he learns to hold up his head. And then to sit. And then to crawl. And then to walk.'

'It's as I said, something new all the time. I'm glad.'

'I'm glad. You can't imagine how happy I am. Oh, Sonny!'

THE PRAM AND THE TWO HOSTILE BROTHERS.
WHEN IS THE NURSING MOTHER'S ALLOWANCE DUE?

It was three days later, on a Saturday. Pinneberg had just come home, and stood a minute by the cot looking at the sleeping Shrimp. He was now sitting at table with Lammchen eating his evening meal.

'D'you think we could go out tomorrow?' he asked. 'It's such nice weather.'

She looked doubtfully at him: 'And leave the baby here alone?'

'But you can't stay indoors until he can walk. You're looking quite pale already.'

'No,' she said, slowly. 'We must get a pram.'

'Of course,' he said. Then, cautiously: 'How much would it cost?'

She shrugged her shoulders. 'Oh, it's not only the pram. We have to have pillows and covers for it.'

Suddenly he was nervous. 'The money's running out.'

'Oh gosh, yes,' she said, echoing his alarm. Then she had an idea: 'You can claim the health insurance money now!'

'Fancy me forgetting that!' he cried. 'Of course.' He thought about it. 'I can't go there. I can't take any more time off. And the lunch-hour's too short.'

'So, write.'

'All right. I'll write to them now. Then I'll run down and put the letter in the box at the Post Office.'

'Listen,' said he, rummaging for their seldom-used writing materials. 'What d'you think, Lammchen, should I go and get a newspaper so we can see where we can get a second-hand pram? People must put ads in.'

'A second-hand pram? For the Shrimp?' she sighed.

'We have to save,' he warned.

'Well, I'll have to see the child who's been in the pram,' she declared. 'We can't put him in any old child's pram.'

'You will be able to see the child,' he said.

He sat down and wrote his letter to the Health Insurance, with his membership number, etc., and put in the discharge letter from the hospital and the note certifying that Lammchen was a nursing mother, and politely requesting that they should forthwith be sent what was due to them out of the confinement and nursing mother's allowance after deduction of the hospital charges.

After some hesitation he underlined the 'forthwith' once. Then again. And signed: 'Respectfully yours, Johannes Pinneberg.'

On Sunday they bought the newspaper and found a number of small ads for prams. Pinneberg set off, and saw a very nice pram, not far from where they lived. He reported on it to Lammchen. 'He's a conductor on a tram. But they seem very decent people. Their little boy is walking now.'

Lammchen wished to be better informed. 'What does the pram look like? Is it high or low?'

'Weell. . . It's a proper pram.'

She tried again. 'Does it have large or small wheels?'

He felt prudence was called for. 'Medium'.

'What colour is it?'

'Now that I didn't get a good look at,' he said, and as she began to laugh, defended himself by saying, 'It wasn't all that light in the kitchen.' Suddenly, he had a flash of inspiration: 'There was white lace round the hood.'

'Oh Lord!' she sighed. 'I wonder what you did notice about this pram.'

'Pardon me! It was a very good pram. For twenty-five marks.'

'I'll have to look at it myself. The type of pram that's in fashion now is low, and deep, with really small wheels.'

Just in case, he said: 'I don't think it'll matter a bit to the Shrimp whether he's pushed around on high wheels or low wheels.'

'He wants something nice,' declared Lammchen.

When the baby had had his feed and was peacefully asleep in his cot, the two prepared to go out. Lammchen stopped on the threshold, returned to look once more at the sleeping child, then went back to the door.

'Leaving him all on his own,' she said. 'Some people just don't know how lucky they are.'

'We'll be back in an hour and a half,' he comforted her. 'He'll probably sleep the whole time, and he can't move.'

'All the same,' she persisted. 'It's not easy.'

Of course the pram was the high sort that had gone out of fashion, very clean, but totally outdated.

A little fair-haired boy was standing nearby looking seriously at the pram. 'It's his pram,' said the mother.

'Twenty-five marks is a lot of money for such an old-fashioned pram,' said Lammchen.

'I can throw in the pillows,' said the woman, 'And the horse-hair mattress. That cost eight marks on its own.'

'Well. . .' said Lammchen, hesitating.

'Twenty-four marks,' said the tram-conductor, with a glance at his wife.

'It's really as good as new,' said the wife. 'And the low prams aren't nearly so practical.'

'What do you think?' asked Lammchen, still hesitating.

'Yes,' he said. 'You can't go searching about.'

'No. . .' said Lammchen. 'Well, all right then. Twenty-four marks with pillows and mattress.'

They bought the pram and took it with them at once. The little boy cried his eyes out at seeing his pram being taken away. His obvious affection for it reconciled Lammchen a little to its out-of-date appearance.

As they walked along the street, no one could tell from the look of the pram that it had only some pillows in it, it might equally well have contained a child.

Pinneberg rested his hand every so often on the side. 'Now we're a real married couple,' he said.

'Yes,' said she. 'We're going to have to leave the pram down in Puttbreese's furniture store all the time. That's a pity.'

'It is,' he said.

When Pinneberg came home on Monday evening from Mandels he asked: 'Have the Insurance sent the money?'

'Not yet,' replied Lammchen. 'It's bound to come tomorrow.'

'Yes,' he said. 'Of course it may not even be there yet.'

But on Tuesday the money still hadn't arrived, and it was coming up to the first. All his salary had gone, and there was only a fifty-mark note left out of their hundred mark reserve.

'We simply mustn't touch that,' said Lammchen. 'That's our last.'

'No,' said Pinneberg, beginning to get vexed. 'The money ought to be here by now. I'll go tomorrow lunchtime and try and speed things up.'

'Why not wait till tomorrow evening,' counselled Lammchen.

'No, I'm going at lunchtime.'

So he went. Time was short, he had to miss his midday meal in the canteen and the journey cost forty pfennigs, but he recognized that anyone who has to pay out money is not generally in so much of a

hurry as the person who is due to receive it. He didn't want to raise
the roof, just speed things up a bit.

So there he was, at the headquarters of the Health Insurance Fund.
It was one of those extraordinarily impressive head office buildings
with a porter, a giant entrance hall and artistically designed counters.

So, along came the little man Pinneberg, and entered the huge,
resplendent, luminous building, wanting his hundred marks, or
maybe it was as much as a hundred and twenty. He had no idea how
much was left over after the hospital charges had been deducted. He
stood in the mammoth hall, as small and shabby a figure as you could
wish for. Pinneberg, my dear man! Are a hundred marks really so
important to you? We deal in millions here, and your hundred marks
are of no importance to us whatever. They have no role in our
scheme of things. That's to say, they do have a role, but let's not talk
about that at the moment. True, this building was erected from the
contributions of people just as small as you, but we'd rather you
didn't think too much about that. We use your contributions exactly
as we are permitted to do by law.

It was something of a comfort to Pinneberg to see employees very
like himself sitting behind the counter: they could be his colleagues.
Otherwise he would have been quite overpowered by all this noble
wood and stone.

Pinneberg looked keenly around. Over there was the right
counter: initial P. A young man was sitting there, thankfully not
behind bars, just on the other side of the counter.

'Pinneberg,' said Pinneberg. 'Johannes. Membership number 606
867. My wife has had a baby, and I've come about the Confinement
and Nursing Mothers'. . .

The young man was busy with a card-index. He didn't have time
to look up. But he stretched out a hand and said 'Membership card.'

'Here,' said Pinneberg. 'I wrote to you. . .'

'Birth certificate,' said the young man, stretching his hand out
again.

Pinneberg said mildly: 'Excuse me, I wrote to you. I sent you the
forms I got from the hospital.'

The young man looked up. He looked at Pinneberg: 'So what
d'you want then?'

'I want to know whether it's been dealt with. Whether the money's been sent. I need it.'

'So do we all.'

Pinneberg asked, even more mildly: 'Has the money been sent to me?'

'I don't know,' said the young man. 'If you applied by post it will be dealt with by post.'

'Could you perhaps find out whether it has been dealt with?'

'Everything's dealt with promptly here.'

'But it ought to have come yesterday.'

'Why yesterday? How do you know?'

'I worked it out. If it's been dealt with promptly.'

'You worked it out! How could you know the way things are handled here? There are various sections.'

'If it's been dealt with promptly. . .'

'Everything's dealt with promptly here, you can be sure of that.'

Pinneberg said gently but firmly: 'So please could you find out whether it's been dealt with or not?'

The young man looked at Pinneberg. Pinneberg looked at the young man. Both of them were smartly dressed. Pinneberg was obliged to look respectable in his job. Both of them had washed and shaved, both had clean nails and both of them were white-collar workers.

But they were enemies, deadly enemies, because one of them was sitting behind the counter and the other was standing in front. The one wanted what he considered to be his rights; the other regarded it as an imposition.

'Lot of fuss about nothing,' grumbled the young man. But as Pinneberg continued to fix him with his eye he got up and disappeared into the background. There was a door there, and the young man went in. Pinneberg watched him go. On the door there was a sign, and Pinneberg's eyes were not good enough to be able to read the writing on it for certain, but the longer he looked, the more convinced he was that it said 'Toilets'.

Pinneberg was enraged. A yard away sat another young man, under the letter 'O'. Pinneberg would like to have asked him about the toilets, but it would have been no use. O would be just the same as P. They were on one side of the counter: he was on the other.

After a fairly long time, actually a very long time, the young man reappeared through the same door, which Pinneberg was fairly certain had 'Toilets' written on it.

Pinneberg looked eagerly at him, but the young man did not look back. He sat down, picked up Pinneberg's membership card, laid it on the counter and said: 'Dealt with.'

'The money's been sent? Yesterday or today?'

'I told you. It's been dealt with by post.'

'When, please?'

'Yesterday.'

Pinneberg looked at the young man again. It was very fishy; that had definitely been the toilets. 'If I don't find the money at home. . .' he threatened.

But the young man had finished with him. He was speaking to his opposite number, the man at 'O', about 'funny people'. Pinneberg looked at his fellow-employee once again. He'd always known that something like this would happen, but it still annoyed him. Then he looked at his watch; he'd have to be really lucky with the tram if he was going to make it back in time.

He was out of luck, of course. First of all the man on the door spotted him, then Mr Jänecke caught him as he rushed breathlessly into the department. Mr Jänecke said: 'Well now, Mr Pinneberg. Not very keen, are you?'

'I'm sorry,' panted Pinneberg. 'I've only been to the Health Insurance. About my wife's confinement.'

'My dear Pinneberg,' said Mr Jänecke firmly, 'you've been telling me about your wife's confinement for a month now. I think it's a great achievement, but next time try to find another excuse.'

And before Pinneberg could bring out a word in reply, he was off, at a stately pace, leaving Pinneberg staring after him.

But in the afternoon Pinneberg did manage at least to have a little chat with Heilbutt behind the big coat-racks. They hadn't had one for a long time, things were not as they used to be between them. There was a barrier. It must have been because Heilbutt had never had a word from Pinneberg about the evening at the baths, let alone an application to join the club. Naturally Heilbutt was too polite to act offended, but there was no longer the same camaraderie.

Pinneberg poured his heart out. First he told him about Jänecke, but at that Heilbutt only shrugged his shoulders: 'Oh, Jänecke, if you're going to take what he says to heart. . .!'

So all right, Pinneberg would stop taking what Jänecke said to heart, but those people at the Health Insurance. . .

'Charming,' said Heilbutt. 'Exactly what you'd expect from those people. First things first though: would fifty marks be a help?'

Pinneberg was moved. 'No, no, Heilbutt. Certainly not. We'll get by. It's just that we've got a right to that money. The birth was three weeks ago now.'

'I wouldn't take any action over the incident you just told me about,' said Heilbutt, thoughtfully. 'The man would just deny it. But if the money isn't there when you get home tonight, I'd complain.'

'That wouldn't help either,' said Pinneberg despondently. 'They can do what they like with us.'

'Oh no, it would be no good complaining to them. But there's a regulatory body for private insurance which they're answerable to. Wait, I'll find their address in the phone book.'

'Ah, now, if there's something like that. . .' said Pinneberg more hopefully.

'You'll see. The money'll be there in a flash.'

When Pinneberg got home to Lammchen his first inquiry was about the money.

Lammchen shrugged her shoulders. 'Nothing. But they've sent us a letter.'

He could hear that insolent voice saying 'Dealt with,' as he tore open the letter. If he had that fellow here now, he'd show him. . .!

It was a letter, plus two nice forms, but no: no money. Money takes time.

Paper. A letter. Two forms. But not the sort you could just sit down and fill in on the spot. Oh no, we aren't going to make it that easy for you. First you need a birth certificate from the town hall, for 'office use'; the ordinary certificate given out by the hospital won't do. Of course. Then you have to sign the form and fill it in properly. The questions are about things which we have in our card index already: how much you earn, when you were born and where you live, but a form is always nice.

Now comes the best part however. All the above could easily be done in a day, but now you have to produce evidence as to which health insurance funds you and your wife have belonged to in the past two years. We know that doctors incline to the opinion that women are generally pregnant for nine months only, but it's better to be safe than sorry, so please could you tell us about the past two years. Perhaps we can then offload the cost onto another establishment.

Please understand, Mr Pinneberg, that this matter cannot be resolved until the relevant documentation has been processed. Thanking you for your patience. . .

Pinneberg looked at Lammchen, and Lammchen looked at him.

'Don't get so worked up,' she said. 'They're like that.'

'Oh God,' groaned Pinneberg. 'The swine. If I could lay my hands on that fellow. . .!'

'Calm down,' said Lammchen. 'We'll write to the insurance places at once. And we'll put in stamped addressed envelopes. . .'

'Another expense!'

'And in two or three days we'll have got everything and we can send it off to them.'

Finally Pinneberg sat down and wrote. It was easy for him, because he had only his one insurance in Ducherow to write to. But Lammchen had unfortunately been with two different places in Platz. Well anyway, those people have got to write to us sometime. . .

'. . . until the relevant documentation has been processed.'

When all the letters had been written, and Lammchen was sitting there peacefully in her red and white dressing-gown, feeding the Shrimp, who drank, and drank, and drank, Pinneberg dipped his pen in the inkpot once again and in his best handwriting wrote a letter of complaint to the supervisory body for private insurance funds.

No, it wasn't exactly a letter of complaint, he wouldn't presume to go that far, more an inquiry: was the Health Insurance really within their rights to make the payment of the Confinement and Nursing Mother's Allowance dependent on the production of those forms? And was it really necessary to go back two years?

The inquiry was followed by a [...]
that I get the money soon? I nee[...]

Lammchen did not hold ou[...]
not going to put themselves o[...]

'But it's unjust!' cried Pinn[...]
has to be paid while she's nu[...]

And for once it seemed a[...]
just three days later he[...]
communication had been[...]
of which would imparted [...]

'You see!' he told Lammchen triump[...]

'Why do they need an inquiry?' asked Lammch[...]
crystal.'

'You'll see,' Pinneberg assured her.

Then followed silence. The fifty-mark note was of course broken
into, but then came pay-day, and a hundred mark note was put back
in. The money would surely come any day now.

But the money did not come, nor did the inquiry seem to have led
to any conclusions. What did come were the certificates from the
health insurance offices in Ducherow and Platz. Pinneberg put
everything together: certificates, forms, the birth certificate which
Lammchen had long since got from the town hall, and took it all to
the post office.

'I'm keen to see what happens now.'

But in reality he wasn't that keen, he had been so indignant, he
hadn't been able to sleep for anger, it had all been so useless. You
couldn't change anything, it was like banging your head against a
wall: it was never going to change.

And then the money came. Very promptly, in fact: straight after
the forms had gone in.

'You see!' he said, once again. Lammchen did see, but she preferred
not to say anything, as that only made him lose his temper. 'Now I'm
keen to see how that Supervisory Body's inquiry turned out. I'll bet
those people at the Insurance Office get torn off a strip.'

'I don't think they'll write to us again,' said Lammchen. 'After all,
we've had the money.'

And it looked as though Lammchen was right. A week went by,

n a third; it was nearly a month. From time to
: 'I don't understand these people. I told them I
, and yet they're taking all this time. There's no

t write again,' repeated Lammchen. But she was wrong
he fourth week they sent a brief, dignified letter to the
at they regarded the matter as closed since Pinneberg had
y received his money from the Insurance.

ut was that all? Pinneberg had also queried whether the Insurance
ere within their rights to demand documents that were so difficult
to get hold of.

To the Supervisory Body that was the end of it. They didn't need
to answer his questions now he had his money.

But it wasn't the end of it for the big bosses of the Health
Insurance. One of the lowliest employees at their resplendent
headquarters, a young man behind the counter in the public hall, had
already seen Pinneberg off very smartly; now they took it upon
themselves to see him off in person. They had written a letter about
this Pinneberg (job-category: salesman) to the Supervisory Body.
And that body now forwarded a copy to him.

What did it say? That his complaint was unfounded. Well, of
course they were bound to say that. But why was it unfounded?
Because this Pinneberg was a dawdler. Proof: he had received the
birth certificate from the town hall on such and such a day, yet he
sent it to the Insurance one week later. 'It is clear from the
documents who was responsible for the delay,' concluded the
Insurance.

'But they don't say a thing about wanting the papers from two
years back!' groaned Pinneberg. 'They asked for all the forms to be
sent in together and the others took that time to come!'

'You see,' said Lammchen.

'Yes, I do see!' cried Pinneberg wildly. 'They're swine. They tell
lies, they falsify things, and make us look like trouble-makers. But
now I'm going to. . .' He fell silent, pondering.

'What?' asked Lammchen.

'I am going to write again to the Supervisory Body,' he said,
solemnly. 'I'm going to tell them that as far as I'm concerned the

The inquiry was followed by a request: Could they please ensure that I get the money soon? I need it.

Lammchen did not hold out much hope for this letter. 'They're not going to put themselves out for us!'

'But it's unjust!' cried Pinneberg. 'The nursing mother's allowance has to be paid while she's nursing. Otherwise there's no sense to it.'

And for once it seemed as though he was going to gain his point: just three days later he received a postcard saying that his communication had been the subject of an inquiry, the conclusions of which would imparted to him in due course.

'You see!' he told Lammchen triumphantly.

'Why do they need an inquiry?' asked Lammchen. 'It's as clear as crystal.'

'You'll see,' Pinneberg assured her.

Then followed silence. The fifty-mark note was of course broken into, but then came pay-day, and a hundred mark note was put back in. The money would surely come any day now.

But the money did not come, nor did the inquiry seem to have led to any conclusions. What did come were the certificates from the health insurance offices in Ducherow and Platz. Pinneberg put everything together: certificates, forms, the birth certificate which Lammchen had long since got from the town hall, and took it all to the post office.

'I'm keen to see what happens now.'

But in reality he wasn't that keen, he had been so indignant, he hadn't been able to sleep for anger, it had all been so useless. You couldn't change anything, it was like banging your head against a wall: it was never going to change.

And then the money came. Very promptly, in fact: straight after the forms had gone in.

'You see!' he said, once again. Lammchen did see, but she preferred not to say anything, as that only made him lose his temper. 'Now I'm keen to see how that Supervisory Body's inquiry turned out. I'll bet those people at the Insurance Office get torn off a strip.'

'I don't think they'll write to us again,' said Lammchen. 'After all, we've had the money.'

And it looked as though Lammchen was right. A week went by,

then another week, then a third; it was nearly a month. From time to time, Pinneberg said: 'I don't understand these people. I told them I needed the money, and yet they're taking all this time. There's no sense in it.'

'They'll not write again,' repeated Lammchen. But she was wrong there. In the fourth week they sent a brief, dignified letter to the effect that they regarded the matter as closed since Pinneberg had already received his money from the Insurance.

But was that all? Pinneberg had also queried whether the Insurance were within their rights to demand documents that were so difficult to get hold of.

To the Supervisory Body that was the end of it. They didn't need to answer his questions now he had his money.

But it wasn't the end of it for the big bosses of the Health Insurance. One of the lowliest employees at their resplendent headquarters, a young man behind the counter in the public hall, had already seen Pinneberg off very smartly; now they took it upon themselves to see him off in person. They had written a letter about this Pinneberg (job-category: salesman) to the Supervisory Body. And that body now forwarded a copy to him.

What did it say? That his complaint was unfounded. Well, of course they were bound to say that. But why was it unfounded? Because this Pinneberg was a dawdler. Proof: he had received the birth certificate from the town hall on such and such a day, yet he sent it to the Insurance one week later. 'It is clear from the documents who was responsible for the delay,' concluded the Insurance.

'But they don't say a thing about wanting the papers from two years back!' groaned Pinneberg. 'They asked for all the forms to be sent in together and the others took that time to come!'

'You see,' said Lammchen.

'Yes, I do see!' cried Pinneberg wildly. 'They're swine. They tell lies, they falsify things, and make us look like trouble-makers. But now I'm going to. . .' He fell silent, pondering.

'What?' asked Lammchen.

'I am going to write again to the Supervisory Body,' he said, solemnly. 'I'm going to tell them that as far as I'm concerned the matter isn't settled, that it isn't about money, but about the way they've misrepresented the case. That that has to be put right! That we have to be treated decently, like human beings.'

'What's the point?' she asked.

'But should they be allowed to do what they like?' he asked, wildly. 'They sit there in their palaces, warm, rich, safe, and run our lives, don't they? And on top of that, are they going to be allowed to put us down and make us look like trouble-makers? I'm not going to let them get away with it. I'll defend myself. I'll do something!'

'No, there's no point,' repeated Lammchen. 'It's not worth it. Just look how worked up you are again. You have to work the whole day. They get to the office feeling perfectly rested, they've got plenty of time to sit and phone the Supervisory people. They're much closer to them than they are to you. In the end you'll just wear yourself out and they'll laugh at you.'

'But you have to do something!' he cried in despair. 'I just can't stand it any more. Do we have to take everything lying down, just let them walk all over us?'

'The only ones we can get at are the ones we don't want to get at,' said Lammchen, taking the baby out of his cot to give him his evening feed. 'I know all that from listening to father. One person on their own can't do anything. All they do is watch him jumping up and down till he's exhausted and laugh.'

'But I'd like to. . .' continued Pinneberg obstinately.

'No,' said Lammchen. 'No. Just stop.'

And she looked so angry that it took Pinneberg by surprise. He couldn't remember seeing her like that before and he quickly looked away.

But then he went to the window and looked out, muttering to himself: 'And next time I am going to vote Communist.'

But Lammchen said nothing, while the baby at her breast drank contentedly.

APRIL BRINGS FEAR BUT HEILBUTT HELPS.
WHERE IS HEILBUTT? GONE

April came in, a typical, changeable April with sun, clouds, and showers of hail, grass turning greener, daisies blooming, bushes sprouting and trees growing. At Mandels Mr Spannfuss was sprouting and growing as well, and every day stories of further economies went round the Gentlemen's Outfitting department. This usually meant one salesman doing the work of two, any emergency being covered by the recruitment of a new apprentice.

Heilbutt now regularly inquired of Pinneberg: 'How are you doing? How much?'

Pinneberg would then look away, and if Heilbutt again asked: 'Tell me how much. I have plenty in hand,' he would at last say, in great embarrassment: 'Sixty.' Or, on one occasion, 'A hundred and ten, but you mustn't. I'll get there.'

And then they wangled it that Pinneberg would come up at the very moment when Heilbutt had just sold a suit or a coat and enter it on his own sales-pad.

They had to watch out, as Jänecke was sniffing around, and Kessler was sniffing around too, eager to tell tales. But they were very careful. They waited for the moment when Kessler was at lunch, and when he once turned up they claimed that Pinneberg had saved the sale, and Heilbutt coolly offered to box Mr Kessler's ears.

But, oh, where were the days when Pinneberg had reckoned himself a good salesman? Nowadays things were different. People had definitely not been so awkward before. A big fat man came in with his wife, demanding an ulster. 'No more than twenty-five marks, young man, understand! A man who plays cards with me got one for twenty, an authentic English one in wool with a woven lining, understand!'

Pinneberg gave a wan smile. 'Perhaps the gentleman was exaggerating his bargain a bit. A genuine English ulster for twenty marks. . .'

'Listen here, young man, you aren't calling my friend a liar, are you? He's a genuine fellow, d'you understand?' The fat man became more and more worked up. 'I don't need you to cast aspersions on one of my card-playing friends, understand!'

Pinneberg tried to apologize.

Kessler gawped. Mr Jänecke lurked behind the clothes-stand to the right. But no one came to his aid. No sale. 'Why do you rub people up the wrong way?' asked Mr Jänecke mildly. 'You used to be quite different, Mr Pinneberg.' Pinneberg knew only too well that he used to be quite different. But it was Mandels' fault. Since that despicable quota system had come in, everyone had lost their nerve. At the beginning of the month it was still all right, people had money and bought this and that. Pinneberg fulfilled his quota easily and was in good spirits: 'This month I'm certainly not going to have to rely on Heilbutt.'

But then there would come the day, or even two, on which not a single buyer showed up. 'Tomorrow I'm going to have to sell three hundred marks' worth,' thought Pinneberg as he left Mandels in the evening.

'Tomorrow I'm going to have to sell three hundred marks' worth,' was his last thought after he'd given Lammchen her goodnight kiss and was lying in the darkness. It wasn't easy to go to sleep with such a thought in his mind, and it was by no means his last waking thought.

'Today I've got to sell three hundred marks' worth,' was on his mind as he woke up, drank his coffee, walked to work and entered the department. All day long: 'Three hundred marks.'

Then along would come a customer; oho, he wants a coat, eighty marks, that's a third of the quota, come along customer, make up your mind! Pinneberg produces masses of coats, tries them on him, says they all look great, and the more excited he gets (make up your mind! make up your mind!), the cooler the customer becomes. He pulls out all the stops, tries crawling: 'You've such splendid taste, sir, everything looks good on you. . .' He can tell he's becoming increasingly disagreeable, that the customer is going off him by the minute, but he can't help it. And then the customer goes away, saying: 'I'll think it over.'

And so Pinneberg would be left standing, in a state of something like collapse. He knew he'd done it all wrong, but he was driven by fear: two to provide for, it's tight enough already, if the money doesn't go round now, what would it be like if. . .?

True, things hadn't got that far yet. Heilbutt, true friend in need that he was, would come up to him without being asked and say: 'How much, Pinneberg?'

He never told him he ought to have done this or that, never told him to pull himself together, never gave him any know-all advice like Jänecke or Mr Spannfuss. He knew Pinneberg could do it, but that he just couldn't do it at the moment. Pinneberg wasn't hard. He was soft. When they squeezed him he went to pieces, turned to porridge.

It wasn't as though he had lost all courage. He pulled himself together again and again and there were good days when he was as on top of the job as he used to be, when every sale succeeded and he began to think he had overcome his fear.

But then the bosses would come along, and say something in passing like: 'Can't you put a bit more zip into your sales, Mr Pinneberg.' Or: 'Why aren't you selling any dark blue suits? Would you prefer us to keep them in the store-room?'

And then they would pass on by and say something, probably the same thing, to the next salesman. Heilbutt was quite right, you ought to pay no attention to it, it was just part of the slave-driving routine they felt obliged to keep up.

No, there was no sense in minding what they said, but could one help it? Pinneberg had sold two hundred and forty marks' worth one day, and this Mr Organizer came along and said 'You look so weary, Mr Pinneberg. You should follow the example of your counterparts over there in the States, they look as cheerful in the evening as they do in the morning. "Keep smiling" is what they say.' (He said it in English, adding a translation forthwith.) 'You can't look tired. A tired-looking salesman is no recommendation for a store.'

He strode off, leaving Pinneberg thinking how much he'd like to punch the swine in the nose. But he made his little bow and kept smiling, and his feeling of confidence was gone.

Yet he was doing comparatively well. He knew of a couple of salesmen who had been summoned to the Personnel Office and either warned, or told to do better, according to their offence.

'He's had the first injection,' the saying went. 'He'll soon be dead.' Then the fear grew, the salesman knew there would be only two more injections, then the end. Unemployed, broke, on welfare, the end.

They hadn't summoned him yet. But without Heilbutt he would long have been ripe for it. Heilbutt was a tower of strength; Heilbutt was impregnable. Heilbutt was able to say to Mr Jänecke: 'Perhaps you'd like to demonstrate the perfect sale to me one day.'

Whereupon Mr Jänecke said to him: 'Don't speak to me in that tone, Mr Heilbutt!' and went away.

And then one day Heilbutt was missing. One minute he was there, he'd sold something, then, in the middle of that April day, he was gone. No one knew where.

Jänecke did perhaps, as he didn't ask after him. And Kessler too, as he did ask after him, so emphatically and so spitefully, as to make it obvious that something out of the ordinary had occurred.

'Do you know where your friend Heilbutt has got to?' he asked Pinneberg.

'Sick,' growled Pinneberg.

'Oh, I wouldn't like to have what he's got!' smirked Kessler.

'What do you know about it then?' asked Pinneberg.

'I don't know anything. Why should I?'

'Come on, man, you tell me. . .'

Kessler was wounded. 'I don't know anything. All I heard was that he'd been called to the Personnel Office. Sacked. Get it?'

'Rubbish!' said Pinneberg, muttering 'Idiot', quite loudly after him.

Why should Heilbutt have got the sack? Why should they have got rid of their best salesman? It made no sense. Anyone rather than Heilbutt.

But next day he was still missing.

'If he isn't there tomorrow, I'll go straight from work to his place,' he told Lammchen.

'Do that,' she said.

But next day came the explanation. It was Mr Jänecke who condescended to enlighten him. 'You were friendly with that man Heilbutt?'

'Still am,' said Pinneberg combatively.

'Ah. Did you know that he had rather strange views?'

'Strange?'

'About nudism.'

'Yes,' said Pinneberg hesitantly. 'He told me about it once. Some naturist club.'

'Do you belong to it?'

'Me? no.'

'No, of course, you're married.' Mr Jänecke paused. 'We had to dismiss your friend Heilbutt. A nasty business he got into there.'

'What!' exclaimed Pinneberg hotly. 'I don't believe it.'

Mr Jänecke only smiled. 'My dear Mr Pinneberg. You don't have a very great understanding of human nature. I've often noticed that from the way you sell.' And, as a parting shot: 'Very nasty. He was having nude photos of himself sold on the street.'

'What?' shouted Pinneberg. He was, after all, a Berliner born and bred, but he'd never come across anyone having nude photos of himself sold on the street.

'But it's true,' said Mr Jänecke. 'It's to your credit that you stand by your friend. Though it doesn't say much for your knowledge of people.'

'I still don't understand,' said Pinneberg. 'Nude photos on the street?'

'We can't be seen to employ a salesman whose nude picture may have fallen into our customers' hands, even our lady customers. With such a memorable face, I ask you!' And with that Jänecke went on his way, smiling amiably at Pinneberg, presumably with the intention of encouraging him, so far as the distance between them permitted.

'So, he told you what happened to your precious Heilbutt? Pretty filthy, I think. Could never stand him myself. Big-mouthed so-and-so.'

'I liked him,' said Pinneberg loudly. 'And if you say anything like that again. . .'

No, Kessler couldn't show Pinneberg the famous nude photo in person, much as we would like to have read its effect on his face. Pinneberg got to see it in the course of the afternoon. The sensation it had created in Gentlemen's Outfitting had quickly spread far beyond the bounds of that department, the salesgirls in Silk

Stockings on the right and Cosmetics on the left were talking about it nineteen to the dozen, and the picture was doing the rounds.

It eventually reached Pinneberg, who had been racking his brains all morning to think how Heilbutt could have nude photos of himself sold on the street. But that wasn't actually it. Mr Jänecke was only partly right; it was in fact a magazine, one of those where you can't tell whether their aim is to be salacious, or to promote the natural life.

On the cover of the magazine, in an oval frame, was Heilbutt, quite unmistakably he, in warlike pose with a spear in his hand. It was an artistic amateur photo, and the subject certainly had a very handsome body – he also just as certainly had not a stitch on. It must have been very exciting for the little salesgirls, many of whom had a crush on Heilbutt, to see him so delightfully unclothed. No one's expectations can have been disappointed. But it was highly revolutionary.

'But who buys that sort of paper?' said Pinneberg to Lasch. 'It's no grounds for dismissal.'

'It'll be Kessler again, sniffed it out,' was Lasch's opinion. 'He had the magazine anyway, and he knew about it before anyone else.'

Pinneberg determined to go to Heilbutt, but not that very evening. That evening he had to talk it over with Lammchen. Pinneberg was only human, and good friends though he and Heilbutt might be, the story did titillate him rather. He bought a copy of the magazine and took it to Lammchen by way of illustration.

'Of course you must go and see him,' she said. 'And don't let anyone slander him while you're around, do you hear?'

'How d'you think he looks?' asked Pinneberg anxiously; he was a touch jealous of his friend's handsome figure.

'He's well built,' said Mrs Pinneberg. 'You're getting a little bit of a belly. And you haven't got such nice hands and feet.'

Pinneberg was embarrassed. 'D'you think so? I think he looks simply marvellous. Couldn't you fall in love with him?'

'I don't think so. Much too dark for me. And then. . .' she put her arm round his neck and smiled at him. 'I'm still in love with you.'

'Still?' he asked. 'Really?'

'Still,' she said. 'Really.'

The next evening, however, he did go to Heilbutt's. The latter was not in the least abashed. 'You heard what happened, Pinneberg? This "summary dismissal" is going to get them into hot water. I've already lodged a complaint with the industrial tribunal.'

'D'you think you'll win?'

'Bound to. I'd win even if I had given permission for them to print the picture. But I can prove that it was published without my consent. They can't hold that against me.'

'But then what? You get three months' pay and you're unemployed.'

'My dear Pinneberg, I'll find something else, and if I don't, I'll set up on my own. I'll survive. I'm not going to live on the dole.'

'I believe you. Will you take me on, if you get your own business?'

'Naturally. You'd be the first I'd ask.'

'And no quotas?'

'Absolutely no quotas! How's it going? It must be difficult. Will you manage on your own?'

'I'll have to,' said Pinneberg, with a blithe confidence he did not entirely feel. 'I'll get by. These last few days have been fine. I'm a hundred and thirty in hand.'

'There you are,' said Heilbutt. 'Perhaps it's a good thing for you that I'm out of the way.'

'No, it would be better if you were there.'

Then Johannes Pinneberg went home. It was a funny thing, but after a while there was nothing more to say to Heilbutt. He was very fond of him, he was an outstandingly decent fellow, but he wasn't, couldn't be an intimate friend. You never got really close to him.

And so he let a long time go by before looking him up again. In fact he had to be actually reminded of him, which happened when he heard them saying in the shop that Heilbutt had won his case against Mandels.

But when he got to Heilbutt's place, he found Heilbutt had moved out.

'I've no idea where to, my young sir. Probably to Dalldorf, or Wittenau they call it now. He was keen enough on the place. And would you believe it, he was still trying to persuade me into his dirty goings-on, at my age.'

Heilbutt was gone.

PINNEBERG IS ARRESTED AND JACHMANN SEES GHOSTS.
RUM WITHOUT TEA

It was evening, a beautiful bright evening in late spring, or early summer. Pinneberg had finished his day's work, he stepped out of Mandels Department Store, called 'See you tomorrow' to his colleagues and was on his way.

A hand descended on his shoulder. 'Pinneberg, you're arrested!'

'Oh, yes?' said Pinneberg, without turning a hair. 'Why's that? Good heavens, it's you, Mr Jachmann! I haven't seen you for ages!'

'That's a clear conscience for you,' said Jachmann in a melancholy tone. 'You didn't even start. Good God, how I envy you young people!'

'Steady on, Mr Jachmann,' said Pinneberg. 'What d'you mean: envy? You just try being in my shoes for three days. At Mandels. . .'

'What about Mandels? I wish I had your job. It's steady, it's secure,' said Jachmann gloomily, walking beside him at a lingering pace. 'Things are so dreary now. So, how's your wife, Romeo?'

'She's very well,' said Pinneberg. 'We've got a little boy now.'

'Good heavens! Really? A boy?' Jachmann was very surprised. 'That was quick. Can you afford it? You're lucky.'

'We can't afford it,' said Pinneberg. 'But if that was it, people like us would never have children. Now we have to manage.'

'Right,' said Jachmann, who had obviously not heard a word. 'Now listen carefully, Pinneberg. Now, we're going to look in the window of that bookshop. . .'

'And?' asked Pinneberg expectantly.

'It's a very instructive book,' said Jachmann very audibly. 'I learned a terrific amount from it.' Then, softly: 'Look to the left, unobtrusively. Unobtrusively, I said!'

'And?' asked Pinneberg again, finding it all very puzzling, and the gigantic Jachmann very much changed. 'What am I meant to be looking at?'

'The stout man in grey with glasses and bushy hair, can you see him?'

'Of course I can. He's walking that way.'

'Good,' said Jachmann. 'Keep your eye on him. And now have an ordinary sort of conversation with me. Don't name any names, especially not mine. Now talk to me!'

Pinneberg racked his brains. 'What can be going on?' he thought. 'What's Jachmann after? He's not said a word about Mother, either.'

'Come on, say something,' Jachmann urged him. 'It looks silly if we walk along without a word. It will be noticed.'

'Noticed? Who by?' thought Pinneberg, and said, 'The weather's quite nice isn't it, Mr. . .'

He'd nearly come out with his name.

'Oh, do be careful!' hissed Jachmann, then continued, loudly: 'Yes, it is really very fine.'

'But a bit of rain wouldn't do any harm,' said Pinneberg, staring intently at the back of the man in grey three paces in front. 'It's terribly dry.'

'Rain would be a good thing,' Jachmann agreed readily. 'But preferably not at the weekend.'

'No, of course not!' said Pinneberg. 'Not at the weekend.'

There his inspiration ran out and nothing more was said. Once he cast a sidelong glance at Jachmann, and reflected that he didn't look as breezily fresh as heretofore. He also noted that he too was staring intently at the grey back.

'For heaven's sake say something, Pinneberg!' said Jachmann nervously. 'You must have something to say. If I hadn't seen a person for six months I'd certainly have a tale or two to tell.'

'Now you've said my name,' stated Pinneberg. 'Where are we going, anyway?'

'To your place, where else? I'm with you, that's the point.'

'But then we ought to have turned left,' observed Pinneberg. 'I live in Alt-Moabit now.'

Jachmann got annoyed. 'So why don't you turn left?'

'I thought we were following the man in grey.'

'Oh God!' exclaimed the giant. 'You haven't a clue, have you?'

'No,' confessed Pinneberg.

'Well, go exactly the same way as if you were going home. I'll explain everything. Now talk to me.'

'We have to turn left agai

'Well do it, then,' said Jac

'We've had a little boy,' s
well. Please couldn't you just
I'm getting more and more id

'You just said my name, f
'Now he's bound to follow us.
round at least.'

Pinneberg said nothing, and
more either. They went one blo
another block further, crossed a
Pinneberg's accustomed route he

The traffic lights turned red, a

PAR

'Nothing alcoholic, Mr J
'My wife's nursing.'
'Oh, nursing. I se
And that means
a life. Must b
into the s
Aft

.... a moment.

'Can you still see him?' asked Jachmann anxiously.

'I thought I wasn't meant to. . . No, I can't see him any more. He
went straight on just now.'

'He did, did he!' said Jachmann, sounding highly relieved and
gratified. 'I must have been wrong. You see ghosts sometimes.'

'Couldn't you please tell me, Mr Jachmann?' began Pinneberg.

'No. That is, later. Of course, later. We'll go to your place first. To
your wife. It's a boy you've got, is it? Or a girl? Splendid! Terrific! Did
it all go well? Of course it would, with a woman like that! D'you
know, Pinneberg, I've never understood how your mother happened
to have a son. It must have been heaven that slipped up, not just the
condom factory. Oh, I beg your pardon. You know me. Is there a
flower-shop anywhere round here? We must pass one somewhere. Or
would your wife prefer sweets?'

'It really isn't necessary, Mr Jachmann. . .'

'I know that, young man, but I'm the one who decides.' And then
he was off! 'Flowers and chocolates. They work on every female
heart. That's to say, they don't work on your mother, but that's
another story, don't let's talk about it. Flowers and sweets. Wait, I'll
go in here.'

'You mustn't. . .'

But Jachmann had already disappeared into the sweetshop. In two
minutes he was out again. 'D'you have any idea what kind of sweets
your wife likes? Cherries in brandy?'

chmann,' said Pinneberg reproachfully.

Who's she nursing? Ah, of course, the baby.
ou can't eat cherries in brandy? I never knew. What
one of the toughest, believe you me!' He disappeared
op, still talking.
a while he came out again, sporting a hefty parcel.
Mr Jachmann!' said Pinneberg dubiously. 'What a lot. I'm not
sure my wife would want. . .'

'Why not? She doesn't have to eat them all at once. I just don't
know her taste. There are so many kinds. Now look out for a flower
shop. . .'

'Please stop, Mr Jachmann. It's quite unnecessary.'

'Unnecessary? You're too young to know. What d'you mean?'

'You don't need to bring my wife flowers as well.'

'Ah, it's the unnecessary that's needed the most. There's a joke
about that, but I won't tell it to you. You don't appreciate that kind
of thing. Aha, here's a flower shop. . .'

Jachmann stopped and thought. 'I don't want to take her cut
flowers. Too much like beheaded corpses. I'd rather take her a pot
plant. That's more her style. Is she as blonde as ever?'

'Mr Jachmann, please. . .'

But he was already off. After a lengthy interval, he returned.

'Now, a flower shop, that would be something for your wife. I
ought to set her up in one. In a good area, where the clients
appreciate being served by a beautiful woman.'

Pinneberg was embarrassed. 'Well, I don't know if you'd call my
wife beautiful. . .'

'Don't talk nonsense Pinneberg. Talk about things you understand. I wonder what you do understand? Beauty – I expect you
believe in the beauty of the movie stars; manicured flesh on the
outside, greed and stupidity on the inside?'

'I haven't been to the cinema for ages,' said Pinneberg in a
melancholy tone.

'Why not? It's essential to go to the cinema. As often as possible.
Every night if you can stand it. It builds up your self-confidence.
No one can put me down: I know they're ten times stupider than I

am. So let's go to the cinema. Straight away! This very evening! What's on? We'll have a look at the next pillar of adverts.'

'But first you were going to buy my wife a shop,' grinned Pinneberg. 'Yes, of course. Actually it's a good idea. It would earn its money back in no time. But. . .' he sighed deeply, gathered two pots of flowers and a parcel of chocolates in one arm, and linked the other through Pinneberg's. 'It's impossible, young man. I'm in shtuck. . .'

'Then you shouldn't be buying up all these shops for us!' cried Pinneberg indignantly.

'Don't talk rubbish! It's not money. I'm stinking rich. For the time being. But I am in shtuck. In other ways. I'll tell you all about it later. You and your Lamb. But I'll tell you one thing. . .' he bent to whisper in Pinneberg's ear: 'Your mother is a bad lot.'

'I've always known that,' replied Pinneberg calmly.

'Oh, you get things all wrong,' said Jachmann, withdrawing his arm. 'She's a bad lot, a real bitch, but she's a splendid woman! No, I'm afraid the flower shop isn't on for the moment.'

Pinneberg tried guesswork: 'Because of the man in grey with the fuzzy beard?'

'What? Which man in grey?' Jachmann laughed. 'Oh Pinneberg, I was pulling your leg. Didn't you know?'

'No,' said Pinneberg. 'And I don't believe you were.'

'Let's drop it then; you'll soon see. And this evening we'll all go to the cinema. No, this evening won't do, we'll just all have a cosy supper together – what have you got for supper?'

'Fried potatoes,' stated Pinneberg. 'And a bloater.'

'And what to drink?'

'Tea,' said Pinneberg.

'With rum?'

'My wife isn't drinking any alcohol.'

'Oh, of course. She's nursing. That's marriage for you. My wife doesn't drink so I don't drink. You poor wretch.'

'But I don't like rum in tea.'

'You imagine that because you're married. If you were a bachelor you'd like it. These are things that are a product of the married state. Don't tell me I've never been married. I know all about it. When I've

been living with a woman, and I've found myself getting into things
like rum without tea. . .'

'Rum without tea,' repeated Pinneberg seriously.

Jachmann didn't notice: 'Things like that, I broke it off then and
there, for ever. However much pain it caused me. So, fried potatoes
and a herring.'

'A bloater.'

'Bloater and tea. I think I'll just pop into that shop for a moment.
But this is absolutely the last.'

And he disappeared into a delicatessen.

When he reappeared, Pinneberg said emphatically: 'One more
thing, Mr Jachmann. . .'

'Oh yes?' said the giant. 'You could carry a parcel for me too while
you're about it.'

'Give it here. The Shrimp is only three months old. He can't see
anything yet or hear anything yet, he doesn't play with anything
yet. . .'

'Why are you telling me all that?'

'In case you have the idea of rushing into a toy-shop and buying
my son a teddy or a puffer-train. Because you'd find me gone when
you came outside.'

'A toy-shop. . .' said Jachmann dreamily. 'Teddy, puffer train,
you're talking just like a father! Do we pass a toy-shop?'

Pinneberg began to laugh. 'I'm going to run away, Mr Jachmann,'
he said.

'You really are a dope, Pinneberg,' sighed Jachmann. 'After all I am
your father in a manner of speaking.'

AN UNWANTED HOUSE-GUEST. JACHMANN
DISCOVERS THE GOOD, WHOLESOME THINGS

Lammchen and Jachmann greeted each other, and Jachmann
dutifully bent over the cot for a moment and remarked: 'Of course
he's a remarkably beautiful child.'

'Takes after his mother,' said Lammchen.

'Takes after his mother,' Jachmann replied.

Then Jachmann unpacked his shopping, and Lammchen, confronted with quite a large amount of fancy food, dutifully exclaimed: 'Oh Mr Jachmann, you shouldn't have!'

Then they ate and they drank (tea, but without the bloater and fried potatoes) and then Jachmann leaned back, and said comfortably, 'Now comes the best bit, the cigar.'

And with untypical vigour Lammchen responded: 'Unfortunately, the best bit's not coming. No one is allowed to smoke in here because of the Shrimp.'

'Seriously?' asked Jachmann.

'Quite seriously,' responded Lammchen firmly. But he gave such a deep sigh that she suggested: 'Why don't you do like my husband and go out and have a puff on the cinema roof for a while? I'll put a candle out for you.'

'Let's do that,' said Jachmann promptly.

The two of them promenaded up and down, Pinneberg with his cigarette, Jachmann with his cigar, both quite silent. The little candle stood on the floor, its small shimmer scarcely reaching to the dusty beams above.

Up and down. Up and down, speechlessly side by side.

And because a cigarette doesn't take as long as a cigar to smoke, Pinneberg was able to slip in and talk over the extraordinary affair with Lammchen.

'So what did he say?' asked Lammchen.

'Nothing at all. He simply came along with me.'

'Did you just happen to meet?'

'I don't know. I think he was lying in wait for me, but I'm not sure.'

'I think it's all very peculiar,' said Lammchen. 'What does he want here?'

'I haven't a clue. First of all he had this obsession that a man in grey was following him.'

'Following him, why?'

'I thought it must be the police. And he's fallen out with Mother. Perhaps it's to do with that.'

'I see,' said Lammchen. 'And he didn't say anything else?'

'Yes, he said he'd like to go to the cinema with us tomorrow evening.'

'Tomorrow evening? Does that mean he wants to stay here? He can't stay the night, we haven't got a bed for him and the oilcloth sofa's too short.'

'Of course he can't stay here. But what if he just doesn't go?'

'In half an hour,' said Lammchen firmly, 'I'm going to feed the Shrimp. And if you haven't told him by then, I will.'

'That'll be fun,' sighed Pinneberg. And he rejoined the silently pacing Jachmann outside.

After a little while Holger Jachmann carefully stamped out the last of his cigar, sighed deeply and said: 'Sometimes I quite like to reflect a while. Normally I prefer to talk, but now and then half an hour's thought does one a lot of good.'

'You're having me on,' protested Pinneberg.

'Not at all, not at all, I was thinking about what I must have been like when I was a small child.'

'And?' asked Pinneberg.

'Oh, I don't know,' said Jachmann hesitantly. 'I don't think I'm like myself at all anymore.' He whistled. 'It could be that I cocked up the whole shebang. I'm monstrously big-headed most of the time; do you know I began in service?'

Pinneberg said nothing.

The giant sighed. 'There's no point in talking about it. You're right there. Let's go in to your wife.'

They went in, and straight away Jachmann was off on his yarns again in high good spirits. 'Well, Mrs Pinneberg, this is the craziest flat in the world. I've seen a few, but nothing so crazy or so cosy as this. . . It's amazing the housing authorities allow it.'

'They don't,' said Pinneberg. 'We live here entirely unofficially.'

'Unofficially?'

'Yes, well, the flat isn't really a flat of course, it's store-rooms. The only one who knows we live here is the person who rented the store-rooms to us. Officially we live at the front with the carpenter.'

'So,' said Jachmann slowly. 'Nobody knows that you live here, not even the police?'

'Nobody,' said Pinneberg emphatically, looking at Lammchen.

'Good,' said Jachmann again, 'Very good.' And he looked round the rooms quite lovingly.

'Mr Jachmann,' said Lammchen, preparing to cast him out of Eden, 'I have to get the baby ready for bed now and feed him.'

'Good,' said Jachmann again. 'Don't let me get in your way. Then let's go to bed straight afterwards. I've run around all over the place today and I'm dreadfully tired. While you're doing that I'll make the sofa into a bed with cushions and chairs.'

The couple looked at each other. Then Pinneberg turned his back and went and drummed on the window panes, his shoulders rocking. But Lammchen said: 'Don't you dare. I'll do your bed.'

'That's all right by me,' said Jachmann. 'Then I can watch you feed him. That's something I've always wanted to see.'

With angry determination Lammchen lifted her son out of his cot and began unwrapping him.

'Come up close, Mr Jachmann,' she said. 'Have a good look.'

The Shrimp began to scream.

'Look, these are what they call nappies. They don't smell very nice.'

'I don't mind,' said Jachmann. 'I've been a soldier, and nothing or nobody ever took away my appetite for one moment.'

Lammchen's shoulders drooped. 'There's nothing to be done with you Mr Jachmann,' she sighed. 'Look, now I rub his bum with oil, with pure, best-quality olive oil.'

'Why are you doing that?'

'So that he doesn't get sore. My son has never got sore.'

'My son has never got sore,' said Jachmann dreamily. 'God, what a ring that has to it! My son has never told a lie. My son has never given me any trouble. How you deal with those nappies is a downright miracle. It must be inborn. A born mother. . .'

Lammchen laughed. 'Don't over do it. You ought to ask my husband about when we first brought him home. And now you must turn round for a moment. . .'

And while Jachmann turned obediently to the window and looked out into the night and the silent garden, where the firelight cast a glow on the gently-moving branches ('Look, it's as though they were chatting to each other, Pinneberg'), Lammchen slipped out of her dress, and slid the straps of her petticoat and vest off her shoulders. Then she wrapped herself in her dressing-gown and put the baby to her breast.

He immediately stopped crying, and with a sigh that was almost a sob, put his lips to her nipple and began to suck. Lammchen looked down at him, and drawn by the sudden silence the two men turned round and gazed silently at mother and child.

Jachmann, who could never stay silent for long, then said, 'Of course I did everything all wrong, Pinneberg. The good simple things. . . the good wholesome things. . .' he banged on his temples. 'You old fool. You old fool!'

And then they all went to bed.

JACHMANN MAKES A DISCOVERY AND THE LITTLE MAN IS KING. WE HAVE EACH OTHER AFTER ALL!

Next morning Pinneberg stood among his trousers, rather heavy in the head. It was none too easy for a newly married young man to contemplate the presence of a visitor like Jachmann in his little home, which was really only one room. He kept on thinking back to how he'd behaved that night when he brought the rent, trying to get to Lammchen's bed.

Well, all right, he had been drunk then, and yesterday evening he had been quite different: really very nice. But he was also capable of anything, and definitely not to be trusted.

The ground burned under Pinneberg's feet as he stood behind his counter. If only he were at home! But of course everything was perfectly in order when he got back. Lammchen was in high good humour; they surveyed the Shrimp, and he called out a brief 'Evening, Mr Jachmann,' in passing to their visitor, who was delving in a case at the window.

The latter replied: ''Evening, my boy. I must just. . .' He was at the door as he spoke and they heard him clattering down the ladder.

'How was he then?' asked Pinneberg.

'Very nice,' said Lammchen. 'He is very nice actually. In the morning he was very nervous, he kept talking about his cases and wanting you to fetch them from the station at the zoo.'

'What did you say?'

'I said he should ask you. He only growled. He went down the ladder three times and came right up again. He jingled his keys at the Shrimp and sang songs. And then he suddenly went.'

'He must have got over whatever was worrying him.'

'And then he came back with his cases, and since then he's been as merry as a lark. Rummaging in his stuff all the time and putting papers on the fire. Oh, and he made a discovery.'

'A discovery?'

'He can't bear to hear the Shrimp crying. He goes quite mad: oh, the poor child, at war with the world already, he can't bear it. I told him he mustn't take it to heart, the Shrimp was only hungry. Then he said I had to feed him, then and there, on the spot. And when I wouldn't, he told me off like anything: parenthood had turned our brains; all this rubbish about scientific childcare was going to our heads. Then he wanted to carry him outside for a walk; then wheel him in the pram. Picture it! Jachmann in the Little Tiergarten with a pram. And when I wouldn't have any of it, and the Shrimp continued to bawl. . .'

She broke off as the Shrimp, acting for all the world as if he had heard his name, raised his voice in a shrill and angry yell.

'There he goes! And now you can see what Jachmann discovered.'

She took a chair and placed it near the cot. And on the cot she put her smart case. And then she got the alarm-clock and put it on the case.

Pinneberg watched intently.

The alarm-clock, which was of the sturdy household variety, was now ticking right next the Shrimp's ear. Its tick was very loud, but it was nonetheless one of those background sounds that didn't impinge when the Shrimp was shrieking. At first the Shrimp simply carried on bellowing, but even he had to pause to draw breath. Then he started up again.

'He hasn't noticed it yet,' whispered Lammchen.

But perhaps he had noticed it. The next pause for breath came earlier and lasted longer. It was as if he was listening: tick-tock, tick-tock. On and on.

Then he began again. But he wasn't crying so wholeheartedly as before. He lay there, quite red from exertion, a wisp of ash-blond hair across his head, his mouth comically creased up. He looked straight ahead of him, probably unseeing, his little fingers spread on the coverlet. No doubt he had a strong desire to cry, he was hungry, there was a rumbling in his stomach, and whenever anything like that happened he cried. But there was this noise next his ear: tick-tock, tick-tock. On and on.

Not all the time though. When he cried, it went away. And when he stopped, it came back. He tried it out. He shrieked for a moment, yes, the tick-tock had gone. He made no sound, yes, the tick-tock came back. And then he stopped crying altogether, he listened. Presumably there was room for nothing else in his head but that tick-tock, tick-tock. The rumbling down below didn't reach up to his brain any more.

'It really seems to work,' whispered Pinneberg. 'What a man Jachmann is, thinking of that.'

'Are you trying out my discovery?' asked Mr Jachmann from the door. 'Does it work?'

'Seems to,' said Pinneberg. 'All that remains to be seen is for how long.'

'How's it going, young lady? Does your spouse know about our programme yet? Does he approve?'

'He hasn't heard a thing. So listen, Sonny. Mr Jachmann is inviting us out for a really grand evening. Cabaret and bar, can you imagine it! And first to the cinema.'

'Well, you've got your wish now, Lammchen,' said Pinneberg. 'You see, Mr Jachmann, Lammchen has always wanted to go out just once in style. Terrific!'

An hour later they were sitting in the cinema, in a box.

It went dark, and then:

A bedroom, two heads on the pillow, one a rosy-cheeked young woman's, breathing softly, the other a man's, rather older, looking careworn even in his sleep.

There appeared the face of an alarm-clock, set for half-past six. The man became restless, turned over and reached for the alarm-clock, still half asleep: twenty-five past. The man sighed, put the alarm back in its place, shut his eyes again.

'He sleeps till the last minute too,' said Pinneberg, disapprovingly.

At the foot of the big bed there was something white: a child's bed. A child lay in it, head on arm, mouth half open.

The alarm went off, you could see the hammer striking the bell: wildly, fiendishly, remorselessly. With one bound the man was up, throwing his legs over the side of the bed. They were thin, calf-less legs with a skimpy growth of black hair.

The audience laughed. 'Real matinée idols don't have hairs on their legs,' explained Jachmann. 'This film's bound to be a flop.'

Perhaps the woman would retrieve it though. She was certainly extremely pretty. She had sat up when the alarm went off, the cover slid back, her nightie opened a little, and in between the overlapping images of sliding coverlet and slipping nightie, there came the momentary sense of having seen her breast. A general sense of well-being, and then she pulled the bedclothes tight around her shoulders and snuggled down again.

'She's a bitch,' said Jachmann. 'The kind of woman whose cleavage you get to see in the first five minutes of the film. Oh Lord, it's all so simple.'

'She is pretty, though!' said Pinneberg.

The man had got into his trousers already. The child was sitting up in bed calling 'Daddy, Teddy!' The man gave him his teddy but now he wanted Dolly. He was in the kitchen, heating the water. He was a thin, meagre-looking man. How he rushed about! Getting Dolly for the child, laying the table for breakfast, spreading bread and butter, then once the water was hot making the tea, shaving, while all the while his wife lay rosy-faced in bed, softly breathing.

Yes, now the wife had got up, she was nice, she wasn't at all the lazy type, she took her own warm water into the bathroom. The man glanced at the clock, played with the child, poured out the tea, looked outside the door to see whether the milk had been delivered yet. It hadn't, but the newspaper had.

Now the woman was ready, she headed straight to her place at the breakfast table. They each took a page of the newspaper, a teacup, bread.

The child called from the bedroom, Dolly had fallen out of bed, the man ran to pick it up.

'This is stupid,' said Lammchen discontentedly.

'Yes, but I'd like to know what happens. It can hardly carry on like this.'

Jachmann said but a single word: 'Money.'

And lo! He was right, old film buff that he was. When the man came back, the woman had found an advert in the paper; something she wanted to buy. The argument began: where was her housekeeping money? Where was his spending money? He showed her his wallet, she showed him her purse. And the calendar on the wall said it was the seventeenth. The milk-lady knocked at the door wanting her money, the pages of the calendar turned over: eighteenth, nineteenth, twentieth, all the way to the thirty-first! The calendar rustled, the few pence that were left lay beside the empty purses, and the man sat with his head in his hand. . .

Oh, how pretty the woman became. She grew more and more lovely, she spoke gently to him, stroked his hair, pulled up his head and offered him her lips, how her eyes shone!

'What a bitch!' said Pinneberg. 'What's he supposed to do?'

The man grew excited too, he took her in his arms. The advertisement appeared then disappeared, fourteen days rustled away on the calendar, next door the child played with his teddy, which was holding Dolly, the meagre bit of money lay on the table. . . the woman sat on the man's lap. . .

Then it was all gone, and out of deepest darkness there arose the ever brightening spectacle of a bank, light streaming from the counters. There was the cashier's desk with its security grille, there lay the bundles of notes, the grille was half open but there was not a soul to be seen. Oh, those bundles full of notes, cylinders of silver and copper coins, a broken bundle of hundred-mark notes opened and spread out fan-wise.

'Money,' said Jachmann composedly. 'And people do love to see it.'

Had Pinneberg heard him? Had Lammchen heard him?

It grew dark again. . . very dark. . . for a long time. . . You could hear people breathe, deeply, in long-drawn-out sighs. Lammchen heard her Sonny's breathing, he heard hers.

The screen lit up again. The best things in life aren't shown in the cinema and the film took up the story again when the wife was quite respectable and wrapped in her dressing-gown. The husband had on his bowler-hat and was kissing the child goodbye. Then the little man went through the big city and jumped on a bus. What a hurry the people were in, how the traffic raced, got into jams, then ploughed along again. Traffic lights changing from red to green to yellow, ten thousand houses with a million windows, and people, people everywhere – and he, the little man, had nothing but a two-and-a-half-room flat at the back, with a wife and child. Nothing else.

A foolish wife, perhaps, who didn't know how to manage the money, but she was his small share of happiness, and he didn't find her foolish. And there awaiting him, with an air of inevitability, was the desk with its four ludicrously tall legs, where he must unavoidably spend his day. That was his place in the inscrutable order of things, and there was no escape.

No, of course he couldn't do it. There was a moment in which the little bank-clerk's hand hovered over the money, like a sparrowhawk over a coop full of chicks, claws spread wide open. Then the hand shut, no, they weren't claws, they were fingers. He was a little bank-clerk, not a bird of prey.

But, lo and behold, this clerk had a friend, the management trainee at the bank, who was of course the son of a real bank director. Nobody had noticed that this trainee had seen the hand turn to claws. And at coffee-break time he took his friend aside and said straight out: 'You need money.' And even though the other denied it and refused all assistance, when he got home he had his pocket full of money. He pulled it all out and laid it on the table, thinking his wife would beam with joy, but she wasn't interested in the money, she was interested in him. She drew him to the sofa, took him in her arms, asking : 'How did you do it? You did that for me? I would never have believed it of you.'

And he couldn't bring himself to tell her the real story. She loved him so much all of a sudden he just couldn't do it. He nodded in silence and gave a meaningful smile. . . She was so excited, so proud of him. . .

What a face that little actor had! That great actor. Pinneberg had seen the face that morning as it lay on the pillow of the marriage-bed, when the alarm-clock said twenty-five past, tired, lined, the face of a careworn man. And now, when the woman he loved admired him for the first time, how his face bloomed; the hangdog look was gone, happiness grew and blossomed like an immense flower radiating sunlight. You poor, little, humble-faced man, this is your lucky break. It's no longer true to say that you've only ever been a nobody. You, too, have been a king!

And now he was indeed a king: her king. Was he hungry? Did his feet hurt from standing so long? How she ran about and waited on him, he was so far above her, the man who had done this thing for her sake! He was never going to have to get up first and put the water on ever again. He was king.

The money lay forgotten on the table.

'Look at him lying there smiling,' Pinneberg whispered breathlessly to Lammchen.

'The poor man,' said Lammchen. 'It can't end well. Is he really happy? Isn't he frightened?'

'Franz Schlüter is a very gifted actor,' was Jachmann's opinion.

No, it couldn't end well. The money was not going to stay forgotten. They didn't think about it on their first spending spree, or the second. What intoxication for the woman to be able to buy everything, everything! What dread for the man, who knew where the money came from.

Then came it came to the third shopping-trip, and the money was running out. She saw a ring. . . and oh! there wasn't enough to buy it. There was a glittering mass of rings in front of them, the salesman wasn't looking, he was serving two customers. What a picture her face was as she nudged her husband: 'Take it!'

Because she believed he would do anything for her. But he was only a little bank-clerk: he couldn't do it. He didn't do it.

Again, what a picture as it dawned on her, and she said to the salesman: we'll look in again. And the man went away, small and grey by her side, and he saw his life before him, a long, endless life with the woman he loved expecting that of him. . . She sulked in silence until all at once – they were sitting in a bar, with a bottle of wine and the last of their money in front of them – all at once she turned around, glowing, flaming, and declared: 'Tomorrow you'll do it again.'

His poor grey face. And that radiant woman.

He had been planning to tell her the truth, but now he nodded his head very slowly and seriously in agreement.

How was he to go on? The management trainee couldn't go on lending him – in truth, giving him – money for ever. He said no. Then the little cashier told his friend why he had to have money, what his wife believed he had done. The trainee laughed, gave him money and said: 'I must meet this wife of yours.'

He did meet her, and what had to happen, happened: he fell in love with her, but she only had eyes for her husband, that brave, reckless man, who would do anything for her. Then the friend got jealous, and at the cabaret table where they were all sitting he told her the truth.

What a fearful moment when the little man came back from the toilet and the two were sitting at the table, and she laughed at him, she laughed insolently and contemptuously in his face.

That laugh said it all: his friend's treachery, his wife's betrayal. His face changed; his eyes widened and filled with tears, his lips trembled.

They laughed.

He stood and looked them.

He looked at her. Perhaps that would have been the moment, when everything was crashing around him, when he could have done something. But he turned round and walked stiffly on his spindly legs to the door, shoulders bowed.

'Oh, Lammchen,' said Pinneberg, clasping her tightly. 'Oh, Lammchen, it's so frightening sometimes. And we're so alone.'

Lammchen nodded slowly in agreement and said softly: 'But we're together.'

'Besides, he had his son,' she added swiftly, to console him. 'The wife certainly wouldn't take him.'

LIFE AND THE FLICKS. UNCLE KNILLI ABDUCTS
MR JACHMANN

It was actually rather a gloomy dinner that the three of them had in their eyrie. Jachmann looked thoughtfully at his two grown-up children, who had lost their appetite even for the unaccustomed luxuries of yesterday's shopping spree.

However, unusually for him, he did not comment upon it, until Lammchen had cleared the table and brought in the Shrimp, when he finally said: 'Oh, kids, kids, look at you, it's enough to make one howl. Even sensitive people shouldn't fall for kitsch like that.'

Pinneberg responded: 'We know it's not true, Mr Jachmann. There isn't a management trainee like that, and there probably isn't a little cashier with a bowler hat either. It was just the actor that got me, what's he called? Schlüter, did you say?'

Lammchen quickly backed him up: 'I know what Sonny means, and you've got to agree with him. The thing is that although it's just a film, people like us have got reason to be frightened, and it's only luck if things go right for a while. Something can always happen that we've got no means of dealing with. The wonder is that it doesn't happen more often.'

'Things are only as dangerous as you let them be,' said Jachmann. 'You don't have to let it get to you. If I'd been that cashier, I'd have simply gone home and got divorced. Then I'd have got married again, a nice young girl. I don't see what the fuss is about. And now I suggest, since the Shrimp seems to be full, and it's past eleven, that we get ourselves ready quickly, and we'll go and cheer you up.'

'I don't know,' said Pinneberg, looking questioningly at his Lammchen. 'Do we want to go out again? I've rather lost the urge.'

Lammchen also shrugged her shoulders.

Jachmann went wild. 'This is unheard-of! Staying at home to mope over hokum like that! No, we're off right now, and you, Pinneberg, clear off, pronto, and get us a taxi while your Lammchen puts on her prettiest dress.'

Pinneberg still looked doubtful, but Lammchen said, 'Go on, Sonny. There's no stopping him.'

Pinneberg went slowly, and then Jachmann did something really nice; he came rushing after him and pressed something into his hand, saying: 'Now put that away. When you go out it's always unpleasant not to have anything in your pocket. Take the bit of silver too. And remember to give your wife some; women always need a bit of small change. Don't say anything, just go and get the taxi quickly.' And then he was off again, and Pinneberg climbed slowly down the ladder thinking: 'He's a good sort really. But I'd prefer to know more about him. Which shows he's not an entirely good sort.' And in his hand he clasped the notes firmly. But once inside the car on his way back to the house he couldn't forbear opening his hand to look at them. He counted them, and said to himself: 'This just isn't on, I'd have to work a month for that. He's mad. I'm telling him right now.'

But he couldn't, as the two were already waiting, and in the car Lammchen started straight into telling him that the Shrimp had dropped off immediately, and she wasn't worried about him, well, only a little bit, and they weren't going to be out all that long, and where were they going to?'

'Listen, Mr Jachmann. . .' began Pinneberg.

But Jachmann said swiftly: 'I'm not taking you to the West End, kids. First: I'm very well known there which spoils the fun. Second: it's gone downhill badly. Now Friedrichstrasse is all laid on for tourists, and very nice, as you will see.'

Then they had a discussion about what sort of a place they wanted to go to first, and Jachmann made Lammchen's mouth water with tales of bars and cabarets and variety shows, throwing in occasional appetisers to Pinneberg. 'Half naked girls! There's something for a newly-married man. Seven beauties with nothing but a little skirt on! What do you say, Pinneberg?'

In the absence of consensus, they decided to accept Jachmann's proposal and stroll down Friedrichstrasse.

They went along in a threesome, Lammchen in the middle linking arms with her two men. They were all now in a wonderful mood, and lingered everywhere, not only outside the Variétés where they admired posters of dazzling, strangely identical-looking girls, but at almost every shop. Pinneberg found it rather boring, but for window-shopping Jachmann was the best companion in the world, able to thrill with Lammchen at the beauty of a Viennese jersey dress, and closely examine twenty-two hats one after the other to see which would suit her best.

'Let's move on a bit,' suggested Pinneberg.

'That's husbands for you!' said Jachmann. 'At first nothing's beautiful enough. Then they don't care what you wear. But I'm beginning to get thirsty. I suggest we cross here.'

They were almost across the street when a car stopped behind them and a high voice squawked: 'That you, Jachmann!?'

Jachmann turned with a start, and called out in astonishment: 'Uncle Knilli, haven't they nabbed you yet?' then broke off and said to the Pinnebergs: 'One moment, kids, I'll be straight back.'

The car had driven close up to the kerb, and Jachmann stood and conversed with the fat, sallow, eunuch-faced man inside, and when they'd had their laugh the conversation got steadily quieter and more serious.

The Pinnebergs stood and waited. Five minutes, ten minutes, they looked in a shop window, and when they'd seen everything in it they waited again.

'I think he might try to get away now,' grumbled Pinneberg. 'He called him Uncle Knilli. Jachmann does know some odd types.'

'He doesn't look at all nice,' confirmed Lammchen. 'Why's he got such a squeaky, squawky voice?'

He was about to explain it to her, when Jachmann came up and said, 'Oh kids, don't be cross. I can't make this evening. I've got to go with Uncle Knilli.'

'Must you?' asked Lammchen doubtfully. 'Mr Jachmann!'

'Business, business. But I'll be with you again tomorrow at noon at the latest. Punctually for lunch. And now just go off together! It will be nicer without me.'

'Mr Jachmann,' said Lammchen again. 'Wouldn't it be better if you stayed with us? I have a feeling. . .'

'I must. I must,' said Jachmann, preparing to get into the car. 'Go without me! Have you still got money, Pinneberg?'

'Go on, get off, Jachmann!' shouted Pinneberg.

And Jachmann murmured: 'Oh, all right. I only thought. . . So tomorrow at noon.'

The taxi was off, and Pinneberg told his Lammchen about the hundred marks or so that Jachmann had stuffed in his pocket an hour ago.

'You'll give that back to him first thing tomorrow!' declared Lammchen emphatically. 'We're going home. Or d'you want to do something?'

'I never did,' said Pinneberg. 'Tomorrow he's getting his money back.'

But it never came to that. A long, long time was to go by, and a great many things were to change in Pinneberg's life, before they were to see Mr Holger Jachmann – who intended to arrive punctually for lunch – again.

THE SHRIMP IS ILL. YOUNG FATHER, WHAT'S THE MATTER?

One night the Pinnebergs were woken by the unaccustomed strains of the baby howling.

'The Shrimp's crying,' whispered Lammchen, quite unnecessarily.

'Yes,' he said quietly, looking at the illuminated face of the alarm clock. 'It's five past three.'

They listened, then Lammchen whispered again. 'He never does this. He can't be hungry.'

'He'll stop soon,' said Pinneberg. 'Let's try to get back to sleep.'

But that turned out to be quite impossible, and after a while Lammchen said: 'Shall I put on the light? He sounds so unhappy.'

But with regard to the Shrimp, Pinneberg was a man of principle. 'Certainly not! D'you hear? Certainly not. We agreed that we wouldn't pay any attention to him if he cried at night, so he knew he had to sleep when it's dark.'

'Yes, but. . .' began Lammchen.

'Certainly not,' declared Pinneberg severely. 'If we once start doing that we may soon be getting up every night. Why did we stick it out the first few nights? He cried for much longer then.'

'It's a different kind of cry. He sounds in pain.'

'We have to hold out, Lammchen. Be sensible.'

They lay in the darkness listening to the baby crying. It went on and on without a break. Sleep was of course out of the question, but it was bound to stop soon, it must stop soon! It didn't. Pinneberg wondered whether the howls did indeed signal pain. It wasn't his angry cry, it wasn't his hungry cry. Could he be in pain. . .?

'Perhaps he's got a tummy-ache?' asked Lammchen softly.

'Why should he? And in any case, what can we do about it? Nothing.'

'I could make him some fennel tea. That always calms him down.'

Pinneberg didn't reply. It wasn't easy to do the best by the Shrimp. He had to be brought up without any mistakes, so that he would turn out a good fellow in all respects. Pinneberg thought hard.

'All right, get up and make him some fennel tea.'

But he got up almost quicker than Lammchen. He turned on the light and the baby quietened down for a moment when he saw it, but then at once recommenced howling. He was dark red.

'My little Shrimp,' said Lammchen, bending over him, then lifted the little parcel out of the cot. 'My little Shrimp, does it hurt? Show Mummy where it hurts.'

Warmed by her body, rocked in her arms, the baby became quiet. He sobbed, was silent, sobbed again and stopped.

'There you are!' cried Pinneberg triumphantly as he fiddled with the spirit stove. 'He only wanted to be picked up.' But Lammchen didn't react. She walked up and down, singing a lullaby that she had brought with her from Platz, in the dialect of that place:

> 'Lullaby, sleep in Mummy's bed,
> Or will you sleep in Dad's instead?
> Lullaby, baby, sleep.'

The baby lay still in her arms, looking up with his bright blue eyes at the ceiling, motionless.

'There, the water's hot,' said Pinneberg ungraciously. 'You brew the tea; I'd rather not get in your way.'

'Hold the baby,' said Lammchen, handing him over. He walked up and down with him, humming, while his wife made the tea and

cooled it. The baby grabbed at his father's face; otherwise he lay as
still as a mouse.

'Have you put sugar in? The tea's not too hot, is it? Let me try it
first. I think you can give it him now.'

The Shrimp had lots of sips from the spoon, and when an
occasional drop ran down the side of his mouth, his father wiped it
off seriously with the sleeve of his nightshirt. 'That's enough, now,'
he said. 'He's quite calm.'

The Shrimp was laid back in his cot. Pinneberg cast a glance at the
clock. 'Nearly four. It's high time we got back to bed if we want to
have a bit more sleep.'

The light went out. The Pinnebergs were gently dropping off.

Then they woke up. The Shrimp was crying.

It was five past four.

'There you are,' said Pinneberg crossly. 'If only we hadn't picked
him up. Now he thinks we're always going to come when he howls.'

Lammchen was Lammchen, she understood that a man who had
to sell all day under the lash of a fixed quota was bound to be touchy
and aggressive. She didn't say a word.

The Shrimp howled.

'Very nice,' said Pinneberg, waxing ironic. 'Just what I needed.
How I'm going to be fresh and ready to sell in the morning, I don't
know.' Then after a moment he burst out in a rage: 'And I'm so
behind! Damned bawling.'

Lammchen said nothing, and the Shrimp howled.

Pinneberg tossed and turned. He listened, and was confirmed in
his first impression that it was indeed the crying of a child in pain.
And of course he knew that he had been talking nonsense, and that
Lammchen knew it too, and he was angry with himself for being so
stupid. But now he hoped she would say something; she must know
he found it hard to start.

'Sonny, I thought he seemed very hot, didn't you?'

'I didn't notice,' growled Pinneberg.

'But he had such red cheeks.'

'That's from crying.'

'No, like definite round red patches. Could he be ill?'

'What could he possibly have?' asked Pinneberg. But this was nonetheless a new angle on the matter, and so he said, rather less churlishly: 'Well, put the light on. You won't be able to stick it out.'

So they put the light on, the Shrimp went for another stroll in Mummy's arms, and once again he calmed down immediately. He swallowed once, and was quiet.

'There you are,' said Pinneberg, annoyed. 'There's no such thing as pains which stop the minute you pick him up.'

'Feel his little hands, they're so hot.'

'That's nothing!' said Pinneberg ungraciously. 'They're hot because he's been screaming. Think how I'd sweat if I were bellowing like that. All my clothes would be dripping wet.'

'But his hands really are very hot. I think the Shrimp is ill.'

Pinneberg felt the baby's hands and his mood changed.

'Yes, they really are very hot. Perhaps he's got a temperature?'

'It's too silly that we haven't got a thermometer.'

'We've always been meaning to buy one but it was the money.'

'Yes,' said Lammchen. 'He has got a fever.'

'Shall we give him some more tea?' asked Pinneberg.

'No, it'll only fill up his little tummy.'

'I still can't believe he's got pains,' said Pinneberg, reverting. 'He's just putting it on, to be carried.'

'But Sonny, we never carry him.'

'Well, let's try it out. You put him in the cot, and you'll see: he'll cry.'

'But. . .'

'Lammchen, put him in the cot. Please, do me a favour, put him in. You'll see.'

Lammchen looked at her husband, then laid the baby in the cot. There was no time to turn the light out. He began crying immediately.

'There you are!' Pinneberg was jubilant. 'Now take him out, and you'll see he'll be quiet immediately.'

Lammchen took the Shrimp out of the cot again, her husband looked on expectantly; the Shrimp continued to cry.

Pinneberg stood frozen as the Shrimp continued to cry. 'That's it!' he cried. 'You've completely spoiled him by carrying him! Now what does his majesty want?'

'He's in pain,' said Lammchen softly. She rocked him, he grew quieter, then started up again. 'Sonny, do me a favour; go back to bed, perhaps you could get a bit of sleep.'

'I wouldn't dream of it!'

'Please, Sonny, do it! I'd be much calmer myself if you would. I can lie down for an hour in the morning, but you have to be fresh.'

Pinneberg looked at her. Then he patted her on the back.

'Well, Lammchen, I will lie down. But call me at once if anything happens.'

But nothing came of that idea. They lay down by turns, they carried him, they sang, they rocked him, all to no avail.

Sometimes the crying died down to a quiet whimpering, then it welled up again. The parents looked at each other across the baby.

'This is awful,' said Pinneberg.

'What pain he must be in!'

'There's no sense to it, a little thing like that in such pain!'

'And I can't help him at all!' And Lammchen suddenly called out very clear and loud, pressing the child to her: 'Oh Shrimp, my little Shrimp, can't I do anything for you?' The baby continued to cry.

'Whatever can be wrong?' murmured Pinneberg.

'It's so awful that he can't tell us! That he can't show us where it is! Little Shrimp, show Mummy where the pain is! Where is it?'

'We're stupid,' raged Pinneberg. 'We don't know anything. If we did, we might be able to help him.'

'And we don't know anyone to ask.'

'I'm going for a doctor,' said Pinneberg, beginning to dress.

'You haven't got a medical certificate.'

'He'll come without one. I'll send it in afterwards.'

'No doctor will come out at five in the morning. When they hear it's a medical-card patient, they say it can wait till tomorrow.'

'He's *got* to come!'

'Sonny love, if you bring him here to the flat, up the ladder, there'll be trouble. He might tell the police we were living here. Actually he wouldn't even come up the ladder, he'd think you were going to do something to him.'

Pinneberg sat down on the edge of the bed, and looked gloomily at Lammchen.

'Oh yes, you're right.' He nodded. 'We've got ourselves into a pretty mess, Mrs Pinneberg. A pretty mess. We never thought about this.'

'Oh come on,' said Lammchen. 'Don't be like that Sonny. It looks bleak at the moment, but it'll get better.'

'It's because we're nobody,' said Pinneberg. 'We're on our own. There are other people just like us all on their own too, everybody thinking he's someone special. If only we were workers at least! They call each other comrade and help each other. . .'

'Oh, I don't know about that,' said Lammchen. 'When I think of the kind of things father talked about, and what he's been through.'

'Well, of course,' said Pinneberg. 'I know they're not perfect either. But at least they're ready for the worst. But people like us, white-collar, we always imagine we're superior. . .'

And the Shrimp cried. And they saw through the panes that the sun was rising. It was growing quite light, and they looked at each other and saw how pale and washed-out and weary they looked.

'Oh love!' said Lammchen. 'My love!' responded Pinneberg, and they held hands.

'Things aren't all bad,' said Lammchen.

'Not so long as we have each other,' he confirmed.

And then they started walking up and down again.

'Now I don't know whether I should feed him or not,' said Lammchen. 'What if there's something wrong with his tummy?'

'Yes, what should you do?' he asked, despairingly. 'It's nearly six.'

'I know, I know,' said Lammchen, with a sudden burst of energy. 'At seven o'clock you go round to the Infant Welfare. They're only ten minutes away, and you beg them and plead with them until a nurse agrees to come back with you.'

'Yes,' said he. 'That's possible. I'll still get to work in time.'

'And we'll let him go hungry till then. A bit of hunger can't hurt him.'

At seven o'clock on the dot a pale-faced young man, with badly-knotted tie, was stumbling around the premises of the municipal Infants' Welfare. There were signs everywhere saying when the consultation times were. There definitely wasn't one now.

He stood hesitating. Lammchen was waiting, but he mustn't antagonise the nurses. What if they were still asleep? What should he do?

A lady went past him and down the stairs. She bore a passing resemblance to the Nothnagel lady he'd met at the baths: middle-aged, fat and Jewish.

'She doesn't look nice,' thought Pinneberg. 'I won't ask her. Besides she's not a nurse.'

The lady had gone down one set of stairs, then she stopped suddenly and puffed back up. She halted in front of Pinneberg and looked at him. 'Now then, young father, what's the matter?' she asked, and smiled.

This was the right one after all: she'd smiled, and called him 'young father'. Heavens, how nice she was! He suddenly realized that there were people who knew who he was and how he felt. This elderly Jewish welfare worker for instance. How many thousand fathers must have hung about on the stairs here! He found he could tell her everything, and she understood and simply nodded and said 'Yes, yes!' Then she opened the door and shouted: 'Ella! Martha! Hanna!'

Heads appeared: 'One of you go with this young father, will you? They're worried.'

And the fat lady nodded to Pinneberg and said. 'Goodbye. It probably isn't anything serious!' And then carried on down the stairs.

After a while a nurse appeared, who said: 'Let's go,' and on the way he was able to describe it all over again, and the nurse didn't seem to find it abnormal either, as she nodded and said, 'It probably isn't anything serious. We'll soon know.'

It was good to have such an experienced person, and it turned out they needn't have worried about the ladder either. The nurse simply said: 'Oho, up into the crow's nest. After you please!' and climbed up the ladder after him with her leather bag just like an old sea-dog. And then she and Lammchen conferred quietly together and looked at the Shrimp who of course now made not a sound. Once Lammchen called over to Pinneberg: 'Sonny, don't you want to be off? It's high time.'

But he only growled 'No, I'll wait now. I may have to fetch something.'

They extracted the baby from his clothes, during which he still remained perfectly quiet, they took his temperature. No, he wasn't feverish, just hot, they took him to the window and opened his mouth. He lay still, and suddenly the nurse said a word and Lammchen peered excitedly at something. And then she shouted in excitement: 'Sonny, Sonny, come here quickly! Our Shrimp has got his first tooth!'

Pinneberg came. He looked into the naked little mouth with the pale-pink gums, and, yes, where Lammchen was pointing there was a little red swelling, with something in it as sharp as a splinter of glass.

'Like a fishbone,' thought Pinneberg. 'A fishbone.'

But he didn't say so, and the two women were looking so expectantly at him, that finally he said: 'So that was why. Everything's all right then. The first tooth.'

And after a while he asked reflectively: 'How many does he have to get?'

'Twenty,' said the nurse.

'So many!' said Pinneberg. 'And will he always howl like that?' 'It depends,' said the nurse consolingly. 'They don't all cry over every tooth.'

'Ah well,' said Pinneberg. 'Now we know.' And suddenly he laughed. He was in a mood between happiness and crying, as though something great and important had happened. 'Thank you, nurse,' he said, nodding to her. 'Thank you. We haven't a clue. Lammchen, do feed him quickly. He must be hungry. I must get to work double-quick. Cheers and thanks, nurse. Goodbye, Lammchen. Good luck, Shrimp.'

And he was off.

IT MAKES NO ODDS. THE INQUISITORS AND MISS FISCHER. ANOTHER STAY OF EXECUTION, PINNEBERG!

Double-quick he went, but it was of no avail. The tram didn't come for ages. Then it came, and all the traffic lights were red, and in Pinneberg all the worries of the night disappeared and his joy that the Shrimp had a tooth and wasn't ill evaporated. And the other fear came back, and spread, and was all-consuming: 'What will Jänecke say to my coming in late?'

'Twenty-seven minutes late – Pinneberg.' The porter didn't react as he noted it down. There were always some late-comers. Some overwhelmed him with pleas. This one was merely pale.

Pinneberg compared the time on his watch: 'I make it only twenty-four.'

'Twenty-seven,' said the porter decisively. 'It makes no odds anyway: twenty-seven or twenty-four.'

He was right there.

Jänecke wasn't in the department. That was one mercy at least. The trouble wasn't going to start up at once.

But it did. Up came Mr Kessler, Pinneberg's colleague and Mandel's most devoted employee, and said: 'You're to go to Mr Lehmann in the Personnel Office straight away.'

'Yes,' said Pinneberg. 'All right.' He felt the need to say something that would show Kessler that he wasn't frightened (though he was), so he said: 'There'll be another stink. I was a bit late in.'

Kessler looked at Pinneberg and smirked, not openly, but his eyes said it all. He said not a word but just looked at him. Then he turned on his heel and marched off.

He went down to the ground floor, and crossed the courtyard. Miss Semmler, sallow and not-so-young, was there as always. She was standing at the half-open door of Mr Lehmann's room. It was obvious what she was doing. She took one step towards Pinneberg and said: 'Wait, Mr Pinneberg.'

And then she took a file, opened it, and took a step back to the door, reading the file of course.

Voices sounded from Mr Lehmann's room. Pinneberg recognized the sharp, precise one: that was Mr Spannfuss. So it wasn't just Mr Lehmann, there was Mr Spannfuss as well, and now another: Mr Jänecke's ringing tones. There was a moment's silence, then a young girl said something in a low voice. She seemed to be crying.

Pinneberg cast an angry look at the door and the Semmler woman, he cleared his throat and made a sign to her to shut the door. But she said 'Shhh!' quite shamelessly. It had brought colour to her cheeks; she had a little red flush, did Miss Semmler.

Mr Jänecke's voice could be heard saying 'So you admit, Miss Fischer, that you are having an affair with Mr Matzdorf?'

Sobs.

'You must answer us,' said Mr Jänecke, in a gently warning tone. 'How can Mr Spannfuss form an opinion when you're so obstinate and won't confess to the truth?' A pause. Then: 'And Mr Lehmann doesn't like it either.'

Miss Fischer sobbed.

'So it's true, isn't it, Miss Fischer,' Mr Jänecke asked patiently once again, 'that you are having an affair with Mr Matzdorf?'

Sobs. Silence.

'Oh come on! Come on!' Mr Jänecke shouted suddenly. 'Is this a sensible way to behave? We know everything, and it would be greatly to your advantage if you simply confessed to your misdeeds.' A short pause, and then Mr Jänecke began again. 'So tell us, what on earth d'you think you were doing?'

Miss Fischer sobbed.

'You must have thought something. As I understand it you were taken on here to sell stockings. Did you think you were hired to have affairs with the other employees?'

No reply.

'And the consequences?' piped up Mr Lehmann suddenly. 'Didn't you think of the consequences? You're only just seventeen, Miss Fischer?' Silence. Silence. Pinneberg took a step towards the door, Miss Semmler looked at him, cross, sallow, but triumphant.

'The door!' said Pinneberg furiously.

A female voice burst out from within, half sobbing, half screaming. 'But it's not an affair! I'm friendly with him, that's all. . .' the words petered out in crying.

'You're lying,' Pinneberg heard Mr Spannfuss say. 'You're lying, Miss Fischer. It says in the letter that you were coming out of a hotel. Shall we inquire at the hotel?'

'Mr Matzdorf has admitted everything!' exclaimed Mr Lehmann.

'Shut the door!' Pinneberg repeated.

'You don't give the orders round here,' responded Miss Semmler crossly.

The girl in the room cried out: 'I have never met him at work.'

'Oh come, come!' said Spannfuss.

'Certainly I haven't! Mr Matzdorf works on the fourth floor and I work on the ground floor. We can't meet.'

'What about lunch-hour?' squawked Mr Lehmann. 'Lunchtime in the canteen?'

'Not then either,' said Miss Fischer hastily. 'Certainly not. Mr Matzdorf's lunch-hour is at a quite different time from mine.'

'Ah,' said Mr Jänecke. 'Well, you certainly seem to know all about that. And no doubt you wished things had been more conveniently arranged. '

'What I do outside work is my own business!' exclaimed the girl. She seemed to have stopped crying.

'That's where you're wrong,' said Mr Spannfuss earnestly. 'Seriously wrong. Mandels feeds you and clothes you, Mandels provides the wherewithal of your very existence. It's not unreasonable to expect that you should think of Mandels first in everything you do and don't do.'

A long pause. 'You meet in a hotel. You could be seen there by a customer. It would be embarrassing for the customer and for you, and injurious for the firm. You could – I have the right to be frank with you – you could get pregnant. According to the present laws we are obliged to carry on employing you. Very injurious to the firm. The salesman is saddled with maintenance, his salary won't cover it, he's worried so he doesn't sell well. Again the firm suffers.' His tone grew more emphatic: 'What you have been doing is so against the interest of the firm of Mandels that we. . .'

Another long pause. Not a word from Miss Fischer. Then Mr Lehmann said quickly: 'Because you have offended against the interest of the firm, we are entitled, under paragraph seven of the contract of employment, to dismiss you without notice. We are making use of this right. You are herewith summarily dismissed, Miss Fischer.'

Silence. Not a sound.

'Go into the Personnel Office next door and you'll get your papers and the rest of your salary.'

'One moment!' called Mr Jänecke, and added hurriedly: 'In case you think we're being unfair to you, Mr Matzdorf is of course being summarily dismissed as well.'

Miss Semmler was at her desk as a young girl came out of Mr Lehmann's room, red-eyed, white-faced. She walked past Pinneberg. 'I have to get my papers here,' she said to Miss Semmler.

'Go in,' said Miss Semmler to Pinneberg.

And Pinneberg went in, with hammering heart. 'Now it's my turn!' he thought.

But it wasn't quite his turn yet. The gentlemen round the desk were acting as if he wasn't there.

'Does that position have to be filled again?' asked Mr Lehmann.

'We can only economize there up to a point,' said Mr Spannfuss. 'The others can cover now while business is slack. But if it livens up, we'll put in a temporary. There are enough hanging about.'

'Of course,' said Mr Lehmann.

The three looked up, and looked at Pinneberg. He took two steps forward.

'Now listen to me, Pinneberg,' said Spannfuss, in a quite different tone. Gone was the serious fatherly concern; he was merely brutal. 'Today you came in half an hour late again. I can't imagine what you're thinking of. I can only suppose you don't care a damn about Mandels and you don't mind if we know it. Well, young man, if that's how you feel about us. . .!' he made a sweeping gesture towards the door.

Pinneberg's assumption had been that they would throw him out no matter what. But suddenly here was hope, and he said in a very low and dejected voice: 'Please excuse me, Mr Spannfuss, my child was ill last night, and I went out to fetch a nurse. . .'

He looked helplessly at the three.

'Your child,' said Mr Spannfuss. 'So this time your child was ill. Four weeks ago, or was it ten?, you were constantly taking time off because of your wife. I expect in two weeks your grandmother will die, and in a month your aunt will break a leg.' He paused, then began again with renewed vigour: 'You overestimate the interest that the firm takes in your private life. Mandels isn't concerned with your private life at all. Please arrange to deal with your little problems outside business hours.'

Another pause, then: 'The firm makes your private life possible, sir! The firm comes first, second and third. After that you do what you like. We take on the burden of providing you with your daily bread. You've got to understand that. You live off us. You're punctual enough collecting your pay at the end of the month.'

He smiled a little, and the other gentlemen smiled. Pinneberg knew it would be a good thing if he smiled too, but with the best will in the world, he couldn't.

Mr Spannfuss wound up with the words: 'Now, take careful note: the next time you're late you'll be thrown out on the street without warning. Then you'll learn what it's like on the dole. Along with all the others. We understand each other, don't we, Mr Pinneberg?'

Pinneberg stared dumbly at him.

Mr Spannfuss smiled. 'Your face may speak volumes, Mr Pinneberg, but I'd still like to hear the confirmation from your own lips: we do understand each other?'

'Yes,' said Pinneberg quietly.

'Good, then you can go.'

Pinneberg went.

MRS MIA PINNEBERG AGAIN. THOSE ARE MY CASES! ARE THE POLICE COMING?

Lammchen was sitting in her little castle darning socks. The Shrimp was lying in his bed, asleep. She was feeling miserable. Sonny had been in such a bad way lately: confused, oppressed, flaring up at one moment, dumbly downcast the next. She'd wanted to give him a treat recently by serving him an egg with his fried potatoes, but when she brought it to the table he flew into a passion and asked if she took them for millionaires, and if it meant nothing to her that he was worrying himself to death.

Afterwards he had moped for days, and spoken so gently to her, his whole being begged for forgiveness. He didn't need to beg for forgiveness, they were one, nothing could come between them, a hasty word might cause unhappiness, but never endanger their marriage.

In the early days things had been very different. They were young, they were in love, there was a ray of light through everything, a gleaming vein of silver in the darkest mineshaft. Now everything was destroyed: mountains of grey rubble with here and there a gleam of light. Then more rubble. Then another gleam. They were still young, they still loved each other, more perhaps, now they were accustomed to each other. But there was a dark shadow over everything; had people like them any right to laugh? How could one really laugh in a world where captains of industry are allowed to line their own pockets and make hundreds of mistakes, whereas the little people who had always done their best were humiliated and squashed?

'A bit more justice would do no harm at all,' thought Lammchen.

This thought was interrupted by sounds of shouting outside. It was Puttbreese, arguing with a woman. Lammchen felt she knew the sharp, piercing tone of that voice, she listened; oh no, she didn't, they were probably just haggling over a cupboard down there.

But then Puttbreese called her. 'Young lady!' he shouted. 'Mrs Pinneberg!' he bellowed.

Lammchen stood up. She went across the boards to the ladder and looked down. Yes, it was that voice. Down below stood Mr Puttbreese with her mother-in-law, Mrs Pinneberg senior, and they didn't seem to be on friendly terms.

'This old girl wants to see you,' said the master-carpenter, pointing with his huge thumb, as he beat a hasty retreat. So hasty in fact, that he slammed the outer door, leaving the two of them in semi-darkness. As her eyes adjusted to it, Lammchen found she was looking down on a familiar brown suit and smart little hat, and a chalk-white fat face.

'Hello, Mama, have you come to call? Sonny's not here.'

'D'you mean to talk to me from up there? Or will you tell me how to come up to you?'

'The ladder, Mama. Right in front of you.'

'Is that the only way?'

'It's the only way, Mama.'

'Very well. Why you wanted to move out of my house I can't imagine. Well, we'll talk about that.'

The ladder was negotiated without difficulty. Mrs Pinneberg wasn't one to be put off by a thing like that. She stood on the roof of the cinema, looking up into the dark and dusty beams. 'Do you live here?'

'No, Mama. Through the door there. May I show you?' She opened the door and Mrs Pinneberg went in and looked around. 'Well, there you are, everyone knows best where they belong. I prefer Spenerstrasse.'

'Yes, Mama,' said Lammchen. Provided Sonny wasn't doing overtime, he could be here in a quarter of an hour. She needed him badly. 'Won't you take your things off, Mama?'

'No, thank you. I'm only stopping two minutes. I don't see there's much call for socializing, the way you treated me.'

'We were really sorry about that. . .' began Lammchen hesitantly.

'I wasn't,' declared Mrs Pinneberg. 'I'm not saying a word about it. But it was very thoughtless of you to leave me in the lurch suddenly like that, without any help in the house. And you've acquired a baby?'

'Yes, we've had our little boy for six months now. He's called Horst.'

'Horst! I suppose it never occurred to you to be careful.'

Lammchen looked her mother-in-law straight in the eye. She was about to tell a lie, but this time her look stayed firm. 'We could have been careful. We didn't want to.'

'Ha. Well, you must know best whether you can afford it. I consider it a bit irresponsible to bring a baby into the world with no prospects. But it's neither here nor there to me. Have a dozen if you want to!'

She went to the cot and looked angrily at the baby. Lammchen had been aware for some time now that her mother-in-law wasn't in a tractable mood. In the past she had at least been more or less polite to her, but now all she wanted was a fight. Perhaps it would be as well if Sonny didn't come too soon.

Mrs Pinneberg had finished with her inspection of the baby.

'What is it, boy or girl?'

'A boy,' said Lammchen. 'Horst.'

'Of course!' said Mrs Marie Pinneberg. 'I thought so. He looks just as unintelligent as his father. Ah well, if it gives you pleasure.'

Lammchen said nothing.

'It's no use sulking with me, child,' said Mrs Pinneberg, unbuttoning her jacket and sitting down. 'I'm only speaking my mind. Ah, there's that expensive dressing-table! It still seems to be your only bit of furniture. I sometimes think one ought to be nicer to that boy; he's really not right in the head. A dressing-table!' And she gave the unlucky object a look fit to crack the veneer.

Lammchen said nothing.

'When's Jachmann coming?' rapped out Mrs Pinneberg so sharply that Lammchen jumped, to her great satisfaction. 'You see, I can find out anything, I found your hidey-hole, I know it all. When's Jachmann coming?'

'Mr Jachmann,' said Lammchen, 'stayed a night or two here several weeks ago. Since then he hasn't been back.'

'Is that so?' sneered Mrs Pinneberg. 'And where is he now?'

'I don't know,' said Lammchen.

'Oh, you don't?' said Mrs Pinneberg, slowly but inexorably gathering steam. She took off her jacket. 'How much does he pay you to keep your mouths shut?'

'I won't answer any such question,' said Lammchen.

'I'm going to send the police round here, my dear child,' said Mrs Pinneberg. 'They'll soon get it out of you. I suppose that card-sharp, that con-man, has told you that he's on the wanted-list, or did he say he was staying here for love of you?'

Lammchen Pinneberg stood and stared out of the window. No, it would be better if Sonny did come soon. She wouldn't be able to throw his mother out; he would.

'You'll soon see what kind of trouble he's got you into. He has to deceive everybody. What he's done to me. . .'

Her voice had taken on another tone.

'I haven't seen Mr Jachmann for over two months,' said Lammchen.

'Lammchen,' said Mrs Pinneberg, 'Lammchen, if you know where he is, tell me, Lammchen!' She paused. 'Lammchen, please tell me: where is he?'

Lammchen looked around and then at her mother-in-law. 'I don't know. I really don't know, Mama!'

The two looked at each other.

'Well, all right then,' said Mrs Pinneberg. 'I'll believe you. I believe you, Lammchen. Did he really only stay here two nights?'

'I think it was only one,' said Lammchen.

'What did he say about me? Tell me, did he speak very badly of me?'

'He didn't say anything,' said Lammchen. 'He didn't speak to me about you at all.'

'Oh,' said her mother-in-law. 'Not a word.' She stared into space. 'Your son's a pretty little boy actually. Can he talk yet?'

'At six months, Mama?'

'No? Don't they talk at that age? I've forgotten it all. I never knew it properly. But. . .' Then she paused. It was a long pause, and it grew longer and longer, weighted with something terrible: rage, fear, menace.

'There!' she said, pointing to the cases which were on top of the wardrobe. 'I know those cases. They're Jachmann's. They're his cases. You liar. You blond, blue-eyed liar, and I believed you! Where is he? When's he coming? You've taken him for yourself, and that dish-rag of a Hans knows all about it. Liar!'

Lammchen was dumbfounded. 'Mama!'

'Those are my cases. He owes me hundreds, thousands, those cases belong to me. He'll soon come if I've got them.'

She pulled a chair up to the wardrobe.

'Mama,' said Lammchen nervously, trying to stop her.

'Will you leave me alone? Leave me alone this instant! Those are my cases!'

She stood on the chair, and pulled on the handle of the first case, but the cornice of the wardrobe was in the way.

'He left the cases behind!' cried Lammchen.

She didn't hear. She pulled. The cornice broke off and the case came down. She could not support its weight and it fell, crashing against the cot. The Shrimp began to scream.

'Leave that alone at once!' shouted Lammchen, with blazing eyes, rushing to her child. 'I'll throw you out.'

'They're my cases!' cried her mother-in-law, pulling at the second one. Lammchen held the crying child in her arms, and forced herself to calm down. He was due for his next feed in half an hour, and she must not get agitated.

'Leave the cases, Mama!' she said. 'They don't belong to you. They have to stay here.'

And to the little boy she hummed:

> 'Lullaby, sleep in Mummy's bed,
> Or will you sleep in Dad's instead?
> Lullaby, baby, sleep.'

'Leave the cases alone, Mama,' she repeated loudly.

'He'll be pleased when he gets back to you tonight.'

The second case fell.

'Ah, there he is now!'

She turned around to face the door as it opened.

However, it was not Jachmann but Pinneberg whom she saw.

'What's going on here?' he asked quietly.

'Mama wants to take Mr Jachmann's cases. She says they belong to her. Mr Jachmann owes her money.'

'Mama can work that out with Jachmann himself, the cases stay here,' said Pinneberg, with a self-control that filled Lammchen with unwonted admiration.

'I knew it,' said Mrs Pinneberg. 'You'd stand up for your wife whatever! You Pinnebergs have always been like that: ninnies. Aren't you ashamed to be such a weakling?'

'Sonny, my love,' implored Lammchen.

But it wasn't necessary. 'It's time for you to go, Mama,' said Pinneberg. 'No, just leave the cases where they are. D'you seriously believe you'll get them down the ladder without me? Now, get moving. D'you want to say goodbye to my wife? You don't have to.'

'I'll set the police on you.'

'Be careful, Mama, mind the doorstep.'

The door banged shut, Lammchen listened to the receding noise, sang 'Lullaby'. 'I hope it hasn't spoiled my milk.'

She bared her breast, the Shrimp smiled and pursed his lips.

He was already feeding when Sonny came back. 'There, she's gone. I wonder if she will send the police? Tell me what happened.'

'You were splendid, Sonny my love,' said Lammchen. 'I'd never have thought it of you. Such self-control!'

Now he was being praised for a real achievement, he was embarrassed. 'Oh no. Go on, tell me what happened.'

And she told him.

'It is possible the police are after Jachmann. I think that bit's true. But if so, Mama will be in it as well. So she's not going to send the police. They would have been here by now anyway.'

The Pinnebergs sat and waited. The baby had his feed, was laid in his cot and went to sleep.

Pinneberg put the suitcases back on top of the wardrobe, got some wood-glue from the master carpenter, and stuck the cornice back on. Lammchen made the evening meal.

And no police came.

SCHLÜTER THE ACTOR, AND THE YOUNG MAN FROM ACKERSTRASSE. IT'S ALL OVER

On the twenty-ninth of September Pinneberg was standing behind his counter in Mandels' Department Store. Today was the twenty-ninth of September and tomorrow was the thirtieth, and there was no thirty-first. Pinneberg was doing some calculations, with a grey and gloomy face. From time to time he took from his pocket a slip of paper on which he had written down his daily takings, looked at it and did some adding-up. There wasn't much to add up. The total remained immutably the same: by the end of tomorrow he would have to have sold five hundred and twenty three and a half marks' worth in order to fulfil his quota.

It was impossible, but of course he had to fulfil it, or what was to become of Lammchen and the child? It was impossible, but when facts are immutable, one hopes for miracles. It was just like in the dim distant past when nasty old Heinemann was giving back their French homework, and Johannes Pinneberg the schoolboy prayed under his desk: 'Oh God, make me only have three mistakes!' (And he knew of seven for certain.)

The salesman Johannes Pinneberg prayed: 'Oh God, make someone come in who wants a set of tails. And an evening coat. And. . . and. . .'

Colleague Kessler sidled up: 'Now then Pinneberg, how are your accounts?'

Pinneberg didn't look up. 'All right, thanks.'

'Really?' drawled Kessler. 'I'm pleased to hear it. Because Jänecke told me when you bungled a sale yesterday that you were very behind and he was going to get rid of you.'

Pinneberg said: 'Thanks for nothing. I'm all right. Jänecke was probably only saying that to spur you on. How are you doing then?'

'Oh, I'm there for this month. That's why I asked you. I wanted to make you an offer.'

Pinneberg stood silent. He hated this man Kessler, this smarmy self-important creep. He hated him so much that even now he couldn't say a word to him, even to ask a favour. After a long pause he said: 'Well, you're home and dry, then.'

'Yes, I don't need to bother now. I needn't sell anything for the next two days,' said Kessler proudly, giving Pinneberg a superior look.

And perhaps, perhaps, Pinneberg might have opened his mouth and asked for help, but at that moment a gentleman came up.

'Could you show me a smoking-jacket, please? Something really warm and practical. It doesn't matter too much about the price, but I don't want a showy colour.'

The man, who was elderly, had looked at both salesman, Pinneberg thought, in fact, that he had looked more at him. So he said 'Of course. If you would. . .'

But colleague Kessler pushed in between. 'If you will come this way, sir. We've got some very nice smoking-jackets in thick wool with a discreet all-over pattern. Let me. . .'

Pinneberg watched them go, thinking to himself: 'Kessler's reached his quota but he still snaffles my customers. But it would have been thirty marks more for me, Kessler.'

Mr Jänecke passed by: 'Not busy? It's getting to be a habit with you. All the others are selling. Anyone would think you were looking forward to the dole.'

Pinneberg looked at Mr Jänecke. It should have been an angry look, but he was so helpless, so cast down, he felt the tears come into his eyes as he whispered: 'Mr Jänecke. . . Oh, Mr Jänecke. . .'

A strange thing then happened, Mr Jänecke, spiteful, ugly Jänecke, realized how helplessly forlorn this human creature was. He said encouragingly: 'Now then, Pinneberg, don't throw in the towel. It will work out. We aren't monsters, after all, you can talk to us. And anyone can have a run of bad luck.'

Then he moved swiftly aside. A gentlemen was coming towards them, looking as though he wanted to buy, a gentlemen with an expressive face, an impressive face. No, he couldn't be a customer, that was a tailor-made suit he was wearing. He wouldn't buy something off the peg.

But the man went straight up to Pinneberg, and Pinneberg was wondering where he had seen him before. Because he had seen him, though he had looked quite different then, and the man said to Pinneberg, touching the rim of his hat: 'Greetings, sir! Greetings! May I ask what you have in the fantasy line?'

The man had a very impressive way of speaking, he rolled his r's and made no attempt to lower his voice, he seemed not to mind that others could hear him.

'Fantasy fabrics?' queried Pinneberg uneasily. 'That's on the second floor.'

The man laughed: a sharply accented Ha-ha-ha. He laughed with his whole face and whole body, stopped, and went back all of a sudden to being expressive and sonorous.

'Oh, not that,' said the gentleman. 'I was asking you whether you could live a fantasy. Could you, for example, imagine yourself as a goldfinch, perched singing on top of this rail of trousers?'

'With difficulty,' said Pinneberg, giving a feeble smile, and thinking: where on earth do I know this nutcase from? It's all a put-on.

'With difficulty,' said the gentleman. 'That's bad. Well, I don't suppose you have much to do with birds in this department.' And he laughed again, his sharp Ha-ha-ha.

And Pinneberg smiled too, although he was getting nervous. Salesmen weren't supposed to be made fun of, he would have to find a gentle but effective way of getting rid of this drunk. Mr Jänecke was still there, behind an array of coats.

'Can I serve you?' asked Pinneberg.

'Serve!' declaimed the other contemptuously. 'Serve! No one is anyone's servant! Now, to another matter. Imagine that a young man comes in here, from Ackerstrasse let's say, with a heap of cash like that, and wants to get himself fitted out from head to toe with new clothes: can you imagine what that young man would choose?'

'I can imagine it very well,' said Pinneberg. 'That sort of thing happens here sometimes.'

'There you are,' said the gentlemen. 'You shouldn't hide your light under a bushel. Fantasy is one of your lines! What sort of material would that young man from Ackerstrasse choose?'

'As bright and showy as possible,' declared Pinneberg with conviction. 'Large checks. Very wide trousers. Jacket as close-fitting as possible. The best thing would be to show you. . .'

'Splendid,' said the other approvingly. 'Splendid. And now show me. This young man from Ackerstrasse really does have a lot of money and does need a whole new outfit.'

'With pleasure. . .' said Pinneberg.

'One moment,' said the other, raising his hand. 'To give you the picture. Look, this is the man who comes in. . .'

The gentleman changed utterly. His face became a picture of impudence and vice, but with a mixture of cowardice and fear in there too. Shoulders hunched, neck drawn in, he seemed to be expecting a policeman with a rubber truncheon round every corner.

'Then, once he has the good suit on. . .'

His face changed in a flash. Yes, it was still impudent and shameless, but like a flower turning to the light, it responded to the brilliance of the rising sun. He too could be smartly dressed, he could afford it, so what the heck!

'You are,' cried Pinneberg breathlessly, 'you are Mr Schlüter! I've seen you in a film. Fancy me not realizing at once!'

The actor was highly gratified. 'Oh yes? Which film did you see me in?'

'What was it called? D'you know, it's the one where you were a bank clerk, and your wife thought you were embezzling money for her, but really it was the management trainee who was giving it to you, who was your friend. . .'

'I know the plot,' said the actor. 'So you liked it? Which bit of mine did you like the best?'

'Oh, there were so many. . . But you know I think the best bit was where you came back to the table after you'd been in the washroom. . .'

The actor nodded.

'While you were away the trainee had told her you hadn't stolen the money and they laughed in your face. And suddenly you went all small. You shrank. It was horrifying.'

'So that was the best bit, but why?' pursued the actor insatiably.

'Because. . . please don't laugh. . . I felt it was so like us. You know things aren't going at all well for ordinary people like us, and it seems to me sometimes as though everyone and everything is making a monkey of us. Life in general, you see what I mean, and one feels so small. . .'

'The voice of the people,' declared the thespian. 'But I'm extremely honoured, Mr. . . what is your name?'

'Pinneberg.'

'The voice of the people, Pinneberg. Well, now let's get back to business and find that outfit. It was all rubbish at the theatrical outfitters. Now we'll see. . .'

And they did see. They waded through all kinds of clothes for half an hour, an hour, until there were mountains lying about. Pinneberg had never been so happy to be a salesman.

'Good man,' muttered the actor from time to time. He was a patient tryer-on. He could try fifteen pairs of trousers, and still be looking forward to the sixteenth.

'A good man this Pinneberg,' he muttered.

They finally did finish however, having examined and tried on everything that the young man from Ackerstrasse might possibly think of wearing. Pinneberg was in seventh heaven. He had hopes that Mr Schlüter might perhaps take more than the one good suit, perhaps he might also take the red-brown coat with the mauve check. He asked breathlessly: 'Well, what shall I put on the bill?'

The actor raised his eyebrows. 'The bill? I was only trying the stuff on. I'm not buying it. What did you think? Don't make such a face. I have given you a bit of work, haven't I. I'll send you tickets for the next première. Do you have a fiancée? I'll send you two tickets.'

Pinneberg said hurriedly in a low voice: 'Mr Schlüter, please do buy the things. You've got such a lot of money. You earn so much. Please buy them! If you go away now and haven't bought anything, they'll blame me and I'll be sacked.'

'You're a funny one,' said the actor. 'Why should I buy the things? For your sake? Nobody does me any favours.'

'Mr Schlüter!' said Pinneberg, his voice growing louder. 'I saw the way you acted that poor little man in the film. You know how things

are for people like us. I've got a wife and child too, you see. The child
is really small, and he's still so happy. If I'm sacked. . .!'

'Good lord, man,' said Mr Schlüter. 'That's your business. I can't
buy suits I've no use for just to keep your child happy.'

'Mr Schlüter!' begged Pinneberg. 'Please do it for my sake. I've
been with you an hour. At least buy the one suit. It's pure Cheviot,
very pleasant to wear and I'm sure you'd be satisfied with it.

'Will you kindly stop it,' said Mr Schlüter. 'This pantomime is
getting boring.'

'Mr Schlüter,' begged Pinneberg, laying his hand on the departing
actor's arm, 'The firm gives us a quota, we have to sell a certain
amount or we're sacked. I'm five hundred marks down. Please,
please, buy something. You know how we feel. You acted it!'

The actor took the salesman's hand from his arm. He said very
loudly: 'Listen, young man, just keep your hands off me. What
you're saying has damn all to do with me.'

Suddenly Mr Jänecke appeared. Of course he would.

'May I help you? I'm the manager of this department.'

'I'm Franz Schlüter, the actor. . .'

Mr Jänecke bowed.

'Strange salesmen you've got here. They manhandle you into
buying. This man claims you force them to do it. That's extortion. It
deserves a letter to the newspapers.'

'The man's a bad salesman,' said Mr Jänecke. 'He's been warned
several times already. I'm very sorry that you just happened to get
him. We'll dismiss him this time. He's useless.'

'My dear sir, that's quite unnecessary. I'm not suggesting that.
Though he did grab my arm. . .'

'He did? Mr Pinneberg, go at once to the Personnel Office and get
your papers. And as for that nonsense about a quota, it's all lies. Only
two hours ago I told this man that if he didn't manage it, well, he
didn't manage it, it wasn't as bad as all that. He's just incompetent. A
thousand apologies, Mr Schlüter.'

Pinneberg followed the two men with his eyes.

He stood and watched them go.

It was all over, all, all over.

LIFE GOES ON

It wasn't all over: life went on. It was November, and fourteen
months had gone by since Pinneberg had ceased work at Mandels.
A dark, cold, wet November, which was all right if the roof was
sound. The roof of the summer-house was sound, thanks to
Pinneberg who had tarred it four weeks ago. Now he was awake,
the hands of the alarm-clock showed a quarter to five. Pinneberg
listened to the November rain pouring and drumming on the
summer-house roof. 'It's water-tight,' he thought. 'I did a good
job there. Perfectly water-tight. At least the rain can't get at
us.'

He was just about to turn over comfortably and go back to sleep
when he realized he had been woken by a sound: the garden gate had
squeaked. Krymna would be knocking in a moment.

Pinneberg shook Lammchen gently by the arm as she lay beside
him in the narrow iron bed, trying to wake her gently. But she
started: 'What's the matter?'

Waking up was no longer the cheerful moment that it used to be
for Lammchen; if she was wakened at an unusual hour it was always
bad news. Pinneberg heard her breathe quickly: 'What's the matter?'
'Quiet!' whispered Pinneberg. 'You'll wake the Shrimp. It's not five
yet.'

'What is it then?' Lammchen asked again, rather impatiently.

'Krymna is coming,' whispered Pinneberg. 'Don't you think I
should go with him?'

'No, no, no,' said Lammchen passionately. 'Listen. We agreed. We
are not going to start stealing. I won't have it.'

'But. . .' Pinneberg objected.

There was a knock outside. 'Pinneberg!' called a voice. 'Are you
coming with us, Pinneberg?'

Pinneberg jumped up, and stood for a moment hesitating.

'Shall I?' he asked, and listened.

But Lammchen did not reply.

'Pinneberg! Come on, lazy bones!' called the man outside.

Pinneberg felt his way in darkness out onto the porch, he could see the dark silhouette of the other man through the glass panes.

'Well, at last! Are you coming or not?'

'I. . .' called Pinneberg through the door, 'I would like. . .'

'So it's no.'

'Please understand, Krymna, I'd like to, but my wife. . . You know women. . .'

'So it's no,' bellowed Krymna outside. 'Don't come, then. We'll go alone.'

Pinneberg watched him go. He could vaguely discern Krymna's squat figure silhouetted against the sky. Then the garden gate squeaked again and Krymna was swallowed up by the night.

Pinneberg sighed again. He was very cold. It couldn't be doing him any good to stand here in his shirt. But he just stood there, staring. Inside the Shrimp called: 'Dad-Dad! Mum-Mum!' He felt his way back quietly into the room. 'Go to sleep, Shrimp,' he said. 'Sleep a little bit longer.' The Shrimp sighed deeply and his father heard him settling himself in bed. 'Dolly,' he whispered softly. 'Dolly. . .'

Pinneberg searched around in the darkness for the little rubber doll. The Shrimp had to hold it when he was going to sleep. He found it. 'Here's Dolly, Shrimp. Hold Dolly tight. Now go to sleep, my Shrimp.' The child made a happy sound, he was contented now, and would be asleep in a moment.

Pinneberg got back into bed himself. He was so cold that he tried not to touch Lammchen so as not to give her a fright.

Then he lay there, unable to get back to sleep, which was barely worth it anyway. He thought about a thousand things. Whether Krymna was very angry with him for not joining the 'wood-gathering' and whether Krymna could do him much harm in the settlement. Then, where would they get the money for briquettes now they didn't have any wood? Then, that he would have to go into Berlin today to draw the dole. Then, that he would have to go to Puttbreese and pay him his six marks. He didn't need the money, he would only drink it; it was enough to drive you mad what people would spend money on when other people needed it so badly. Then Pinneberg reflected that Heilbutt also had to have his ten marks today, and then the dole would be all gone. Where they were to get food and heating for the next week heaven only knew; only heaven probably didn't know either.

And so it had been going on week after week. Month after month. That was what was so discouraging, that it went on so endlessly. Hadn't he once believed that it was all over? The worst thing was that it went on. And on, and on, with no end in sight.

Gradually Pinneberg grew warm and sleepy. There'd be no harm in grabbing a little more sleep. Sleep was always worth it. And then the alarm rang: it was seven o'clock. Pinneberg was awake on the instant, and the Shrimp shouted enthusiastically: 'Tick-tock! Tick-tock! Tick-tock!' over and over until the clock was turned off. Lammchen continued to sleep.

Pinneberg lit the little petrol lamp with the blue glass shade. Now the day was off on its course, there would be a lot of things to do in the next half hour. He ran to and fro, got into his trousers, the Shrimp demanded his 'Ca-ca'. Daddy brought him the 'Ca-ca', his best toy, a cigarette tin full of old playing cards. The little cylindrical stove and the fire were soon alight. He went out to the pump in the garden for water, washed, made the coffee, cut and spread the bed – Lammchen continued to sleep.

Did he think about that film he'd seen so long ago? There had been a woman asleep in bed, she was rosy, the man ran about and did things – but, oh, Lammchen wasn't rosy, Lammchen had to work all day and she was pale and tired; Lammchen balanced the books. It wasn't like the film.

Pinneberg dressed the little boy and said, turning to the bed, 'Time to get up now, Lammchen.'

'Yes,' she said obediently, and began dressing. 'What did Krymna say?'

'Nothing. But he was very annoyed.'

'Let him be annoyed. We're not starting on that sort of thing.'

'But you know,' said Pinneberg cautiously. 'Nothing can happen. Six to eight men always go together to get the wood. No forester would dare go up to them.'

'That's neither here nor there,' declared Lammchen. 'That's not the sort of thing we do and we're not going to do it.'

'But where are we going to get the money for the coal?'

'I'm going to the Kramers all day today to darn socks. That's three marks. And I may be going to the Rechlins tomorrow to repair their linen. Three more marks. And I've already got three days booked next week. I'm getting going nicely here.'

The room seemed to get brighter as she spoke. It was like a breath of fresh air.

'It's a tough job,' he said. 'Nine hours darning socks, and so little money!'

'You have to include the food,' she said. 'I get plenty at the Kramers. I'll bring some for you both this evening.'

'You should eat your own food,' said Pinneberg.

'I get plenty at the Kramers,' she repeated.

It was now completely light, the sun had risen. He blew out the lamp and they sat down at the table for coffee. The Shrimp alternated between his father's lap and his mother's. He drank his milk, he ate his bread, his eyes gleamed with pleasure at the arrival of a new day.

'When you go into the town today,' said Lammchen, 'you could bring him back a quarter of a pound of nice butter. I think it's not good for him always having margarine. He's having trouble cutting his teeth.'

'I have to go and give Puttbreese his six marks too.'

'Yes, you must. Don't forget.'

'And Heilbutt has to have his ten marks rent. The day after tomorrow is the first.'

'Right,' said Lammchen.

'And then that's the end of the dole. I'll only have the fare left.'

'I'll give you five marks to take with you,' said Lammchen. 'I'm getting three more today. Then you can get the butter, and be sure to get some of the five pfennig-bananas on Alexanderplatz. The robbers here charge fifteen. Who's going to pay that?'

'All right,' he said. 'Mind you don't get in too late so that the boy isn't alone so long.'

'I'll see what I can do. I may be back here by half-past five. You leave at one?'

'Yes,' he said. 'I have to be at the Labour Exchange at two.'

'It'll work out,' she said. 'It isn't very nice having to leave him alone in the house. But it's always worked out so far.'

'So far,' he said.

'You mustn't say that kind of thing,' she said. 'Why should we always be unlucky? Now I have the mending and the darning, we're getting by.'

'Getting by,' he said slowly. 'Yes we are, of course.'

'Oh Sonny!' she cried. 'Things will be different. Just keep your pecker up. It will get better.'

'I didn't marry you,' he said stubbornly, 'for you to keep me.'

'I don't keep you,' she said. 'How could I on three marks? What nonsense!' She reflected. 'Listen, Sonny, you could do something to help me.' She hesitated. 'It isn't pleasant, but it would be a great help to me.'

'Yes, what?' he said expectantly. 'Anything.'

'I did some mending at the Ruschs' in Gartenstrasse three weeks ago. Two days: six marks. I still haven't had the money.'

'Do you want me to go?'

'Yes,' she said. 'But you mustn't make a scene. Promise me.'

'No, no,' he said. 'I'll be able to get the money.'

'Good,' she said. 'That's a weight off my mind. Now I must go. Cheers, Sonny love. Cheers, my little Shrimp.'

'Cheers, my girl,' he said, 'Don't overdo the darning. One pair of socks more or less won't make any difference. Say bye-bye, Shrimp!'

'Cheers, my little Shrimp!' said she. 'And this evening we must definitely make a plan for what we're going to grow in the garden next spring. We want to have such a lot of vegetables! Think about it anyway.'

'You're great,' he said. 'You really are the greatest. Yes I will think about it. Cheers, wife.'

'Cheers, husband.'

He held the child in his arms and they watched her as she went down the garden path. They shouted, laughed, waved. Then the garden gate squeaked. Lammchen went down the path between the allotments. Sometimes she disappeared behind a summer-house and then the Shrimp called: 'Mum-Mum!'

'Mum-Mum's coming back soon,' his father comforted him.

But finally she was no longer to be seen, and the two went into the house.

MAN AS WOMAN. NICE WATER AND A BLIND SHRIMP.
A BATTLE OVER SIX MARKS

Pinneberg put the child on the ground and gave him a newspaper while he himself set about tidying the room. It was a big newspaper for such a small child, and he was a long time unfolding it. The room was only small: three metres by three, and there was nothing in it but a bed, two chairs, a table and the dressing-table. That was everything.

The Shrimp had found the pictures inside the paper, and gave an eager 'Pic!,' followed by a joyful 'Ei Ei!'

Pinneberg acknowledged the find. 'Those are pictures, my Shrimp,' he said. When the baby found someone he thought was a man he said 'Dad-Dad'. All women were greeted with 'Mum-Mum'. There were lots of them in the paper and he was bubbling with good humour.

Pinneberg put the feather-beds out of the window to air, tidied the room, then went next door into the kitchen. It was pocket-handkerchief-sized, three metres long by one and a half wide, and the stove was the smallest stove in existence, with only one burner. It was Lammchen's greatest affliction. He tidied in the kitchen and washed up. He didn't mind doing that, or mopping and sweeping. But his next task was the one he objected to: peeling potatoes for lunch and scrubbing carrots.

After a while Pinneberg had finished all his work, and he walked a while in the garden looking at the surrounding land. The minute size of the summer-house with its little glassed-in porch made the allotment around it seem all the bigger. It was almost a thousand metres square, but the ground wasn't in good shape. Nothing had been done to it since Heilbutt inherited it three years back. It might be possible to rescue the strawberries, but it would mean a fearful amount of digging, as it was full of weeds, couch-grass and thistles.

The sky had cleared after the morning rain, it was fresh but it would do the Shrimp good to go out.

Pinneberg went inside. 'Well, little Shrimp, now we're going out,' he said, dressing the little boy in his woollen jumper and grey leggings, and putting on his white woolly hat.

The Shrimp cried eagerly: 'Ca-Ca!' and his father ga[...] him. They had to go out with him. On every outing [...] something in his hand. The boy's little pushchair w[...] the veranda; they had exchanged it for the pram in the [...] in, my Shrimp,' said Pinneberg, and the Shrimp got i[...]

They set off slowly. Pinneberg went a different way from the usual. He didn't want to go past Krymna's summer-house today, there would only be trouble. In his present hopeless mood, Pinneberg would have preferred to get by without any trouble, but it was not always possible. The population of the huge group of allotments – three thousand in all – shrank to fifty people at most in winter. Anyone who was in any way able to scrape together the money for a room or who could find refuge with relations had fled from the cold, the dirt and the loneliness into town.

However those who had stayed behind, the poorest, the toughest and the bravest, felt they belonged together. The trouble was that they did not belong together: they were either Communists or Nazis, so there were continual arguments and fights.

Pinneberg had not yet been able to decide in favour of one or the other, and he had thought that would be the easiest way to slide through. But sometimes it actually seemed the most difficult.

There was vigorous sawing and chopping in some of the houses; that was the Communists who had been out on the night expedition with Krymna. They quickly cut the wood into bits, so that if the local constable did ever make a check there would be no proof. If Pinneberg said a polite 'Good morning' to them, they replied 'Mornin'', briefly and sullenly, none of them really friendly. No doubt they were annoyed with him. Pinneberg was uneasy.

At last they came into the village itself with its long paved streets and rows of little villas. Pinneberg undid the strap of the pushchair and said to the Shrimp: 'Get out! Get out!' He glanced at his father with a mischievous look in his blue eyes.

'Get out,' repeated Pinneberg. 'And push.'

The Shrimp looked at his father, stretched a leg out of the pushchair, smiled and withdrew it.

'Get out, Shrimp,' said Pinneberg in a warning tone.

The Shrimp lay back as though he wanted to go to sleep.

'All right,' said Pinneberg. 'Then Dad-Dad's going on alone.'

The Shrimp peeped at him but didn't move.

Pinneberg went on slowly, leaving the little pushchair with the child in it behind him. He went ten steps, twenty steps: nothing. He went ten more steps, slowly, and then the child shouted: 'Dad-Dad! Dad-Dad!'

Pinneberg turned round. The Shrimp had got out of the pushchair, but he made no move to follow his father, he held up the strap for Pinneberg to attach.

He went back and did as required. Now the little boy's sense of order was satisfied. He pushed the pushchair along beside his father for some time. After a while they crossed a bridge over a wide, swift stream flowing through a field. On both sides of the bridge there was an embankment where you could get down into the field.

Pinneberg left the pushchair on the path, grasped the Shrimp by the hand and climbed with him down the embankment to the stream. The recent rain had filled the stream, it rushed murkily along its course churning up swirls of foam.

Holding the Shrimp by the hand, Pinneberg went to the edge of the stream, and they both looked long and silently at the hurrying water. After a while Pinneberg said: 'That's water, my Shrimp. Nice water.'

The child gave a small sound that betokened approval. Pinneberg repeated the sentence several times, to the Shrimp's unfailing satisfaction.

It seemed ungracious to be standing dispensing information to the child from on high, so he squatted and said again 'That's water, nice, friendly water, Shrimp.'

When the child saw his father squatting, he thought that must be part of the activity and squatted too. And so they both looked at the water for a time in a squatting position. Then they went on. The Shrimp had got tired of pushing and went along by himself. He began by walking alongside his father and the pushchair, then he found things to look at: some hens, a shop window, an iron drain cover that caught his eye in the expanse of pavement. Pinneberg waited a while, then went slowly on, then stopped and called and beckoned to the Shrimp. He trotted eagerly ten steps in his father's direction then laughed at him, turned around and went back to his drain cover.

This happened several times, until his father had got quite a way ahead: much too long a way it seemed to the Shrimp. He called to his father, but the latter just kept on going. The child stood stamping from one leg to the other getting very insistent. He grabbed the edge of his woolly hat and pulled it with one jerk down over his face, so that he couldn't see. At the same time he cried out very loudly: 'Dad-Dad!'

Pinneberg looked around. There stood his little son in the middle of the road, the hat completely covering his face, tottering this way and that, ready to fall at any moment. Pinneberg ran and ran to get there before it happened, his heart beating wildly, thinking to himself: 'One and a half years old and he thought of that all on his own. He makes himself blind so that I have to fetch him.'

He pulled the hat off the child's face; the Shrimp beamed at him. 'What a noodle you are, Shrimp, what a noodle!' he said over and over again, moved to tears.

Now they came to Gartenstrasse, where Rusch the factory-owner lived, whose wife had owed Lammchen six marks for three weeks now. Pinneberg inwardly repeated his promise not to make a scene and firmly resolved not to do so. He rang the bell.

The villa was set back from the road, with a front garden. It was a fine big villa with a fine big orchard behind, very much to Pinneberg's taste.

He surveyed the place in detail, gradually becoming aware that nobody was answering the bell. He rang it again.

This time a window in the villa opened, and a woman shouted to him: 'What d'you want? We've nothing to give you.'

'My wife did some mending for you,' said Pinneberg. 'I've come for the six marks.'

'Come back tomorrow!' shouted the woman in reply and shut the window.

Pinneberg stood for a while pondering how much latitude was permitted him by his promise to Lammchen. The Shrimp sat quite still in his pushchair, sensing no doubt that his father was cross.

Then Pinneberg pressed the bell-button again; at length. But nothing stirred. Pinneberg thought again. He was on the point of leaving when he reflected what eighteen hours of mending and darning meant, and he jammed his elbow on the bell-button. He stood there quite a long time and some passers-by stared at him. But he remained rooted to the spot, and the Shrimp didn't utter a sound.

Finally the window did open again and the woman shouted: 'Get away from the bell this instant or I'll call the constable.'

Pinneberg took away his elbow and shouted back: 'You do that! Then I'll tell him. . .'

But the window had already shut. So Pinneberg began ringing again. He had always been a mild, peace-loving person, but enough was enough. It would in fact have been very undesirable for him to get mixed up with the police in his present situation, but he didn't care. It was also altogether too cold to leave the Shrimp so long in his pushchair, but that didn't deter him either. Insignificant he might be compared with the manufacturer Rusch, but he wanted his six marks and he was going to ring the bell till he got them.

The door opened and the woman headed straight for him in a towering rage. She had two mastiffs on a lead, a black one and a grey one. Presumably they watched over the house and grounds at night. The animals had grasped that he was an enemy; they pulled at their leads and growled menacingly.

'I'll let the dogs loose,' said the woman, 'if you don't get on your way this minute!'

'When I get six marks,' said Pinneberg.

The woman grew even more furious when she perceived that the threat of the dogs didn't work, as she could not really let them loose. If she did, they would be over the railings in a minute and would have torn the man apart. And the man knew that just as well as she did.

'You must be used to waiting,' she said.

'I am,' said Pinneberg, and stayed put.

'You're unemployed,' said the woman contemptuously. 'One can see that. I'll tell them about you. You have to declare what your wife earns on the side. That's deception.'

'Fine,' said Pinneberg.

'I'll deduct income tax and health insurance from your wife's money,' said the woman, calming the dogs.

'You do that,' said Pinneberg. 'And I'll come round tomorrow for the receipts from the tax office and the health insurance.'

'Let your wife try coming to me for work again!' shouted the woman.

'That'll be six marks,' said Pinneberg.

'Of all shameless louts. . .' said the woman. 'If my husband were here. . .'

'But he's not,' said Pinneberg.

And then the six marks appeared. There they lay, three two mark pieces, on top of the iron railing. Pinneberg couldn't pick them up at once, the woman had to go back with her dogs first. Then he took them.

'Thank you very much,' he said, raising his hat.

'Mmm, mmm,' said the Shrimp.

'Yes, money,' cried Pinneberg. 'It's money, little Shrimp. And now let's go home.'

He moved off slowly with the pushchair, never turning round once to look at the woman or the villa; he was tired, and desolate, and sad.

The Shrimp chatted and crowed.

His father did answer him every so often, but it wasn't the right sort of answer and in the end the Shrimp too fell silent.

WHY THE PINNEBERGS DON'T LIVE WHERE THEY LIVE.
JOACHIM HEILBUTT'S PICTURE AGENCY. LEHMANN GETS
THE CHOP

Two hours later Pinneberg had cooked a meal for himself and the Shrimp. They had eaten it together and then he had put the Shrimp to bed. Now he was waiting behind the partially-closed kitchen door for the child to go to sleep. He wasn't ready to go to sleep yet, however, and he kept calling him: 'Dad-Dad! Dad-Dad!' but Pinneberg stood stock still and waited.

The time was approaching when he would have to go to the

station. He had to get the one-o'clock train if he was to be there
punctually for the payment of his unemployment benefit, and the
thought of being unpunctual, with the best excuse in the world, was
simply grotesque.

The Shrimp was still calling: 'Dad-Dad, Dad-Dad!'

He could, of course, simply go. He had tied the child into his little
bed, nothing could happen to him, but he felt easier in his mind
when he was asleep. It wasn't pleasant to think of the child calling in
vain for five hours, perhaps six, the whole afternoon till Lammchen
came back.

Pinneberg peeped through the door. The Shrimp had gone quiet.
He was asleep. Pinneberg crept silently out of the summer-house,
he locked up, then stood for a moment at the window to hear
whether the Shrimp had woken up when he shut the door.
Silence.

Pinneberg set off at a trot. He might still get the train, but it wasn't
likely. No, actually he had to catch it. Their great mistake of course
had been to hang onto their expensive flat at Puttbreese's a year after
he lost his job. Forty marks rent on ninety marks income. It had been
madness, but they just couldn't resign themselves to giving up that
one last thing, their own home: the space to be alone together. . .
forty marks rent, and the last of his wages went on it, and Jachmann's
money went on it, and then there was nothing more, and that went
on it. Debts. And Puttbreese stood there saying: 'Now, young man,
where's the money. Or shall we start moving you out? I told you free
removal was on offer – onto the street.'

It was Lammchen who always mollified the master-carpenter.
'You'll pay, young woman,' said Puttbreese. 'But what that young
man of yours is about I don't know. I'd have found work long
ago. . .'

Anxiety and arrears mounted up, and impotent hatred for the man
in the blue overalls. Finally Pinneberg hadn't dared to go home. He
sat all day long in some park or other, or wandered aimlessly through
the streets seeing in the shops how many good things there were for
good money. While doing this it occurred to him that he might as
well try to find Heilbutt. He had only made the one attempt, at Mrs
Witt's, but there were also the police to try, the electoral roll, the

register of residents. It wasn't just to keep himself busy that
Pinneberg was casting his net for Heilbutt. At the back of his mind
was that conversation he had had with Heilbutt once about the
business of his own that Heilbutt was going to start, and the first man
he was going to employ.

It hadn't turned out to be very difficult to find him. He still lived
in Berlin; he had recorded his change of address in the proper
manner, but now he no longer lived in the East. He had made it into
the centre of town. 'Joachim Heilbutt Picture Agency' it said on the
door.

Heilbutt had indeed got his own business. Here was a man who
hadn't allowed himself to be walked over, but had still got on. And
Heilbutt had also been perfectly willing to employ his erstwhile
colleague and friend. But a commission-only job was all he had to
offer. A respectable rate of commission was agreed, but after two days
of earning nothing Pinneberg gave the job back.

Oh, he didn't deny that there was money to be earned there, but he
wasn't capable of it, he didn't have it in him. It wasn't that he was
prudish, he just couldn't do the job.

Heilbutt had come to grief over a nude photo. Because of a nude
photo he had been forced out of a job that was absorbing in itself and
not without prospects. Where other people would have avoided
nude photos like the plague, Heilbutt made his stumbling-block into
the cornerstone of his existence. He possessed an extraordinarily
valuable and varied collection of nude photos: not models of easy
virtue with used bodies, but fresh young girls, vivacious women –
Heilbutt had become a dealer in nude photos.

He was a careful man; a bit of retouching, a different head didn't
cost the world and nobody could point to a photo and say: 'Surely
that's. . .' But plenty of people would stop and wonder: 'Could that
be. . .?'

Heilbutt tried the small ads, but there was too much competition
in the field. He did some business but not enough. Heilbutt had
three young people going around town (Pinneberg had been the
fourth for two days) selling these photos to dubious girls and seedy
landladies, to the porters of certain small hotels and the toilet
attendants of certain restaurants. It was big business and it was

getting bigger as Heilbutt learned what the customers required. There was no telling how big the appetite for these things was in a city of four million people. The possibilities were endless.

Heilbutt was sorry that his friend Pinneberg hadn't been able to commit himself to the enterprise. It had a big future. Heilbutt reflected that there were times when even the best of wives could hold a man back: the best were actually the worst in that respect. Pinneberg had simply found it too distasteful to have to listen to some old toilet-attendant telling him what his customers thought of the last collection, and what aspects of the photos had to be more distinct and why. Once upon a time Heilbutt had been a naturist, he didn't deny it, but he said: 'I'm a practical man, Pinneberg. I live life as it is.'

But he also added: 'I won't let myself be kicked, Pinneberg. I am who I am, and people can take it or leave it.'

No, there had been no quarrel between them. Heilbutt had understood his friend's position very well. 'It doesn't suit you, that's all. But what are we to do with you now?'

That was Heilbutt all over: a friend in need. He and Pinneberg didn't exactly belong together any more, they'd never really done so in fact, but he saw the need for help and wanted to give it.

And then it was that Heilbutt thought of this summer-house. It was rather a long way off, forty kilometres to the East, right out of Berlin, but with its own piece of land. 'I was left it by some aunt or other three years ago, Pinneberg. What am I to do with a summer-house? You could live there, and plant your own vegetables and potatoes.'

'The fresh air would be great for the Shrimp,' Pinneberg had said.

'You needn't pay any rent,' Heilbutt had said. 'The thing's standing empty, and you can put the garden in order for me. There's just the expenses involved, like the land and the road taxes and I don't know what else I have to pay. . .'

Heilbutt reckoned it up. 'So shall we say ten marks a month? Is that too much for you?'

'No, no,' said Pinneberg. 'It's wonderful, Heilbutt.' He thought about all these things as he was sitting in the train – he had in fact managed to catch it – staring at his ticket. It was a yellow ticket and

cost fifty pfennigs. The return journey cost fi
since Pinneberg had to travel in to the labour ex
a week, that was two marks out of his eighteen m
at once. His blood boiled each time he paid for a

There were in fact special cheap tickets for sma
order to get one Pinneberg had to live where he actua
that he wasn't allowed to do. There was also a labour ex
village where he lived. He would have been able to sign o
he been allowed to live there. For the purposes of s
Pinneberg lived at Puttbreese's, today, tomorrow and for all
whether he could afford the rent or not.

He had unwelcome but constantly-recurring memories o
time in July and August when he had gone from pillar to
trying to get permission to move out of town to the settleme
and be transferred from the Berlin labour exchange to the on
out there.

'Only if you can prove that you have a prospect of work out there.
Otherwise they won't accept you.'

No, he couldn't do that. 'But I won't find any work here either!'

'You can't know that. Anyway it was here that you became
unemployed, not there.'

'But this saves me thirty marks rent a month.'

'That has nothing to do with it. That's not our concern.'

'The landlord here is throwing me out!'

'Then the city authorities will find you another home. You only
have to register with the police as homeless.'

'But I've even got some land with the summer-house! I could grow
my own vegetables and potatoes!'

'A summer-house. You must know it's forbidden by law to live in
summer-houses?!'

So, there was nothing to be done. The Pinnebergs still officially
lived in Berlin at Puttbreese's, and Pinneberg had to travel into town
twice a week for his money – and go to the hated Puttbreese every
fortnight with six marks to pay off his rent arrears.

Sitting in the train for an hour, Pinneberg had gathered up the fuel
for quite a lively blaze of rage, hate and bitterness. But it was only a
little blaze, and once he was in the grey monotonous crowd that

hange, a crowd with so many
nted by the same fears, the
t was the point? He was
ig past the counters, so
e off; they didn't have a
instead of just the one.
oney and clear off. We
thing so special that we

inters and out onto the
eese. Puttbreese was in his

ese', said Pinneberg, in an attempt at
ouse-carpenter as well?'

ng man,' said Puttbreese, blinking. 'I'm not

n't,' agreed Pinneberg.

your son up to?' asked Puttbreese. 'What's he going to be?'
uldn't tell you for sure,' said Pinneberg. 'Here's the money.'
Six marks,' confirmed the master-carpenter. 'There's forty-two
still to come. But your young lady is in order.'

'She is,' agreed Pinneberg.

'You say that as if it was your doing. But it's got nothing to do with
you.'

'I know,' said Pinneberg peaceably. 'Any post?'

'Post!' exclaimed the master-carpenter. 'Post for you! A job-offer
perhaps? A man was here.'

'A man?'

'Yes, a man, young fellow. At least I think it was. All quiet in
town?'

'What d'you mean: all quiet?'

'The police were having a punch-up with the Communists again.
Or the Nazis. Broke some shop-windows in town. Didn't you see
any of it?'

'No,' said Pinneberg. 'I didn't. What did the man want?'

'No idea. Are you a Communist?'

'Me? No.'

'That's odd. If I were you, I'd be a Communist.'

'Are you one?'

'Me? Certainly not. I'm a tradesman, how could I be a Communist?'

'I suppose not. What did the man want?'

'Which man? Oh, stop bothering me about him. He stood around here jawing for half an hour. I gave him your address.'

'The one out there?'

'Certainly, young fellow. The one out there. He knew this one. He came here.'

'But we expressly agreed. . .' began Pinneberg heatedly.

'It will be all right, young man. Your wife won't mind. You haven't got a ladder in your summer-house, have you? Otherwise I'd be out there one day. Very nice thighs your wife has. . .'

'Oh, go to. . .' began Pinneberg, flying into a rage. 'Will you just tell me what the man wanted?'

'You should take off your collar,' taunted the master-carpenter. 'The thing's grubby. Out of work for over a year and still walking around in a stiff collar. There's no helping people like you.'

'You can just st. . .' screamed Pinneberg, and slammed the workshop door from the outside.

Whereupon the master-carpenter stuck out his red head. 'Come along, young man, and have a whisky with me. Cheer me up, you do, more than I can say for most.'

Pinneberg wandered off at random, raging inwardly at allowing himself to be made a fool of by the master-carpenter yet again. It was the same every time. He always resolved only to exchange a few words with him, and it always turned out the same. What a feeble clod he was; he never learned, and people could do what they liked with him.

He stopped in front of a dress-shop where there was a fine big mirror. He could see himself full-length, and he saw that he no longer looked at all respectable. His light grey trousers were spotted with roof-tar. His coat was worn and the colour had faded, his shoes were patched all over. Puttbreese was right; it was ridiculous to be wearing a collar. He was unemployed and down in the world, as anyone could tell from twenty steps away. His hand went sharply to his neck and he tore off collar and tie and put them in his coat pocket. He didn't actually look much different. There wasn't much left to spoil in his appearance. Heilbutt wouldn't say anything, but he'd look volumes.

Ah, there goes the police-car. So there'd been more trouble with the Communists, or the Nazis. You had to hand it to those fellows for spirit. He'd like to be able to look at a newspaper once in a while, he had no idea what was going on. For all he knew deepest peace might be reigning on German soil; out there in the summer-house you didn't hear anything.

No, no, if things settled down he would notice. The labour exchange didn't yet look as though they would have to cut back the staff for want of custom.

Well, you could ruminate all day like that, it wasn't very amusing and it didn't cheer Pinneberg up, but what else was there to do in a city where nothing related to you, but concentrate on yourself and your own worries? Shops where you couldn't buy anything, cinemas you couldn't go into, cafés for people able to pay, museums for people who were respectably dressed; homes for other people, public agencies where they cheated you. No, Pinneberg preferred to stay at home minding his own business.

Yet he was happy as he climbed the steps to Heilbutt's place. It was coming up to six; he hoped that Lammchen was at home now, and that no harm had come to the Shrimp. . .

He rang the bell.

A girl opened the door. A very nice young girl in an art-silk blouse. She hadn't been there a month ago. 'May I help you?'

'I'd like to see Mr Heilbutt. My name's Pinneberg.'

And seeing her hesitate he said, irately: 'I'm a friend of his.'

'Come in,' said the young girl, letting him into the hall. 'Could you wait a minute, please?'

He could. The young girl disappeared behind a white door with an inscription saying 'Office'.

It was a very respectable hall, with walls covered in red hessian. No sign of nude photos, very respectable pictures, engravings Pinneberg thought, or woodcuts. It was scarcely conceivable that a year and half ago they had been colleagues at Mandels, both selling suits.

And now here was Heilbutt: 'Good evening, Pinneberg. Nice of you to come round,' he said. 'Come in. Marie, bring us some tea in my study!'

So, they weren't going to go into the office. It transpired that since Pinneberg's last visit Heilbutt had acquired not only the young girl but also a study, with book shelves and Persian rugs and an enormous desk; precisely the gentleman's room that Pinneberg had dreamed of all his born days but would never possess.

'Sit down,' said Heilbutt. 'I see you're looking round. I have bought a few bits of furniture. One has to. Personally I don't care about such things, you remember at old Mrs Witt's. . .'

'But this here is something,' said Pinneberg, full of admiration. 'I think it's fabulous. All these books. . .'

'Ah, well, the books. . .' began Heilbutt, but then changed the subject. 'Well, are you getting on all right out there?'

'Yes, very much so. We're very content, Heilbutt. My wife has found a bit of work, darning and mending, that sort of thing. Things are better now.'

'Well that's good,' said Heilbutt. 'Put it all down there, Marie, I'll see to it. That'll be all, thank you.

'Help yourself, please, Pinneberg. Have a cake. These are supposed to be the right ones for tea. See if you like them. I don't understand these things and I don't care.'

Suddenly: 'Is it getting very cold out there?'

'No, no,' said Pinneberg hastily. 'Not very. The little stove heats very well. The rooms are only small, so it's cosy most of the time. Here's the rent.'

'Oh, right, the rent. Is it time already?'

Heilbutt took the note and folded it, but didn't put it in his pocket. 'You tarred the roof, Pinneberg, didn't you?'

'Yes indeed. I did. And it was a very good thing you gave me the money to do it. I didn't realize until I started, but it wasn't watertight at all. When it started raining this autumn it would have come in in buckets.'

'Is it watertight now?'

'Yes, thank heaven, Heilbutt. It won't let a drop in.'

'You know,' said Heilbutt. 'I ought to tell you something that I read. . . Do you have heat on all day?'

'No,' said Pinneberg hesitantly, not quite sure what Heilbutt was driving at. 'We have the stove on in the mornings a bit, and then again in the afternoon so that it's warm in the evening. The weather's not that cold yet.'

'And do you know how much briquettes cost out there?' asked Heilbutt.

'Not exactly,' said Pinneberg. 'Since the last emergency decree they're supposed to have got cheaper. Perhaps one mark sixty. Or one mark fifty-five? Really, I don't know.'

'I read in a building journal recently,' said Heilbutt, playing with the note, 'that you can easily get dry rot in that sort of weekend home. And I'd advise you to heat it properly.'

'Yes, we can. . .' said Pinneberg.

'That was what I wanted to ask you,' said Heilbutt. 'I wouldn't want the house to deteriorate. If you'd please be kind enough to have the heating on all day, so that the walls dry out thoroughly, I'll give you this ten mark note back to start with. Then you could perhaps bring me the coal bill as a receipt on the first of next month?'

'No, no,' said Pinneberg hurriedly, swallowing hard. 'You mustn't, Heilbutt. You'd just be giving me the rent back every time. You've helped us enough already, starting at Mandels.'

'But Pinneberg!' said Heilbutt, seeming perfectly astonished. 'Help you – it's in my own interest to have the roof tarred and the place heated. You can't call it help. You're helping yourself.' And he shook his head as he looked at him.

'Heilbutt!' exclaimed Pinneberg. 'I understand what you're saying, but. . .'

'Oh, now listen to this,' said Heilbutt. 'Have I told you who I met from Mandels?'

'No,' said Pinneberg. 'But. . .?'

'No? You'll never guess. I met Lehmann, our former boss and head of Personnel.'

'And?' asked Pinneberg. 'Did you talk to him?'

'Of course I did, that's to say he talked to me. He poured out his heart to me.'

'Why's that? He's surely got nothing to complain about.'

'He got the chop,' said Heilbutt emphatically. 'Sacked by Mr Spannfuss. Just like us.'

'Good grief,' said Pinneberg, in bewilderment. 'Lehmann sacked. Heilbutt, you must tell me all about it. If you don't mind I'll help myself to another cigarette.'

PINNEBERG AS THE CAUSE OF THE TROUBLE.
THE FORGOTTEN BUTTER AND THE POLICEMAN.
NO NIGHT IS DARK ENOUGH

It was getting on for seven when Pinneberg stepped out onto the street again. The conversation with Heilbutt had livened him up and saddened him all at once. So, Lehmann had fallen, the mighty Mr Lehmann who Pinneberg remembered so well sitting grandly behind his shiny desk, and saying, 'We don't deal in fertilizers.'

Lehmann had tormented Pinneberg when he was in his power, then along came Spannfuss and did the same to him. And Spannfuss, for all his combat-training, would go the same way. That was the way of the world, and it was small consolation that it happened to everyone in the end.

What had brought about Mr Lehmann's fall? According to rumour, and if you accepted the official reason, the cause of his dismissal had been that man Pinneberg. Mr Spannfuss, efficient as ever, had sniffed out that the head of Personnel had been exceeding the authority given to him by putting in his own favourites – at a time of staff-cuts! He had claimed that they came from branches in Hamburg, Fulda or Breslau, and Spannfuss had discovered these claims to be false.

In truth everybody knew that had only been the official reason for his dismissal. Favourites were always put in, and now Mr Spannfuss was sowing his own favourites throughout the business. But a precondition for being able to do so in peace was the sacking of Mr Lehmann. What had for twenty years been common knowledge, in the twenty-first filled the cup to overflowing. He'd committed actual forgery, hadn't he?'

'Comes from the Breslau branch', he had written in Pinneberg's
personnel file, when in fact he had come from Kleinholz's in
Ducherow. Lehmann could in fact be grateful to Mr Spannfuss;
criminal prosecution was by no means beyond the bounds of
possibility. Now he just had to keep his mouth shut.

But, oh, how he opened his mouth when he encountered his ex-
salesman Heilbutt! Hadn't he been friends with that man – stocky
little chap, what was his name? Pinneberg. They'd stuck their knife
into him too, the poor fool. Because he hadn't sold enough? That was
a joke. After Heilbutt had left, Pinneberg had been the only one in the
department who had got anywhere near the quota. No doubt that was
why he had particular 'friends' among the other salesmen, no doubt
that was why there was a letter in his personnel file – anonymous of
course – saying that he was a member of a Nazi storm troop!

Lehmann had always thought it was rubbish, otherwise how could
Pinneberg be a friend of Heilbutt of all people? But it was useless to
argue, Spannfuss only believed his own men, Jänecke and Kessler,
apart from which it was widely accepted that Pinneberg was the one
who had persistently drawn swastikas and 'death to the Jews' on the
walls of the employees' toilets, and a gallows with a fat Jew hanging
on it with 'The New Improved Mandel' written underneath. It had
stopped when Pinneberg left, the loo walls now remaining spotlessly
white. And that was the sort of man whom Mr Lehmann had
installed on the pretence that he came from Breslau!

Pinneberg had been Lehmann's downfall, and Kessler had been
Pinneberg's downfall. So much for being a good salesman, and
loving the job, putting as much effort into selling a pair of cotton
trousers for six and a half marks as an evening suit for a hundred and
twenty. Oh yes, there was solidarity among white-collar workers, the
solidarity of the envious towards the capable!

He was the man it had all happened to, and he was angry still, but
that anger, he sensed as he went along Friedrichstrasse, was growing
old. You could rage about it, but finally what was the point? That was
the way things were.

In former days Pinneberg had often strolled along Friedrichstrasse,
it was his home ground, and so he noticed that there were many
more prostitutes than there used to be. Of course they weren't all

prostitutes, there was a lot of unfair competition these days. He'd heard in the shop a year and a half ago that many unemployed men's wives walked the streets to earn a few marks.

That was plain to see; many of them were such hopeless cases, utterly charmless, or else if they were pretty they had such greedy faces: greedy for money.

Pinneberg thought of Lammchen and the Shrimp. 'We aren't so badly off,' she was always saying. And she was certainly right.

The police seemed to be still on the alert. There were two at all the places where one usually stood, and you kept meeting pairs of them patrolling the pavements. Pinneberg had nothing against the police in principle. They had to exist of course, especially the traffic police, but he did find that their well-nourished and well-dressed appearance was a provocation, and so was their behaviour. They walked around among the public as his teacher had used to walk among the pupils: you behave properly or else. . .!

Oh, let them!

This was the fourth time that Pinneberg had strode up and down the stretch of Friedrichstrasse in between the Leipziger and Linden intersections. He couldn't go back home yet, he simply couldn't. Once he was home, everything was finished again. At home the ashes of life smouldered hopelessly on, but here something could happen! The prostitutes weren't giving him a second glance, though. He was out of the question for the ones round here, with his faded coat and his dirty trousers, and his collarless shirt. If he wanted one of their kind he'd have to go down to the Schlesische Station, where the girls didn't mind how a man looked provided he had money. But did he want a prostitute?

Perhaps. He didn't know. He didn't think about it.

What he was sure he wanted was the chance to tell someone what it used to be like, and what nice suits he had had, and how wonderful the Shrimp was.

The Shrimp!

So he had gone and forgotten his butter and bananas after all, and it was nine o'clock, too late for the shops. Pinneberg was furious with himself, and even more sorry than angry. He couldn't go back without them, what would Lammchen think of him? Perhaps he could

still get into one of the shops by the back door. There was a big
delicatessen, brilliantly illuminated. Pinneberg pressed his nose flat
against the window, perhaps there was someone still there whose
attention he could attract by knocking. He had to get his butter and
bananas!

A voice beside him said, in a low tone: 'Move along there!'
Pinneberg started, alarmed, and looked around him. There was a
policeman standing beside him.

Was he was speaking to him?

'Move along, d'you hear!' shouted the policeman.

There were other people standing by the shop window, well-
dressed ladies and gentlemen, but the policeman wasn't talking to
them. There was no doubt that it was Pinneberg he meant.

Pinneberg was thoroughly confused. 'What? Why? Aren't I
allowed to. . .?'

He was stammering. He simply didn't understand.

'Are you going to go now?' asked the policeman. 'Or shall I. . .?'

He had the strap of his rubber truncheon over his wrist. His grip
tightened on it slightly.

Everyone was staring at Pinneberg. More people stopped to look, a
regular crowd of spectators. They looked on expectantly, they
weren't taking sides; shop windows had been broken here and in
Leipzigerstrasse yesterday.

The policeman had dark eyebrows, keen bright eyes, red cheeks, a
decisive nose and small black moustache.

'You going to move?' he asked calmly.

Pinneberg tried to speak; he looked at the policeman, his lips
trembled; he looked at the people. They were standing right up to
the shop window, well-dressed people, respectable people, people
who earned money.

But reflected in the window was another figure: a pale outline
without a collar, in a shabby coat, with trousers besmirched with tar.

And suddenly Pinneberg understood everything. Faced with this
policeman, these respectable people, this bright shop window, he
understood that he was on the outside now, that he didn't belong
here any more, and that it was perfectly correct to chase him away.
Down the slippery slope, sunk without trace, utterly destroyed.

Order and cleanliness, gone; work, material security, gone; making progress and hope, gone. Poverty is not just misery, poverty is an offence, poverty is a stain, poverty is suspect.

'Shall I help you on your way?' said the policeman.

Pinneberg complied abjectly; his mind a blur, he turned to go down the pavement in the direction of Friedrichstrasse Station. He only wanted to be on the train and on the way home to Lammchen.

He received a blow on the shoulders. It wasn't a hard blow, but enough to knock him into the gutter.

'Clear off, you!' said the policeman. 'Get a move on, will you.'

And Pinneberg started to move. He trotted along the gutter at the side of the road; he thought about a lot of things: arson, bombs, assassination. He thought that this was the end with Lammchen and the Shrimp, that it was the end of everything. . . but then he thought of nothing at all.

He came to the intersection with Jägerstrasse. He wanted to cross over to the station, to Lammchen and the Shrimp, the only place where he was somebody. . .

The policeman gave him a shove. 'That way, you!'

He pointed into Jägerstrasse.

Once again Pinneberg tried to object: he had to get to his train. 'But I have to. . .' he said.

'That way, d'y hear,' repeated the policeman, pushing him into Jägerstrasse. 'Now you clear off and sharp, young fellow-my-lad!' And he gave Pinneberg a hefty swipe.

Pinneberg began to run, he ran very fast. He noticed that they were no longer following him, but he did not dare to look round. He ran along the road he was on, straight ahead into the dark night, which isn't absolutely dark anywhere.

After a long, long time he slowed down. He stopped, he looked round. There was no one there. No police. Gingerly he raised one foot and put it on the pavement. Then the other. He was off the road and onto the pavement.

Then Pinneberg went on his way, one step at a time, through Berlin. But nowhere was completely dark, and going past policemen was particularly difficult.

A VISITOR IN A CAR. TWO PEOPLE WAIT IN THE NIGHT.
LAMMCHEN IS OUT OF THE QUESTION

On road 87a, in front of allotment 375, stood a car: a taxi from
Berlin. As for the driver, he had been sitting in the Pinneberg's
summer house for some hours, filling up the entire kitchen.

The man had drunk a pot of coffee, then smoked a cigar, then
walked for a while in the garden, but there was nothing to see out
there in the darkness. He had then gone back into the kitchen, drunk
another pot of coffee and smoked another cigar.

But the people in the room were still talking, in particular the big
fair man who jawed and jawed. The cab driver could have listened in
if he'd wanted to, but he wasn't interested. In a taxi there's almost
always a gap in the glass panel separating the driver's seat from the
interior, and one can hear enough intimate conversations in the
course of a week to last a lifetime.

After a while the man decided to act. He stood up and knocked on
the door. 'Aren't we leaving soon, sir?'

'Why!' shouted the fair man. 'Don't you want to earn some
money?'

'I do,' said the cab-driver. 'But the waiting costs a lot of money.'

'It's my money that it costs,' said the big man. 'You sit right
down again on your backside, and see if you can still recite the
Catechism. That's the kind of thing it's almost impossible to forget.
Try it.'

'Well, all right,' said the driver. 'In that case I'll have a nap.'

'All right by me,' said the fair man.

Lammchen said: 'I really can't understand where Sonny has got to.
He's always here by eight at the latest.'

'He'll come soon,' said Jachmann. 'How is the young father then,
little mother?'

'Lord,' sighed Lammchen. 'It's not easy for him. When you've
been unemployed for fourteen months. . .'

'That'll change,' declared Jachmann. 'Now I'm back on the scene,
something will turn up.'

'Were you away on a trip, Mr Jachmann?' asked Lammchen.

'Yes, I've been away a little.' Jachmann stood up, and went to the Shrimp's bedside. 'It's a mystery to me how a father can stay out when he has something like that lying here at home.'

'Ah, Mr Jachmann,' said Lammchen. 'Of course the Shrimp is wonderful, but you can't build your whole life round a child. What happens is that I go out sewing in the day. . .'

'But you shouldn't! That must stop now.'

'. . . I go out sewing in the day and he looks after the house, and the meals, and the child. He doesn't complain, he even gets pleasure out of it, but what sort of a life is it for him? What d'you think, Mr Jachmann? D'you think it's going to be like this from now on with the men at home doing the housework while the women work? It's impossible!'

'Oh come, how d'you work that out? During the war the women did the work while the men killed each other, and everybody thought that was all right. It works better this way round.'

'Not everybody thought it was all right.'

'Nearly everybody, young lady. People are like that. They don't learn from experience, they keep on doing the same stupid things. Me too.' Jachmann paused. 'I'm moving back in with your mother-in-law.'

Lammchen said hesitantly. 'Well, you must know what's best, Mr Jachmann. It may not be so stupid. After all she is clever and amusing.'

'Of course it's stupid,' said Jachmann angrily. 'It's damn stupid. You don't know the half, young lady! You have no idea. But let's say no more about it. . .'

He sank into thought.

After a long while Lammchen said. 'You mustn't wait, Mr Jachmann. The ten o'clock train has gone through now. I really believe that Sonny's got up to mischief tonight. He did have rather a lot of money on him.'

'What? A lot of money? D'you still have a lot of money?'

Lammchen laughed. 'What we call a lot of money, Jachmann. Twenty marks. Twenty-five marks. He can go out on that.'

'He can,' said Jachmann sadly.

And after that there was another long silence.

Then Jachmann lifted his head and said: 'Worried?'

'Of course I'm worried. You'll see what two years and those people have done to him. And he's such a decent chap.'

'He is.'

'It wasn't necessary to walk all over him like they did. And now if he begins to drink. . .'

Jachmann thought about it. 'He won't,' he said. 'Pinneberg has always had a freshness about him. Serious drinking is a squalid business; he won't go in for it. Maybe the odd night on the tiles but not real drinking. . .'

'The half-past-ten train has gone by,' said Lammchen. 'Now I am getting worried.'

'You mustn't,' said Jachmann. 'He'll struggle through.'

'Through what?' asked Lammchen angrily. 'What will he struggle through? None of what you're saying makes sense, Jachmann. It's just to comfort me. The worst thing is actually that he's stuck out here with nothing to struggle for. All he can do is wait, but what for? There is nothing. It's a life spent waiting.'

Jachmann gave her a long look. He had turned his great leonine head quite round and looked her full in the face.

'You must stop thinking about the trains, Lammchen,' he said. 'Your husband will come back. I'm sure of it.'

'It isn't just the drink,' said Lammchen. 'Drinking would be bad, but not very bad. But he's so down, you see, something might happen to him. He was at Puttbreese's today, and Puttbreese might have been mean to him. A thing like that can knock him right over these days. He can't stand much more. He might. . .'

She gave him a big-eyed stare. And then suddenly her eyes filled with tears. They ran, large and bright, down her cheeks. The gentle, strong mouth began to quiver, lost its firmness. 'Jachmann,' she whispered, 'he might. . .'

Jachmann had stood up, and placed himself half behind her. He gripped her by the shoulders. 'No, young lady, no!' he said. 'That couldn't happen. He wouldn't do that.'

'Anything can happen.' She broke free. 'You'd better go home. You're wasting your money waiting. You caught us at a bad time.'

Jachmann didn't answer. He kept pacing two steps forward, two steps back. On the table was the tin cigarette-case with the old playing-cards so beloved of the Shrimp.

'What did you say your young chap called those cards?'

'Which young chap? Oh, the Shrimp. He calls them "Ca-ca".'

'Shall I read the ca-ca-cards for you?' said Jachmann, smiling. 'Wait and see, your future is quite different from what you think.'

'Leave off,' said Lammchen. 'A small gift of money will come into the house. That's next week's unemployment benefit.'

'My funds are rather low at the moment,' said Jachmann. 'But eighty marks, maybe ninety, I'd be glad to give –' he corrected himself – 'lend, I mean.'

'It's nice of you, Jachmann,' said Lammchen. 'We could certainly use it. But you know, money isn't the answer. We can get by, and money isn't what's needed. It's work that would help Sonny, a bit of hope. Money? No.'

'Is it because I'm going back to your mother-in-law?' he asked, looking searchingly at her.

'That too,' she said. 'I have to keep things away from him if they're going to add to his misery. You must understand that, Jachmann?'

'I do understand,' he said.

'But the main thing is that money really doesn't help. How does it change things being able to live a bit better for six or eight weeks? Not at all.'

'Perhaps I could get him a job?' reflected Jachmann.

'Oh, Mr Jachmann, you mean well. But don't put yourself out. If he does get something, it mustn't be through lying or fraud. He's got to lose his fear, feel free again.'

'Well. . .' said Jachmann sadly. 'If you want the luxury of getting something today without lying or fraud, there I can't help you!'

'You see,' said Lammchen eagerly, 'they steal wood around here for fuel. I don't find that specially wrong, but I told Sonny: you mustn't. He shan't go down, Jachmann, I won't let him. That's one thing he's got to keep. It's a luxury, maybe, but it's our only luxury, and I'm going to hold onto it, and then nothing bad can happen to us, Jachmann.'

'Young lady,' said Jachmann. 'I. . .'

'Look at the Shrimp there in his little bed. Supposing things did get better, and Sonny got back on his feet and had a job he liked, and earned money again. What if he had to keep thinking: you did that, you were like that? It isn't the wood, Jachmann, it isn't the law. What sort of law is it that can smash up everything for us with impunity, and we can be sent to gaol for three marks' worth of wood? That's a laugh. Of course it's no disgrace.'

'Young lady. . .' Jachmann tried to break in.

'But Sonny,' pursued Lammchen passionately, 'he can't laugh over it. He takes after his father, he's not like his mother at all. Mama's told me ten times over what a stickler his father was. He was chief clerk in a lawyer's and everything at work had to be right, down to the last jot. His whole private life was the same. If he got a bill in the morning, he went straight out in the evening to pay it. "If I were to die," he used to say, "and the bill wasn't paid, someone could say I'd been a dishonourable man." And Sonny is exactly like that. So that's why it's not a luxury, Jachmann. He has to hang on to that. He may sometimes think he can be like the others, but he can't. He has to keep his hands clean. So I make sure it's so and that he never again takes a job that's built on dishonesty.'

'What am I doing sitting here?' said Jachmann. 'What am I waiting for? You're doing all right. You're right, young lady, you're absolutely right. I'm going home.'

But he didn't go. He didn't even get up from his chair, he looked Lammchen full in the face. 'This morning at six, young lady, I was let out of gaol. I did time for a year, young lady,' said Jachmann.

'Jachmann,' said Lammchen. 'Ever since you didn't come back that night, I've imagined something of the kind. It wasn't my first thought, but it seemed possible. I mean,' Lammchen didn't know how to put it. 'You're that sort of. . .'

'Of course I'm that sort,' said Jachmann.

'To the few people you like you're nice, and to all the rest I think you're probably not nice at all.'

'Exactly!' said Jachmann. 'You I like, young lady.'

'Then you enjoy living and having a lot of money, and you have to have things going on around you, and you have to have plans. . .

Well, all that's your business. But when Mama told me you were wanted by the police, I realized it must be so.'

'And d'you know who informed on me?'

'Mama, wasn't it?'

'Of course it was Mama. Mrs Marie, otherwise known as Mia Pinneberg. I went astray a bit, you know, Lammchen, and Mama's a devil when she's jealous. She landed in it too, but not badly, four weeks.'

'And now you're going back to her? Actually, I do understand why. You belong together.'

'Right, young lady. We belong together. And she is a splendid woman for all that. I like her for being so greedy and so egotistical. Did you know that Mama's got over thirty thousand marks in the bank?'

'What? Over thirty thousand?'

'What d'you think of that? Mama's clever. Mama prepares for the future. She thinks about her old age and doesn't want to be dependent on anybody. No, I'm going back to her. For a man like me she's the best pal in the world, through thick and thin, game for anything.'

There was a silence, and then Jachmann stood up suddenly and said 'Well, good night, Lammchen. I'll be off.'

'Good night, Jachmann, and I hope things go well, really well for you.'

Jachmann shrugged his shoulders. 'The cream's gone when you reach fifty, Lammchen. There nothing left but skimmed milk, just watery stuff.' He paused, then said softly. 'I suppose you're out of the question for me, Lammchen?'

Lammchen smiled at him, from the depths of her heart. 'Yes, Jachmann, I am. Sonny and I. . .'

'Well, don't worry about your young man! He'll come. He'll be here in a moment! Cheers, my Lammchen. Perhaps we'll meet again!'

'Certainly we'll meet again. When things are going better for us. Now go, and don't forget your cases. They were the main reason.'

'They were the main reason, young lady. Right as always. Absolutely right.'

A BUSH BETWEEN THE BUSHES.
AND THE OLD LOVE

Lammchen went out into the garden with him, the sleepy driver couldn't get the cold engine going at once, and they stood in silence next to the car. Then they shook hands and said goodbye once again, and Lammchen watched the light of the headlamps getting farther and farther away. She heard the noise of the engine for a little while longer, and then all was still and dark around her.

The sky was starry-clear, there was a slight frost. In the whole settlement, so far as she could see, there was no light, only behind her, in the window of her own summer-house, there was the soft reddish glow of the petrol lamp.

Lammchen stood there, the Shrimp slept – was she waiting? What was there to wait for? The last train had gone through; the earliest Sonny could now come was next morning. He must have got up to something. So she hadn't been spared that either. She'd been spared nothing. She could lie down and go to sleep. Or stay awake. It didn't matter. Who cared?

Lammchen didn't go inside. She stood still. There was something in this silent night which made her heart uneasy. There were the stars, glittering in the cold air, they were friendly enough. The bushes in the garden and the next door garden had clumped together into a mass of black, the neighbour's summer-house was like a great dark animal.

No wind, no sound, nothing but a train going down the line in the far distance, which only made it stiller and more soundless here. And Lammchen knew she was not alone. Someone else was here outside in the darkness like her, immobile. Could she hear breathing? No. And yet there was someone.

There was one lilac bush, and another. Since when was there something between the two?

Lammchen took a step forward, her heart was hammering, but she asked quite calmly: 'Sonny, is that you?'

The bush that shouldn't be there remained motionless. Then it moved, hesitantly, and Sonny asked hoarsely, dragging out the words: 'Has he gone?' 'Yes, Jachmann's gone. Have you been waiting here a long time?'

Pinneberg did not answer.

For a while they stood silent. Lammchen would have liked to be able to make out his face, but there was nothing to be seen. And yet a sense of danger emanated from the motionless figure, something darker than the night, something more threatening than the strange immobility of the man she knew so well. Lammchen stood silent.

Then she said lightly: 'Shall we go in? I'm getting cold.'

He did not reply.

Lammchen understood. Something had happened. It wasn't that he had been drinking. Or not only that he had been drinking, because he might have done that as well. Something else had happened, something bad.

There stood her man, her beloved young man, in the darkness, like a wounded animal, and did not trust himself to come into the light. They had crushed him at last.

She said: 'Jachmann only came for his cases. He's not coming back.'

But Pinneberg did not answer.

They stood for a while again; Lammchen heard a car going along the high road, up hill and down dale, very distant at first then humming nearer, very loud, then growing farther away till it disappeared. She thought: 'What shall I say? If only he'd speak!'

She said: 'You know I went to do some darning at the Kramers today?'

He did not answer.

'I didn't actually do any darning. She'd got some material there and I cut it out to her figure. I'm making her a housecoat. She's very satisfied and she's going to let me have her old sewing-machine cheap and recommend me to all her friends. I'll get eight marks for making a dress, maybe ten.'

She waited. She waited a long time. She said cautiously. 'We might be able to make a good bit of money out of that. Perhaps we're out of the mire.'

He made a movement, but then he stood still again and still said nothing.

Lammchen waited, heavy-hearted, it was cold. She couldn't comfort him any further, she was at a loss. It was all useless. What help was it to struggle? What for? He might as well have gone out with the others to steal wood.

She bent back her head once again, and saw the sky full of stars. It was still and solemn, but terribly strange and huge and far away. 'The Shrimp kept asking for you all afternoon. He's suddenly begun saying Daddy instead of Dad-Dad,' she said.

Sonny said nothing.

'Oh Sonny! Sonny!' she cried. 'What is it? Say something to your Lammchen! Do I no longer exist? Are we both quite alone?'

But, oh, nothing helped. He came no nearer, he said nothing, he seemed to be getting farther and farther away.

The cold had risen in Lammchen, penetrated her through and through, nothing was left. Behind her was the warm reddish brightness of the summer-house window, where the Shrimp was sleeping. But oh, even children pass, they belong to us only a short while – six years? ten years? Nothing lasted but being alone.

She went towards the reddish brightness; she had to, what else was there?

Behind her, a far-off voice cried: 'Lammchen!'

She continued on her way, nothing could help any more, so she went on.

'Lammchen!'

She went on. There was the summer-house, there the door, only one more step, her hand was on the latch.

She felt herself grasped tight, it was Sonny who held her, he sobbed and stammered: 'Oh Lammchen, what have they done to me. . . the police. . . they knocked me off the pavement. . . they chased me away. . . how can I look anyone in the face. . .?'

And suddenly the cold had gone, an immeasurably gentle green wave lifted her up and him with her. They glided up together; the stars glittered very near; she whispered: 'But you can look at me! Always, always! You're with me, we're together. . .'

The wave rose and rose. It was the beach at night between Lensahn and Wiek, the one other time when the stars had been so near. It was the old joy, it was the old love. Higher and higher, from the tarnished earth to the stars.

And then they both went into the house where the Shrimp was sleeping.

In its first issue of 1932 the *Berliner Illustrierte Zeitung* launched the new year with two pieces of vivid photoreportage, one entitled 'Unemployed between 14 and 21', the other 'Shelter for the Night'. The titles, like the accompanying photographs, speak for themselves. The camera, so often focused in Berlin's illustrated weeklies on the glitzy aspects of city-life, was exploring the darker recesses, the wretchedness of lives lived – to adapt lines from the film of Brecht's *Threepenny Opera* – not visibly in the light but invisibly in the dark. Later in 1932 the same weekly produced a documentation in pictures of 'Berlin Cave-dwellers', the Berlin poor living in unspeakably primitive huts and hovels. Three camera-essays from the same source in the same year – three occasions for despair and perhaps anger, three outrages recorded. Yet the overall impression is of impotence and inaction: grounds for anger, it seems, are plentiful; solutions are harder to come by.

But there were other responses to social horror-stories. 'Food first, then Rent' is the slogan on a dank wall in a gloomy backyard depicted in a left-wing weekly for women, *Woman's Way*, from the same year. The woman's way seems to have been more purposeful – graffiti protestations on walls were obviously not enough. A poem accompanies the photograph, a song by the Communist versifier Erich Weinert entitled 'Bright Song from a Dark Yard':

> Old and young are on the dole,
> But they don't just sit and stare,
> Hoping it will all just go away,
> They raise the alarm in every street.
> You old folk and youngsters, come out of your night!
> When the people finally wake in the slums,
> Their iron bonds will burst apart!
> On each pale face there's a glow of hope,
> As the children strike up their new song,
> The Song of the Hammer and Sickle.

A different strain indeed – utopian perhaps, propagandistic for sure, but at least far removed from impotence and inaction.

By 1932, the year in which all these photographic records of deprivation appeared, the Great Slump, set in train by the Wall Street Crash of 24 October 1929, was in its third year. A newspaper graph published in mid-1932 charted the course of the slump in Germany from late 1929 to the present: unemployment had risen from 1.4 million to 6 million, wages had decreased by fifty per cent, production by forty per cent. *Red Pepper*, a Communist satirical journal, found a pictorial equivalent for the state of the Weimar Republic (it had in the event less than a year of life left in it): a policeman guards a shop whose fascia reads 'German Republic Ltd' and whose window is empty save for stickers reading 'Stock-taking Sale, cheaper than ever', 'Everything to clear!' and labels lying around – 'Pensions', 'Wages and Salaries', 'Social Welfare'.

At a time when the prospect, like that shop-window, looked bleak, when poverty, conflict and social disorder were endemic, it is hardly surprising that there were conflicting recipes spanning the entire political spectrum. They ranged from National Socialists, destined, of course, to assume power, who, if the occasion demanded it – and the crisis of 1932 did – could put an extra shine on the Socialist part of their name ('National Socialism is socialism only for form's sake' was Brecht's later verdict) to the Communists, to whom solidarity with the workers and with those deprived of work came perhaps more easily – in 1932 eighty-five per cent of party members in Germany were unemployed. The common thread, linking the photoreportage and the Weinert poem, the Communist cartoon depicting the empty Republic shop and Nazi posters offering work and bread, was unemployment. In 1932 forty-two per cent of German workers were unemployed (corresponding figures for Britain are twenty-two per cent, for Denmark thirty-two per cent). On 1 June 1932 Chancellor Brüning, who for two years had responded to a worsening situation with ineffectual emergency-measures, was replaced by von Papen who promptly cut unemployment-support. On 10 June 1932 *Little Man – What Now?* appeared.

It is worth emphasizing the social upheavals, the explosive mixture of despair and revolutionary zeal, that surrounded Fallada as he wrote and published his novel – he had begun work in October 1931 – not because he aims at any kind of total picture. The time-span of his narrative is close to that of the Slump itself, but the principal actors, whether politicians or industrialists, are absent. Fallada – leaving his readers, as it were, to fill in the all-too-familiar background – has chosen characters whose perspective is narrow, even blinkered, people for whom the major political issues, if they arise at all (and Johannes Pinneberg, his central character, encounters Nazis and anti-Nazis), are incidental, reduced to virtual invisibility in the day-to-day struggle to stay above the bread-line. 'The terror of those on the margin of employment . . . the agony of those who are never secure' – this was Fallada's theme in the eyes of *The Spectator*, reviewing the first English translation which appeared less than twelve months after the German edition.

Timing was obviously crucial: in the right hands at the right time the angle of the 'Little Man' can, however indirectly, prove revelatory. Charlie Chaplin, after all, expressed the state of an entire age – his immensely popular *City Lights* (1931) was showing in Berlin in 1932 – and not just the state of tramps. Literary history is indeed rich in examples of bestsellers whose success suggests that the voice of the half-hidden victims can ring more eloquently and reach further than the voice of the victimisers. Hašek's *Good Soldier Schweyk* and Remarque's *All Quiet on the Western Front* offer a bottom-up view of war, Anne Frank, whose diary opened millions of eyes to the Holocaust, had, to put it mildly, a restricted view of the world. Fallada's Little Man is a distant relative, certainly his enduring success has been on a comparable scale: translated into over twenty languages, twice filmed – once in Germany, once in the USA – within two years of its appearance, by which time half a million copies had been sold world-wide – 'The Book of the Year is now the Film of the Year', a film poster for the American version proclaimed, 'Learn about Life from Little Man and his Wife' – thus the publicity from Universal Pictures. Enduring success is one thing, immediate impact is something different, and clearly the immediate impact of Fallada's novel was undeniable. Film rights were sold within a month, indeed Fallada was working on a film version in the days immediately up to publication. At his death four unpublished film-outlines were found, entitled *Keep your Head*

High!, of which the longest, thirty-one handwritten pages, was written between 6 and 10 June 1932. The fact that some fifty provincial
German newspapers serialized the novel points to a readership that
was diffuse and by nature immeasurable and to a resonance that
resists final analysis.

'Never,' said the redoubtable critic Herbert Jhering, 'has the
success of a book been easier to explain.' The statistics record the scale
of that success; those who fuelled the success, the reviewers, help to
explain it. To many of its most enthusiastic reviewers the novel's
strength lay in its close-up characterization. But these were not characters in a vacuum: timing – that critical year 1932 – gave them a
context and, with that context, urgent topicality. Thus even the
Communists, to whom Pinneberg's passivity, his opting-out of
revolutionary engagement, was anathema, could still commend his
relevance. One of their number, Jürgen Kuczynski, recalled later, 'we
found the novel completely unpolitical and yet full of a political
actuality'. The leading literary journal, *The Literary World*, reviewed
the novel in July 1932, and the review is worth quoting at length because it underlines the interaction between the book and its circumstances, between small lives in close-up and large issues at a distance:

When a few decades ago a Russian newspaper serialized Tol-
stoy's *Anna Karenina*, complete strangers talked in the street and
in trains, exchanging opinions about the characters in the novel
and their fate. A man of exceptional gifts was expressing what all
felt. When Fallada's novel *Little Man – What Now?* appeared in
the *Vossische Zeitung*, author and publisher were bombarded
with letters seeking to express the passionate involvement of
readers in the fate of the people in the novel. One man was
expressing what all were suffering. One man was giving shape
to what all could sense. That is how the miracle occurred that
we no longer believed possible: a fragmented society, a moun-
tain of conflicting interests, a nation which appeared to share
nothing save poverty and the hatred of each against each that
poverty gives rise to, this ill-treated people acquired in Fallada's
novel a book for the people. It concerns everyone . . . Thanks to
Fallada's keen sense of reality, his powers of observation, his gift

of catching the flavour of ordinary speech and his boldness in conveying unvarnished what he has heard, he has created a book for our time and about our time . . . Any foreigner seeking to form a picture of present-day Germany will find it in this story of the little white-collar worker and his wife much more than in newspapers or party meetings or manifestos.

The suggestion that authenticity was one of the virtues of *Little Man – What Now?* had already been made by Ernst Rowohlt, Fallada's publisher, in their publicity material: 'The marital bliss, the joy of fatherhood, happiness at work and the hunger for work, the despair and the love of Johannes Pinneberg, a little white-collar worker, one of millions. The novel is no novel, it is the life of all of us here and now.' Critics bore out what Rowohlt were claiming in advance: here was the quintessential 'novel of *pauvreté*', as one reviewer put it; Fallada was 'an unusual expert in the use of detail'; for Hermann Hesse, whose own fictional world was far removed from that of Fallada, he deserved high praise for 'having reported so realistically, so truthfully, with such closeness to life'.

Fallada himself once admitted that he could depict only what he saw, not what might happen, and shortly before his death he stressed the importance of a certain kind of authenticity. He had, he claimed, sampled and studied life before writing books. What sounds like a dispassionate reiteration of old truths about life and experience being the best teachers conceals the high price that Fallada paid for the sampling and the study. By the time that *Little Man – What Now?* was published he had spent nineteen months in a mental hospital and a total of over two years in prison. By the end of his life he had been variously institutionalized for some seven and a half years. The anguish began early: school was a torment, he was isolated, was bullied by those around him and a prey to constant, serious illness. To keep away from school he inflicted illness on himself by drinking quantities of vinegar, which produced a deathly pallor. In October 1911 at the age of eighteen he fought a duel with a fellow-pupil, killed him, failed to kill himself (this was not his first suicide attempt) and was charged with murder. From January 1912 until October 1913 he was confined in an institution. Soon after his release he became a morphine addict.

During the next ten years he was repeatedly a patient at treatment-centres for drug-addiction but proved uncooperative. In 1924 and again between 1926 and 1928 he had two spells in prison, having been twice convicted of embezzlement, crimes committed in order to finance his addiction.

Contradicting the self-destructive urges that the young Fallada manifested – and yet perhaps complementing them – were his precocious literary ambitions. While still a schoolboy he had, according to one of his teachers, no academic goals, learned little, but was seized with the desire to achieve fame as a writer. His first attempt to fulfil that ambition yielded *Young Goedeschal: A Novel of Puberty*, completed in 1918 and published in 1920. It is not easy to discern the author of *Little Man – What Now?* in the hectic hyperbole of this immature piece, indeed Fallada subsequently disowned both this and his second novel, *Anton and Gerda*, published in 1923, requesting that available copies be pulped. In *Goedeschal* disorder is not in society but in the blood, in the turmoil of adolescence, in a hothouse sensibility that soon palls. Of Johannes Pinneberg, the later Little Man, who is more sober than soul-searching, there is no sign, yet there may be much of Fallada himself in the febrile, volatile central character:

> The icy wind sweeping down the street bit into his fevered face. Kai's hand shot up, passed smoothingly across his face, and it was as if cracks had opened in his cheeks, a deep, jagged cleft seemed to gape open on his forehead and inside it his blood was singing, pressing out of every vein, white, foaming, scornful of the cold, and every heart-beat drove it to ever wilder turbulence. It sang, it yelled, it stormed in him.

Fallada's case was too tragic and too complex to permit slick summary diagnosis, nevertheless it might be suggested that *Young Goedeschal*, for all its weaknesses, explores the youthful sources of the disabling extremism that was to plague Fallada himself.

However, the life that Fallada claimed to have sampled and studied had its less painful aspects, embracing more than nervous breakdowns, drug-addiction and crime. Looking back in 1946 in an essay 'How I became a writer', which was found after his death, Fallada points to a positive consequence of what had at first been seen by his father and others as a course of physical and psychological rehabilitation – work and training on farms and estates in Mecklenburg, Silesia and West Prussia through the first half of the 1920s:

> I was with people almost all the time, I stood behind endless rows of women talking away while they chopped turnips and dug potatoes, and I heard the women and girls talking away. It went on from dawn till dusk . . . I could not avoid it, I had to listen and I learned how they talk and what they talk about, what their worries are and what problems they have. And as I was only a very minor official and not riding around on horseback – I just had a bike now and then to save time – they had no inhibitions about talking to me and I learned to talk to everybody.

From the adolescent's pounding blood to the trainee-inspector on his bike is a long road and it is the latter that ultimately, after a long, unproductive interval, bore fruit. It is a clear case of experience, gained first on those farming-estates and then in a newspaper-office, providing the material for documentary fiction.

In 1929 Fallada, by now a reporter on a local newspaper in Neumünster, Schleswig-Holstein, the town in which, the previous year, he had completed two years in prison, experienced at close hand the increasingly violent confrontation between the over-taxed, under-resourced small-farmers of Schleswig-Holstein and the authorities. By 1930 he had moved to Berlin, working part-time for his old publisher Ernst Rowohlt, and began to write a novel around those experiences, *Bauern, Bonzen und Bomben* (a title which has been ingeniously translated as *Farmers, Functionaries and Fireworks*). The novel, Fallada's third, was published in 1931, having already reached a large public and gained pre-publication publicity via serialization in a leading Cologne journal. The novel launched – or re-launched – Fallada as a writer. It was commended not least for its authoritative documentary perspective on events through characters who were by no means locked in parochialism – one leading critic, Kurt Tucholsky, saw the work indeed as a 'political manual of Fauna Germanica'. But the novel is also rooted at many levels in Fallada's private circumstances. The events – Fallada shifts the stage from Schleswig-Holstein to Pomerania – are witnessed through a local newspaper-office and they involve, among

others, a local journalist Max Tredup. Tredup is not the central figure
but he is important as the first in a line of 'little men' which, most
obviously, includes Tredup's immediate successor in Fallada's fictional world, Johannes Pinneberg. Tredup is a victim, a wretched,
despised figure, seeking – and failing – to improve his shaky financial
state, to protect his family, to survive in an uneasy world. His fate is
ultimately more tragic than Pinneberg's – he is killed by mistake – but
the affinity, both to Pinneberg and to Fallada's own circumstances, is
striking.

In 1929 those circumstances had changed. In June of that year Fallada married Anna Issel, daughter of a working-class family. She was
a sane, sound, practically-minded twenty-eight-year-old, employed
in a milliner' shop and she is generally held to have had a stabilizing
influence on Fallada and to have been a model for the equally level-
headed Lammchen in *Little Man – What Now?* In March 1930 a son
was born. Fallada later recollected the straitened circumstances in
which the trio had to live: 'Those were times of dreadful anxiety!
Instead of making progress we were up to our ears – up to our hair –
in debt! We had nothing, except worries and sleepless nights!' But
Fallada was no longer alone, no longer – or not yet again – addicted
to drink or drugs. If anything, writing itself had become a source of
intoxication, a means of escape:

> It was often like an intoxication, but one above all the forms of
> intoxication that material substances can deliver. Even the worst
> hours, when I was in utter despair about how to continue the
> novel, were far better than my most beautiful free hours. No,
> that's what it was, I had taken a poison that I could not shake out
> of my mind or my body, I was thirsty for it, I wanted to drink
> more of it, to drink it always, every day for the rest of my life.

And *Little Man – What Now?* was written in sixteen weeks.

Fallada's writing, meeting as it clearly did a personal need, offered
a kind of therapy. What sounds from his own account like an escape
from reality might seem to inhibit every impulse towards gritty realism, but for Fallada, it might be said, even the humdrum, the ins-
and-outs of lives lived at the margin of society, had an intoxicating
fascination. Not that the escapism is always under control, there are

moments in *Little Man – What Now?* when escapes are escapes into idylls, however imperilled and short-lived they might be. Thus Romantic colours suffuse the end of the novel:

> And suddenly the cold had gone, an immeasurable gentle green wave lifted her up and him with her. They glided up together; the stars glittered very near; she whispered: 'But you can look at me! Always, always! You're with me, we're together. . .'
>
> The wave rose and rose. It was the beach at night between Lensahn and Wiek, the one other time when the stars had been so near. It was the old joy, it was the old love. Higher and higher, from the tarnished earth to the stars.
>
> And then they both went into the house where the Shrimp was sleeping.

At such a point the imaginative freedom of fiction seems to be colliding with the harsher exigencies of the lives that Fallada has been recording. Indeed he seems, when he came to recollect the year between *Farmers, Functionaries and Fireworks* and *Little Man – What Now?* to have overlaid fact with fiction. He did not, as he later alleged, lose his job in 1931, he resigned in 1932. Times were indeed hard, resources very limited, but by the winter of 1931, when he began work on *Little Man – What Now?*, his circumstances in his little house in a Berlin suburb, bought with the proceeds of *Farmers, Functionaries and Fireworks*, were not comparable with the desperate poverty of Pinneberg. When Fallada later describes his mode of life he comes close to indulgent romanticizing nostalgia:

> Every morning, while Suse did the housework, I went out, pushing my son in his pram . . . I pushed him through Altenhagen, I pushed him through Neuenhagen, I pushed him through Bollensdorf . . . Everywhere we appeared, the pram and me, we were part of the landscape. In a greengrocers Suse heard that we had a name – I was just called 'the poor out-of-work man with his baby.'

Intoxication, romanticizing and personal therapy aside, Fallada clearly had acquired and had put to use in *Farmers, Functionaries and Fireworks* and in *Little Man – What Now?* detailed knowledge of lives that he had at most only half shared and an ability to capture the essence of those lives, the temporary pleasures and the enduring ordeals. In fulfilling that life-long and exclusive ambition to be a writer Fallada was not, in other words, rejecting the skills in listening and in observation that had been valuably practised first on the women chopping turnips and then, more recently, on events recorded in the Neumünster paper.

But neither acquired skills nor the fruitful conjunction of opportunity, experience and the 1932 crisis can quite account for the success of *Little Man – What Now?* Observation and close-up realism were among the virtues singled out by reviewers whom we have quoted, reviewers who also stressed the novel's social relevance, the general significance, the symptomatic character, of the seemingly insignificant lives led by its central figures. But two other factors, the one bearing on Fallada's manner, the other on his subject-matter, help to explain the impact of the novel and, in so doing, link it with contemporary trends.

First, the manner. Fallada's much-praised authenticity is inseparable from a major cultural shift in Germany in the late 1920s. No change during these admittedly changeable years was quite so far-reaching as that towards what came to be called 'Neue Sachlichkeit', a term variously rendered as neo-realism, new objectivity, new sobriety. The term had gained currency in 1925 when G. F. Hartlaub, a gallery-director, opened an exhibition in Mannheim under that title. In that same year Expressionism, the polar opposite of realism, was pronounced dead in a famous essay by the art-critic Franz Roh. Cinema and photography were soon seeking to exploit the realistic rather than the visionary, the transcendent potential of the camera. Painting too exemplifies the move towards what the art-historian Wieland Schmied has called 'a new attentiveness to the world of objects'. In literature the change was equally marked through the cultivation of coolness of gesture, of undemonstrative language, in the foregrounding of fact and authenticity, in the cult of reportage.

In 1926 the journal *The Literary World* conducted an inquiry among leading writers on the question 'whether literature, narrative prose in particular, is being decisively influenced by Neue Sachlichkeit and reportage'. That the question was being asked at all is significant. Opinions might vary, but there was no denying the fact that Neue Sachlichkeit, however construed, was an influence to be reckoned with. As the Austrian novelist and feuilletonist Joseph Roth put it: 'Nowadays only what is recognizably documentary is recognized at all.' There is a hint of ruefulness in Roth's observation and, indeed, this was no cut-and-dried affair. Writers, including contributors to the debate initiated by *The Literary World*, had misgivings about the extent and the nature of the interaction between the differing modes of narrative fiction on the one hand, reportage on the other. The risk could be 'Fact-poets', as they were disparagingly called. The world of facts, the evidence of the senses, needed to be mediated creatively in order to be grasped, otherwise the facts defeat the understanding – '700 Intellectuals Revering An Oil-tank', thus the title of a poem by Brecht, caricaturing what he felt to be the uncomprehending stance of the out-and-out realists. Plain documentation, Brecht suggested elsewhere, is not enough – a photograph of the Krupp-works or AEG tells us nothing about the reality.

Fallada was no theorist, nor was he at the heart of any of the numerous debates about the possible limits of realism. Yet it is difficult to read *Little Man – What Now?* without sensing that issues currently under discussion were finding practical expression in his attempt to achieve a balance between the claims of fiction, of imaginative shaping, on the one hand, and the claims of documentary realism on the other. In the case of *Little Man – What Now?* the link between Fallada and that discussion is in fact neither coincidental nor tenuous. He read with keen interest the study of Siegfried Kracauer on *White-collar Workers* (*Die Angestellten*) which appeared to considerable acclaim in 1930. Kracauer, in hundreds of feuilleton essays a wide-ranging and incisive analyst of Weimar culture, wrote his study in an attempt to reconcile the need for documentation and the need for a creative shaping of the evidence. In an introductory chapter of *White-collar Workers* he recognizes the pervasive influence of Neue Sachlichkeit:

> Writers hardly acknowledge any loftier ambition than to report – reproducing what you observe has top priority. There is a hunger for immediacy which is without doubt a consequence of being undernourished through a diet of German idealism.

In words that echo Brecht's comment on photography, Kracauer
expresses thoughts that Fallada might well have found congenial:

> A hundred reports from a factory cannot be added up to make
> the reality of the factory – they remain for ever a hundred
> factory-views. Reality is a construction. Of course life must be
> observed, so that reality can emerge. But reality is in no way
> contained in the more or less fortuitous sequence of observa-
> tions that make up reportage, rather it resides exclusively in the
> mosaic which gathers together discrete observations by grasping
> their real meaning. Reportage photographs life, a mosaic of this
> kind produces a picture of it.

Kracauer was one of many critics who around 1930 argued that
reportage – 'Sachlichkeit' – was essential but inadequate and that literature required more. And Fallada was not the first to produce a
bestseller that was praised for both its recording power and its imaginative scope. In 1929 Alfred Döblin had produced the classic Berlin
novel, *Berlin Alexanderplatz*, embracing both small fictional lives and
the monster-city. Erich Kästner, whose world-wide best-seller *Emil
and the Detectives* (1930) placed a bunch of children in a carefully
documented Berlin world, created in *Fabian* (1931) a central character who registers with vivid irony the particularities of Berlin-life but
is tragically unable to withstand its pressures.

The affinity between Fallada's novel and Kracauer's study is, however, exceptionally close – and here we move from the question of
literary manner to that of subject-matter – because both are concerned with the world of the white-collar workers (Kracauer's term, the
'Angestellten', occurs throughout Fallada's novel). To explore that
world was to Kracauer to venture into the unknown.

Whether Fallada had a similar sense of pioneering is a question
that must remain unanswered, although his reviewers had no doubt
that he was focusing on a world that most writers ignored. To Kracauer the white-collar worker – twenty per cent of all workers and
numbering three and a half million – was a vast underclass, un-
defined hitherto and, in contrast to the proletariat, overlooked:

> Hundreds of thousands of white-collar workers crowd the
> streets of Berlin daily and yet their life is more of a mystery than

that of the primitive tribes whose customs they marvel at in the cinema.

Kracauer's sense of exploration and discovery certainly fired his own enquiry and it may well help to explain the excitement that greeted Fallada's novel. Kracauer's own 'little expedition' is, he claims, 'perhaps more adventurous than a film-trip to Africa. For by seeking out the white-collar worker it leads us to the heart of the city'.

Kracauer's study is important and directly relevant to Fallada's novel not simply because it scrutinizes the lives and the economic conditions of white-collar workers and places them centre-stage, but also because their lives are seen to have a tragic dimension. They are in an important sense homeless, more homeless indeed than the industrial worker – as Mr Morschel, Lammchen's father, puts it in the novel: 'You don't stick together; you've got no solidarity. So they can push you around just as they like.' Kracauer, it might be said, is mapping out the territory that is inhabited by Lammchen's family on the one hand, proletarians with 'solidarity', and Pinneberg, very much more adrift, in Kracauer's sense 'homeless'. When Kracauer summarizes the comparison between proletariat and white-collar worker he supplies a context for *Little Man – What Now?* in advance of the novel itself:

> The average worker, whom many a white-collar worker likes to look down on, is often not only materially but also existentially his superior. His life as a class-conscious proletarian is roofed over by popular Marxist concepts telling him where he belongs. Admittedly the roof is now leaking mightily.
>
> The mass of white-collar workers differs from the industrial proletariat in that they are intellectually homeless. They cannot connect with the proletarian comrades, and the haven of middle-class values and feelings where they once lived has collapsed . . . they live without tenets that they can respect and without a goal that they can ascertain.

Not only does Kracauer sketch out the emotional and existential deprivation that is the lot of the white-collar worker, he also focuses on individual cases at least as ominous as any that Fallada came to flesh out. The Union of White-collar Workers sent out a questionnaire to its unemployed members in early 1929, and the brief résumés of some who replied are harrowingly succinct:

> 39 years, married, three children (14, 12, 9). No earnings for three years. Future? Work, mad-house or gas-tap.
>
> Future hopeless, no prospects. A quick death would be the best – thus writes a thirty-two year old married man, father of two children.

Fallada avoids such extremes, but they cannot have been unknown to either him or his readers. 'One unemployed less,' a woman remarks as a young man throws himself from a tenement window in the opening sequence of Brecht's only film, *Kuhle Wampe*. The film appeared in 1932, the same year as *Little Man – What Now?*

Topicality of theme and of method, relevance across the spectrum from cultural theorist to general reader, variously fuelled the success of Fallada's novel. Contexts – economic, political, literary or cultural – are, of course, crucial but timeliness at whatever level is no substitute for intrinsic merit, and the reasons for Fallada's success must be sought between the covers of the book itself. Or even, to begin with, on the binding of the first edition, which contains a drawing by George Grosz. This is not Grosz the creator of nightmare grotesques, pillorying the inequalities of the Weimar Republic. Here a young girl, smiling, dangles a little toy over a cheery-looking baby in a basket. Not a hint of trouble, no sign of hardship. But a clue to a part of the book's appeal.

Fallada's narrative soon puts the Grosz idyll in perspective – the novel has hardly started before Johannes Pinneberg, waiting outside the doctor's consulting-room, winces violently as he hears Lammchen 'in a high, clear voice that was almost a shriek' call out '"No, no, no!" And once again, "No!" And then, very softly, but he still heard it: "Oh God."' Fallada begins with a disaster, an unwanted pregnancy, unwelcome to a couple who are hard-up and not yet married. Within moments, however, they are planning marriage and Pinneberg's bleak despair has been replaced:

> Her eyes lit up. She had dark blue eyes with a green tinge. And now they were fairly overflowing with light.

As if all the Christmas trees of her life were glowing inside her, thought Pinneberg, so moved that he felt embarrassed.

In a very short space Fallada has staged a disaster and then softened the blow. It is a technique that he employs throughout the novel – life is cruel but the Pinnebergs survive, or rather, for this is the common pattern, Lammchen's innate fortitude banishes the gloom. Grosz's drawing is, in other words, not after all so misleading – the tower of strength in the Pinneberg household is not Pinneberg but Lammchen, and it takes Pinneberg – and Fallada's reader – some time to realize how strong she in fact is:

She stood there, all determination, aggressive, with red cheeks and flashing eyes, her head thrown back.

Pinneberg said slowly: 'You know, Lammchen, I'd thought you were quite different. Much gentler . . .'

She laughed, sprang over to him, ran her hand through his hair. 'Of course I'm different from what you thought I was. Did you really think I could be all sugar and spice when I've been going out to work since I left school, and had the sort of father and brother I've had, as well as that bitch of a boss and those workmates of mine?'

Without that central contrast *Little Man – What Now?* would lose a source of tension, would indeed lose its character as a story not of destruction but of survival. And the contrast has another advantage – Pinneberg's despair may time and again be mollified by Lammchen, but it is voiced, it is eloquently present in the novel. It can be a passing comment – 'It just suddenly makes you angry, the way things are set up' – or it can be a sustained, rhetorical diatribe:

He was one of millions. Ministers made speeches to him, enjoined him to tighten his belt, to make sacrifices, to feel German, to put his money in the savings-bank and to vote for the constitutional party.

Sometimes he did, sometimes he didn't, according to the circumstances, but he didn't believe what they said. Not in the least. His innermost conviction was: they all want something *from* me, but not *for* me. It's all the same to them whether I live or die. They couldn't care less whether I can afford to go to the cinema or not, whether Lammchen can get proper food or has too much excitement, whether the Shrimp is happy or miserable. Nobody gives a damn.

At such a moment Pinneberg's misery is a misery shared; close-up becomes wide-angle.

If Pinneberg and Lammchen are at the heart of the novel and must in the end account in large measure for its popularity, this does not mean that Fallada presents them solely in terms of the polarity of despair and hope. Most important is his refusal to let their troubles overwhelm the novel or dictate its tone. Indeed his refusal to take them or their troubles entirely seriously may be risky – irony and humour can defuse an explosive theme, and the critical, revolutionary Left, while acknowledging his skill, found his mixed feelings unpalatable. But the humour is inescapably a part of the whole from the moment when Pinneberg, at the start of the novel, having slipped up on birth-control, calls pessaries 'pessoirs' and Lammchen takes off her blouse for an abdominal examination. Lammchen, for all her resourcefulness, can be comically incompetent, cooking a pound of peas in five litres of water and producing what Pinneberg ruefully calls 'hot water'. Pinneberg too, put upon and put down by those with whom he works, predisposed to expect the worst, nevertheless is a source of or an accessory to humour. His early job with Kleinholz, bagging grain, lands him in a richly comic set-up where a drunken father, fearsome mother and pathetic daughter have one goal – to marry the daughter off. When mother, dressed in slippers and dressing-gown, hounds her drunken husband off a dance-floor she is 'a force of nature, a tornado, a volcanic eruption' and the reader is a long way from slumps and cash-flow problems. Pinneberg's own mother, Mia Pinneberg, whose past, unforgotten by her son, is as suspect as her present, is a comic figure, ferocity incarnate, locked, whenever they meet, in a war of words with her disapproving son. The disapproval is itself important: Pinneberg's moral stance – he resists a host of temptations and exhibits more than once a straightforward integrity – could easily become too good to be true, but the integrity is being put to the test in encounters with people, Kleinholz,

Mia Pinneberg, Jachmann, who are themselves at least in part comic. And the comedy can take unexpected turns – Heilbutt, staunch helper of the Pinnebergs, reduces the by no means strait-laced Pinneberg to cringing embarrassment by suggesting and, worse still, demonstrating that the answer to the dreadful state of Germany is not politics but nudism.

Fallada adopts a variety of tones of voice towards his central figures, but his narrative embraces more than the plight of individuals, even though the title – devised not by him but by a colleague – seems to reinforce the individual focus. At his death Fallada left a five-page manuscript-talk, possibly intended for radio and almost certainly written in 1932. It brings us close to the time when, at extraordinary speed, Fallada wrote the novel. He admits that *Farmers, Functionaries and Fireworks* had been a laborious enterprise and that he had been sustained by the pleasurable anticipation of writing something wholly different, something less crisis-torn, 'a story about a marriage, a quite simple good little marriage – a baby is born: two are happy, three are happy.' But complications of a less idyllic kind intruded:

> There are these two young people that we've been having such pleasant dreams about – what, by the way, are they going to live on? Well he's going to earn his money, our new hero Pinneberg. Earn his money at a time like this? . . . So I said to my wife: 'You know, it's not going to be so straightforward for these two young people. I can see difficulties. I'm going to have to collect material about the situation of white-collar workers.'

The route, as we have seen, led to Siegfried Kracauer. In Fallada's response to the external reality pressing in, as it were, on his characters lies, of course, the 'Sachlichkeit' of his novel, but it is easy, in reading *Little Man – What Now?*, to understate the documentation that underlies the story because Fallada himself does not overstate the socio-critical case. The life of white-collar workers, whether bagging grain or selling men's clothes, is closely observed, the financial exploitation is accurately measured. Stores such as Mandel's were the glory of Weimar Berlin, glorified in song, celebrated in giant neon lights, in vast posters and even in spectacular stage-musicals. Fallada exposes the hierarchies that were endemic, the dog-eat-dog rivalries and painful insecurities that the bright lights concealed. And there is exactitude underpinning the humdrum penny-pinching of Lammchen and Pinneberg – the exact price of a cigarette can be crucial – and when Lammchen produces a shopping-list of essentials it is an integral part of the narrative texture, not a piece of down-to-earth documentation tacked on for effect.

Fallada is economical with his facts, avoiding the temptation to root his fiction in a copious spread of documentation. This is most obvious in his treatment of what, after all, is the setting for most of Pinneberg's troubles – Berlin. Berlin as myth, as endlessly fascinating, endlessly documented metropolis, figures in countless films and literary works of the time. At first sight the two-part structure of the novel – 'The Small Town' and 'Berlin' – seems to build a contrast and a sense of climax into the narrative. But Fallada creates no climax, does not make the arrival in Berlin into a grand occasion of the kind experienced by Erich Kästner's Emil who arrives by train or by Alfred Döblin's Franz Biberkopf who emerges from prison, or by the wordless camera in Walter Ruttmann's film *Berlin, Symphony of a City*, speeding through the suburbs by train into the waking city. Arrival in Berlin for Pinneberg and his wife means above all, after the briefest mention of a 'mêlée of pedestrians and trams', a first encounter with the formidable Mia Pinneberg, not a detailed encounter with a vibrant, vivid metropolis. There is consistency in this – the lives lived by the couple connect only tangentially with the big city, where they see it, they only glimpse it – and then for personal reasons. Thus Johannes in the Tiergarten:

> . . . with the winding blowing out of all corners and a lot of ugly brownish-yellow leaves, it looked particularly desolate. It wasn't empty, far from it. Masses of people were there, clothed in grey, and sallow-faced. Unemployed people, waiting for something, they didn't themselves know what, for who waited for work any more . . .?

or Lammchen flat-hunting, noting that 'it's a wide world and Berlin's a big city' but seeing only what matters to her:

> And the sleek cars roared by, and there were delicatessens, and

people who earned so much they didn't know how to spend it all. No, Lammchen didn't understand it.

. . . Recently she'd been going ever further east and north, where there were endless frightful blocks of flats, overcrowded, malodorous, noisy.

Berlin, a cold, unglamourous place, rejects Pinneberg shortly before the end of the novel, when he is roughly handled by the police in the Friedrichstraße and realizes 'he was on the outside now, that he didn't belong here any more'.

Yet the novel closes on a momentarily upbeat note, more open-endedly than in Fallada's first, unpublished version in which Johannes brings in a prostitute from the street and Lammchen makes them all a cup of coffee. At least in this earlier version the novel ended with a kind of social intervention, but even here the scope for action is limited, the basic predicament stays unresolved. Any answer to the question in the title might, in any case, have reduced the lasting success of *Little Man – What Now?* – answers often date more quickly than questions. Certainly when the centenary of Fallada's birth was celebrated in 1993 commentators were quick to praise Fallada's avoidance of slick answers, his portrayal of helplessness. The state of mind of workers in Eastern Germany threatened with unemployment could – thus the *Tageszeitung* – be understood through Fallada's novel. Fallada, *Die Welt* suggested, is as much a mouthpiece of the powerless victims as ever.

Fallada himself preferred to leave the *What Now?* question unanswered. Yet for him the sheer indestructibility of Lammchen was a kind of answer. A partial answer no doubt and not one for the proponents of root-and-branch policies, but an answer that nevertheless deserves to be heeded:

People have said to me: 'Why have you no answer to the question "What Now?"' Lammchen is my answer, I know no better one. Happiness and misery, worries and a child, worries about a child, the ups and downs of life, no more, no less.

PHILIP BRADY

THIS IS A MELVILLE HOUSE ◉ HYBRIDBOOK

HybridBooks are a union of print and electronic media designed to provide a unique reading experience by offering additional curated material—Illuminations—which expand the world of the book through text and illustrations.

Scan the code or follow the link below to gain access to the Illuminations for *Little Man, What Now?* by Hans Fallada, which include never before translated essays and letters by the author, and commentary from translator and Fallada scholar Geoff Wilkes.

The Illuminations include:
- "How I Became a Writer" by Hans Fallada, never before published in English
- The secret history of the Fallada Archive: the former archivist reveals how it was controlled by the Stasi—the East German secret police
- An exclusive interview with Dr. Ulrich Ditzen, Fallada's son
- "The Goose Girl" and "Hans in Luck" by the Brothers Grimm— the stories from which Fallada took his pen name
- A selection of Fallada's personal letters that shed light on his turbulent life
- And much more

Download a QR code reader in your smartphone's app store, or visit
mhpbooks.com/fallada973

Additional HybridBooks by Hans Fallada available from Melville House:
EVERY MAN DIES ALONE • THE DRINKER • WOLF AMONG WOLVES